IMMEDIATE RECORDS

LABELS UNLIMITED

IMMEDIATE RECORDS

LABELS UNLIMITED

SIMON SPENCE

black dog publishing
london uk

'I LOATHE THEM BOTH'

MUSIC PRESS

NATIONAL PRESS

ANDREW OLDHAM IN *MUSIC ECHO*, 1965

CONTENTS

8	THE NEW TESTAMENT
16	LAUNCH OF IMMEDIATE
24	EARLY SINGLES
34	"ALL MICK"
38	KEITH GOES SOLO
42	WHO?
46	MOTHER CYN
48	I KNOW EXACTLY WHAT I WANT
54	GOD ONLY KNOWS
58	TWICE AS MUCH
64	FIRST LADY OF IMMEDIATE
68	HERE COME THE NICE
76	EURO VISION
84	IT'S ALL OVER NOW
88	WOULD YOU BELIEVE
94	OGDEN'S NUT GONE FLAKE
106	AMERICA
118	TONY AND THE HAMBURGERS
124	A BOMB ON THE BUS
128	STILL A TWINKLE
134	IF PARADISE IS HALF AS NICE
142	HUMBLE PIE
154	THE AMERICAN DREAM
160	DRUGS, DRUGS AND MORE DRUGS
166	JUDGE FOR YOURSELF
174	A BIT ABOUT ME
180	DISCOGRAPHY
188	ACKNOWLEDGEMENTS
190	COLOPHON

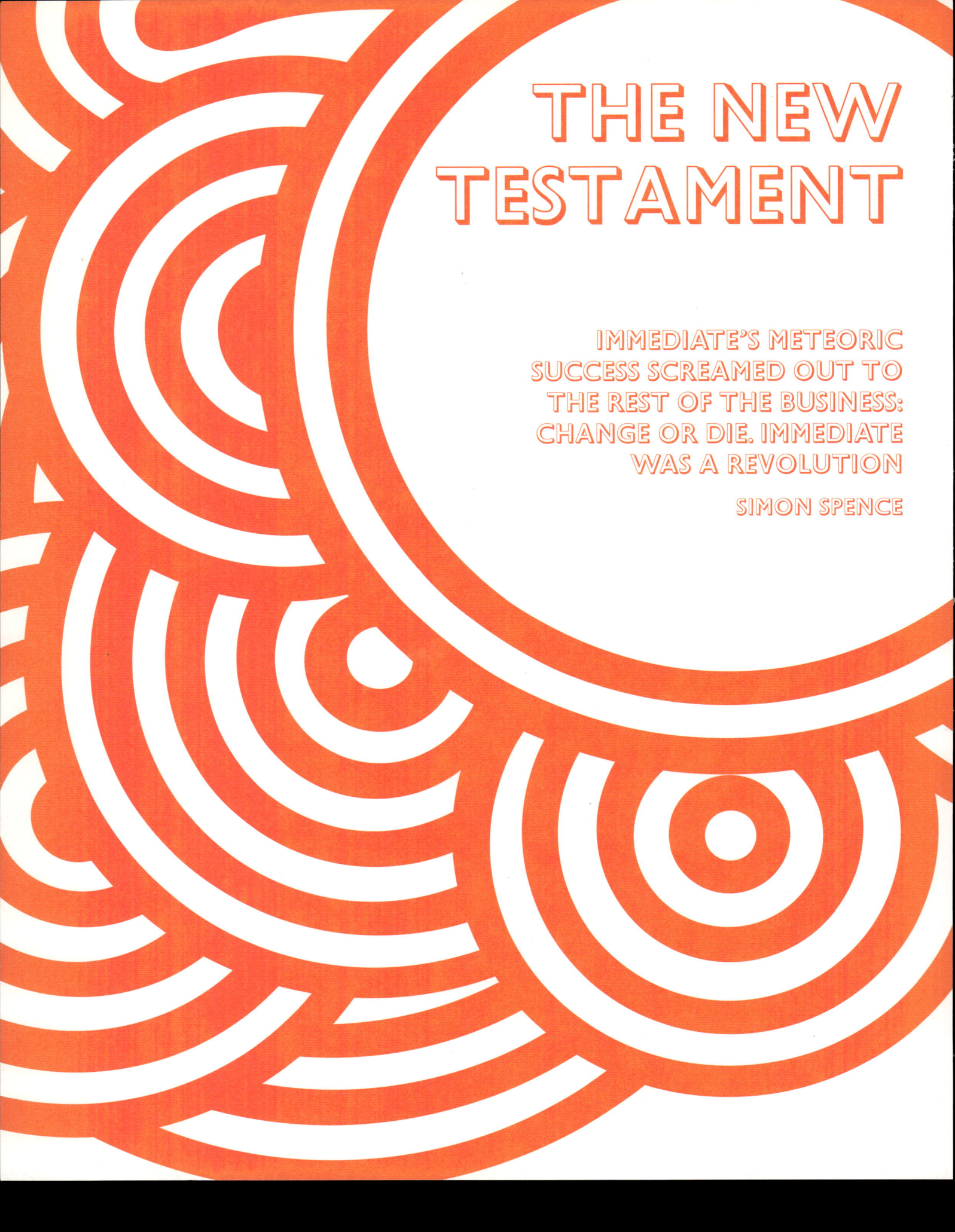

THE NEW TESTAMENT

IMMEDIATE'S METEORIC SUCCESS SCREAMED OUT TO THE REST OF THE BUSINESS: CHANGE OR DIE. IMMEDIATE WAS A REVOLUTION

SIMON SPENCE

There is little of Andrew Loog Oldham's Immediate adventure in his two volumes of autobiography: *Stoned* and *2Stoned*. Oldham and myself spent almost a decade, 1991–2000, working together on these books chronicling his legendary 1960s exploits as manager and producer of Rolling Stones. For me, musically and culturally, the story of Immediate was equal to any of Oldham's achievements with the band and the two —Immediate label and Rolling Stones—seemed deeply entwined. Sure, it ended badly (with the liquidation of the company in 1970) but so had Oldham's relationship with Rolling Stones (which ended in estrangement mid-1967). While the split with the band seemed to still resonate, he was always more light-hearted about the spectacular crash he had steered Immediate toward. We talked about the label in depth; I had done the research and interviewed scores of people but, come publication, I was surprised by his decision to leave it all on the cutting room floor. Was it just a shrewd editing job? After all, *Stoned* and *2Stoned* are regularly featured in the lists of best music books of all time. Or was there more to it? With Rolling Stones, Oldham retains a healthy percentage of the 1960s recordings he made with them, earning him hundreds of thousands annually. With Immediate there is no such happy ending, even though hits such as "Lazy Sunday" or "First Cut Is The Deepest" are as much common currency as "Paint It Black" or "The Last Time". Between 1975 and 1995, a series of ill-fated and hotly contested deals involving rights relating to the music of Immediate had robbed an "out to lunch" (as he describes it) Oldham of ownership of the label's back catalogue and the riches that went with it. While he had been able to clear his conscience regarding the Rolling Stones in *Stoned* and *2Stoned*, Immediate's "dirty laundry", as he called it, was still in the wash, with several original artists complaining about being ripped off over re-issues of their work and some contention over who was doing the ripping off.

In 2002, Oldham appeared at London's High Court to launch a legal battle over the ownership of the label's back catalogue, whereupon his victory would make all well and clean. He lost the case and the legal bills alone cost him £370,000. Afterwards, almost relieved, Oldham told me he thought the label was "shit" anyway. Still, at the beginning of it all, in 1965, he was as excited about the launch of Immediate as he was the current Rolling Stones number one "Satisfaction". Immediate was going to be a giant two fingers to the British music business that even topped his controversial handling of the Rolling Stones. For a start, everyone involved was in their early 20s, maddeningly hip, and deeply committed to destroying the established old farts network that had controlled the 1960s industry thus far. Drugs, sex, lunacy and scamming co-existed under the Immediate roof.

Immediate's outlandish and controversial posturing, and a core production team made up of Mick Jagger, Keith Richards, Andrew Loog Oldham, Jimmy Page and Steve Marriott, attracted a crowd of daring, young British talent, forging the hippest and hottest

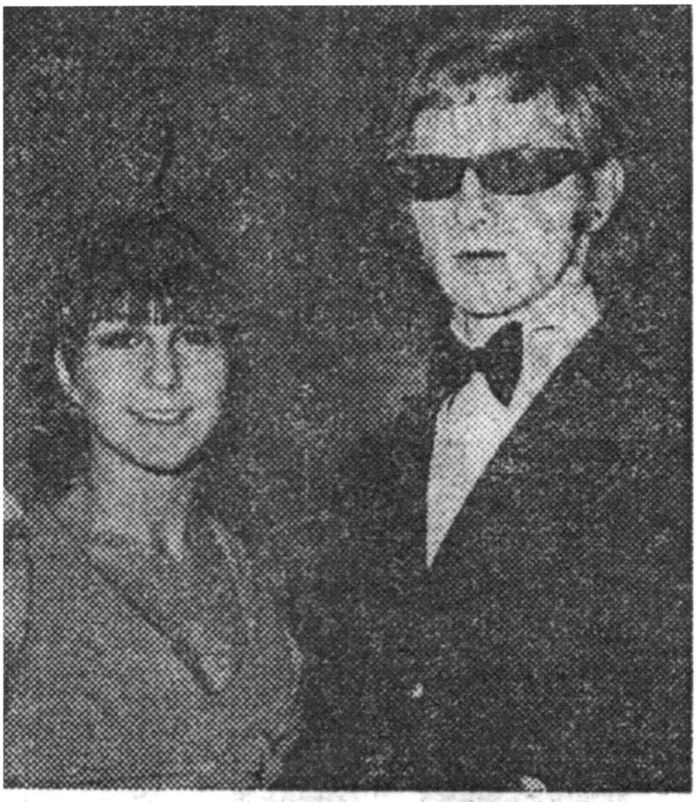

Andrew Oldham, co-manager of the Rolling Stones pop group, brings his bride Sheila to the show.

scene in London for the golden years of the 1960s. Immediate's meteoric success screamed out to the rest of the business: change or die. Many of them already seemed to work in funeral parlours. Immediate was a revolution.

What follows is largely picked up off the cutting room floor of my research and interviews for *Stoned* and *2Stoned*. When dealing with the cash figures in this book, it's easiest and approximately right to multiply all UK 1960s amounts by 20 to come up with numbers that would apply today. For US figures multiply by ten.

Introducing Andrew Loog Oldham and Tony Calder

In early 1965, Immediate Records was an idea germinating in the minds of two young men barely out of their teens. They were Andrew Loog Oldham, 21, the ultra-hip manager and producer of the second most successful, outrageous and controversial act in the UK: the Rolling Stones, and Tony Calder, his business partner, 22, who handles the pair's PR Company, Image. Calder is sometime manager of Marianne Faithfull, who Oldham launched to stardom a year earlier with the single "As Tears Go By". Oldham and Calder finish each other's sentences and compliment one another physically too. Oldham is exceptionally tall, slim and fair-haired, whereas Calder is dark-haired and shorter with thick-rimmed glasses. Oldham's personal style veers wildly to the extreme while Calder is essentially the suit in the background.

Two years earlier, Oldham had signed Rolling Stones to Decca Records in the UK. Since then, like The Beatles manager, Brian Epstein, he had been quick to establish a wider 'stable' of acts, and most of that product had also been put out by Decca, such as the Marianne Faithfull material, The Nashville Teens, Tony Jackson (The Searchers' lead singer), Vashti, The Mighty Avengers and The Poets. The bosses at Decca thought Oldham was "mad as a hatter", despite how much money Rolling Stones were making for them, and they made no secret of their dislike for him. For Oldham, the feeling was mutual.

When he came to London from his hometown of Southampton at 18, Calder had actually worked at Decca as Sales and Marketing trainee. He quit soon after, bored and disgusted, when they failed to properly promote the single "Runaway" by Del Shannon, a track he was crazy for. He had then worked for DJ Jimmy Savile and his hugely popular Off The Record dancehall tours.

Calder went in to public relations and was touting a very young, pre-Small Faces Steve Marriott when he met Oldham for the first time in 1963. They hit it off and quickly formed the public relations company Image. It was pop's first independent PR company, handling accounts for Brian Epstein's Liverpool stable, Manchester-based Kennedy Street Enterprises' roster (Herman's Hermits, Freddie and The Dreamers, The Hollies, Dave Berry, The Mighty Avengers and Wayne Fontana and The Mindbenders), and also looking after Rolling Stones, Gene Pitney, Georgie Fame, Kenny Lynch, Phil Spector, The Beach Boys and television programme *American Bandstand*'s Dick Clark.

In Oldham's first volume of memoirs, *Stoned*, Andy Wickham, who left EMI's press office to assist at Image, remembered Calder as "like a dog-track bookie" who "seemed to think only in terms of deals and he reeked of danger". Tony Hall, who led Decca's Promotions department, told me: "I remember Calder rubbing his hands together, 'who can we screw up now, who can we cut up'. Oldham was seen to change when Calder came on to the scene. There was an extra element. Together they used try and come up with every conceivable scam." Tony Calder said: "Our attitude towards the business in the UK was fuck them all, they were all old men."

Oldham is no angel. His chauffeur, Reg King, who had previously worked for Brian Epstein and Lionel Bart, became notorious for driving Oldham around town in an open-top, powder blue, Chevrolet Impala. "At a time" noted Keith Richards, "when you didn't see that many powder blue Chevys on the street". There were endless rumours about King and Oldham: either out of their heads on speed pills and dope engaging in gun-foolery

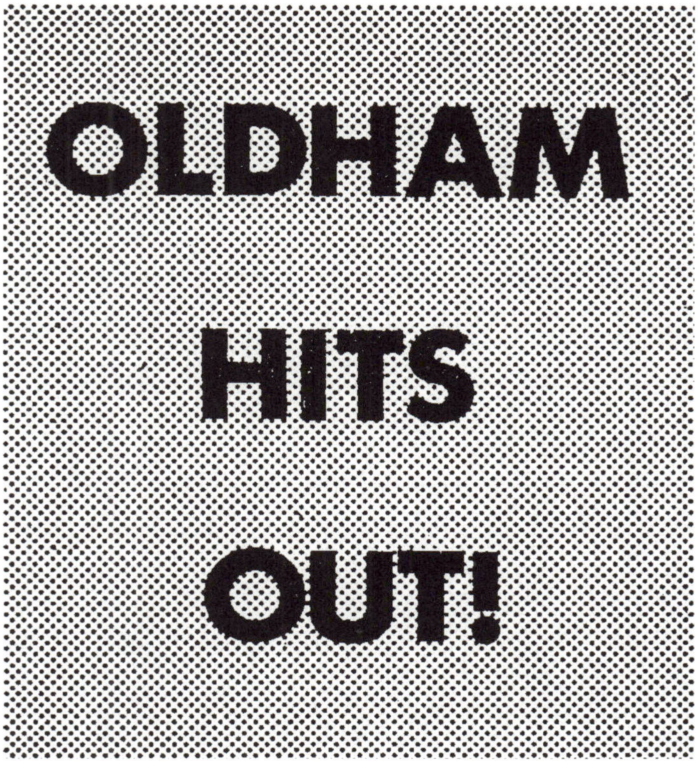
OLDHAM
HITS
OUT!

OUR ATTITUDE TOWARDS THE BUSINESS IN THE UK WAS FUCK THEM ALL. THEY WERE ALL OLD MEN

TONY CALDER

OPPOSITE: ANDREW OLDHAM AND HIS WIFE SHEILA ATTEND THE PREMIER OF *MAGGIE MAY*, *DAILY MIRROR*, 1964

LEFT: THE STRAPLINE OF *DISC AND MUSIC ECHO* "OLDHAM HITS OUT!" COLUMN

RIGHT: THE ORIGINAL THREE ARTISTS ON THE IMMEDIATE LABEL, 1964

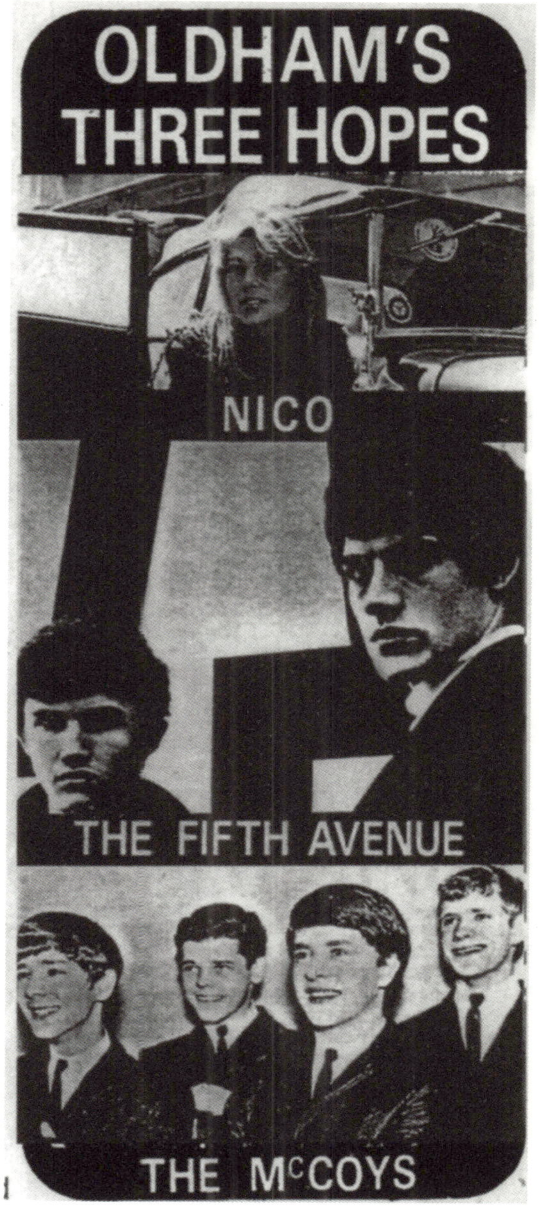
OLDHAM'S
THREE HOPES
NICO
THE FIFTH AVENUE
THE McCOYS

TONY CALDER WAS LIKE A DOG-TRACK BOOKIE WHO SEEMED TO ONLY THINK IN TERMS OF DEALS AND REEKED OF DANGER

ANDY WICKHAM

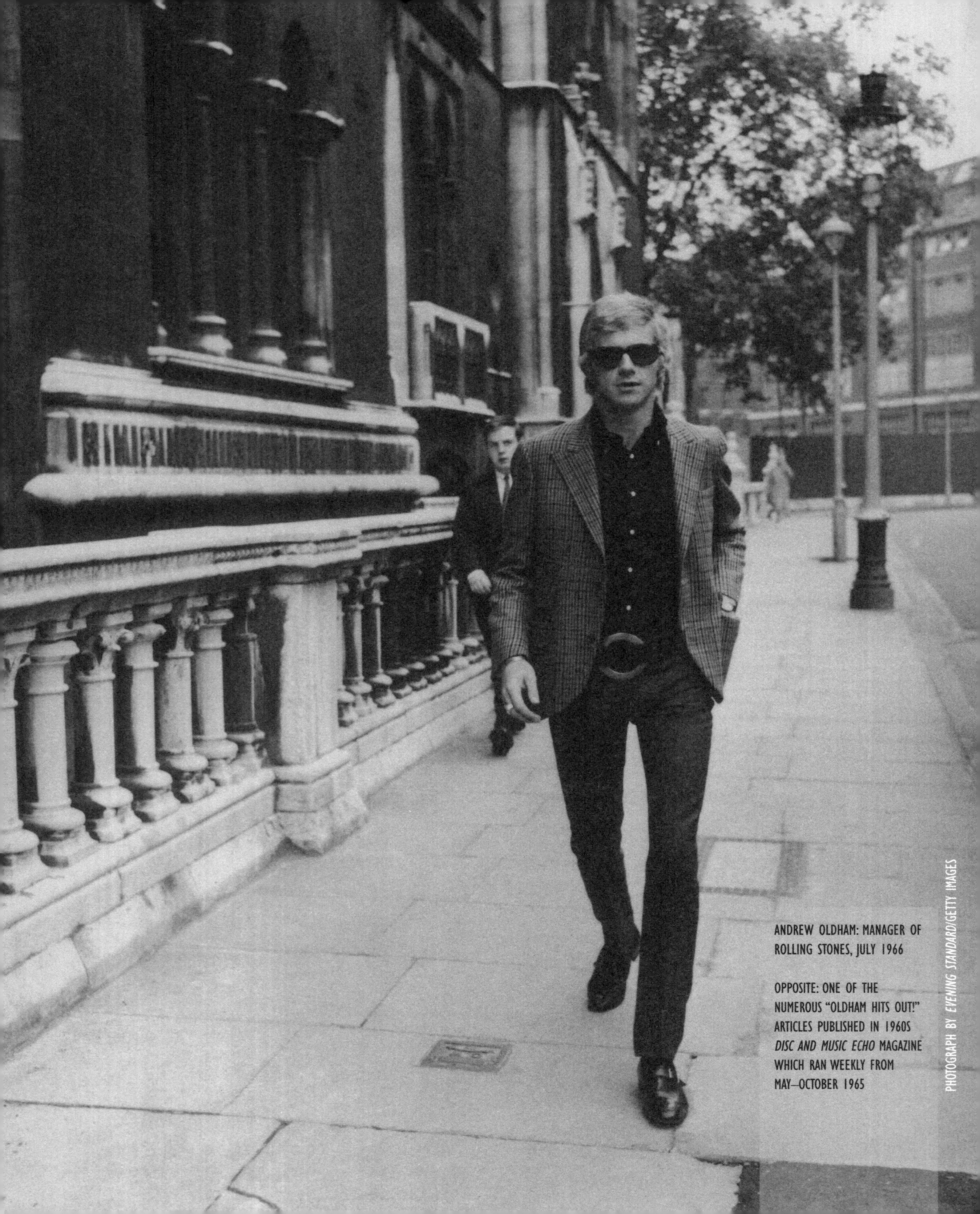

ANDREW OLDHAM: MANAGER OF ROLLING STONES, JULY 1966

OPPOSITE: ONE OF THE NUMEROUS "OLDHAM HITS OUT!" ARTICLES PUBLISHED IN 1960S *DISC AND MUSIC ECHO* MAGAZINE WHICH RAN WEEKLY FROM MAY–OCTOBER 1965

PHOTOGRAPH BY *EVENING STANDARD*/GETTY IMAGES

OLDHAM HITS OUT!

Marianne Faithfull (above): "I am accused of copying her style with my new singer VASHTI."

Andrew Oldham Britain's most controversial pop music columnist

ACCUSATIONS, presumptions and rumours have been flying round these last few weeks about the supposed battle between MARIANNE FAITHFUL and THE NASHVILLE TEENS over the song they both recorded 'Little Bird.'

At this stage of the battle, it seems to be over, with Marianne Faithful in the Top Ten – way ahead of the Nashvilles. And as so much has been said about the duel between the two discs, I feel I ought to explain the real story behind the record.

When I took over The Nashville Teens and set up the first recording date, my idea was to cut the old EDDIE COCHRAN hit 'Summertime Blues,' an old JIM REEVES number and generally work on LP material. But once in the studio, the idea of "Summertime Blues" just didn't work out. The song and the playing didn't have the required atmosphere of sound. So we sat and puzzled our heads and then Art and Ray pulled out a JOHN D. LOUDERMILK LP whcih had provided the first two big smash hits 'Tobacco Road' and 'Google Eye' and said there was a number they would like to do on it because they felt the original melody-and lyrics weren't up to scratch. I listened to them, listened to the number and agreed and we started work on the song.

Even at the time, I felt the title was familiar, but couldn't place it. It was only after the session when I realised why. The title was, in fact, scheduled to be MFs next British release.

My first reaction was to put it on an L.P. the problem was that in my estimation, the record had turned out to be so great that I could not resist putting out my version of the song. This I did. And I received numerous calls from people who thought I was getting at my former artiste by releasing the record and also through my new artiste VASHTI whose first record is released this week and who is supposed apparently, to sound and look like Marianne.

Vashti

It is a mistake on the part of these people to judge my actions by their own standards. I felt that my version of 'Little Bird' was so great I had to release it. I still beleive in this. But judging by the current chart positions of the two records, that in the long run are the only true yardstick of good and bad in the music industry, I am wrong.

As regards Vashti, I am accused of copying the Marianne Faithful sound, and without wanting to sound presumptious, should like to point out that the Marianne Faithful sound, is in fact, the Andrew Oldham sound and that I am in this business with one view – to make good, artistically satisfying records and make money. And if the music business thinks that if I see a girl singer whose voice is reminiscent of Marianne's that I should turn round and say 'People might confuse her with Marianne. I'd better not record her' they have another think coming. As far as I am concerned, I have just done another recording which is a profession of a sound that I created; a sound which gave Marianne Faithful her first hit.

'Top Gear'

On to other, happier subjects. It is a great shame that 'Top Gear' has been taken off the air. BERNIE ANDREWS is a very fair minded, creative producer and I hope it is not too long before the B.B.C. have the sense to give him his head again and he can come up with another fine show. Because, as I mentioned two weeks ago, this and ALAN FREEMAN'S Pick of the Pops are the only great shows on the B.B.C. and it needs more programmes like this.

Chris Curtis

I heard a record CHRIS CURTIS produced with EDEN KANE this week. In my estimation Chris has always been a great talent and has a very shrewd knowledge of the British pop scene. His record with Kane shows great maturity of mind and the sounds are odd but interesting. Hope it'll be a big, big hit for him. By the way, congratulations to MICKEY MOST on receiving six gold discs in New York.

As the fuss over record sales dropping goes on, I'd like to add my bit. As record sales reach their all time low standard and records reach their all time high, the days when follow up records could be the same song backwards are over. Which is going to make the business a much, much healthier place to be in.

or smashing car windows and punching pedestrians while driving on pavements or the wrong way down one-way streets. King, an expert joint roller, kept a truncheon in the car (Keith Richards had given him the sobriquet "the Butcher" as rumour went round that he was a killer).

With the Butcher in tow, Oldham had slammed down windowsills on journalist's fingers, kicked music promoters to a pulp in the Scotch of St James nightclub and assaulted Bill Cotton, the head of BBC light entertainment. The fracas with Cotton served to enhance the Rolling Stones' surly performance on fading BBC pop show *Juke Box Jury*, which left middle-England choking, a performance about which Oldham said: "If they'd have gone down well it would have set our work back four or five months."

Prior to launching Immediate, Oldham made no secret of his loathing toward the state of the British music industry. In a centre spread splash in *The Sun* he attacked the "nine to five mentality" at the four dominant major labels of the time (EMI, Decca, Pye and Philips), criticising the old men staffers who after a day of 'pop' go home to listen to "some good music". He declared: "Pop music is an art just as creative as making a classical record."

In the popular music weekly, *Melody Maker*, Oldham was asked to review the current week's single and "the *enfant terrible* of British pop, cavorted and sang, stamped his feet, clapped his hands and exploded with venom as he expounded his views on each new release". "It's awful; I can't stand listening to it anymore", he exclaimed: "This is a tired old format of making records. The song's nowhere and I hate everything about it.... It's so bad it makes me sick."

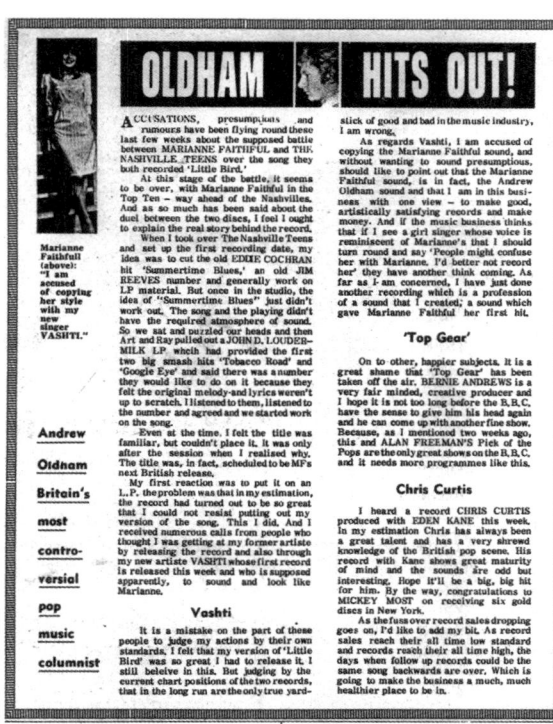

In May 1965, Oldham started to criticise what he called the "stalwarts in the business who have no idea what is going on" from a new weekly position as 'Britain's Most Controversial' music columnist in—the three hundred thousand circulation—*Disc and Music Echo* magazine (an arrangement that ran until October 1965). In these columns he was vocal in his opinion of commercial radio stations. For Oldham, the pirates stations, Caroline and London, were a "breath of fresh air". At the same time, Sir Joseph Lockwood, chairman of EMI Records, Decca boss Sir Edward Lewis and the BBC were all strongly denouncing pirate radio as illegal.

Through his continuous outbursts and public rants Oldham had become as famous— perhaps more famous—than any Rolling Stone. His name blared out from the cover of their singles and profiles of him peppered the media. In a *Daily Mirror* spread—with the huge headline, "Nut or Genius?"—he hinted at his vision for Immediate, saying his future plans included:

> Buying a house in North London, a sort of House of Talent. I will have writers there and music arrangers. It will house only artists and equipment to produce my records, a complete unit of talent. Writers will have their own rooms with electric pianos. This may sound expensive but they will be my writers, my artists, my publishing company, and therefore my production.

Oldham's major inspirations to this end lay in the US, where he had made regular visits—with and without the Rolling Stones—forging valuable business contacts. He had soaked up the influence of US producers such as Phil Spector and Bob Crewe, and bathed his ears in the 15 or so independent radio stations in New York. Most relevantly he had seen how independent record labels, such as Chess, Philles, Roulette, Atlantic and Motown, owned a massive slice of the US business, alongside the major labels, CBS, RCA and Capitol.

Inspired by the US independent scenes key players and propelled by their poor treatment at the hands of the major labels in the UK, Calder and Oldham both recall Immediate coming to life sometime in July 1965. In the back seats of Oldham's new motors—a white Lincoln Continental with red leather seats—Immediate was born on the way to a television recording of *Ready Steady Go!*. King screeched the Lincoln to a stop and Calder ran into a pay phone box to call the head of Philips, Leslie Gould, demanding he backed their vision for Immediate. Gould did. As Oldham reflected:

> The UK industry was just plodding along and I was fed up with being mocked as crazy. Tony and I agreed and decided that controlling the making of music was one thing, now we wanted to control the destiny of the music: the meeting of image, aura, art and commerce.

CONTROLLING THE MAKING OF MUSIC WAS ONE THING, NOW WE WANTED TO CONTROL THE DESTINY OF MUSIC: THE MEETING OF IMAGE, AURA, ART AND COMMERCE

ANDREW OLDHAM

This strange ma

NUT OR GENIUS?

IN America tonight, appearing on the Ed Sullivan Show, the Rolling Stones ride a wave of hysteria outstripping even Beatlemania.

The propulsion behind this avalanche of Stones is Andrew Loog Oldham, their co-manager, who was seen on Juke Box Jury last night.

He is a long-haired gangling youth who uses make-up and swears like a dyspeptic drill sergeant. Some say he is as mad as a five-bob watch. Others acclaim him as a genius of pop.

With his girlish looks, one would never think that he had ever been booted out of an English public school or tossed into a French jail for vagrancy.

But that's Oldham all right. A man who owns four musical companies—two for making money; two for artistic amusement.

Add to this his discovery of Marianne Faithfull, a 17-year-old convent girl he has turned into a disc star, and the publicity drive he used to help boost the Beatles to the top.

Funny

Andrew Oldham IS TWENTY. Here is the "genius" himself in full flood:

I shared a flat with the Stones once, and I know they haven't time to live it up. They work very hard. They rehearse at the studio when they're cutting a new disc: never at home.

How did you come to be living with the Stones?

My mother kicked me out. I turned up on their doorstep saying would they take me in. It was very funny considering I was their manager.

We lived in a £9-a-week furnished flat in North London and knocked off the milk and sugar we saw from other flats.

Rows

Do the Stones ever row with each other?

Any group row from time to time. But it never gets enough to cause the Stones to break-up.

There is no jealousy if one gets more audience attention than the others. Mick Jagger as the vocalist naturally has the TV cameras on him more than the others, but it doesn't mean he is the popular one always.

When did you discover the Stones?

After I left the Beatles. I was having a bad time, earning about £8 a week.

One day a friend told me there was a great group playing at Richmond. I went to see them. They were the Rolling Stones. With a partner, Eric Easton, who supplied

An interview by Jack Bentley and Matt White

the finance, we sig
them up.

*What were the Sto
like then?*

The same as now.
thought they were
natural progression to
Beatles. I've alw
believed that teena
don't want to share
boom with adults. I ne
trained them. T
smoke, they drink, th
get drunk, they go
clubs. So what's wron

'Kicked Out

*All your life you
refused to be disciplin*

True, I never bothe
much about study. I'
just interested in
music—that's why I
kicked out of Welli
borough public school.

*You don't like conv
tion, do you?*

No, it's just for she
I've never been di
plined.

*Have you ever h
psychiatric treatment*

I went to a psychiat
At group therapy I
tened to a bloke tell
us how he was frighte
to kiss his girl-friend
cause he had acne.
didn't have time to lis
to the others. It was
very funny.

Do you have fears?

Only misgivings.
quite confident of w
I'm about to do. As lo
as I know it's good,
do it. If somebody t
me to change someth
on a record I wouldn't

*If you are not afr
why do you wear d
glasses day and night*

Maybe to withdraw
hind them into myself.

Do you get drunk?

Yes, but never if
depressed. I have a dea
wish, too.

*What about the lo
hair?*

It's to set us aside fr
convention. I don't rega
myself as perfectly m

DAILY MIRROR SPREAD, 1964, QUESTIONING WHETHER ANDREW OLDHAM IS A "NUT OR GENIUS"

...ho set the Stones rolling

Andrew Oldham, wife Sheila and Genius, his dog. They will NOT be living in Oldham's creative dream—the House of Talent—when it becomes reality.

HIS DREAM.. A HOUSE OF TALENT

...line, but there is nothing necessary to be nice to feminine about me.

If I work hard most of the night and get up looking pale, I use make-up. I'm pale and everybody round me looks sunned, I feel sick.

It's a mental thing. If I make up in the mirror it makes you feel good. Lots of fellows I know use eye-drops in their eyes to make them sparkle. If men want to look attractive to other people and themselves, why shouldn't they?

Money

You don't think it necessary to be nice to people?

No, I don't dig that "hello" bit. The record companies are only interested in money. The artists only love you so long as you're making money for them.

You know nothing about music academically?

I don't read music. But I call myself an artist, cause I think pop music is an art just as creative as making a classical record.

However, the first record I produced outside the Stones was a disaster. I made two more flops then I got a hit and went mad. By that stage, I knew I was talented.

It has been reported that the Rolling Stones could make £300,000 a year.

If I said it was a lie, someone would prove that they could. As long as I'm getting my bit from them I'm quite happy.

Can we ask what is your bit?

It's not for the record.

Would you consider yourself a genius?

To me, a genius is somebody who excels all others. Financially and professionally, I have excelled in England—not in America. But artistically I believe I have there, too.

I am the best pop record producer in Britain. There are only two pop producing geniuses in the record world—both Americans.

What about the Stones?

Before they became famous, we finished a late-night recording session and drove to a castle belonging to a friend near Hastings.

We got there and found bricks piled up ready for building extensions. We bricked up this chap's front door. When he woke, he couldn't get out.

Later, we found swords and started having fights all along the battlements. We even went to Dover Castle and fought with swords there, too. The police moved us off.

Trouble

Have the Stones ever had much trouble with the police?

Not in this country. But in one American city the Stones were pretending to drink whisky—it was really Coke—in a local theatre where liquor was forbidden. A cop knocked the glasses out of their hands.

How did the Americans react to your long hair?

It wasn't easy. They all want to be clean-cut Americans. They used to shout at us: "Hey, fairy." They want to fight.

Don't you think some of your jokes go too far?

Maybe. At an American airport I got into an empty wheelchair and folded my legs up under me to look as if I had none.

The Stones pushed me around and everyone was sympathetic. Then suddenly the Stones left me and I was alone.

Then I saw why. In another wheelchair was a real cripple. He smiled at me and I had to smile back.

That made me feel bad. For about ten seconds I really believed I had no legs.

But later, when the Stones wheeled me into the airport restaurant the waiter fussed over me.

I asked where the men's room was. When he pointed, I got up and walked to it. You should have seen his face.

What are your future plans?

I am now buying a house in North London. This will be a sort of House of Talent.

I will have writers there and music arrangers. It will house only artists and equipment to produce my records. A complete unit of talent.

Writers will have their own rooms with electric pianos.

'Better off'

This will be a bit costly?

Yes, but I'll be financially better off because they will be my writers, my publishing company, my artists, and therefore my production.

Will your wife and you be living in this House of Talent?

No.

DISCS

TOP POPS

Figures in brackets are mid-week ratings.

1	(1)	Oh, Pretty Woman	—Roy Orbison
2	(2)	(There's) Always Something There to Remind Me	—Sandie Shaw
3	(3)	Where Did Our Love Go	—Supremes
4	(4)	The Wedding	—Julie Rogers
5	(7)	Walk Away	—Matt Monro
6	(8)	We're Through	—Hollies
7	(9)	How Soon?	—Henry Mancini
8	(5)	I'm Into Something Good	—Herman's Hermits
9	(6)	When You Walk in the Room	—Searchers
10	(13)	The Twelfth Of Never	—Cliff Richard

(Figures supplied by Melody Maker)

♪ THE 46TH LORD PARAMOUNT SEIGNIORY of Holderness, John Chichester, Constable, is the first of ye olde landed gentry of England to try for the jackpot of popdom, writes Jack Bentley.

His discoveries: The Hullaballoos. They live on his 6,000-acre estate in Yorkshire—the King of France once stayed there—and play like olde-tyme minstrels with a modern beat.

Their first record, I'm Gonna Love You Too (Columbia), looks like joining the upper crust of the charts.

♪ IT'S AN UNUSUAL FATHER who would sell his house to finance his boy's pop career. But Captain Plant, from Eastbourne, Sussex, did just that for his son, Richard, who is a member of a group with the singular name of Shelley.

Group leader, Stu Hinchcliffe, also made a sacrifice by giving up a Soccer career with Eastbourne United.

After hearing the boys' first disc, I Will Be Wishing (Pye), I think all concerned have made a shrewd move.

♪ QUICKIES. Elvis Presley made Ain't That Loving You Baby (RCA) six years ago, but it's just been released. Personally, I like the way Elvis sang six years ago. ... Also made moons ago but never released here is Doris Troy's, Whatcha Gonna Do About It (Atlantic). Odds on you're going to do a lot about it. ... Don't miss the Fourmost with Baby I Need Your Loving (Parlophone), the late Jim Reeves singing There's a Heartache Following Me (RCA Victor), and Ray Charles's Smack Dab in the Middle (HMV).

♪ PREDICTION SPOT: The Merseybeats make what Tin Pan Alley calls "sleepers"—hits that take a while to get off the deck. But Last Night (Fontana) is already on the right track to the top.

REVIEWS

WHEN Joseph Levine first bought the film rights of Harold Robbins' story of seduction, adultery, lesbianism and other best-selling kinks called THE CARPETBAGGERS, I asked him how he was going to clean it up for the screen.

His answer was: "I'll clean it up all right. It'll be a great movie." Certainly the scissors came out, but what is left in this tale of an American tycoon torn 'twixt boardroom and bedroom is a high budget bore.

Carroll Baker, George Peppard and Martha Hyer are the stars, but the only performer who scintillates is unknown actress Elizabeth Ashley.—(X) Plaza.

★ THE SCREEN'S favourite female amateur 'tec, Margaret Rutherford, bumbles her way delightfully to the solution of the crime in MURDER MOST FOUL. It's another of her homicide howlers that will slay audiences everywhere.—(C) Empire.

5182. Elegantly fashioned in 9-ct. gold, this lovely Tudor Royal watch is set on a flexible 9-ct. gold bracelet. £37.10.0.

A beautiful watch
To say so much
So perfectly. A Tudor watch.
Elegantly gold ...
So right for a feminine woman ...
A Tudor watch.
Skilfully made by Swiss craftsmen,
Backed by the famous name of Rolex.
A gold Tudor watch
Is the most wonderful gift in the world.

TUDOR

We shall be delighted to send an illustrated catalogue of our full range of watches on hearing from you

THE ROLEX WATCH COMPANY LTD (Founder: H. Wilsdorf),
1 Green Street, Mayfair, London, W.1

LAUNCH OF IMMEDIATE

In early August 1965 Oldham penned another of his weekly *Disc and Music Echo* columns running under the headline "Oldham Hits Out". It was basically a statement of intent on behalf of Immediate, in which he admitted that:

On many occasions I have run down the large record companies over issues such as pirate stations, their promotion and their tastes. And many readers have written in and said that if I was so disturbed by the state of the existing record companies why didn't I do something about it. I have!

On the twentieth of this month the first of three records released by my own record company, Immediate Records, is to be launched. I would like to tell you a little about the activities and the functions of Immediate Records, and about some of the things we are trying to do.

Immediate records will operate in the same way as any good small independent in America, with the accent on promotion and product not board meetings. We will try to set a standard of only quality records and it is our intention to release from the initial week no more than two records a week. My partner in this venture is Mr Tony Calder, who apart from being the Vice President of the Former Managers of Marianne Faithfull (I am the President), has the most successful publicity and promotions operation going, which has handled artists like Herman's, The Beach Boys, Wayne Fontana and The Mindbenders and Marianne Faithfull. Tony will be applying his genius for promotion, his years of experience in the retail and distribution side of Decca and his years as consultant to one of the largest chain of ballrooms, in our new venture. We are very, very excited by our first three records and I would like to point out that this record company is no hobby horse for my own products.

Immediate Records represents a growth in my activities and whereas up to now, I have just admired producer's products, I now have the opportunity, through Immediate Records, to be their associate. We will be bringing in new producers while our main hope lies with the top session guitarist turned producer, Jimmy Page, and my two friends, Mick Jagger and Keith Richard. All these three, I believe, will develop and become fine hit-making producers.

Our first record is from the new independent company in America headed by that gigantic hit-maker and songwriter Bert Berns who wrote "Twist and Shout" and produces the hits of Them, The Drifters, Solomon Burke, Ben E King and many other top flight R&B artists.

Bert's new label Bang! is already a smash in America, and I am happy to be able to form an association with him. Our first record on the label is "Hang On Sloopy" by The McCoys. I have always believed the success of record lies in two places, the mind and the feet. This one definitely leans towards feet and is one of the most infectious, danceable records I have heard in a long time with all

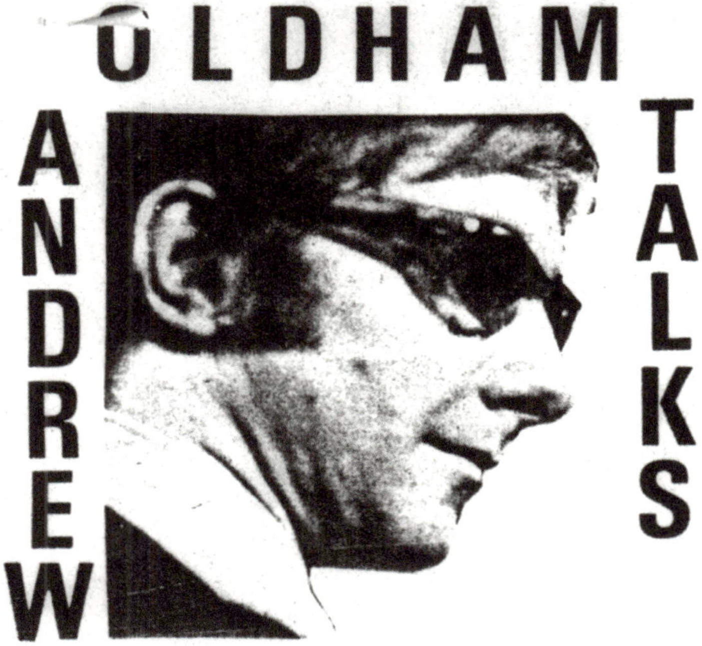
OLDHAM
ANDREW
TALKS

GRAPHIC OF ANDREW OLDHAM IN THIS ARTICLE FROM *NME*, SEPTEMBER 1965

IMLP 001
IMMEDIATE
HANG ON SLOOPY
By THE McCOYS
SLOOPY LIVES IN A VERY BAD PART OF TOWN...
EVERYBODY I KNOW... TRYS TO PUT MY SLOOPY DOWN.
SLOOPY I DON'T CARE WHAT YOUR DADDY DO...
CAUSE YOU KNOW SLOOPY, GIRL... I'M IN LOVE WITH YOU
BANG RECORDS
A FELDMAN, GOLDSTEIN, GOTTEHRER PRODUCTION

—McCOYS—

THE McCOYS, whose U.S. hit "Hang on Sloopy" is doing likewise here on ANDREW OLDHAM's new Immediate label, will probably visit the U.K. in December.

Provisional dates are from the 5th to the 9th. And Immediate Records plan to rush-release the group's LP, cut in America last week.

The McCoys, who hail from Indiana, owe their success to U.S. group THE STRANGELOVES (their "I Want Candy" was covered here by BRIAN POOLE).

After making a name for themselves in the Mid-West, the McCoys – Ricky Zehringer (17), brother Randy (16), Randy Hobbs (18) and Ronnie Brandon (18) – played with the Strangeloves in Dayton, Ohio.

They made such an impression that the Strangeloves persuaded the McCoys' parents to let them go to New York. Next day, the group recorded their hit disc.

Ricky, lead vocalist, lead guitar and group spokesman, is a spare-time guitar teacher and artist. Brother Randy boasts the title of The Only Drummer in the World Who Plays Standing Up– he got into the habit when, as a child, he couldn't reach the pedals sitting on a stool.

Randy Hobbs plays bass guitar, sings lead in DYLAN numbers and . . . is notoriously fond of Hamburgers.

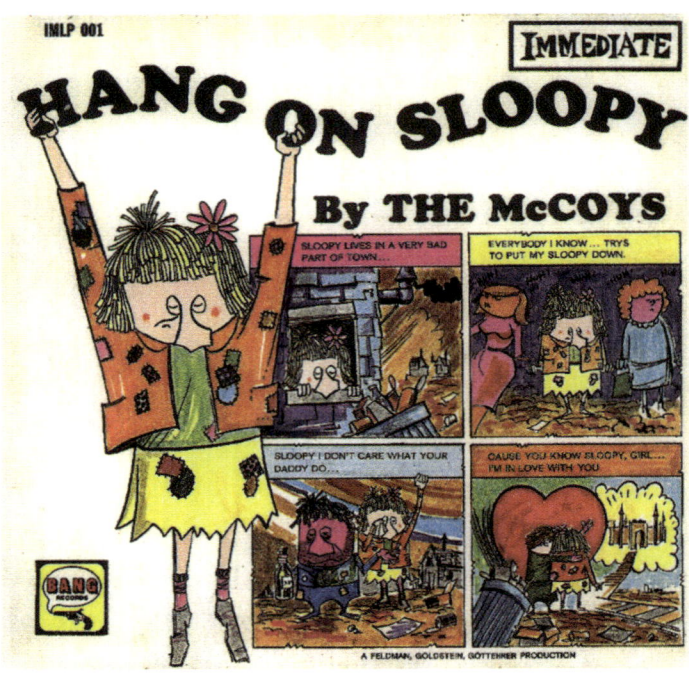

> the feel of a "Twist and Shout" or "Louie Louie".
> Our second record is by a new group called Fifth Avenue produced by Jimmy Page. The song is the Pete Seeger folk classic "The Bells of Rhymney". The third record I produced myself. It features a very talented artist who you all saw on Ready Steady Go! a few weeks ago called Nico. Nico has recorded a great song by Gordon Lightfoot who composed the Peter, Paul and Mary smash "For Loving Me". Now Gordon had come up with a brand new song "I'm Not Saying".

In an *NME* interview, the same week, Oldham expanded on the concept:

> It is our policy to only put out releases that will be promoted by every means possible, contrary to the policy of the major labels in the country. We believe that success lies in dispensing with the accepted tradition and going against the current trend, which is to deal with pop merchandise in a stiff and unimaginative manner. We want to give an aura of youth. There's no room in business for an old-club atmosphere. One must adopt streamlined [US] methods of selling and promotion.
>
> The business has changed. Four years ago I was a fan when the big guys in blue suits dressed a kid in white and advertised him as a star. We believed in them. Today young people are setting the trend for kids of their own age. The group boom has broken every rule that applied to pop. What we're seeing is not just a musical phenomena, it's a social phenomenon.

On the evening of 20 August, the Immediate launch party was held at Wolf Mankowitz's upmarket Pickwick club tucked away off Charing Cross Road in Soho. Wolf was the father of new Rolling Stones photographer Gered Mankowitz and had written one of Oldham's favourite pop texts, *Expresso Bongo*.

Pickwick, the refined night space come restaurant, was more accustomed to hosting the higher echelons of the film industry than the new pop aristocracy. During the night there was music and dancing but everyone stayed sharp, handsomely tailored and subtly illuminated. Rolling Stones, Eric Clapton and Jimmy Page mixed it up with new US act The Byrds and two very loud, savvy, New York Lindas: Stein and Goldner. Linda Stein was the wife of Seymour Stein—a young, Brill Building, go-getter who had originally hooked Oldham up with Bert Berns and "Hang On Sloopy". Seymour Stein (now one of the most famous US music industry executives) was also trying to get Immediate the UK rights to King Records, home to soul legend, James Brown. Linda Goldner was the daughter of infamous Red Bird Records boss George Goldner (who Seymour worked for at the Brill) and was assistant to Artie Ripp, boss at the newest and hippest New York independent label, Kama Sutra Records. Marianne Faithfull and Oldham's latest discovery, ice queen Nico, lent the party a different layer of exoticness. Faithfull and Nico, along with Oldham's wife, Sheila, and Keith Richards's girlfriend, Linda Keith, passed around marijuana. Calder was there with a young Steve Marriott, who was hitting on Mick Jagger's girl, Chrissie Shrimpton.

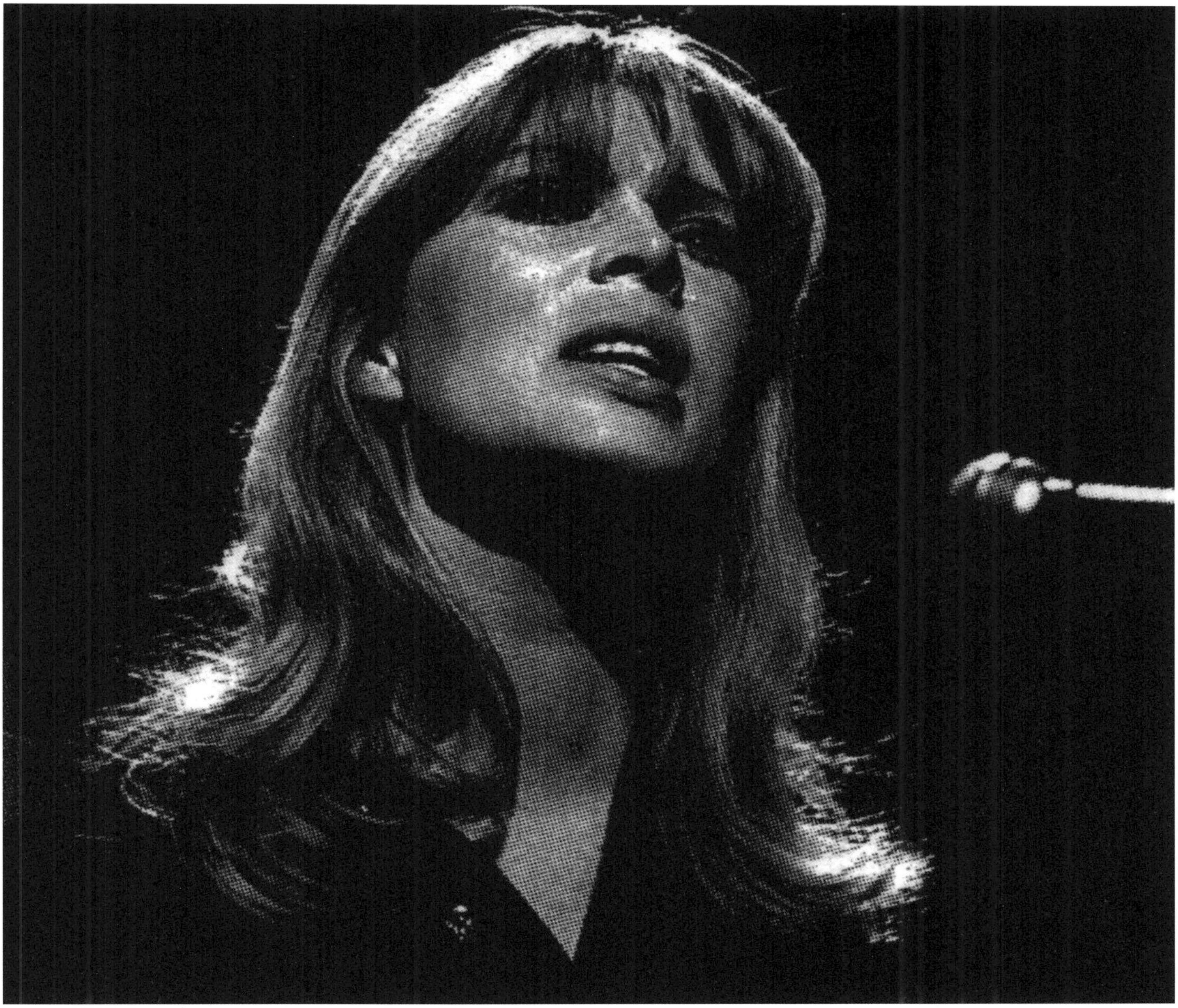

OPPOSITE TOP: THE ARTWORK FOR HIT SINGLE "HANG ON SLOOPY" BY THE MCCOYS, NOVEMBER 1965

OPPOSITE BOTTOM: THE MCCOYS ARE PRAISED IN THIS *NME* ARTICLE, SEPTEMBER 1965

NICO PERFORMS LIVE, 1965

The Who's managers, Kit Lambert and Chris Stamp, who kept offices in the same apartment block as Immediate, were all ears on how to retaliate against the music business and make their own millions. Their fresh-faced charge, Pete Townshend partied for five minutes but was a little in awe of Keith Richards and had taken too much speed to enjoy the lush surrounds. Of the Rolling Stones, Charlie was dapper, Bill was on the pull and Brian shook his blonde hair a lot and grinned his leery grin.

The party happily coincided with the release of Rolling Stones' "Satisfaction" in the UK. The track had already been released in the US and was a massive hit there: a first US number one for the band. Everyone at the party was blown away by "Satisfaction", and it required little hype from Oldham, who was busy working his new label, Immediate: "The most exciting thing for me since Rolling Stones made their chart debut", he told producer Mickie Most, as reported by *NME*.

The following day a full-page advert appeared in *NME*, *Melody Maker*, *Record Mirror,* and *Disc and Music Echo*, heralding the start of Immediate. It was over the top in extremis; at the time even new records by major acts were afforded no more than a quarter page advert. The advert, utilising distinctive typography, read:

"BIG ROCKETS FLY HIGH; OUT OF REACH.
THEY CAN'T SEE YOU, NOR YOU THEM.
YOU CAN SEE SMALL ROCKETS
THEY CAN SEE YOU
THAT IS CONTACT!"
FIRST RELEASES
HANG ON SLOOPY
THE McCOYS
IM 001
THE BELLS OF RHYMNEY
THE FIFTH AVENUE
IM 002
I'M NOT SAYIN'
NICO
IM 003
IMMEDIATE RECORDS
A NEW RECORD COMPANY OF TOMORROW TODAY
IMMEDIATE RECORD COMPANY LIMITED
IMMEDIATE RECORDS ARE DISTRIBUTED SOLELY BY PHILIPS RECORDS LIMITED
Philips Records Ltd., Beddington Farm Road, Purley Way, Croydon, Surrey. P.O. Box 90
Philips Records Ltd., Floodgate Street, Birmingham 5. P.O. Box 131. MIDLAND 8411
Philips Records Ltd., Lloyd House, 18 Lloyd Street, Manchester 2. P.O. Box 450.
Philips Records Ltd., 26 Bothwell Street, Glasgow C.2. CENTRAL 1617/8

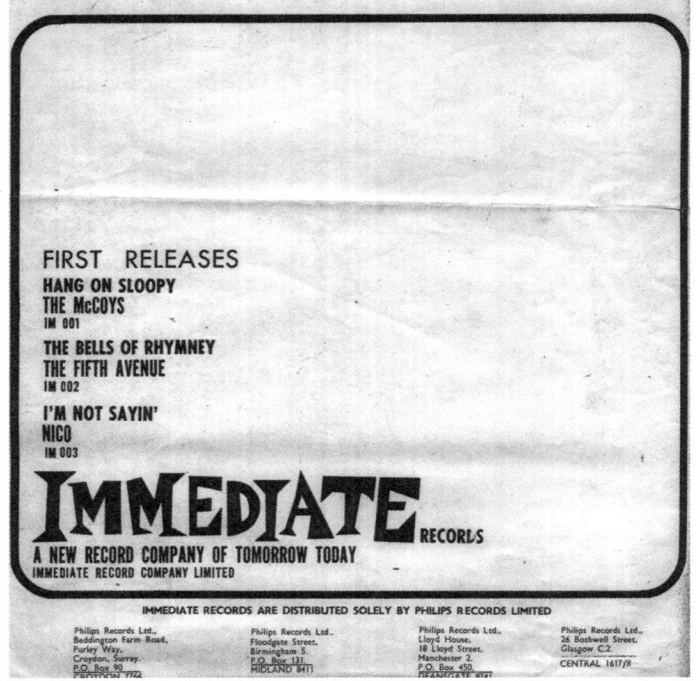

"Satisfaction" shot to the top of the UK chart, brushing aside The Walker Brother's "Make It Easy On Yourself", becoming the Rolling Stones fourth consecutive UK number one.

With the backing of pirate radio stations, London and Caroline, The McCoys' "Hang On Sloopy" became Immediate's first hit. By early October the song had replaced "Satisfaction" at number one on many charts. Already a number one in the US, the single was another first for the history books: a bicoastal independent chart-topper. The McCoys consisted of three non-descript teens from the US; the youngest (a stand-up drummer) was just 17 years old. Immediate announced that The McCoys would tour the UK later in the year.

During "Hang On Sloopy's" nine-week chart life, Immediate sold roughly 180,000 copies of the single—a phenomenal start. While The McCoys's bubblegum pop was the 'sound' of the Immediate launch, the label's 'look' came courtesy of Nico, who was ready and available for promotion in London. The international fashion model had heard Oldham was looking for girls "to turn into stars" after his success with Marianne Faithfull. Her real name was Christa Paffgen; she was German, gracefully tall, with long blonde hair and an incredible bone structure. It was easy to see why Brian Jones had fallen for her when they met in Paris after a Rolling Stones show at the Olympia. Years later Nico would document her relationship with Jones in vivid, vicious terms: how he knocked her around, leaving her bleeding and bruised, once trying to pin a brooch to her vaginal lips, even fucking her with a loaded gun and pouring hot wax on her nipples.

Nico used Jones to get to Oldham, who was impressed enough by her modelling credentials, film work in Fellini's *La Dolce Vita*, and friendship with Bob Dylan, to give her her first recording break. He remembers signing Nico to a deal in LA, while there recording "Satisfaction". In Richard Witts' book, *Nico, The Life and Lies of an Icon*, Nico claimed that Oldham took her to a secluded toilet where they each snorted a line of high-grade speed. Nico recalled him saying:

> It's time to do a deal. I'm going to start up a Rolling Stones record company. They'll be the producers and so will I, and we'll be able to give the breaks to people we love, like you, Nico. Once we've got the business sorted out with the legal people there'll be a contract for you. I'm thinking three singles for a start.

Originally Nico had wanted to record the song Dylan had written for her, "I'll Keep It With Mine". The sentiment and tempo were too downbeat for a debut but could work out as a follow-up single, Oldham told her. Jones reassured a disappointed Nico that his manager, Oldham, "knew the trade inside out". Nico wondered what trade he meant. "The drugs trade I think", she told Witts.

After recording Nico singing a cover of Dylan's "Blowin' in the Wind", a track he had already cut with Marianne Faithfull on vocals, Oldham cherry-picked Gordon Lightfoot's, "I'm Not

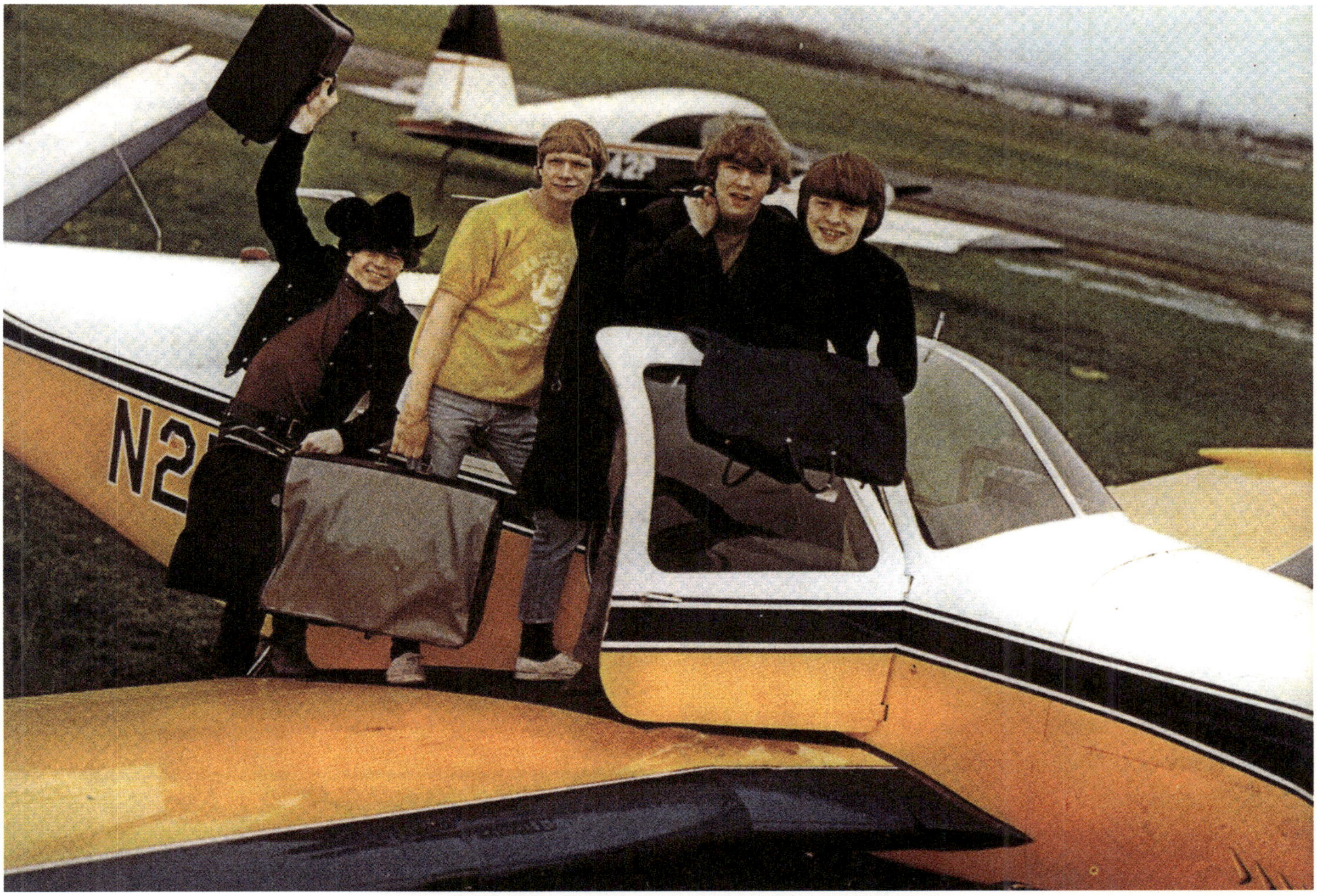

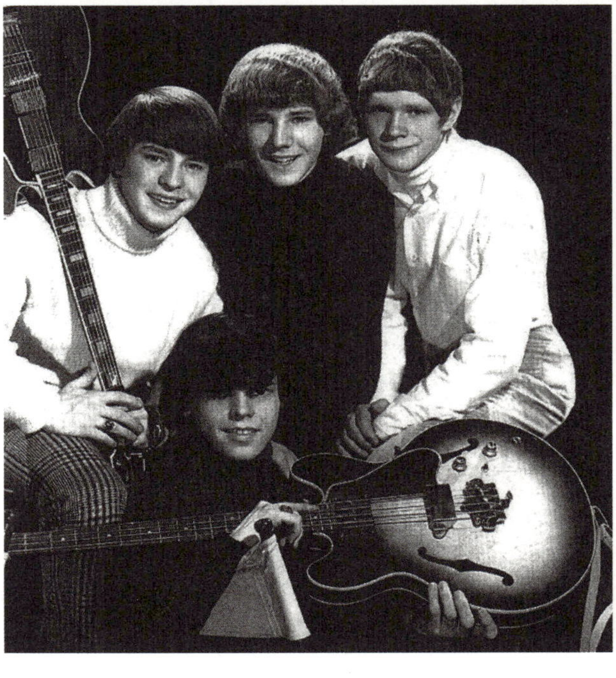

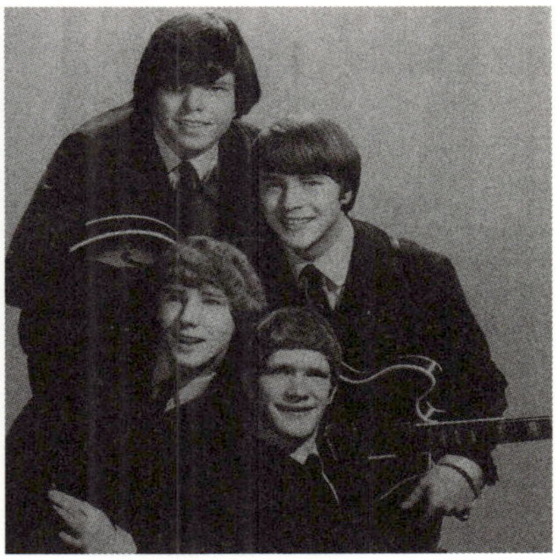

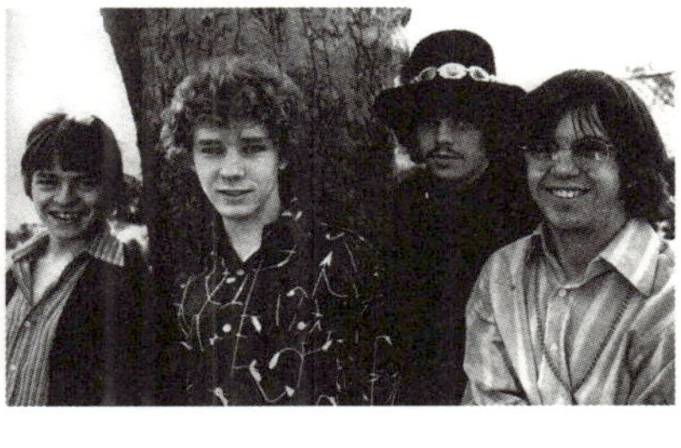

OPPOSITE: IMMEDIATE PRESS RELEASE, 1965

PROMOTIONAL SHOTS OF THE MCCOYS WHILST PROMOTING "HANG ON SLOOPY", CIRCA 1965

WHAT HAS TRUTH GOT TO DO WITH POP?

ROLLING STONES DISCOVERER ANDREW OLDHAM SLAMS AT RSG's NEW POLICY

So "Ready Steady Go" has changed its policy: no more miming to records! Well I'd say there's only a handful of groups in this country who are capable of giving top quality performances when playing live in the TV studio. This means that to maintain a standard comparable to the mimed "RSG" these top acts will have to rotate far too quickly. The Rolling Stones have no intention of going on TV every four weeks. That much exposure would reduce their value—they'd no longer be an event on TV. Besides, they—like the other top groups—are too busy.

Solo singers, of course, are something else. Here the problem is to provide them with large and competent orchestras, otherwise the singers' live performances are bound to sound inferior to their records. After all, a record these days is a very produced thing, heavily orchestrated and often using various recording studio sound effects. Any singer who goes on a stage—on TV or in a theatre—without these aids, accompanied by an ordinary band without a string section, has got be extra good to compensate for the deficiencies. It's not like a group, who can make the same sort of sound on or off record. I know very few singers who can sound as good in the flesh as they can on record. Orbison, Pitney, Springfield and one or two more, that's all.

SILLY

What strikes me as particularly silly in all this talk about the superiority of a live show to a mimed one is the implication that there is something more Truthful about being live. What's truth got to do with it?

The basic formula of pop records is making a sound that hits people in the face, makes them take notice, and helps fill their leisure hours. The business of pop music is meant to have an aura of glamour around it. Truth doesn't enter the picture. What matters is the product, however it's achieved. Sometimes it's a straight recorded performance, sometimes it's an engineering job, requiring the splicing together of many bits of tape from numerous takes of a number. If this juggling weren't done, quite a few careers would never have got started. Marianne Faithfull's a marvellous artiste NOW but there had to be a lot of splicing on her first record.

Sandie Shaw had two hit records before anybody heard her sing in public and getting a very good reviews.

Once the Stones were on "Saturday Club" and I said to the sound engineer: "Put a little more echo on that, will you?" D'you know—he went off in a huff, saying I was cheating the public! Fantastic! Most times, when you do a radio show anywhere in the world, the engineer says proudly: "Wasn't that like the record?" Which, of course, is the thing to aim at. Yet when I asked this man to try to make a performance like the record he complained. It's the sort of mentality you run into in this country far too often. You get some producer coming to a show from "Woman's Hour" or "Midland Theatre" who knows little and cares less about the sort of sound the public wants to hear. Incidentally, I must say that on "Ready Steady Go" recently I met a TV director, an American called Martin Lindsay Hogg, who got some very good camera shots and was one of the very few TV directors who was seriously concerned about getting the right sound: the Stones don't do any TV shows live where the sound is not good and I can't sit in the control booth and take care of it.

ANDREW OLDHAM—the new image, minus tinted glasses. (RM Pic.).

With all these strange notions about Truth going around it pays to be vigilant. Since the basic thing in the pop music industry is to make money by keeping people happy it's difficult to see how some of these phoney controversies about Truth and so on ever get started. I mean, miming was always the standard practice in the great Hollywood musicals and nobody said those movies were cheating the public. Really, the only thing that can be said against miming is that it shouldn't be done if the artiste can't mime accurately. I agree that the least a TV producer should expect is that an artiste should know his own record.

The worldwide success of British pop has given the business here a great feeling of self-importance. It's not justified. America is still the centre of the pop scene and I'm fully aware that I'm not as talented as the best American record producers by any stretch of the imagination. I agree with Marshall Chess who told me recently he thought British pop music is still in the third grade of high school. In America they're at the top of the school.

So how is it that we Britons have done so well lately? I think it's because a change is required every half decade. The business gets too clever for the public every so often and has to be brought back down to the basics—I Love You, I Need You, Don't Leave Me. In the States they'd got to clever refinements like Will You Love Me Tomorrow? The Beatles came along with their semi-naive messages and conquered. I don't mean that The Beatles themselves are naive, I'm talking about the content of such songs as She Loves You.

The r & b scene in America has always stayed pretty down to earth, as far as lyrics go, and that's one explanation of why the Stones have become so popular. They're basic.

Finally, I'd just like to say how much I admire Tony Hatch's new Searchers' record, "Goodbye My Love." It will prove even bigger than his "Downtown" and I think it will be number one all over the world.

ROY ORBISON
GOODNIGHT

HLU 9951

TWINKLE
GOLDEN LIGHTS
F 12076 DECCA

ACNE, BOILS, PIMPLES

DO THEY CAUSE YOU

If so get together NOW with fast working MASCOPIL. A 30-day treatment of MASCOPIL is guaranteed to clear up existing skin troubles and prevent them returning. MASCOPIL gets to the source of the trouble—within the system!

Just 2 tiny pills a day—what could be simpler? No more sticky creams or ointments, unpleasant squeezing or unsightly plasters—but most important of all—NO MORE EMBARRASSMENT Mr. F. P., of Norwich writes: "... after only one supply of MASCOPIL, the spots have all gone. It's lovely to go out and mix with people again. I must write and tell you what a wonderful discovery you have made For a descriptive leaflet and a 30-day treatment just send 8/6 (post free) to:
CROWN DRUG CO.
(Manufacturing Chemists Est. 1908)

OLDHAM DEBATES TRUTH IN POP AFTER TELEVISION SHOW READY STEADY GO! GOES LIVE, MARCH 1965

Sayin'" for Nico's Immediate debut. Canadian Lightfoot had written hits for Elvis Presley, Johnny Cash, and Barbara Streisand and was managed by Albert Grossman (who was also Bob Dylan's manager). Three months before her twenty-eighth birthday, Nico was the oldest person present during recording at Regent Sound, the basement demo studio in Denmark Street, Soho's 'Tin Pan Alley', where Oldham had also cut his first Rolling Stones hits. Assembled as backing for Nico were Brian Jones, Oldham's regular guitar/bass duo of Jimmy Page and John Paul Jones and arranger, Art Greenslade, who down-pitched the backing, allowing the monotoned Nico to half chant, half curse her way through the lyrics. In her hands, they took on an eerie despondency. Oldham jotted down some intensely gloomy lyrics for the b-side, "The Last Mile", which Jimmy Page quickly shaped into a passable song. Nico had appeared on (the then live) *Ready Steady Go!* to promote the single but it had turned into a disaster. Her timing was out and the band and orchestra, conducted by Art Greenslade, were only half way done by the time she had finished the lyric. Still, her stunning looks, exotic European accent and vacant pose, were a hit with the press and photos of her—sometimes happily posing with Oldham and Calder—were valuable publicity for Immediate.

A pop video was filmed of Nico lip-synching and swaying to the song by the river Thames, but chart success proved elusive for "I'm Not Sayin'" and when Brian Jones introduced her to Andy Warhol, she decided to jump ship. Warhol took "I'm Not Sayin'" as her audition for *de facto* Factory membership and would soon launch her alongside The Velvet Underground. Oldham didn't bear her any grudges because, as Immediate took its first strides, personalities were what the label required and she had notably been one of them. Oldham remembers:

> We served each other well for those few minutes in 1965 when she allowed us to unsuccessfully emulate the advanced copy of [Bob Lind's] "Elusive Butterfly" we had and some of the stellar Jackie de Shannon demos we loved. The McCoys with "Hang On Sloopy" went to number one for us but were unavailable and ugly. Nico helped us promote ourselves, and she understood the rhythm of life, did the movie and moved on to the next part.

When he agreed to join the label as 'staff producer', Jimmy Page, was already one of the top session guitarists on the London recording scene. He had been nicknamed "little Jimmy" so as not be confused with "big Jim" Sullivan, the other pre-eminent session guitarist of the time. Oldham had used Page on many past recordings, including his Andrew Loog Oldham Orchestra albums. Oldham also frequently used session bass player, John Baldwin, in the studio, re-naming him John Paul Jones and promoting him to arranger, giving him his first major break. Page and Jones, who cofounded Led Zeppelin four years later, often played together on early Immediate recordings. Oldham praised the 21-year-old Page in the press as "exceptionally talented" with "a big career ahead" but 'little Jimmy' was friendlier with Calder. The pair had been on a wild LA trip together, checking in at independent label Liberty Records (who had released "Elusive Butterfly"), another influence on early Immediate style. Page was a fan of Liberty's sexy new act, Jackie De Shannon, who had hit in the US with "Needles and Pins". He wrote the song "Come Stay With Me" for her which, back in the UK, Calder recorded with Marianne Faithfull. However, for contractual reasons Faithfull stayed with Decca and was never an Immediate act. For his first Immediate single Page had taken vocal duo, Fifth Avenue, into the studio to harmonise over his guitar on a cover of the Pete Seeger written "The Bells of Rhymney". The Byrds had covered the same song as the centrepiece for their debut album and the sound of the Immediate single was almost identical. Page "arranged produced and conducted" the release and wrote the moody b-side, "Just Like Anyone Would Do", with its recurring guitar motif hook. Questioned about it, over a decade later by 1970s rock magazine *Trouser Press*, Page said:

> It's got a fantastic sound on it. I used a double pick-up on the acoustic guitar; it had nice Beach Boys type harmonies. The band was just session musicians that happened to be around.
>
> Jackie De Shannon was playing guitar and she said, 'I've never found a guitarist who could adapt so quickly to the sort of things I'm doing.' She had these odd licks and she said: "It's usually a big struggle to get these things across." I didn't know what she was talking about, because I had been quite used to adapting. We wrote a few songs together, and they ended up getting done by Marianne Faithfull, PJ Proby, and Esther Phillips or one of those coloured artists did a few. I started receiving royalty statements, which was very unusual for me at the time, seeing the names of different people who had covered your songs. I just knew him, Oldham. I knew all the crooks. Better not print that he might sue me. Actually I love Oldham; he's one of the few producers I really respect.

"Everything Jimmy Page wanted to do for Immediate we let him", said Calder. "He was a lovely fella. His mum used to ring up our office and say, 'Is my Jimmy there?' She would be at home waiting up for him."

I LOVE OLDHAM, HE'S ONE OF THE FEW PRODUCERS I RESPECT
JIMMY PAGE

EARLY SINGLES

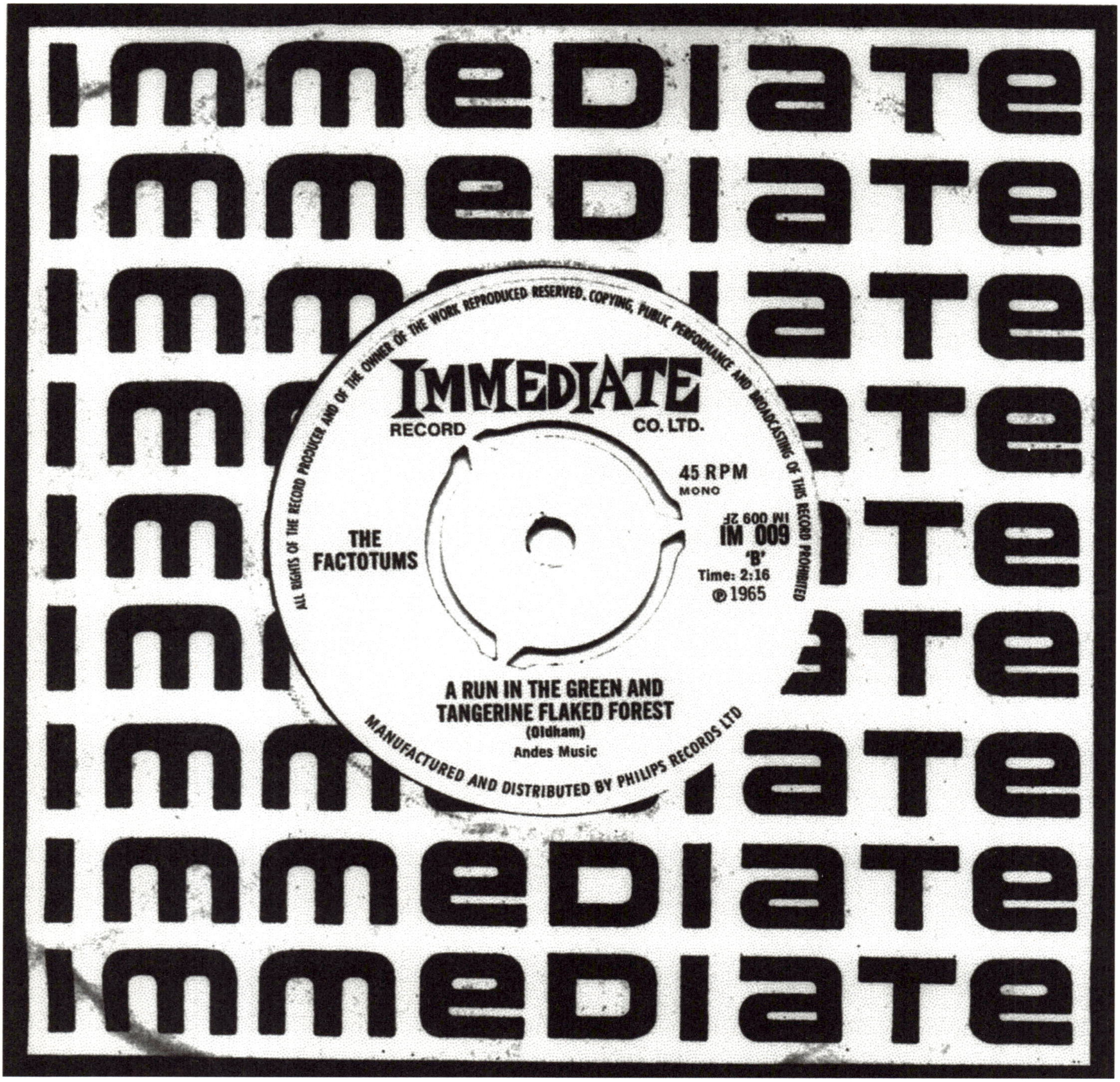
IMMEDIATE
ALL RIGHTS OF THE RECORD PRODUCER AND OF THE OWNER OF THE WORK REPRODUCED RESERVED. COPYING, PUBLIC PERFORMANCE AND BROADCASTING OF THIS RECORD PROHIBITED
IMMEDIATE
RECORD CO. LTD.
45 RPM
MONO
THE FACTOTUMS
IM 009
'B'
Time: 2:16
℗ 1965
A RUN IN THE GREEN AND TANGERINE FLAKED FOREST
(Oldham)
Andes Music
MANUFACTURED AND DISTRIBUTED BY PHILIPS RECORDS LTD

Over the final months of 1965, with Jimmy Page heavy involved, Immediate released 20 more singles by an odd ragbag of artists in a bewildering diversity of styles. Page produced a Liverpudlian outfit, The Masterminds, who were discovered by Oldham and Rolling Stones after a gig in Liverpool. The Masterminds created a passable homage cover of a Bob Dylan's "She Belongs To Me". Calder then hooked him up with teenage, early psychedelic outfit, Les Fleurs De Lys, for a cute cover of Buddy Holly's "Moondreams". Oldham chipped in with a great everything-but-the-kitchen-sink production of a Kennedy Street Enterprises act, The Factotums, on a cover of a track he had heard on an Ivy League single, "In My Lonely Room"; writing his own piss-take b-side for the release, "Run In The Green And Tangerine Flaked Forest".

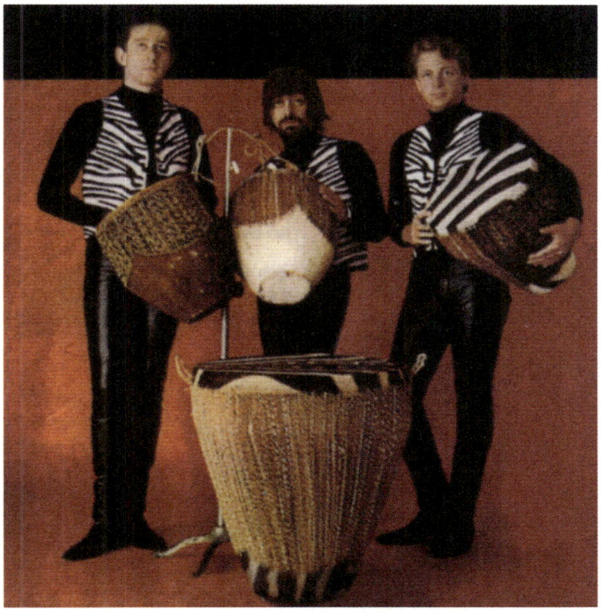

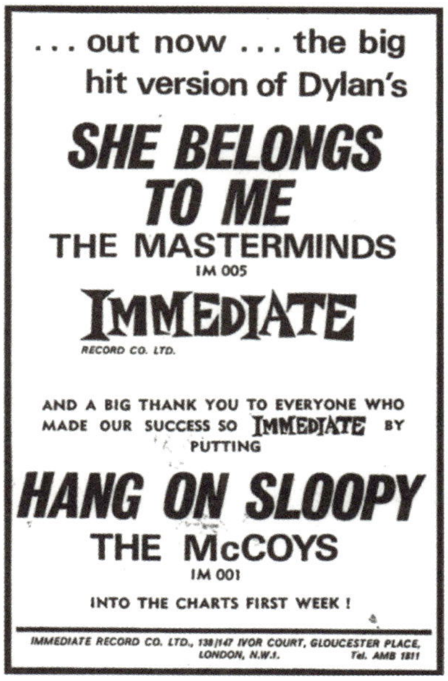

... out now ... the big hit version of Dylan's
SHE BELONGS TO ME
THE MASTERMINDS
IM 005
IMMEDIATE
RECORD CO. LTD.
AND A BIG THANK YOU TO EVERYONE WHO MADE OUR SUCCESS SO IMMEDIATE BY PUTTING
HANG ON SLOOPY
THE McCOYS
IM 001
INTO THE CHARTS FIRST WEEK !
IMMEDIATE RECORD CO. LTD., 138/147 IVOR COURT, GLOUCESTER PLACE, LONDON, N.W.1. Tel. AMB 1811

OPPOSITE: "A RUN IN THE GREEN AND TANGERINE FLAKED FOREST" BY THE FACTOTUMS WAS ONE OF IMMEDIATE'S EARLIEST RELEASES, 1965

TOP: IMMEDIATE BAND THE STRANGELOVES, 1965

BOTTOM: PROMOTIONAL MATERIAL FOR THE MASTERMINDS' "SHE BELONGS TO ME" AND THE MCCOYS "HANG ON SLOOPY" FEATURED IN *NME*, 1965

The Yardbirds production team, Giorgio Gomeslky and Paul Samwell-Smith, directed the release of another Kennedy Street Enterprises act, The Mockingbirds, who were managed by Herman's Hermits manager, Harvey Lisberg. Their haunting single "You Stole My Love" was written by their lead singer, the 19-year-old George Gouldman, who had already written massive hits for The Yardbirds, "For My Love"—a US Top 10 entry—and The Hollies, "Look Thru Any Window".

Courtesy of Bert Berns's Bang! label came the bubblegum beat of "Cara-Lin" by The Strangeloves. Also from the US, via a deal with Hercules records, came the Dylan *pastiche*, "Down And Out" by Joey Levine, who would go on to front acts for bubblegum label Buddha, and Barbara Lynn's smallish cult R&B hit "You Can't Buy Me Love", through a deal with Jamie Records. In the early 1960s Lynn had a hit US number one as an 18-year-old with her R&B classic, "You'll Lose A Good Thing", and Rolling Stones recorded another of her hits "We've Got a Good Thing Goin'".

The Kinks and Who producer, Shel Talmy, recorded Van Lenton's single "Gotta Get Away", a Cilla Black-style easy-listening outing. There were also The Golden Apples of the Sun, a group supposedly managed by photographer, David Bailey, fronted by a girl with great pipes, with an Oldham produced cover of Curtis Mayfield's "Monkey Time". Teenager, Greg Phillips, had been dropped in Oldham's lap by his show business pal Lionel Bart. Aged 14, Phillips starred in a film with Dirk Bogarde and Judy Garland, and the latter had become a sort of surrogate mother to Phillips in London. Phillips was friends with another former child actor, Steve Marriott, and, over the past few years, had cut a few singles for Pye between acting jobs. Jimmy Page and Oldham co-produced a single for Phillips, a cover of Billy Joe Royal's version of MOR hit "Down in the Boondock", which was a US smash that Oldham was led to understand would not be given a release in the UK. However, a few weeks after Immediate put out Phillip's version, the original was made available in the UK and Greg lost the chart battle.

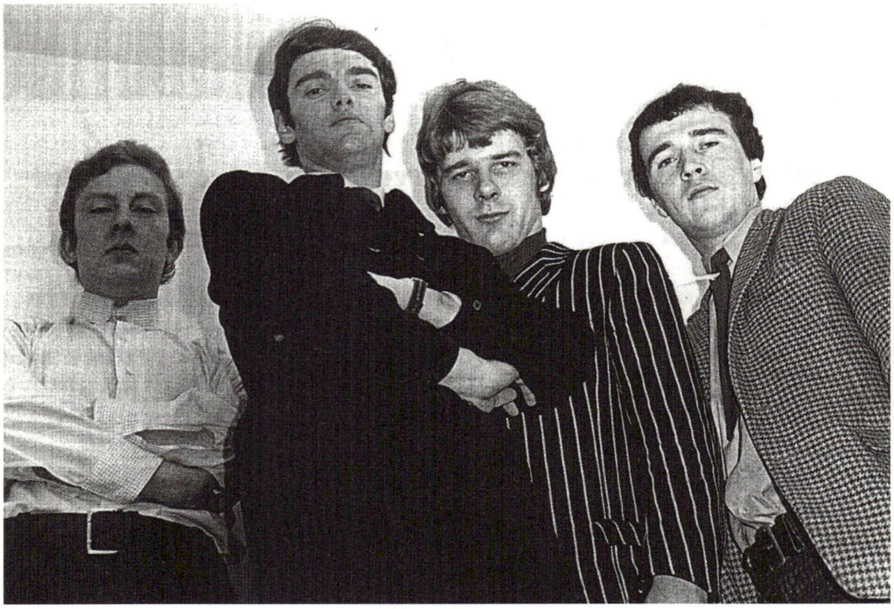

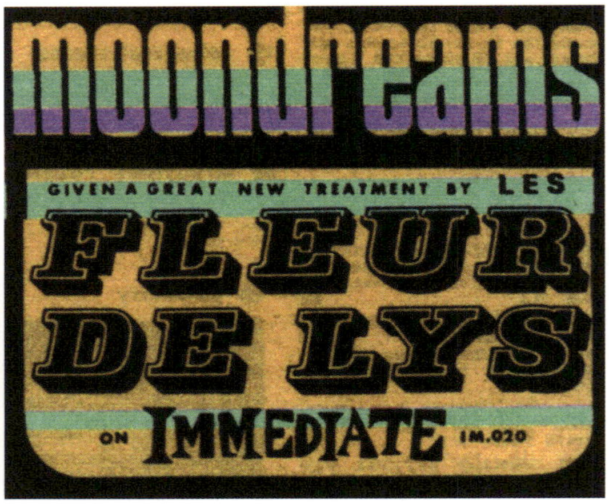
moondreams
GIVEN A GREAT NEW TREATMENT BY LES
FLEUR DE LYS
ON IMMEDIATE IM.020

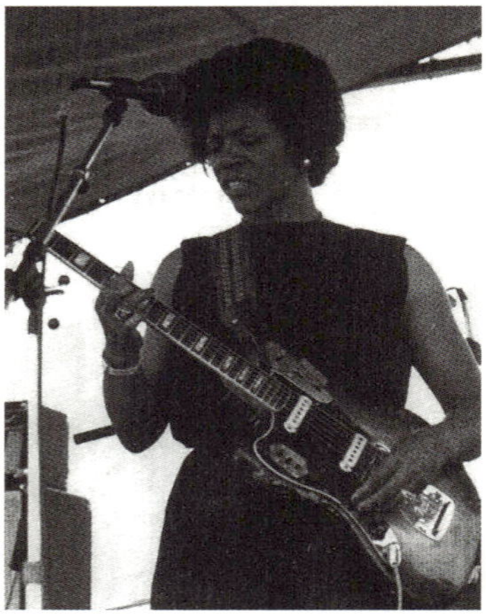

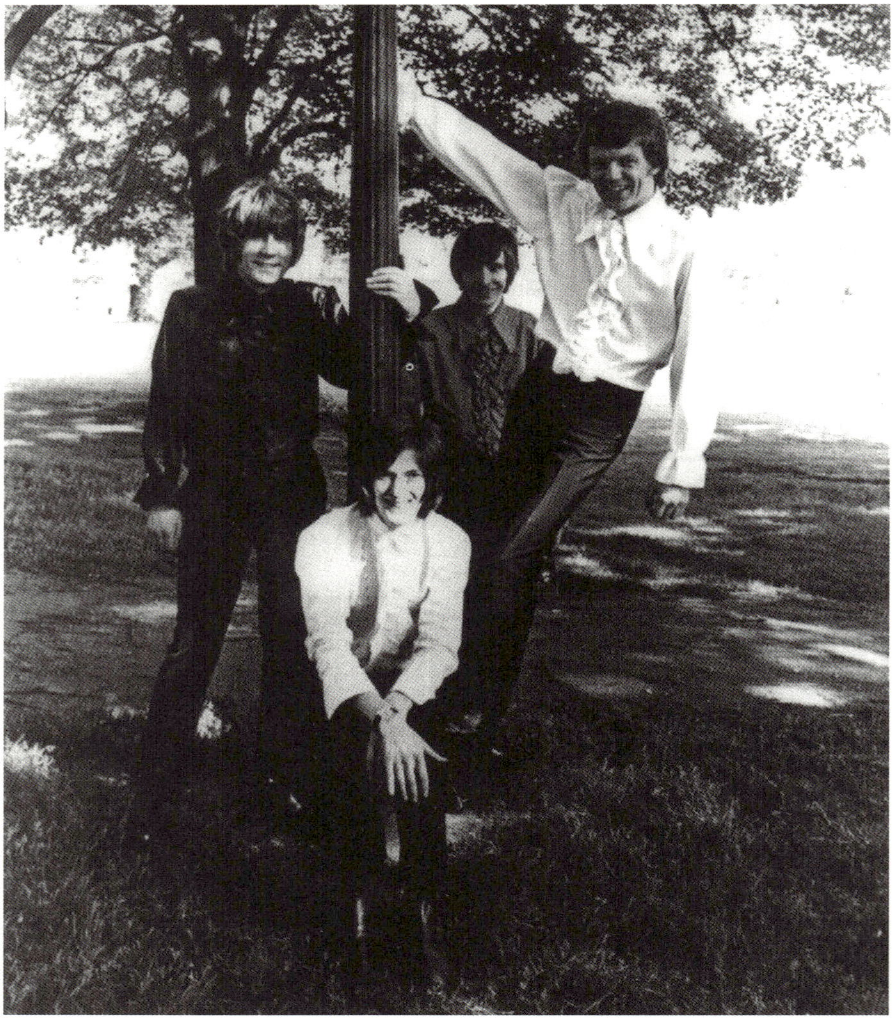

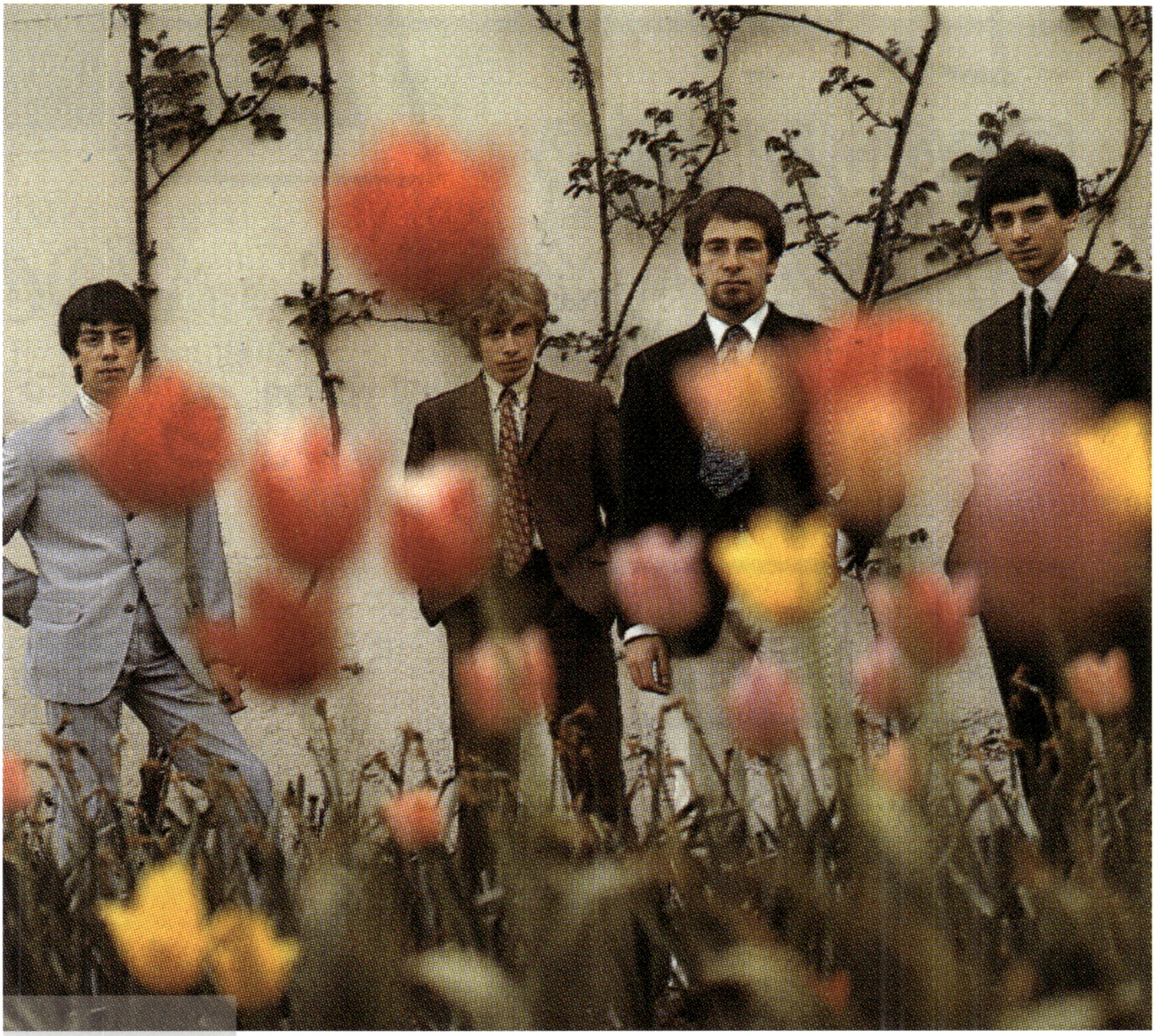

OPPOSITE: CLOCKWISE FROM THE TOP: THE FACTOTUMS, FLEUR DE LYS PROMOTIONAL MATERIAL, FLEUR DE LYS THEMSELVES AND BARBARA LYNN, ALL TAKEN IN LATE 1965

IN THE GARDEN: THE MOCKINGBIRDS WITH GRAHAM GOLDMAN (IN THE BLUE SUIT), OCTOBER 1965

THE WEIRD EARLY SINGLES GAVE THE LABEL A CULT APPEAL. THE LABEL FELT ESTABLISHED ALREADY

SIMON SPENCE

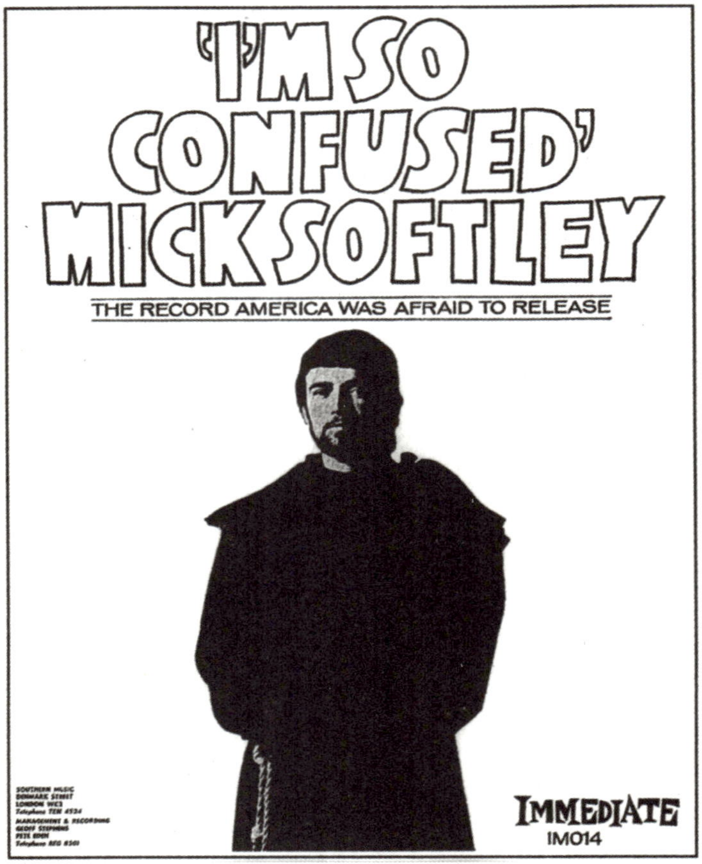
'I'M SO CONFUSED'
MICK SOFTLEY
THE RECORD AMERICA WAS AFRAID TO RELEASE
IMMEDIATE
IM014

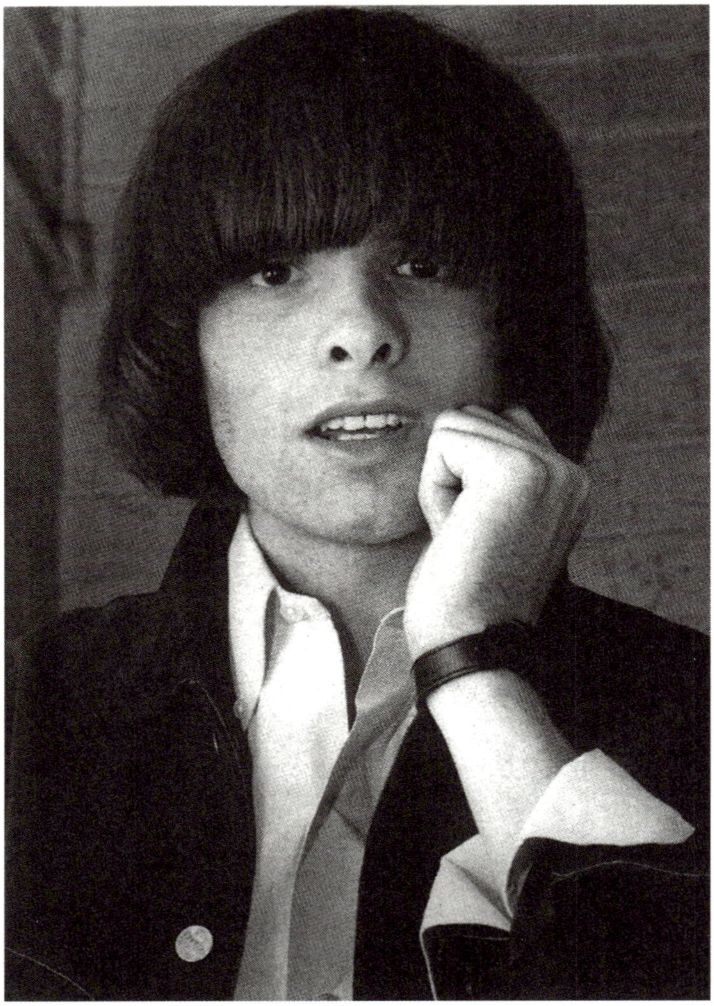

OLDHAM HAS BUILT THE ROLLING STONES SUPREMELY SUCCESSFULLY, LAUNCHED A PROMISING NEW LABEL, IMMEDIATE, AND ADDS GREAT ATMOSPHERE IN RECORDING SESSIONS

DENNY CORDELL

LEFT: MICK SOFTLY PROMOTIONAL MATERIAL, NOVEMBER 1965

RIGHT: THE HANDSOME DAVID ANTHONY OF CHARLES DICKENS, CIRCA 1965

"Folk plus protest equal hits", Oldham noted in one of his final *Disc and Music Echo* columns, as Dylan, The Byrds and Barry McGuire's "Eve Of Destruction" rose in the US.

Immediate signed Mick Softly, a folkesque songwriter friend of Donovan ("Britain's Dylan"), and released his single "I'm So Confused", produced by Donovan's managers, Geoff Stephens and Peter Eden. Immediate's press releases were often as entertaining as their records, and for his Dylan impersonating release, Softly was suggested to have been a Jesuit novice who now insisted on wearing a monk's habit on all television appearances.

Immediate also pressed up the Julian Protest Quintet's instrumental version of "Satisfaction", with a comically mean b-side written by Oldham, aptly named "Like A Bob Dylan" in response to Dylan's breakthrough cut, "Like A Rolling Stone". More laughs came courtesy of comic, Jimmy Tarbuck, the new MC on ITV's top show, *Sunday Night At The London Palladium*. Oldham took him into the studio with Art Greenslade arranging to produce a cover of the Ricky Nelson hit, "Someday You'll Want Me To Want", which he had seen Cher perform a big band

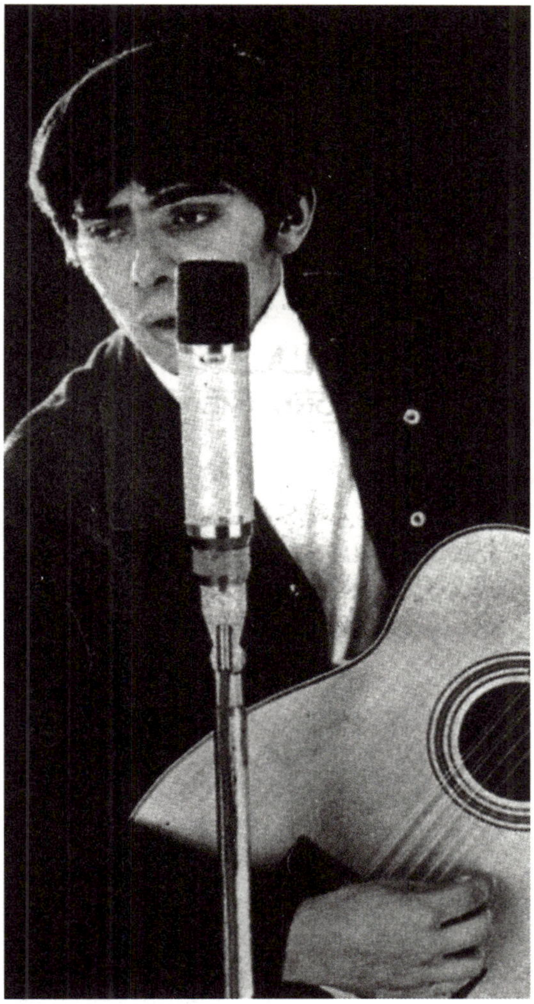

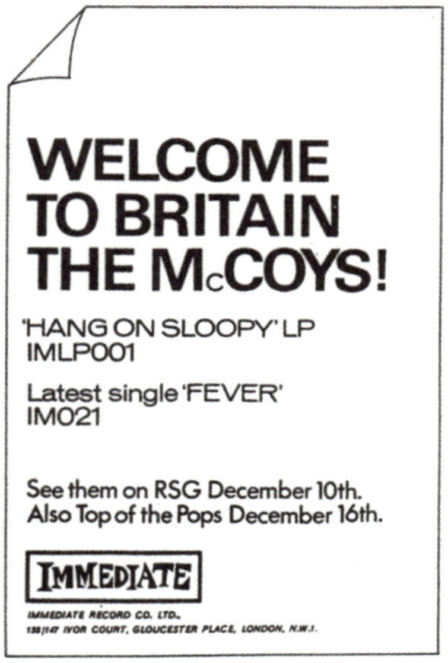
WELCOME TO BRITAIN THE McCOYS!
'HANG ON SLOOPY' LP
IMLP001
Latest single 'FEVER'
IM021
See them on RSG December 10th.
Also Top of the Pops December 16th.
IMMEDIATE
IMMEDIATE RECORD CO. LTD.
138/147 IVOR COURT, GLOUCESTER PLACE, LONDON, N.W.1.

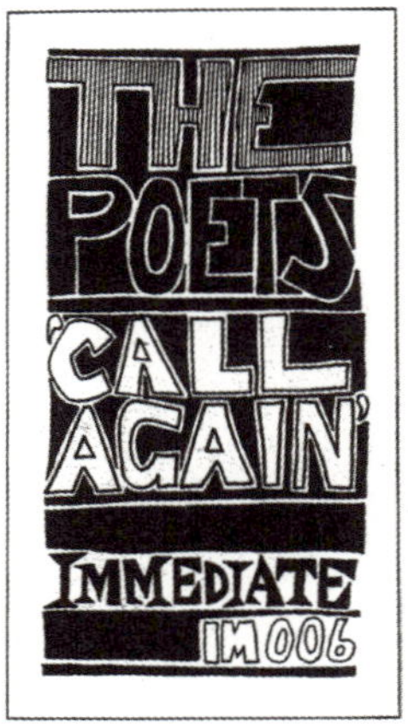
THE POETS
'CALL AGAIN'
IMMEDIATE
IM006

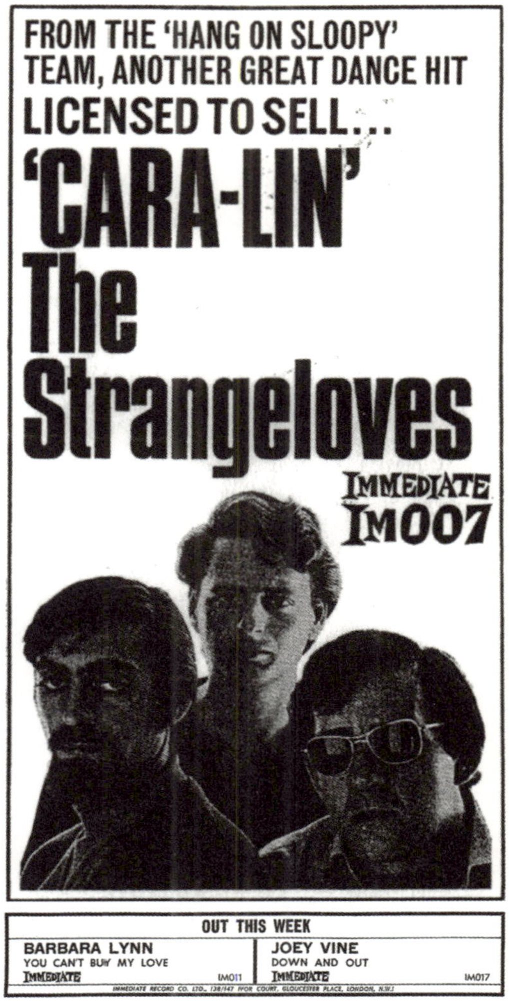
FROM THE 'HANG ON SLOOPY' TEAM, ANOTHER GREAT DANCE HIT
LICENSED TO SELL...
'CARA-LIN'
The Strangeloves
IMMEDIATE
IM007
OUT THIS WEEK
BARBARA LYNN
YOU CAN'T BUY MY LOVE
IMMEDIATE
IM011
JOEY VINE
DOWN AND OUT
IMMEDIATE
IM017

WE WEREN'T IN IT FOR THE MONEY, IT WAS JUST FUN

TONY KING

CLOCKWISE FROM TOP: GLYN JOHNS, PROMOTIONAL ADVERTISING FOR THE MCCOYS, THE STRANGELOVES PROMOTING "CARA-LIN" AND THE IMMEDIATE ADVERTISING FOR JOHN LENNON ENDORSED BAND THE POET'S AND THEIR SINGLE "CALL AGAIN", CIRCA 1965

version. The b-side of the Tarbuck single was a Jagger/Richards song, "We're Wasting Time". Greenslade recalled: "It was Jimmy's first record, I went in and he was absolutely crapping his pants, he was so scared." Another Mick and Keith song, "So Much In Love", was used as an a-side for an act called Charles Dickens, fronted by fashion photographer, David Anthony.

The Rolling Stones' previous recording engineer, Glyn Johns', went from the control booth to the vocal booth for his debut single, a deep-voiced croon cover of the Shadows recent hit "Mary-Anne". Unfortunately sales of the single were less than the number of promotional copies sent to the press and radio.

The McCoys arrived in London to promote their "Hang On Sloopy" follow-up, "Fever", and their debut UK album, *The McCoys*. A ten-day visit included performances on television programmes, *Ready Steady Go!* and *Top of the Pops*. The single was a little too cabaret inspired but the b-side "Sorrow" was a top five hit. Unfortunately for Immediate the chart position was achieved when "Sorrow" was covered by The Merseys a year later. "Sorrow" was later revamped by David Bowie on his 1970s *Pin-Ups* album.

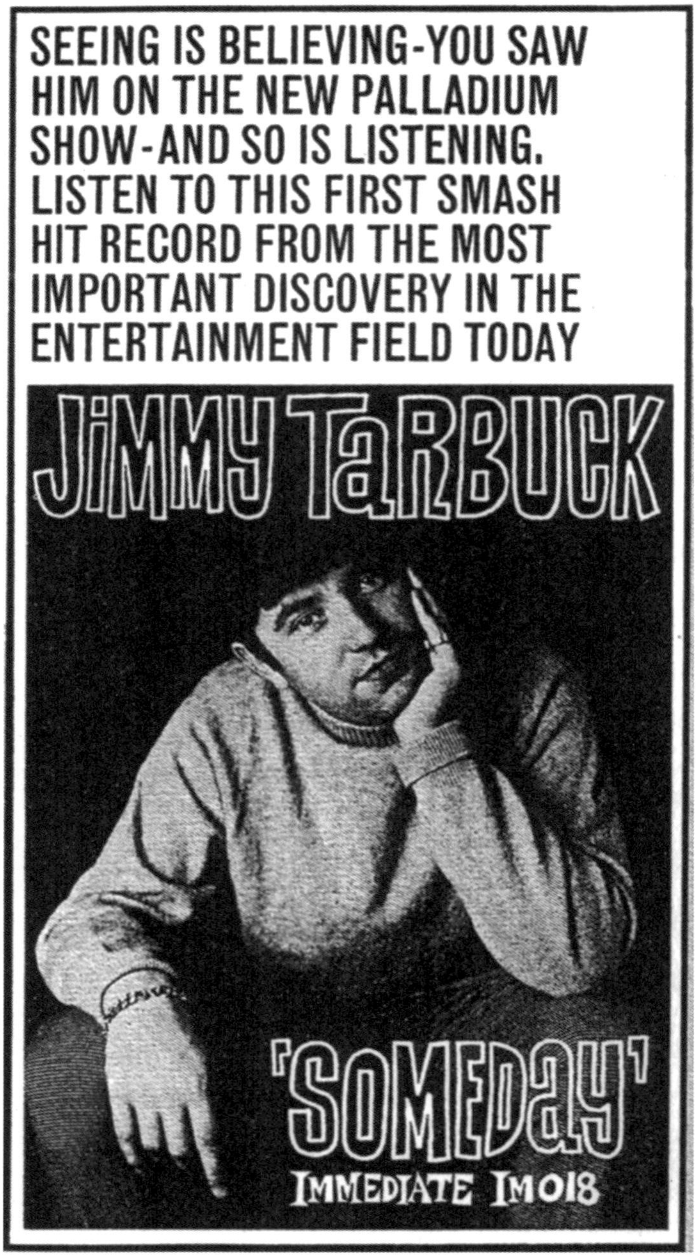
SEEING IS BELIEVING-YOU SAW HIM ON THE NEW PALLADIUM SHOW-AND SO IS LISTENING. LISTEN TO THIS FIRST SMASH HIT RECORD FROM THE MOST IMPORTANT DISCOVERY IN THE ENTERTAINMENT FIELD TODAY
JIMMY TARBUCK
'SOMEDAY'
IMMEDIATE IM018

Oldham had discovered The Poets in Glasgow when he eloped to marry his teenage bride, Sheila Klein, in 1964. The Poets early work with Oldham (released by Decca) had been endorsed by John Lennon and now they recorded their debut Immediate single "Call Again". Oldham once again enjoyed their droning sound and the fact that they performed original material, the stark simplicity of which afforded him a lot of space in which to indulge his Phil Spector doppelganger, with reverb and additional percussion. Singer, George Gallagher, remembered "wide boy trickster" Tony Calder handing out the group's £8 a week Immediate wage.

Immediate also raided Soho's trendy "Hammond and horns urban R&B" scene (the UK's hottest underground movement) for talent and signed up two of the leading lights, John Mayall and Chris Farlowe. Both men were regulars at the Flamingo Club on Wardour Street, London, a live distraction for wild crowds of mods, jazzers, US servicemen, prostitutes and pimps; all getting their kicks to a steamy mix of Blue Note, Jamaican Blue Beat, American Stax and Tamla Motown music.

Guitarist and singer/songwriter, John Mayall, had moved down from Manchester and made a name for himself in London with his Bluesbreakers outfit featuring Eric Clapton on guitar and Jack Bruce on bass—men who later became two thirds of the band Cream. Mayall was managed by no-nonsense Flamingo Club boss, Rik Gunnell, who also looked after the careers of Chris Farlowe, Alan Price (who had just departed from The Animals), Geno Washington and The Shotgun Express. John Mayall and the Bluesbreakers recorded the evil, horror inspired, "I'm Your Witchdoctor" for Immediate. Written by Mayall and produced by Jimmy Page, the song is an outstanding example of British "blues" at its best, sounding like Jim Hendrix several years in advance.

At first glance Chris Farlowe was just a rat-faced shouter but Otis Redding apparently rated him and he arrived at Immediate with his own hot backing group, The Thunderbirds, featuring Albert Lee on guitar and Nicky Hopkins on piano. Farlowe had been a regular on the Hamburg scene in the early 1960s before signing to Gunnell and had already recorded for Decca, EMI and Sue, but, aged 25, was still looking for his first hit. His withdrawn EMI single "Buzz With The Fuzz" had won him many mod votes, including those of Paul McCartney, Steve Winwood and Georgie Fame. The Animals vocalist, Eric Burden, was also a Farlowe fan and the two performed on an episode of *Ready Steady Go!* devoted to the music of Otis Reading. Burden was persuaded in to the studio to produce Farlowe's debut single for Immediate, the bluesy "The Fool". Oldham praised Farlowe in *NME*, saying: "He's the first since Mick Jagger who can really sing and, with the right pushing, he could become not only an R&B singer but an all-round entertainer." Mick Jagger was also a fan and, toward the end of 1965, the Rolling Stones singer went public with his involvement at Immediate, announcing he had become Farlowe's new producer, along with Oldham and Keith Richards under the guise of We Three Producers. At IBC studios, with Art Greenslade's arranging, they cut a four track EP, "In The Midnight Hour". The title track was recorded as well as "Mr Pitiful", a cover

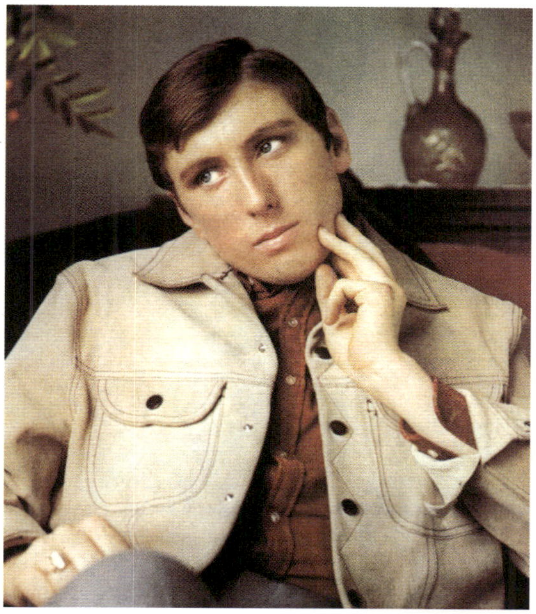

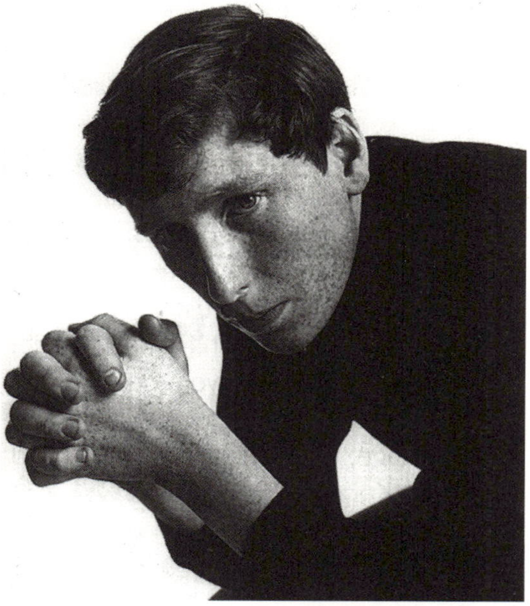

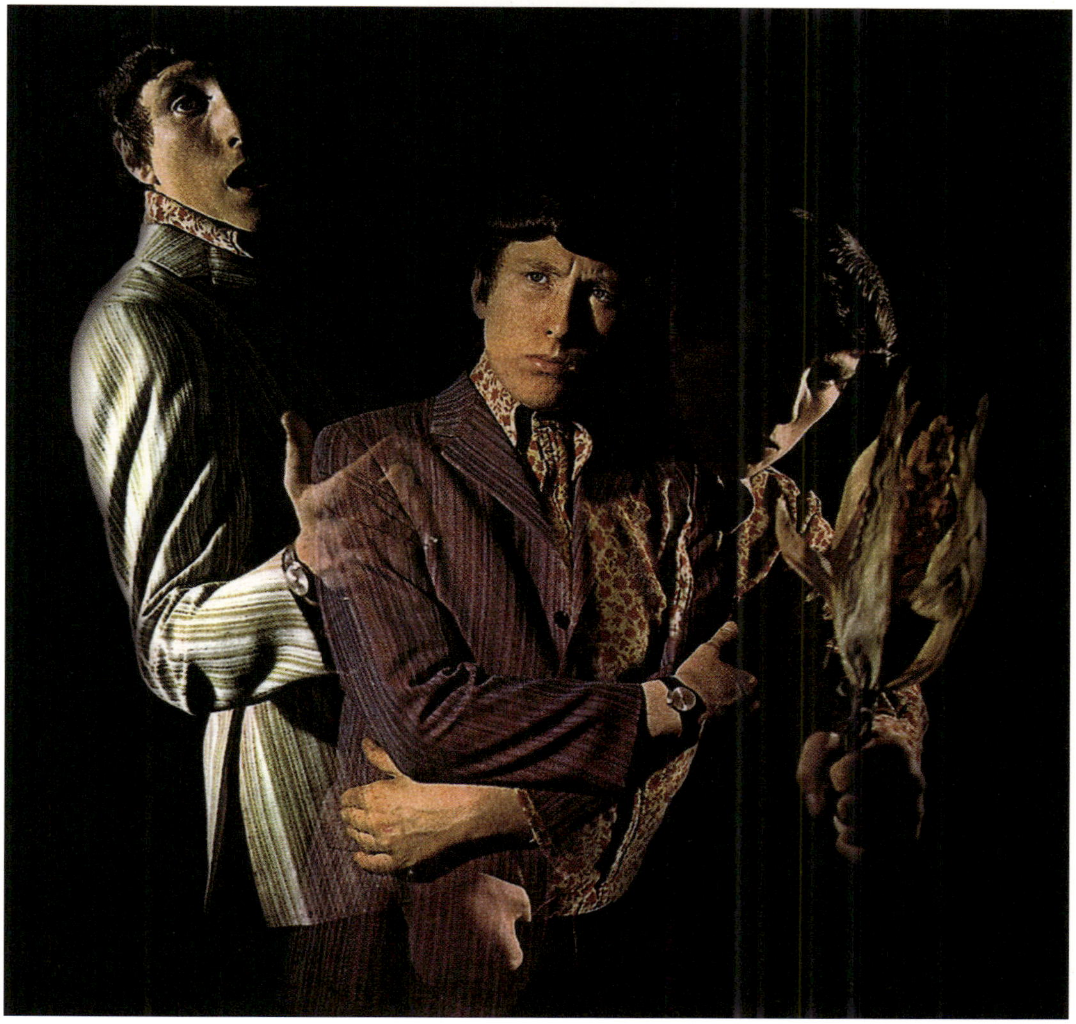

OPPOSITE: JIMMY TARBUCK PROMOTING "SOMEDAY". ART GREENSLADE RECALLS: "IT WAS JIMMY'S FIRST RECORD, I WENT IN AND HE WAS ABSOLUTELY CRAPPING HIS PANTS, HE WAS SO SCARED." OCTOBER 1965

PROMOTIONAL SHOTS FOR CHRIS FARLOWE, 1965

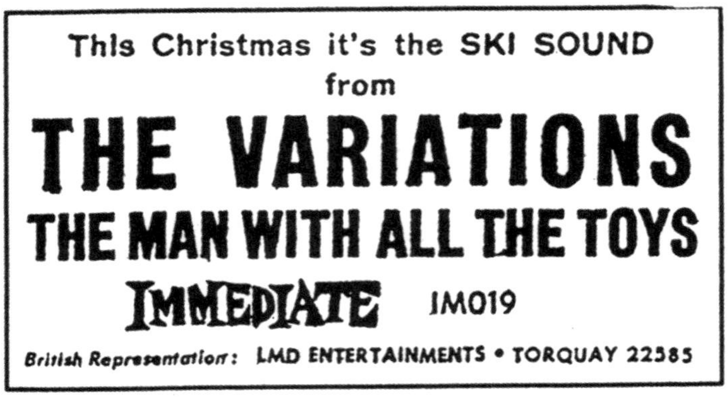
This Christmas it's the SKI SOUND
from
THE VARIATIONS
THE MAN WITH ALL THE TOYS
IMMEDIATE IM019
British Representation: LMD ENTERTAINMENTS • TORQUAY 22585

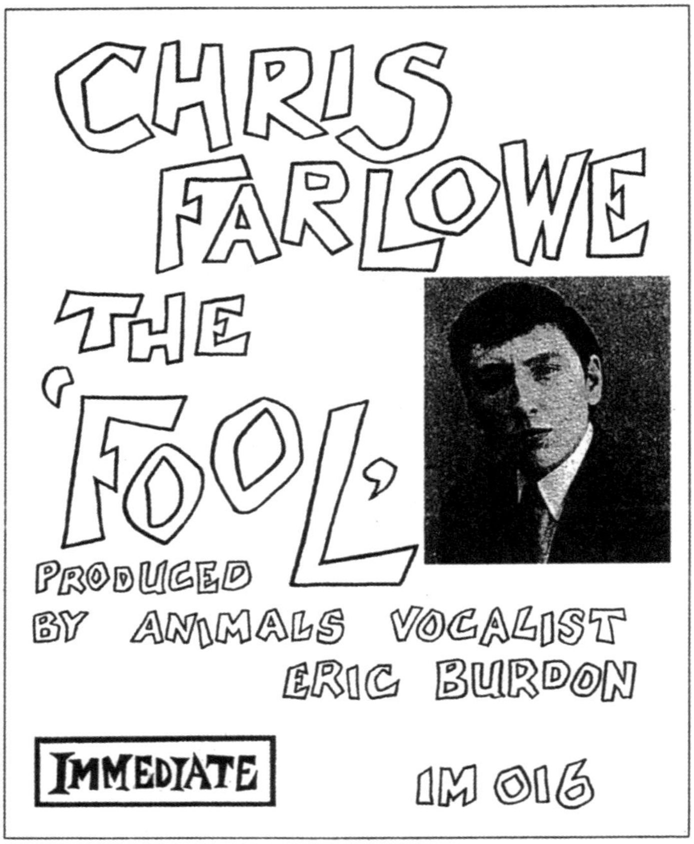
CHRIS FARLOWE
THE 'FOOL'
PRODUCED BY ANIMALS VOCALIST ERIC BURDON
IMMEDIATE
IM 016

TOP: IMMEDIATE PROMOTION FOR THE VARIATIONS' DEBUT, "THE MAN WITH ALL THE TOYS", DECEMBER 1965

BOTTOM: CHRIS FARLOWE'S "THE FOOL", OCTOBER 1965

of "Satisfaction" and an obscure Anthony Newley track "Who Can I Turn To?". Despite the EP retailing at around double the price of a single, it made number 21 in the singles chart, as well as a high entry in the EP charts.

Immediate's final release of 1965 was a pop-tastic "Christmas" single. Produced by a teenage Gary Glitter, then going by the name of Paul Raven (real name Paul Gadd), and advertised as "The Ski Sound", The Variations covered Brian Wilson's "The Man With All The Toys", a track taken from the Beach Boys Christmas Album. Rounding off the year, Immediate took out more full-page music press simply wishing the UK record industry merry Christmas.

In *NME*, "Whiter Shade Of Pale" recording manager Denny Cordell, named Oldham as "definitely Mr 1965", saying, "he has built the Rolling Stones supremely, successfully launched a promising new label, Immediate, and adds great atmosphere at recording sessions". Decca Promotions manager, Tony Hall, rounding up his year in *Record Mirror* gave, "full hallmarks for the one and only Andrew Oldham, who has consistently enlivened (if often infuriated) the record business this year—under the frighteningly astute guidance of Allen Klein—and who had the guts to start Britain's first real independent label."

I asked Oldham if he could elaborate on some of these early Immediate releases but he merely pointed to his hectic late 1965 schedule with Rolling Stones. On his behalf, hard-nosed US lawyer, Allen Klein, was renegotiating the group's deal with Decca, as their new single "Get Off Of My Cloud" followed "Satisfaction" to number one in the US and UK charts (their fifth consecutive UK number one, equalling the tally of Elvis and The Beatles). The "wonderful pressure of success", as Oldham called it, was relentless. The most time-consuming aspect was a Klein-arranged mammoth end of 1965 US tour. The six week tour, covering 35 cities, clinched the Rolling Stones arrival in the top league of US entertainers, grossing them a massive $1.5 million. Oldham was also working overtime to facilitate the growing demands for Rolling Stones product in the US, patching together an album, *December's Children (And Everybody's)* and a single "As Tears Go By", for the Christmas market. In the UK, a new album *Out of Our Heads* topped the charts. There were also five *Top of the Pops* and three *Ready Steady Go!* appearances to oversee—including a *Ready Steady Go!* Rolling Stones special, on which Oldham and Jagger dueted on Sonny and Cher's "I Got You Babe".

With Calder at the wheel—and excluding "Hang On Sloopy" and the Rolling Stones-promoted Chris Farlowe EP—none of these early Immediate singles troubled the Top 20. Calder explained to me how, at the time, "working a record" was a case of testing the waters with radio DJs by sending out promos and, if nobody was keen, just moving on to the next. He had encouraged this turnover of singles and acts to "try and establish ourselves". Calder could pursue this policy partly due to the innovative deal Immediate had with Philips, who manufactured and distributed Immediate records for a 17.5 per cent share of profits. Philips, unusually for the business, paid up every 30 days on records sold, whereas

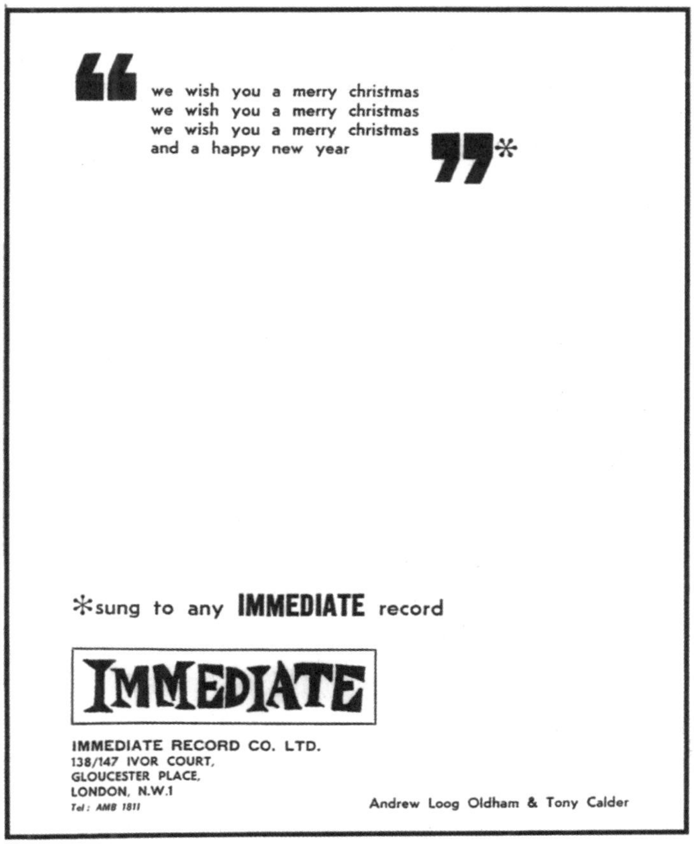
“we wish you a merry christmas
we wish you a merry christmas
we wish you a merry christmas
and a happy new year”*
*sung to any IMMEDIATE record
IMMEDIATE
IMMEDIATE RECORD CO. LTD.
138/147 IVOR COURT,
GLOUCESTER PLACE,
LONDON, N.W.1
Tel: AMB 1811
Andrew Loog Oldham & Tony Calder

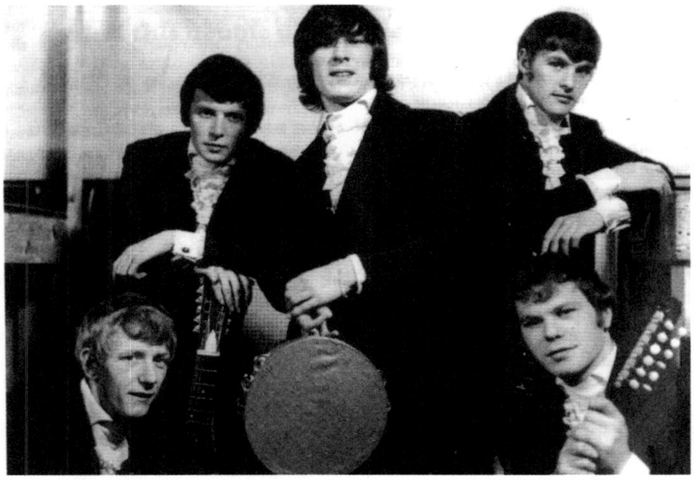

TOP: IMMEDIATE WISHES THE MUSIC INDUSTRY A MERRY CHRISTMAS, 1965

BOTTOM: IMMEDIATE BAND THE POETS, WHO OLDHAM DISCOVERED DURING HIS HONEYMOON, OCTOBER 1965

the Rolling Stones, for instance, had been forced to wait 18 long months before getting their first record royalties from Decca. This meant there was a constant feed of Immediate money for Calder to juggle with. Calder's tactics had been successful, even if Oldham would have preferred another hit, the weird early singles had given the label cult appeal. Alongside the number one straight out of the trap and the hard-to-ignore adverts, the label felt established already.

Busy with Rolling Stones, Oldham had hired Tony King to work alongside Calder as Immediate's new Head of Promotions. A young gay man in his early 20s, King had worked for Decca in promotions and as a personal assistant to Roy Orbison. King worked from Oldham's office at 138 Ivor Court, Gloucester Place, W1, from where the Rolling Stones business was also conducted. Calder was situated at number 147, a floor above, in the same ritzy residential apartment block near Baker Street, overlooking Regent's Park. Both offices were rented weekly for £50. The Immediate 'engine room', with its black and white tiled floor, was considered to be Calder's office, where he also lived with his girlfriend Josie. Oldham's office at 138 was more creative. One interviewer noted Oldham, in 138, "poised on a chair he had had made to spec for £80", curtains drawn, decked out in tight sludge-green corduroys, suede Clark's desert boots, pyjama-style, striped shirt with a chunky silver identity bracelet, his long blonde hair curling over a tan suede jacket. Here, the marijuana leaf wallpaper was complimented by brown and green velvet décor. 138 was a good bolthole in central London and King recalls often arriving at work to find Keith Richards and other acts asleep in the bedroom. Tony King remembers:

> I worked hard promoting "Hang On Sloopy", pulling in favours. We weren't in it for the money, it was just fun. I did all the mailing myself, I did all the packing of the envelopes. I had a tiny office and I was just furiously stuffing envelopes full of records, sticking on stamps and taking them to the post office, running around town delivering them to the BBC. I loved doing it. I would do it till midnight or 2am. There was a lot of pot [marijuana] around, I was the official potholder. I had to go around the corner to these two call girls, who always had really good stuff, and I would keep different types of grass in different drawers in the office. Tony's job was to whip up the troops, he used to piss people off most of the time. Once he was shouting, "I want work!". Oldham and I burst out laughing and it became a sort of catchphrase in the office. Tony was important to Oldham but Oldham was dismissive toward him much of the time. He thought of him as a good joke. Tony was hard-edged, hard-nosed in business, he could be Oldham's bad guy. When there was dirty work to be done Tony could do it and Oldham would still look okay.

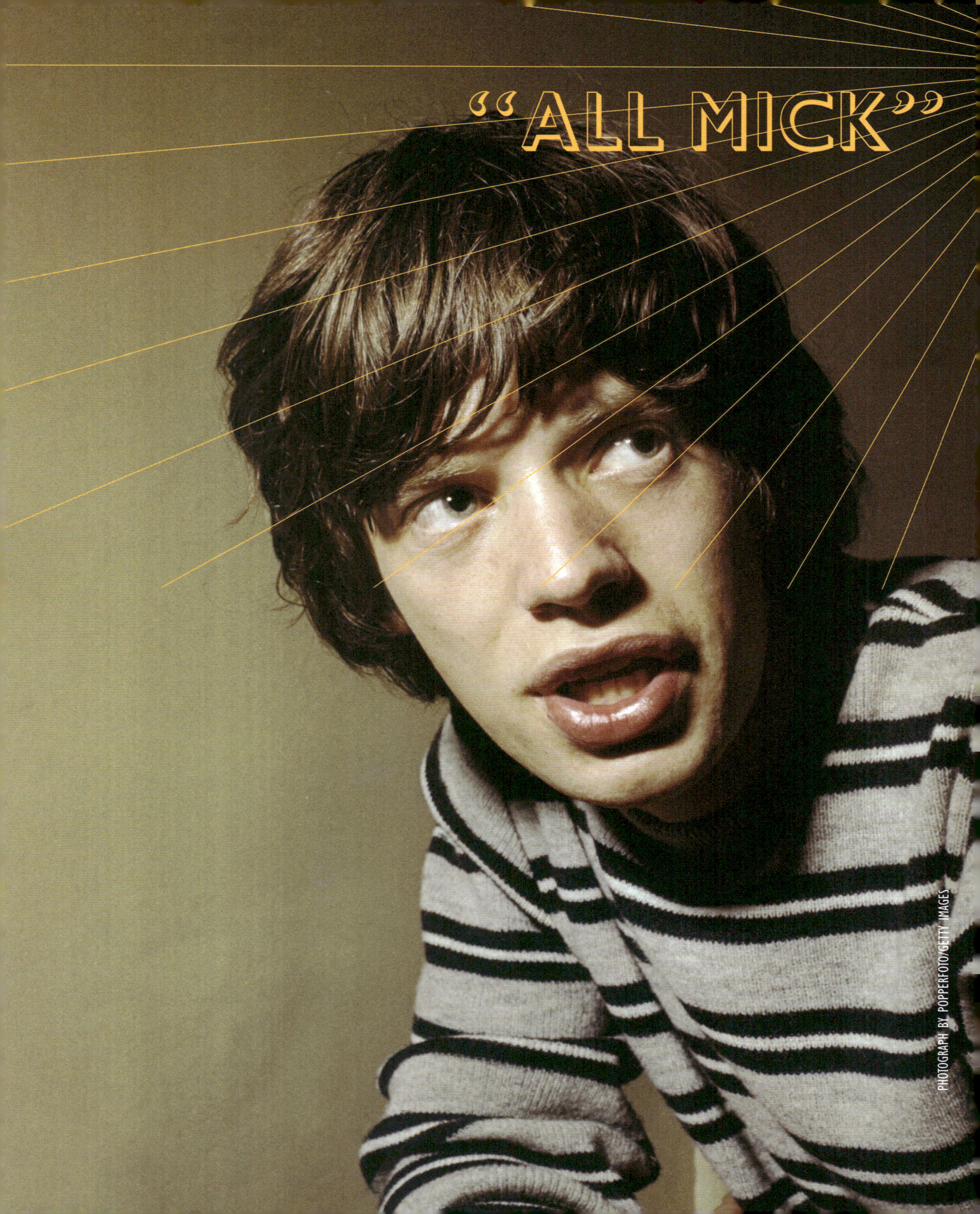
"ALL MICK"

PHOTOGRAPH BY POPPERFOTO/GETTY IMAGES

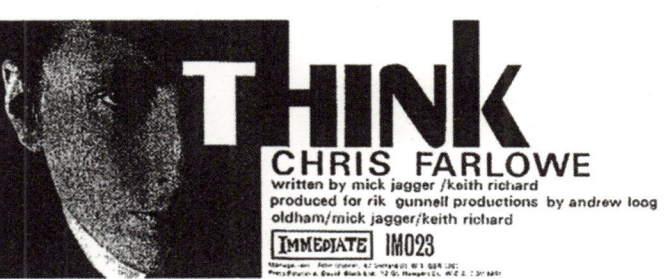

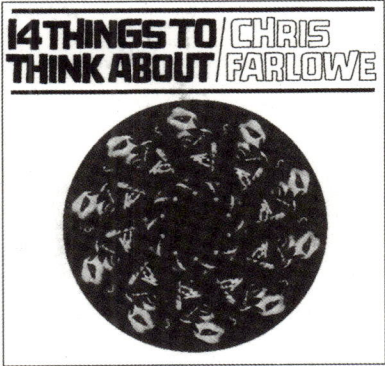

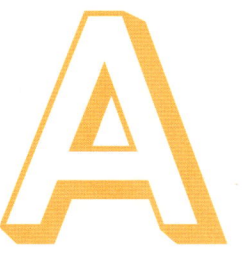

After prising Chris Farlowe away from the constraints of his backing group, The Thunderbirds, Immediate set about making him the label's first official 'star'. Pop music and culture were not really Farlowe's style, but he was smartly dressed and, from certain angles, looked pretty sharp. Covering "Satisfaction" on the recent Jagger/Richards/Oldham produced EP had given Farlowe a taste of what was to come. On his new Immediate single he covered the Jagger/Richards song, "Think", which the Rolling Stones had recently recorded in Hollywood for inclusion on an album in the making. For extra Immediate kudos Jagger sang backing vocals and had a hand in producing, again under the name We Three Producers. The explosive, trumpet-driven single was swiftly followed by a debut album, *14 Things To Think About*, made up of an old mix of Thunderbirds-backed blues and soul standards and more modern touches such as covers of Dylan's, "It's All Over Now Baby Blue" and The Beatles', "Yesterday".

THINK
CHRIS FARLOWE
written by mick jagger /keith richard
produced for rik gunnell productions by andrew loog oldham/mick jagger/keith richard
IMMEDIATE IM023

14 THINGS TO THINK ABOUT
CHRIS FARLOWE

THE BUTCHER'S FINAL ACT OF MADNESS WAS MOWING DOWN ROLLING STONES FANS AFTER A GIG

SIMON SPENCE

OPPOSITE: THE DASHING MICK JAGGER IN 1964

TOP: ADVERTISING FOR CHRIS FARLOWE'S "THINK", 1966

BOTTOM: FARLOWE'S CRITICALLY ACCLAIMED ALBUM "14 THINGS TO TALK ABOUT", 1966

In an early January 1966 edition of *Melody Maker*, Farlowe was photographed for the cover with his manager, Rik Gunnell, holding a gun to the his head, as a new contract with Gunnel Management, was signed. The paper reported Farlowe was guaranteed £50,000 (from Immediate) over the next five years, one of the era's first big buck deals—and everyone understood Gunnell was not a man to be messed about when it came to cash. Oldham now had money to burn after Allen Klein had extracted £600,000 from Decca to extend the label's relationship with Rolling Stones for two more years. Klein also bandied about the phenomenal figure of £5 million in future guarantees. Oldham was declared a 'paper millionaire' and was quick to start ripping it up.

Oldham added a new motor to his car fleet—already a Chevvy, a Lincoln and a maroon Sunbeam Tiger convertible with V8 engine—a gleaming black £19,000 black Rolls Royce Phantom 5. He was only the third British owner of this top of the range motor, after the Queen and John Lennon. The car came with blacked-out windows, telephone, record player and bar. However, Oldham's violent psychopath chauffeur, Reg 'the Butcher' King, would not enjoy driving the Rolls Royce, having just got a five year driving ban. The Butcher's final act of madness was mowing down Rolling Stones fans while reversing Oldham and the group away from a crazed crowd waiting backdoor after a gig. Oldham's new chauffeur, Eddie Reed, would be ever present for the rest of the decade, at the wheel of the Rolls Royce.

Gunnell told *Melody Maker* about his dealings with Immediate: "Oldham came to me and said he wanted to record John Mayall, I said, 'Okay, but take Chris because he's a great talent and I'm going to develop him'." Farlowe recalled singing at Gunnell's Flamingo Club while Oldham worked the bar in the early 1960s and now thought it a little bit weird to be working for him. "Mind you", he added, "he knows what he is doing".

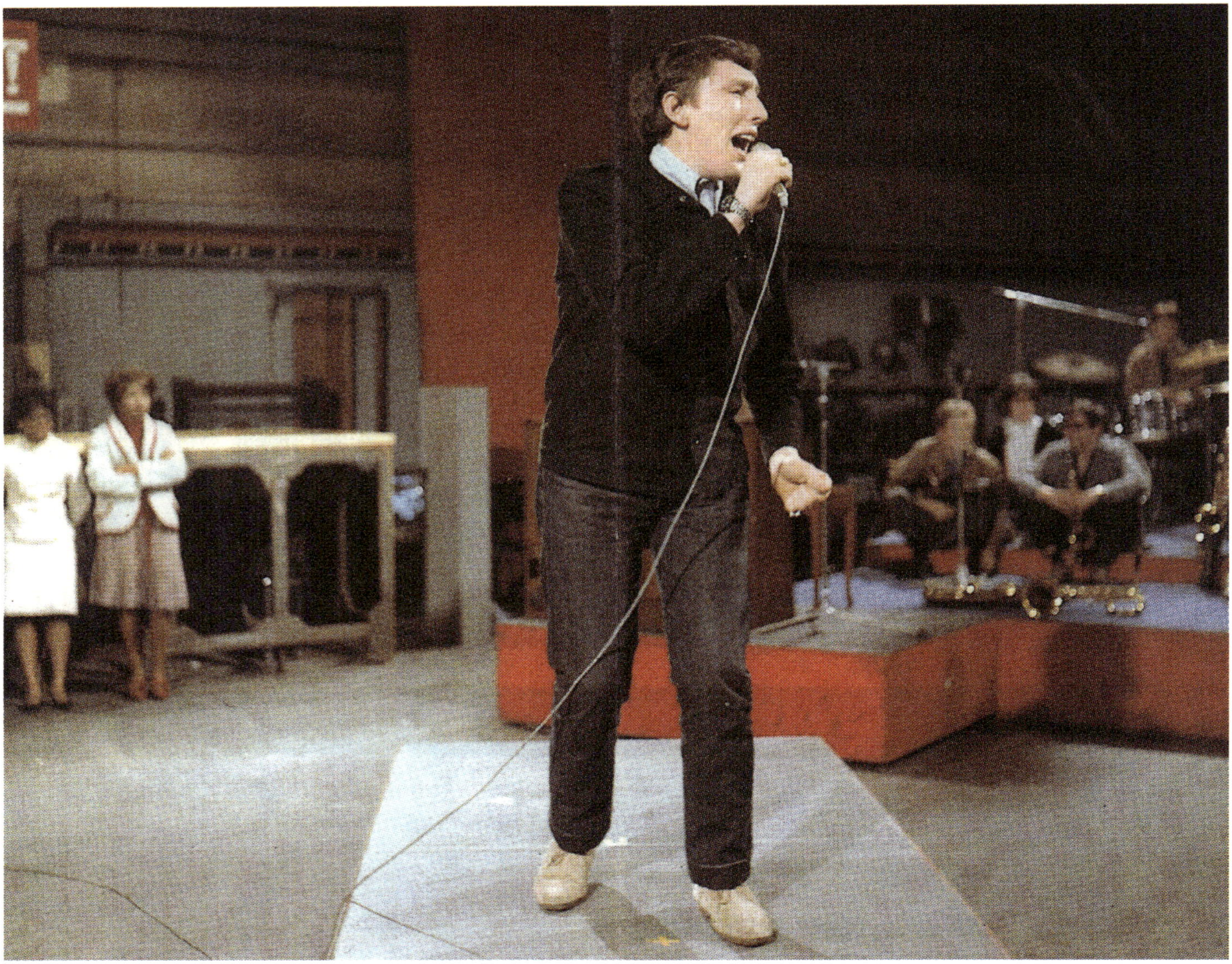

FARLOWE TOLD THE PRESS THE PRODUCTION WAS 'ALL MICK', BUT IT WAS ACTUALLY CREDITED AS 'AN ANDREW LOOG OLDHAM PRODUCTION'

SIMON SPENCE

IMMEDIATE's first No. 1 record was Chris Farlowe's 'Out Of Time' written by Mick Jagger & Keith Richard and produced by Mick Jagger. Released from the same team, Chris Farlowe's 'Ride On Baby'

IMMEDIATE

IM038.

TOP: CHRIS FARLOWE APPEARS ON *READY STEADY GO!*, 1967

BOTTOM: IMMEDIATE CELEBRATE THE SUCCESS OF FARLOWE'S SINGLE "OUT OF TIME", OCTOBER 1966

Oldham rounded off the backslapping when he said: "That man (Farlowe) is so humble. It's refreshing to find someone who retains an air of humility after being helped."

Farlowe's second Immediate single, "Think" sold a respectable 23,000 copies in its first week, but its failure to break the Top 20 had both Oldham and Jagger spitting feathers in the press about the way the British charts were compiled, implying their was either a fix or conspiracy. Jagger's heavy involvement upped the stakes for Immediate and Farlowe's next recording was a cover of the Jagger/Richards classic "Out Of Time", a song which, like "Think", they had cut during the new album sessions in Hollywood, but one perhaps good enough to have been a Rolling Stones single. Adverts for the Farlowe "Out Of Time" single featured a photo of Jagger draping an arm over the singer, with Mick's involvement as producer heavily strap-lined.

Oldham's regular arranger, Art Greenslade, who also worked with The Kinks, Dusty Springfield, Shirley Bassey, Johnny Halliday and Serge Gainsborough, told me:

> My first big hit with Immediate was Chris Farlowe: "Out Of Time".... We went in and did the track but Mick couldn't get Chris' voice on it. I stopped up at Immediate later and Andrew said: 'Well, Art what do you think of this?' He had taken Chris Farlowe in and done it. Andrew must have worked hard in there, Chris Farlowe couldn't sing his way out of a paper bag. I'm sure Andrew must have done it, where you get an artist singing and you can do a sentence at a time, stitching it all together. He must have done it in pieces.

As Tony Calder recalls:

> They all thought "Out Of Time" was a b-side. I told Andrew, 'That's an a'. He said, 'No, you do as I tell you.' I said, 'Okay' and just took the tapes and put it out. When it went to number one, Mick gave this interview about how long they had spent working on it and how it was all Mick's' idea. That to me was the real introduction to how great artists really are.

Tony King remembers:

> "Out Of Time" with Chris Farlowe was fucking hard work, it didn't go to number one by itself. We were very lucky, we got a hell of a lot of radio and television because it was Mick and Keith's song. We got Mick and Keith to do backing vocals on Ready Steady Go!. They wrote it, produced it and promoted it. There was a great Gered Mankowitz snap of Jagger and Farlowe in the adverts, possibly there was a fleet of cars dashing around to crucial shops buying up records.

Two hundred thousand copies of "Out Of Time" gave Immediate their second number one hit. Tony Calder told the BBC that Mick Jagger and Keith Richards—although unsure about their newly acquired roles at Immediate—were definitely on board. "I told them", he said, "if we say you can do it, you can do it!".

Jagger next announced he was taking exclusive control of recording Farlowe. First came a single, another Jagger/Richard original "Ride On Baby", recorded by Rolling Stones during what was to become the *Aftermath* album sessions, but not included on the LP. It was another Top 20 hit and Farlowe told the press the production was "all Mick", but it was actually credited as "an Andrew Loog Oldham Production". It was followed by the "Mick Jagger produced" album, *The Art Of Chris Farlowe*, which had reportedly cost a then, wildly extravagant, £17,000 to make. Farlowe admitted he didn't really have a hand in choosing the songs at Immediate, recalling: "Mick was involved with Immediate and it was a natural things for him to get involved musically in the production side of things. When he was producing my album, Ike and Tina Turner did the backing vocals on "North, South East and West"."

The sleeve notes for *The Art Of Chris Farlowe*, written by Oldham state:

> *The Art of Chris Farlowe* is now apparent and the emergence of Mick Jagger, the singer, as Jagger, the producer, has come from the combination of Farlowe's singing talent and both Jagger's rapport and communication with his public, and his growing understanding of today's sound. The songwriting team of Jagger and Richard; the arrangements of Art Greenslade, under the mind of Jagger, has finally given Chris Farlowe the recognition he deserves and with two big hits behind him. We are proud to present his second album with Immediate; proud of Chris Farlowe, the artists, and Mick Jagger, the producer, and proud of this album that speaks for itself: so listen to *The Art of Chris Farlowe*.

Oldham and Jagger promoted *The Art of Chris Farlowe* together, conducting interviews at the trendy Trattoria Terrazzo restaurant in Soho, where Oldham's movie idol, Laurence Harvey, and crooner Frank Sinatra (when he was in town), often ate. Despite their efforts *The Art of Chris Farlowe* only sold about five thousand copies in the UK, enough to take it in to the Top 20 but hardly the sensation everybody expected. "Andrew doesn't interfere but I accept his advice on sessions as he would accept mine on a Rolling Stones session", Jagger told the press. The situation with the Rolling Stones at Immediate gave Oldham the chance to push any talents Mick and Keith had. "From pissing to producing", he said.

KEITH GOES SOLO

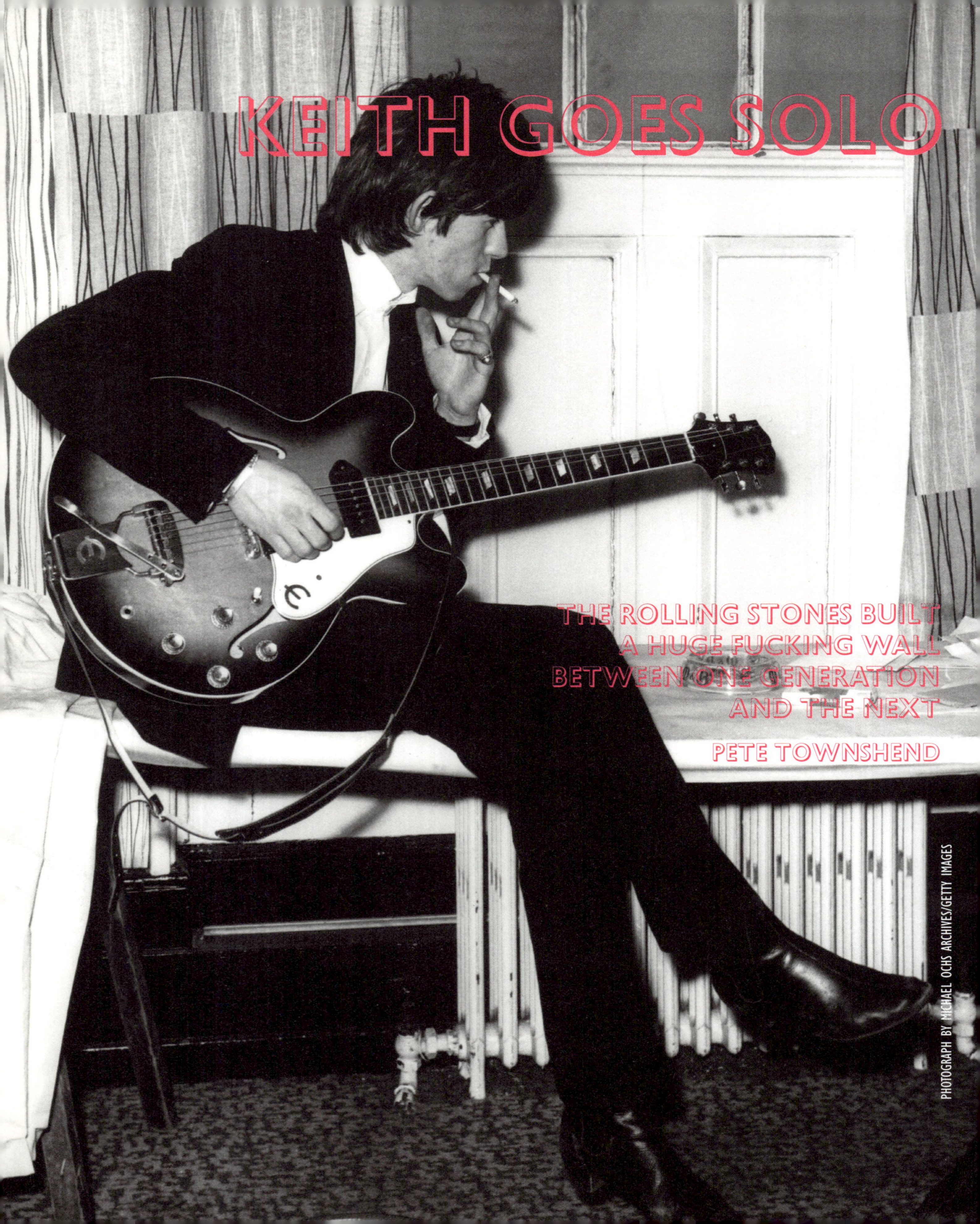

THE ROLLING STONES BUILT
A HUGE FUCKING WALL
BETWEEN ONE GENERATION
AND THE NEXT

PETE TOWNSHEND

PHOTOGRAPH BY MICHAEL OCHS ARCHIVES/GETTY IMAGES

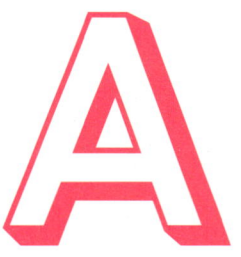

A first for any Beatle or Rolling Stone, was Keith Richards' debut solo album, *Today's Pop Symphony*, a "new conception of today's hits in classical style", by The Aranbee Pop Orchestra under the direction of Keith Richards. Richards had gone cold on recording under the title of the Keith Richard Orchestra, as everybody at Immediate had originally wanted. Oldham had a huge soft spot for the shy-looking Richards, who, as a Rolling Stone, was often left in the shadow of Jagger and the magnificent Brian Jones. It was Oldham who had purposefully knocked the 's' off Keith's surname from the very early days, as an attempt to market him in homage to Cliff Richard.

TODAYS POP SYMPHONY
a new conception of todays hits in classical style
THE ARANBEE POP SYMPHONY ORCHESTRA
UNDER THE DIRECTION OF KEITH RICHARD
IMMEDIATE

'Directed and produced' by Keith, the album featured string-laden rock and orchestral versions of several Jagger/Richard originals, including "Play With Fire", "Mother's Little Helper", "Sittin' on a Fence", and "Take It or Leave It", plus similar styled versions of The Four Seasons' "Rag Doll", Sonny and Cher's "I Got You Babe", two Beatles numbers, "There's a Place" and "We Can Work It Out", plus "In the Midnight Hour" and "I Don't Want To Go On Without You" by Berns and Wexler. The front cover featured a cartoon of Richards alongside Mozart, Beethoven, the Beatles, and Sonny and Cher, with a handsome photograph of Richards on the back. "If anyone thinks Keith's talents are limited, they will be forced to think again", Oldham told the press. "It's just something I've always wanted to do", Keith said. "He's just trying to prove he's a musician not just a rock'n'roll guitarist", added Mick. Oldham's sleeve notes for the album read:

IMMEDIATE
STEREO
NEBCD 411
TODAYS POP SYMPHONY
a new conception of todays hits in classical style
THE ARANBEE POP SYMPHONY ORCHESTRA
UNDER THE DIRECTION OF KEITH RICHARD
SEQUEL RECORDS

> Everybody in the pop industry is involved in the quick racket of hit records; a song comes and weeks later it is forgotten. But in a span of hits, regardless of the opinion of the so-called experts, great songs are written and should be remembered for they stand up on their own on any field against any competition. Here is a selection of today's hits in a stimulating album conceived by Rolling Stone, Keith Richard, who displays an outstanding sympathy and understanding for both his own art form and that of the classics and blends the two together in a great marriage of song and sound. This is an album that Immediate are proud to be associated with, a compliment to the industry that has been so good to us.

The album reached a respectable number 11 but there were doubts over the validity of Richards' involvement. This was a time when Jagger, Richards and Oldham were very close and had been dubbed the "unholy trinity" by the rest of the Rolling Stones. In his autobiography, *Stone Alone*, Bill Wyman wrote how he "always doubted that Keith had anything to do with its production or instigation". He added: "I think it was probably Oldham's idea and execution, purely an Oldham projection of Keith to promote the album and to boost his public image, yet another round in Oldham's campaign to increase Keith's profile."

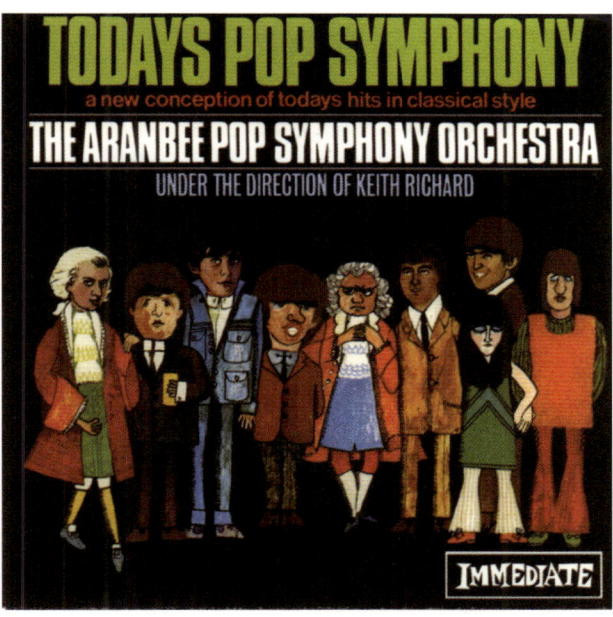

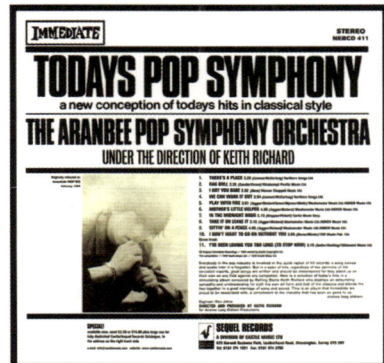

OPPOSITE: GUITARIST KEITH RICHARDS OF, ROLLING STONES, SMOKES A CIGARETTE WHILE PLAYING HIS EPIPHONE HOLLOW BODY ELECTRIC GUITAR IN 1966.

KEITH RICHARDS VENTURES AWAY FROM ROLLING STONES AND PRODUCES *TODAY'S POP SYMPHONY*, 1966

THE WONDERFUL WORLD OF SAM COOKE
IMMEDIATE
IMLP 002

The crazy world of the SIXTH ROLLING STONE

by RAY COLEM

'I have no brain for money'

HIS PLUSHY SUITE OF OFFICES IS EIGHT FLOORS UP IN THE POP NO - MAN'S - LAND OF LONDON'S REGENTS PARK. HERE, ANDREW LOOG OLDHAM IS KING.

The sixth Rolling Stone is 22 and an extraordinary top pop person. For three turbulent years he has guided the scene's most controversial group along the trouble-torn path to fame and fortune.

And today, the Stones are back near the top of the chart, as if by divine right.

"Yes, I'm rich," he says proudly. "So are the Stones. Put it this way—we need never work again. But we couldn't pack it in. I suppose it's because we all have big egos and we enjoy the fame and success of it all so much . . ."

To hear Andrew Oldham talking about ego is refreshing and realistic. He is drowned by complexes and a burning determination to succeed.

That the Rolling Stones have survived the turmoil, the smears, and the "great unwashed" image is due largely to their manager's willingness to take on all-comers. And to his unnerving belief in the whole Stones bonanza.

Mick, Keith, Brian, Bill and Charlie couldn't fail to make it with Andrew Oldham in the wings as their manager. He is infuriatingly hip, and a devastating exhibitionist out to prove himself. He has, he says, many enemies.

Oldham runs a Rolls-Royce (equipped with record player, cocktail cabinet and 'phone), a Sunbeam Tiger, an MGB and a Lincoln. He employs 12 people, runs Immediate Records, and often works a 13-hour day, leaving his office at 9 p.m.

When the Stones burst on the scene amid a battery of cameras and rebel images, Oldham said how he despised the attitude of many people in the pop backrooms. "They just treat it as a 9 to 5 job, then go home to watch the telly," he said.

Now, despite all the trappings, he is married, with a year-old son, and laughs at his old image. "I was an angry young man years ago simply because I hadn't got any money. Now, I suppose, I'm very nearly one of the people I hated so much. You grow up fast in this business or you get left behind."

Just a bum

He attributes his financial success to his link-up with American Allen Klein, his business manager. "I know how to handle things artistically and creatively," says Andrew, "but Allen knows how to convert my ideas into cash. Without his business brain, I'd be nowhere —just a bum with good ideas that would keep misfiring. I have no brain for money."

His association with the Stones is fascinating. He and the other Stones are acutely aware of Jagger's overshadowing image.

"Mick is the focal point and we all know it. But he has been exploited by people. He says things that the Press pounces on, and the singer out in front always seems to get the limelight more than others."

Oldham's devotion to the Stones does not blind him to other talents. He spends an enormous amount of time studying the scene for new people, and some people intrigue him.

"Ray Davies ought to be much bigger—he has a face with the pathos of a clown, and he ought to be trying to be an Anthony Newley, or bigger. Ray Davies is a rarity.

"Pete Townshend is another who fascinates me—he represents total escapism to the fans."

But Oldham snorts at any talk of a Stones v. Walker Brothers comparison.

"There can't be any comparison between the two groups. The Walkers' fans are much younger, and I'm not sure that their fans will grow up with them in the same way that ours have grown with us. The Stones can easily reach the Cliff Richard stage of carrying a lot of fans with them as years go by.

"We are going into the film, 'Only Lovers Left Alive,' very seriously. I think we could win an Academy Award if we play it properly. The Stones will become actors, not just pop stars trying to do it."

And he rebuffs criticism that the Stones are following the Beatles career pattern. "If by that people mean that Brian Jones is using a sitar like George Harrison, and we are making a film, just like the Beatles did, that's really stupid.

"The Stones get on with the Beatles very well. There need never be a clash between release of singles because we talk about it quite openly. Mick might well meet Paul somewhere and say: 'When are you putting your new single out?' And when Paul tells him, Mick might say: 'Oh, we'll make sure we don't clash then.'

"There's no point in clashing, and there's no reason why that sort of relationship shouldn't go on."

IMMEDIATE IMLP002

THE WONDERFUL WORLD OF SAM COOKE

SIDE ONE
1. THAT'S HEAVEN TO ME (Cooke)
2. DEEP RIVER (Cooke)
3. I THANK GOD (Hoffman / Blake / Lewis)
4. HEAVEN IS MY HOME (Cooke)
5. GOD IS STANDING BY (Taylor)
6. PASS ME NOT (Harris)

SIDE TWO
1. STEAL AWAY (Cooke)
2. MUST JESUS BEAR HIS CROSS ALONE (Cooke)
3. LEAD ME JESUS (Cooke / Crume)
4. TROUBLE IN MIND (Fickling)
5. SOMETIMES (Harris)
6. SOMEBODY (Harris)

SAR RECORDS

IMMEDIATE RECORD COMPANY LIMITED, 138/147 IVOR COURT, GLOUCESTER PLACE, LONDON NW1

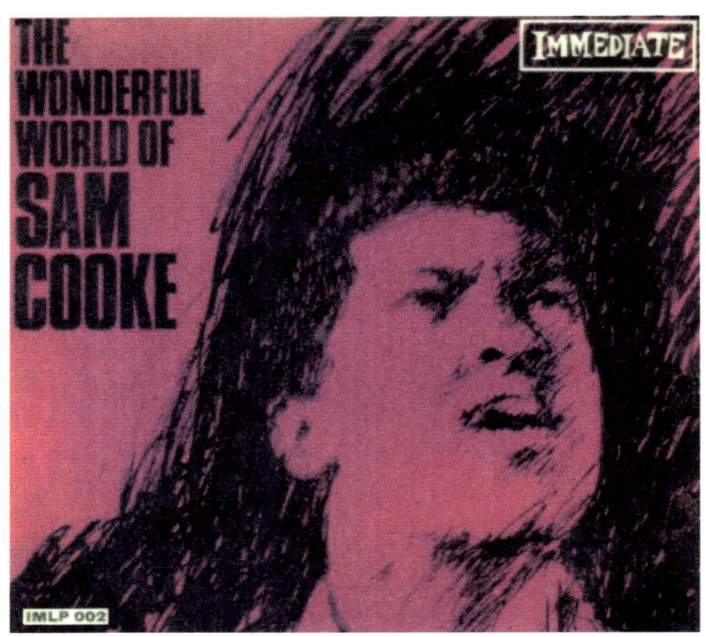

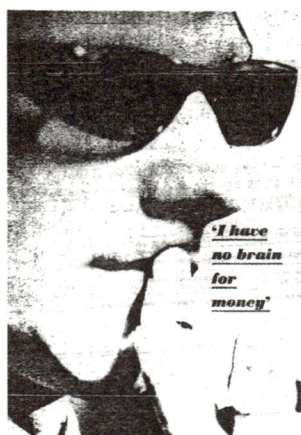

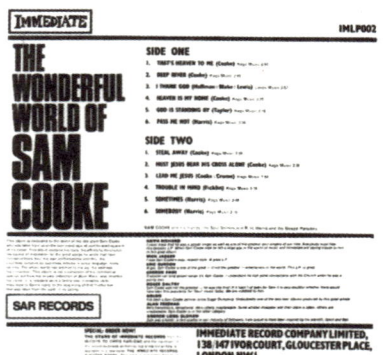

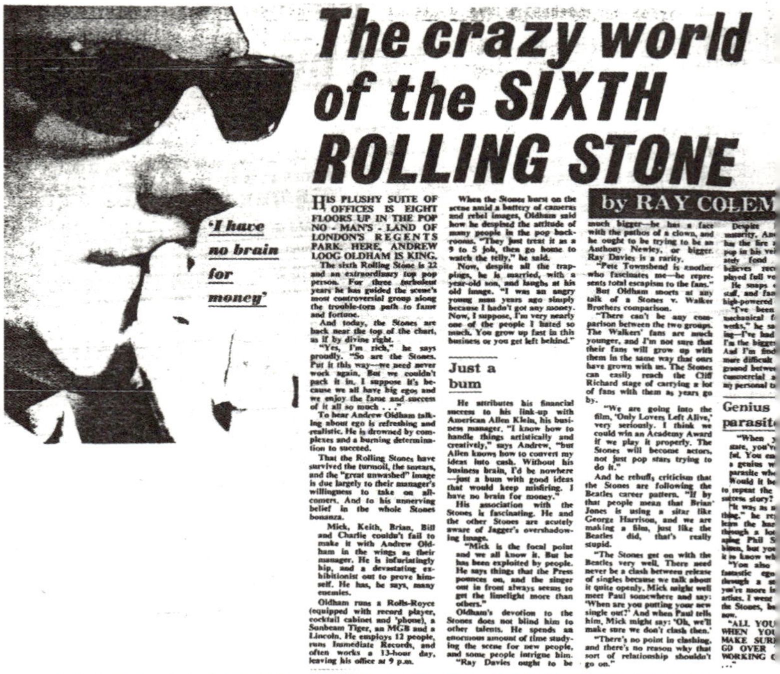

> **WE WORK ON THE PRINCIPLE THAT IF YOU ARE GOING TO KICK CONFORMITY IN THE TEETH, YOU MAY AS WELL USE BOTH FEET**
>
> **ANDREW OLDHAM**

> **WHEN YOU GET TO THIS STAGE YOU'VE GOT TO BE CAREFUL. YOU END UP A GENIUS THAT'S BROKE OR A PARASITE THAT'S A MILLIONAIRE**
>
> **ANDREW OLDHAM**

LEFT: *THE WONDERFUL WORLD OF SAM COOKE* LP, JANUARY 1966

RIGHT: "THE CRAZY WORLD OF THE SIXTH ROLLING STONE" *NME*, JUNE 1966

Oldham maintains that Richards planned and produced *Today's Pop Symphony* and doesn't consider it important, nor does he remember, who originated the idea. Recorded in a two day session at IBC studios, engineered by Glyn Johns and arranged by Mike Leander, it sounded like a stringed-out version of the Andrew Loog Oldham Orchestra, whose three albums to date had been largely made up of surging orchestral rock arrangements of Oldham's favourite pop songs, often those of the Rolling Stones.

Keith's album was followed by the first UK posthumous album release of soul legend, Sam Cooke, who had recently been shot dead in his prime. The album sleeve of *The Wonderful World of Sam Cooke* came plastered with plaudits from Jagger, Richards, Eric Burdon, Georgie Fame, Roger Daltrey, Alan Freeman and many more. Oldham, who had been a fan since acting as PR on the 1962 Don Arden-promoted Cooke/Little Richard UK package tour, wrote:

> This album is dedicated to the talent of the late great Sam Cooke, who was taken from us a little over a year ago, at just the starting point of his career. This album explains his roots,

his affinity to the church, his source of inspiration for the great songs he wrote that have thrilled millions through his own performances and through the countless versions by countless artists in every language, every country. The whole world has warmed to his joy, his sadness, and his conviction. This album is not a collection of his commercial outings but from the private collection of Allen Klein, who directed his career. It is released as a family tree, it enables us to trace back to Sam's roots, to his beginning of that fruitful tree that was take from the earth in its spring. Sam was a rare leader, a rare quality in our industry of followers. I am proud to have been inspired by his warmth, talent and feel.

The album, made up of obscure Cooke material, went Top 20 and a single, "That's Heaven To Me", was pressed up. The Cooke album had been given to Immediate by Oldham's new Rolling Stones business manager, Allen Klein—who still owns Sam Cooke's astonishing back catalogue of hits.

Klein, having just scored Rolling Stones a massive new megabucks deal with Decca, was becoming an increasingly influential figure in the lives of many UK acts. He already controlled producer Mickie Most's recordings (Herman's Hermits, the Animals and Donovan), and was now 'in with' The Kinks and Marianne Faithfull. Klein secured Oldham over-rides on Faithfull's work for the US, and it briefly looked as if she would be leaving Decca and joining Immediate with Oldham taking "executive control". Oldham bought a Mini as a sweetener for Faithfull and, while he was at it, bought a specially built mini replica of the Phantom 5 from himself. Faithfull told the press: "I am happy to return to the fold. I like and have a very high regard for Andrew."

Klein also helped Immediate get a distribution in the US for Chris Farlowe's "Out Of Time" hit with major label MGM, who it was rumoured Bob Dylan may be joining. In the US, as well as administering Sam Cooke's music publishing, Klein was also now in negotiations to buy Roulette Records boss Morris Levy's Philadelphia label, Cameo Parkway, and looking in to securing Immediate rights on MGM product in the UK. When Farlowe's "Out Of Time" was put out via MGM in the US the single hit the Top 40 but one of Klein's promotional men had got his dates mixed up; done his job too well. He had reported high distributor and radio station activity to chart compilers *Billboard*, *Cashbox* and *Record World* when the record wasn't even available yet. There were a lot of red faces at Immediate and two weeks later, when "Out Of Time" was pressed, a lot of stations were afraid to touch the record in case it looked like they'd been bought. In London, Oldham encouraged the rumour and myth building around Klein whose casual, pump-healed approach disguised a ferocious business diligence. With suspicions that the Mafia were heavily involved in the US business, especially in "promotions" where there was a lot of "here's the money, play the record, fuck you" action going on, Oldham enjoyed pumping up Klein's gangster image. Klein, a meaty, dark-haired immigrant New Yorker in his early 30s, kept it brief when he told the press: "Andrew manages the [Rolling] Stones and I manage him."

Oldham, at the time 22, reflected on Klein's impact upon his life:

> I was an angry young man years ago simply because I hadn't got any money. Now, I suppose, I'm very nearly one of the people I hated so much. You grow up fast in this business or you get left behind. I know how to handle things artistically and creatively but Allen Klein knows how to convert my ideas into cash. Without his business brain I would go nowhere—just a bum with good ideas that would keep misfiring. I have no brain for money. I've been very cold for the past few weeks. Quite worrying, I've had the attitude that I'm the biggest con of all time. And I'm finding it more and more difficult to find a common ground between what I know is commercial and what offends my personal taste.

> When you get to this stage, you've got to be careful. You end up either a genius that's broke or a parasite that's a millionaire. It was as much luck as anything to get to the top. I had to learn the hard way and pass through a lot of phases—like aping Phil Spector. You get bitten but you must experience it to know where you're going. You also have to have a fantastic ego and you go through a stage of thinking you're more important than the artists. I went through this with the Rolling Stones, but I'm sorted now. All you have to do when you arrive is make sure you don't go over the top. I'm working on that now. Yes, I'm rich and so are The [Rolling] Stones. Put it this way: we need never work again. But we couldn't pack it in. I suppose we all have big egos and we enjoy the fame and success of it all so much. Mick is the focal point and we all know it. The Rolling Stones can easily reach the Cliff Richard stage of carrying a lot of fans with them as years go by.

In this interview, Oldham—a manic depressive, with shock therapy to look forward to—sounds nothing like the PT Barnum show seller the press had become accustomed to. In an earlier 'black mood' he had announced he was quitting show business, only to reconsider a week later: both pronouncements well publicised by interviews with the press. Now Oldham is rich beyond his wildest dreams, "need never work again", and wonders where his artistic talent is leading him. At his own personal crossroads, he reached deep to produce another Mick and Keith monster, "19th Nervous Breakdown". It was harder and harsher than anything Oldham had produced with the group before, dense and malevolent, a storm brewing on Charlie's massive cymbal crashes and Keith's over-amped flourishes. As ugly as it was, it was another UK number one.

"The [Rolling] Stones are still social outcasts", Oldham reminded the press, in more familiar, expansive mood. "We work on the principle that if you are going to kick conformity in the teeth, you may as well use both feet." The single, the group's sixth consecutive UK number one, went to number two in the US. The new album *Aftermath*, recorded entirely in LA and which featured "Think" and "Out Of Time" (both already singles for Chris Farlowe), also went straight to number one in the UK charts, staying there for two months. In the US a "hits" album package *Big Hits (High Tide And Green Grass)* went to number two. Pete Townshend told me. "The [Rolling] Stones built a huge fucking wall between one generation and the next." In early 1966, Oldham was pissing all over that wall.

WHO?

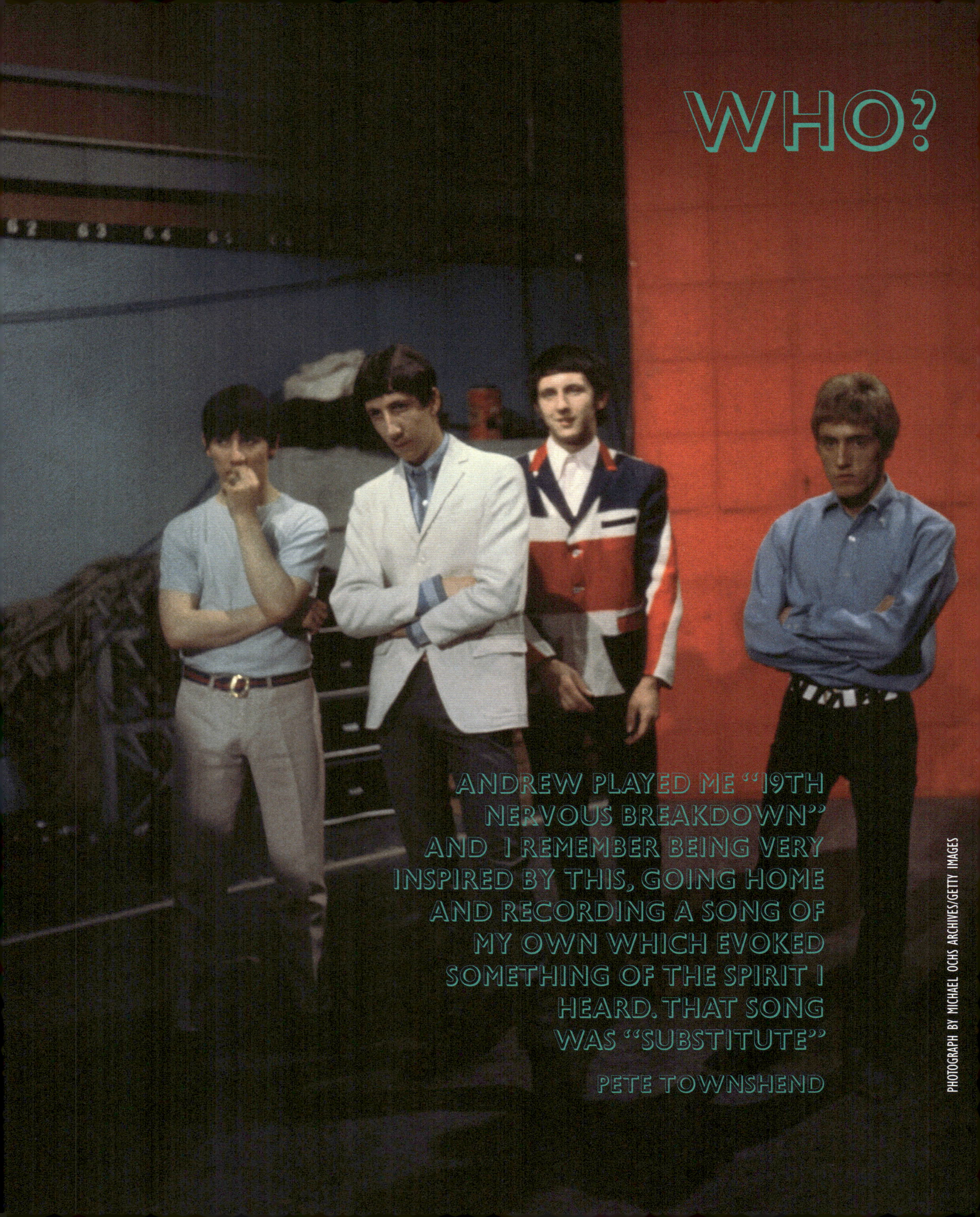

ANDREW PLAYED ME "19TH NERVOUS BREAKDOWN" AND I REMEMBER BEING VERY INSPIRED BY THIS, GOING HOME AND RECORDING A SONG OF MY OWN WHICH EVOKED SOMETHING OF THE SPIRIT I HEARD. THAT SONG WAS "SUBSTITUTE"

PETE TOWNSHEND

PHOTOGRAPH BY MICHAEL OCHS ARCHIVES/GETTY IMAGES

AN INSTANT SMASH FOR YOUR PARTY!

'CIRCLES' BY The Fleur de Lys

IMMEDIATE IM032

Avenue Artistes Limited, 1 Cherry Walk, Shirley, Southampton Tel: 74268

Scotland's No1 group
THE POETS
'BABY DON'T YOU DO IT' IM024
OUT TODAY-BUY NOW!
DIRECTION:IMMEDIATE ARTISTES
IMMEDIATE

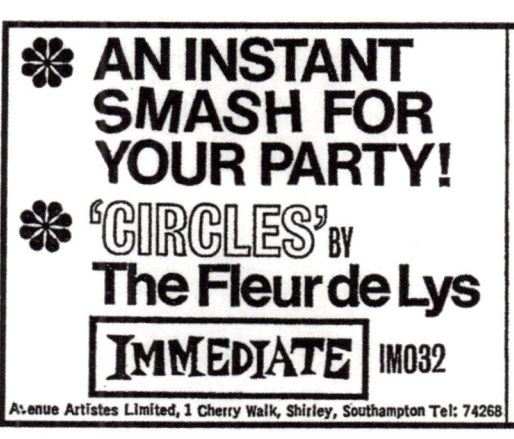

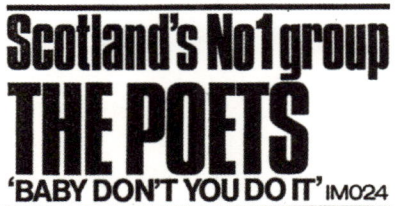

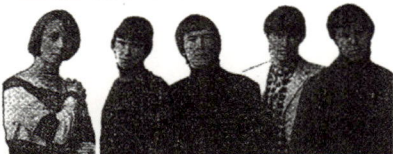

OPPOSITE: THE WHO, LONDON, 1965, LEFT TO RIGHT: KEITH MOON, PETE TOWNSHEND, JOHN ENTWHISTLE AND ROGER DALTREY, 1965

TOP: IMMEDIATE PROMOTIONAL MATERIAL FOR "CIRCLES" BY THE FLEUR DE LYS, 1966

BOTTOM: "SCOTLAND'S NUMBER ONE GROUP", THE POETS ADVERTISE THEIR RELEASE "BABY DON'T YOU DO IT", 1966

Oldham had been teenage pals with The Who's original manager Peter 'the Face' Meaden, and the group's new managers, Kit Lambert and Chris Stamp, kept an office at Ivor Court, in the same apartment block as Immediate. Oldham arranged—by phone from the back of the Phantom Roller—for an incredulous Townshend to fly over to New York to meet Allen Klein on a yacht on the Hudson River to discuss The Who's future. It was hot gossip in the music business that Lambert and Stamp had, in Stamp's words, "fucked up" with the deal they allowed The Who's producer, Shel Talmy, to make for the group's recordings. Talmy, from the US, had signed the group to Decca US (a separate entity to Decca UK) and The Who's singles came out via Brunswick in the UK. Rumours quickly circulated that The Who were signing to Immediate. Townshend gave the label a song, "Circles", and Tony Calder made a rare appearance in the studio with Jimmy Page to produce a version with The Fleur De Lys. Page laid down a fuzz guitar lead line on the distinctive The Who-esqe track that lyrically spoke of typical Townshend teenage confusion. "Peter Townshend is another who fascinates me", Oldham told the press: "He represents total escapism to the fans". Immediate encouraged such rumours. One week The Who were signing, the next it was The Warriors, or Birds, or there was going to be a "tribute" album to Jim Reeves, with various Immediate acts recording one of his songs: a project, if it had been realised, that would have set the precedent for the now all-too-common tribute albums.

Klein had tossed about the idea of Oldham coming on board with The Who as "executive producer" but eventually Townshend stuck with Lambert and Stamp, who soon rectified the group's relationship with Shel by getting rid of the producer. There was no small amount of fall-out back in London about Klein's brusque attempt to land The Who and much bad-mouthing of Oldham, particularly by The Who's managers. Even so, trying to sign the band was an audacious move, signalling that Immediate already felt they could compete with the major labels for top acts.

Back on *terra firma* The Poets received more warm applause for a Gary Glitter/Andesound production and the ultimate mod version—despite also being cut by The Who and Small Faces—of the Holland/Dozier/Holland's "Baby Don't Do It". However, The Poets were short-changed as Tony Calder preferred to promote new priority Immediate acts such as early-Velvets-looking duo, London Waits, with their baroque instrumental version of the theme tune to the BBC1 programme, *Softly Softly*. He also pushed the legendary Creation, featuring Ron Wood of The Birds, on a Shel Talmy produced track, also called "Creation". Another new signing to Immediate, New York's Goldie, fresh from leaving her backing group The Gingerbreads, was also thought to have much potential. She had recorded a great version of the aching Goffin/King number "Goin' Back" with Oldham producing. Unfortunately Dusty Springfield had also got hold of and recorded the song. Springfield was coming off the back of a number one with "You

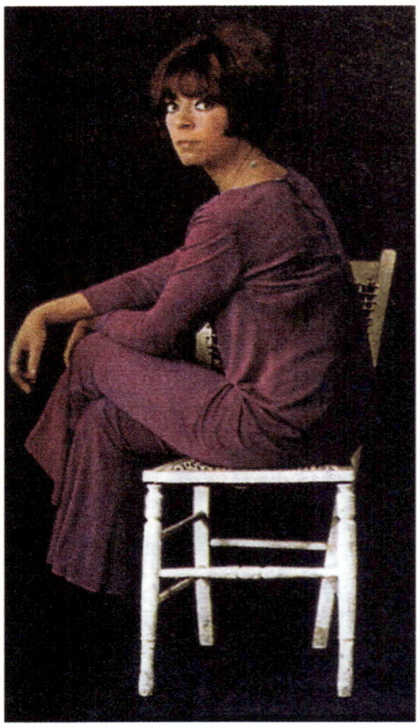

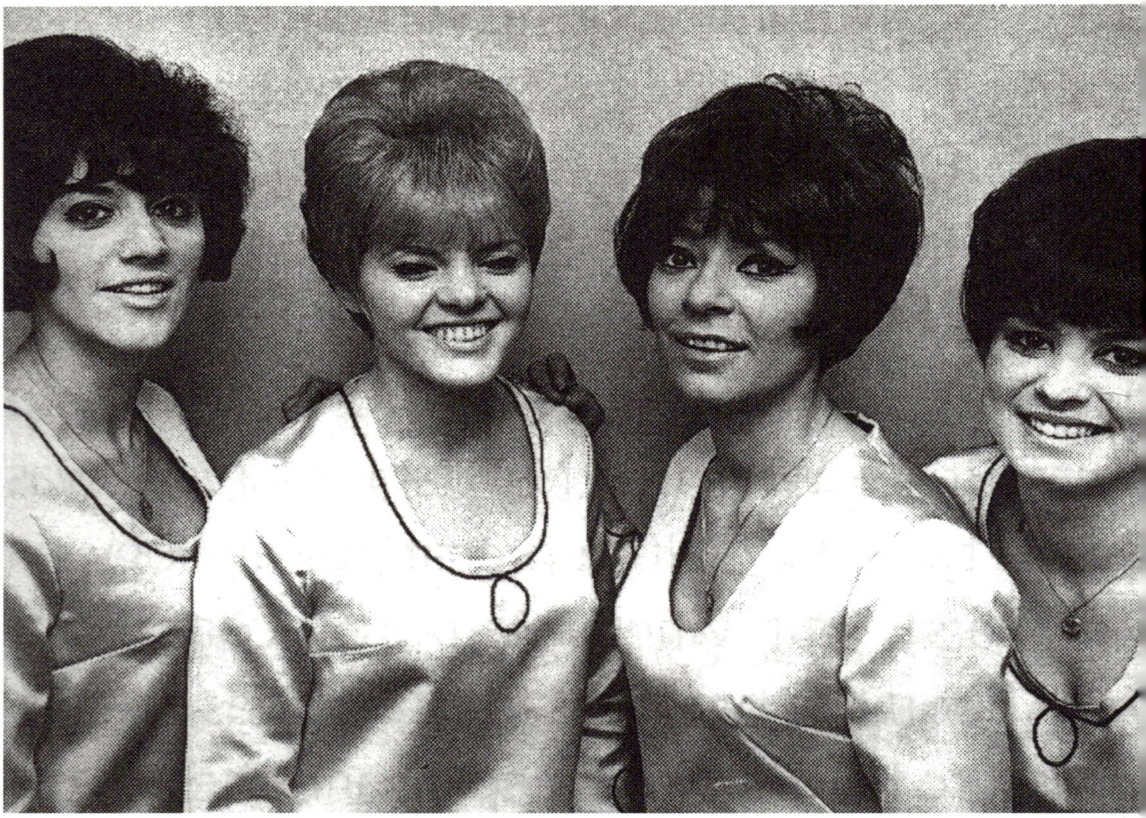

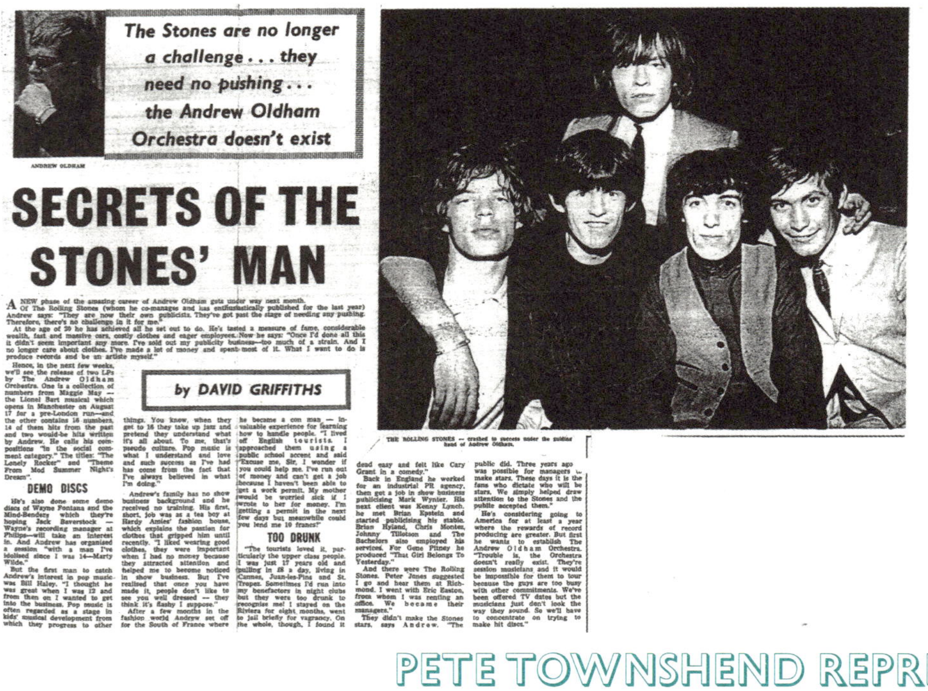

The Stones are no longer a challenge . . . they need no pushing . . . the Andrew Oldham Orchestra doesn't exist

ANDREW OLDHAM

SECRETS OF THE STONES' MAN

A NEW phase of the amazing career of Andrew Oldham gets under way next month. Of The Rolling Stones (whom he co-manages and has enthusiastically publicised for the last year) Andrew says: "They are now their own publicists. They've got past the stage of needing any pushing. Therefore, there's no challenge in it for me."

At the age of 20 he has achieved all he set out to do. He's tasted a measure of fame, considerable wealth, fast and massive cars, costly clothes and eager employees. Now he says: "Once I'd done all this it didn't seem important any more. I've sold out my publicity business—too much of a strain. And I no longer care about clothes. I've made a lot of money and spent most of it. What I want to do is produce records and be an artiste myself."

by DAVID GRIFFITHS

Hence, in the next few weeks, we'll see the release of two LPs by The Andrew Oldham Orchestra. One is a collection of numbers from Maggie May — the Lionel Bart musical which opens in Manchester on August 17 for a pre-London run—and the other contains 16 numbers, 14 of them hits from the past and two would-be hits written by Andrew. He calls his compositions "in the social comment category." The titles: "The Lonely Rocker" and "Theme From Mod Summer Night's Dream".

DEMO DISCS

He's also done some demo discs of Wayne Fontana and the Mind-Benders which they're hoping Jack Baverstock — Wayne's recording manager at Philips—will take an interest in. And Andrew has organised a session "with a man I've idolised since I was 14—Marty Wilde."

But the first man to catch Andrew's interest in pop music was Bill Haley. "I thought he was great when I was 12 and from then on I wanted to get into the business. Pop music is often regarded as a stage in kids' musical development from which they progress to other things. You know, when they get to 16 they take up jazz and pretend they understand what it's all about. To me, that's pseudo culture. Pop music is what I understand and love and such success as I've had has come from the fact that I've always believed in what I'm doing."

Andrew's family has no show business background and he received no training. His first, short, job was as a tea boy at Hardy Amies' fashion house, which explains the passion for clothes that gripped him until recently. "I liked wearing good clothes, they were important when I had no money because they attracted attention and helped me to become noticed in show business. But I've realised that once you have made it, people don't like to see you well dressed — they think it's flashy I suppose."

After a few months in the fashion world Andrew set off for the South of France where he became a con man — invaluable experience for learning how to handle people. "I lived off English tourists. I approached them using a public school accent and said "Excuse me, Sir, I wonder if you could help me. I've run out of money and can't get a job because I haven't been able to get a work permit. My mother would be worried sick if I wrote to her for money. I'm getting a permit in the next few days but meanwhile could you lend me 10 francs?"

TOO DRUNK

"The tourists loved it, particularly the upper class people. I was just 17 years old and pulling in £8 a day, living in Cannes, Juan-les-Pins and St. Tropez. Sometimes I'd run into my benefactors in night clubs but they were too drunk to recognise me! I stayed on the Riviera for eight months, went to jail briefly for vagrancy. On the whole, though, I found it dead easy and felt like Cary Grant in a comedy."

Back in England he worked for an industrial PR agency, then got a job in show business publicising Mark Wynter. His next client was Kenny Lynch, he met Brian Epstein and started publicising his stable. Brian Hyland, Chris Montez, Johnny Tillotson and The Bachelors also employed his services. For Gene Pitney he produced "That Girl Belongs To Yesterday."

And there were The Rolling Stones. Peter Jones suggested I go and hear them at Richmond. I went with Eric Easton, from whom I was renting an office. We became their managers."

They didn't make the Stones stars, says Andrew. "The public did. Three years ago was possible for managers to make stars. These days it is the fans who dictate who will be stars. We simply helped draw attention to the Stones and the public accepted them."

He's considering going to America for at least a year where the rewards of record producing are greater. But first he wants to establish The Andrew Oldham Orchestra. "Trouble is, the Orchestra doesn't really exist. They're session musicians and it would be impossible for them to tour because the guys are too busy with other commitments. We've been offered TV dates but the musicians just don't look the way they sound. So we'll have to concentrate on trying to make hit discs."

THE ROLLING STONES — crashed to success under the guiding hand of Andrew Oldham.

CLOCKWISE FROM ABOVE: GOLDIE ALONE, 1966, AND WITH HER GINGERBREADS, 1967, AND MORE OLDHAM-OBSESSED PRESS IN THE MEDIA, AUGUST 1964

OPPOSITE: OLDHAM PUTS THE FINISHING TOUCHES TO THE ROLLING STONES' SONGBOOK, JULY 1966

PETE TOWNSHEND REPRESENTS TOTAL ESCAPISM TO THE FANS

ANDREW OLDHAM

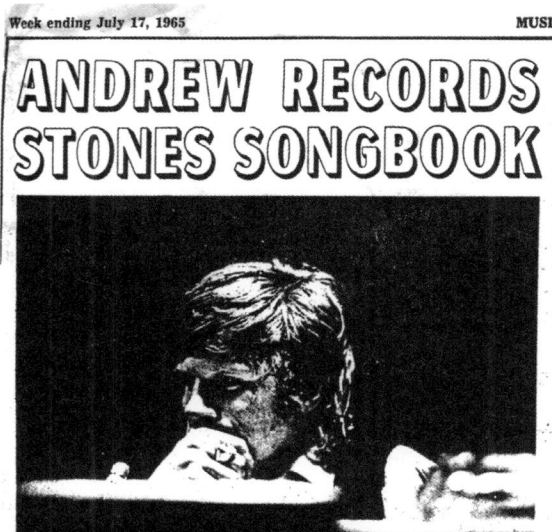

Week ending July 17, 1965 — MUSIC

ANDREW RECORDS STONES SONGBOOK

Andrew Oldham in a pensive mood, pictured during his recording session by Clive Bubly.

THE Andrew Oldham Orchestra and chorus have recorded "The Rolling Stones' Songbook Album." The L.P. recorded on July 3 and 4 at Pye Studios for Decca is set for August release both here and in the States.

Eight of the 12 titles set for the L.P. are Stones originals—"The Last Time," "Tell Me," "As Tears Go By," "Satisfaction," "Play With Fire," "Heart Of Stones," "Blue Turns To Grey" and "Congratulations."

The other four include two Oldham compositions, "Theme For A Rolling Stone" and "Stonamova."

The remaining titles are "You'd Better Move On" (Alexander) and "Time Is On My Side" (Britten House Music).

The idea is, says Andrew Oldham, "to prove that The Stones' music is not just a noise, but that their melodies and idiom can stand up in any form."

Likely title set for the L.P. is "The Rolling Stones' Songbook."

Don't Have To Say You Love Me" and when her version of "Goin' Back" was released, Goldie's version was lost. Goldie wasn't interested in dueting with Chris Farlowe and left Immediate three months later to record for Chris Blackwell at Island Records. In the 1970s she produced the first Dead Boys albums.

Amidst all this action with the Rolling Stones and Immediate, Oldham found time to make his fourth solo album. This was the one he considered his bible, "with the [Rolling] Stones as disciples and the songs as testaments". *The Rolling Stones Songbook* was the final instalment from the Andrew Loog Oldham Orchestra. Oldham urged the Immediate staff to promote his angel-voiced chorused and over-blown orchestrated versions of Jagger/Richards songs, "The Last Time" (the version which providing the string riff for The Verve's "Bittersweet Symphony"), "Blue Turns To Grey", "(I Can't Get No) Satisfaction", "Heart Of Stone", "Tell Me", "Congratulations", "Play With Fire", and two he had helped them write, "As Tears Go By" and "Theme For A Rolling Stone", (both collaborative Oldham/Jagger/Richard tracks). "A fantastic new album containing a dozen Rolling Stones numbers presented in subtle orchestral arrangements" ran the advert. "The idea is to prove that the [Rolling] Stones music is not just a noise, but the melodies and idiom can stand up in any form", Oldham told the press.

The Rolling Stones Songbook was out on Decca, rather than Immediate, but working another label's records was nothing unusual at Ivor Court. Oldham's best friend in LA, Lou Adler, was manager of Johnny Rivers and the Mamas and Papas. Adler lived in the hip Bel Air, on Stone Canyon Road, and was the owner of Sunset Strip's most happening clubs, Whisky A-Go-Go, Roxy and Rainbow. With his partner, Herb Alpert (who went on to form A&M records), and Sam Cooke he had also co-written "Wonderful World". PR, Andy Wickham, had left Image and Immediate to work at Lou's new independent label, Dunhill, who had a massive hit on their hands with "Eve of Destruction" by Barry McGuire.

Through Adler, Immediate had picked up the tacky track by The Turtles, "You Baby", a US Top 20, for UK release. It was written by PF Sloan and Steve Barri, who had also penned "Eve Of Destruction" and who worked for Lou Adler's publishing company Trousdale. Oldham had been a huge fan of The Turtles far superior previous smash, "Happy Together". Immediate staff were told to forget "You Baby" and prioritise the new Mamas and Papas UK single, "California Dreamin'", even though it was coming out on EMI in the UK. They placed another full pager in the press that read:

California Dreamin' by the mamas and papas
is more relative today
than the general election
which can only bring more bigotry,
unfulfilled promises
and the ultimate big bringdown.
"California Dreamin'" won't put the country
 back on it's feet
but it will give you a helluva lift
for two minutes and thirty two seconds
and sometimes that can be a long time.

Andrew Loog Oldham, a bystander

p.s., I didn't write it, John Phillips did; I don't publish it, Trousdale do; I didn't produce it, Lou Adler did; and I don't release it, RCA do—I just like it...

Lou Adler recounts:

I remember when the Mamas and Papas first went to the UK, they went over on a boat. Why? There was no way of figuring out the reasons for [their] actions. Going on a boat could have been destructive or perhaps John reckoned they could rehearse on the way over. I went with Andrew to meet them and [Mama] Cass was arrested for a blanket she had taken off the boat and the police took her to local jail. It was great publicity. Andrew helped break the Mamas and Papas in the UK, he definitely did, without a doubt. I'm sure the advert was just part of it. He never discussed it, never called and said, 'look I would like to take an advert or I'm thinking about it'. You would just open up the paper up and there it was. He was laying the foundation for us.

By their own creation, and by association, Immediate had placed themselves at the very centre of the 1966 London pop scene, ruling the dancefloor with a kitsch and bewitching, frenzy of heavy beats and pop baroque.

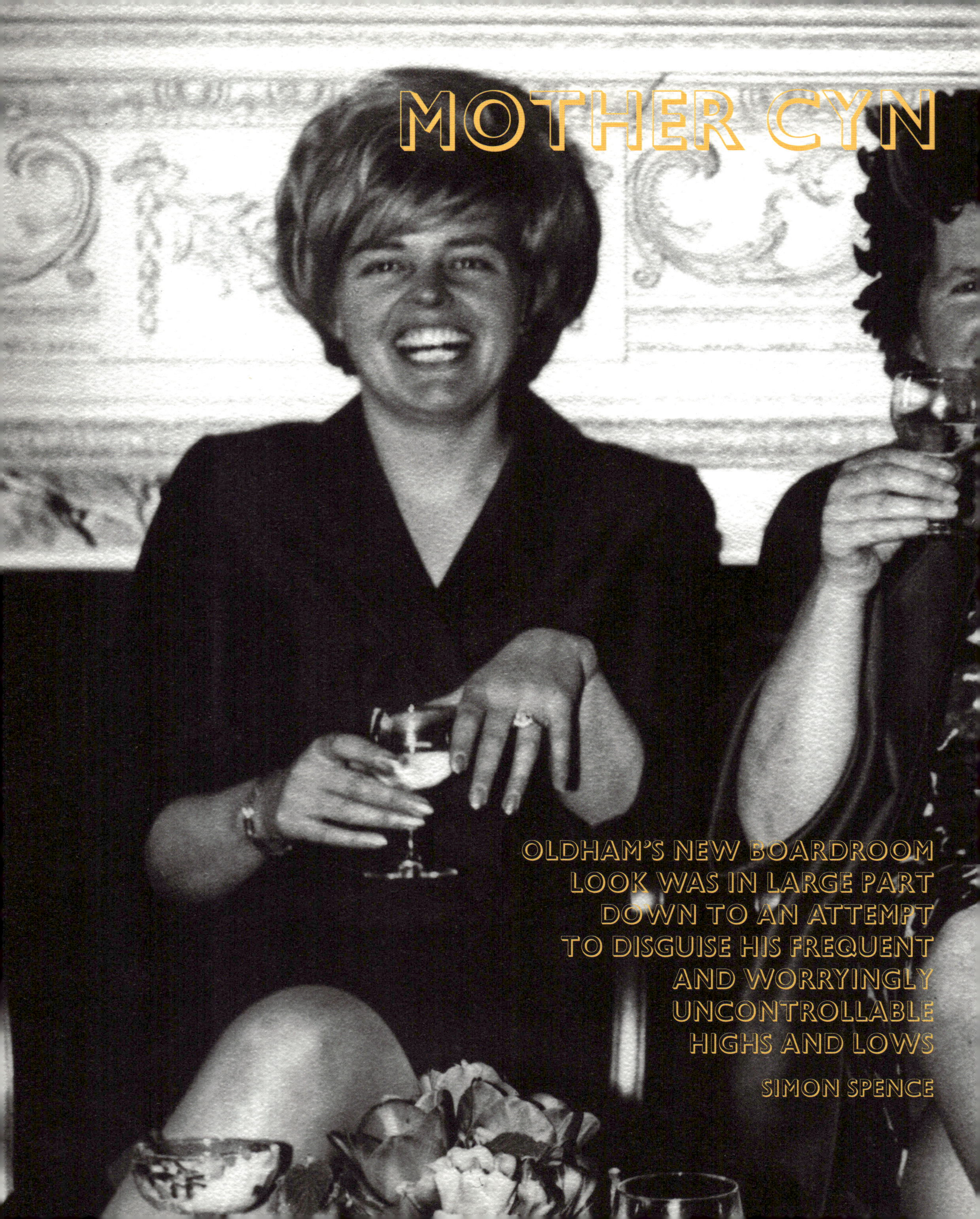

MOTHER CYN

OLDHAM'S NEW BOARDROOM LOOK WAS IN LARGE PART DOWN TO AN ATTEMPT TO DISGUISE HIS FREQUENT AND WORRYINGLY UNCONTROLLABLE HIGHS AND LOWS

SIMON SPENCE

The success of the Rolling Stones was at a zenith, Immediate was the most happening record label in London, and Oldham was well into the throes of a full-on drug and drink addiction with marijuana, vodka, amphetamines and sleepers on heavy rotation. The Ivor Court offices were often in chaos, thanks to his absence or presence, threatening to spiral out of control as the staff too freely indulged in following their leader. It was fun but bad for business. Rather wisely, Oldham appointed himself a new personal assistant, Cynthia Gainsford, who was engaged to 'sixth' Stone, Ian Stewart (who had been sacked by Oldham from the original Rolling Stones line-up for not looking the part). Cynthia had previously worked for Alan Freeman and admired Oldham's style as he added an Aston Martin and grey Lotus to his car fleet. Under Gainsford, Oldham forgot his main style of long leather coats, silk Thea Porter Cossack blouses and hexagonal sunglasses and adopted a ferocious, boardroom look in Roland Melandari suits, smartly clipped hair, bandit moustache and glasses with clear lenses to put on when reading contracts. Cynthia Gainsford remembers:

> My value was social. I was never a secretary or anything like that. I couldn't type or do shorthand but I had very good contacts in the business and he [Oldham] needed somebody to block the public out. He started drinking, he had this globe you would open, full of vodka and Kalhúa, which made Black Russians. For a while he absolutely adored Black Russians, part of my job was to pour drinks and things. 138 Ivor Court was much more showbizzy than Calder's 147 office. Really Andrew was an owl, he would come in latish in the mornings sometimes and work until late. After I married Stew he would say things like, "oh darling you can't go home', even though it was nine o'clock at night. I was always sort of watching over Andrew in a way.

"Before Cynthia arrived at Ivor Court it was fun", Tony King told me, "then Cynthia organised everything, kept everything in order. I think he [Oldham] rather liked the idea of having a high-powered female personal assistant, she was quite ferocious and kept all sorts of people out of the office." King left Immediate soon after Cynthia joined.

The 'Cassius Clay of record makers'—as Oldham was dubbed in the press—was also getting speed injections from Harley Street's infamous Doctor Robertson and his new boardroom look was in large part down to an attempt to disguise his frequent and worryingly uncontrollable highs and lows. Life was moving fast. Allen Klein had arranged another mammoth Rolling Stones tour of the US—the last with the original line-up—covering 29 cities in 27 days. That summer, in 1966, in Hollywood at RCA studios on Sunset Strip, Oldham recorded a new single, "Paint It Black" with the Rolling Stones. LA was boiling over, with riots happening right on the RCA studios' doorstep. It was a far cry from the previous year's Watts riots but nonetheless shocking. The riots were sparked by hundreds of kids congregating on the Strip expecting to party and causing traffic problems. Permits and licenses for clubs were withdrawn and a 10pm curfew for anyone under 18 was zealously enforced. As the riots grew harsher—"Long Hair Nightmare" screamed the *LA Times*—one of the few winners appeared to be Buffalo Springfield, whose song, "For What It's Worth", became an anthem for the city's youth movement.

"Paint It Black" was the Rolling Stones seventh consecutive UK number one on advance orders of 300,000. According to Oldham it was "completely different from anything the boys have done as a single before". It was also a huge number one in the US where its beating sense of dark neurosis sent crowds crazy on the US tour; riots in some cities were so intense that Oldham and the band were often lucky to escape with their lives. After experiences such as being buried under a five deep stage invasion when one venue's stage collapsed, the group were allowed their first proper break in three years. Jagger flew to Mexico, Richards stayed in New York, Bill Wyman and his wife went off to Florida, Charlie Watts to the Greek Islands and Brian Jones to Tangier with Anita Pallenberg. There was no rest for Oldham, as he charged into a new era at Immediate, leaving behind the Ivor Court apartments, and moving the whole outfit to a new address: Immediate House, 63–69 New Oxford Street, WC1.

OPPOSITE: CYNTHIA GAINSFORD, CIRCA 1965

I KNOW EXACTLY WHAT I WANT

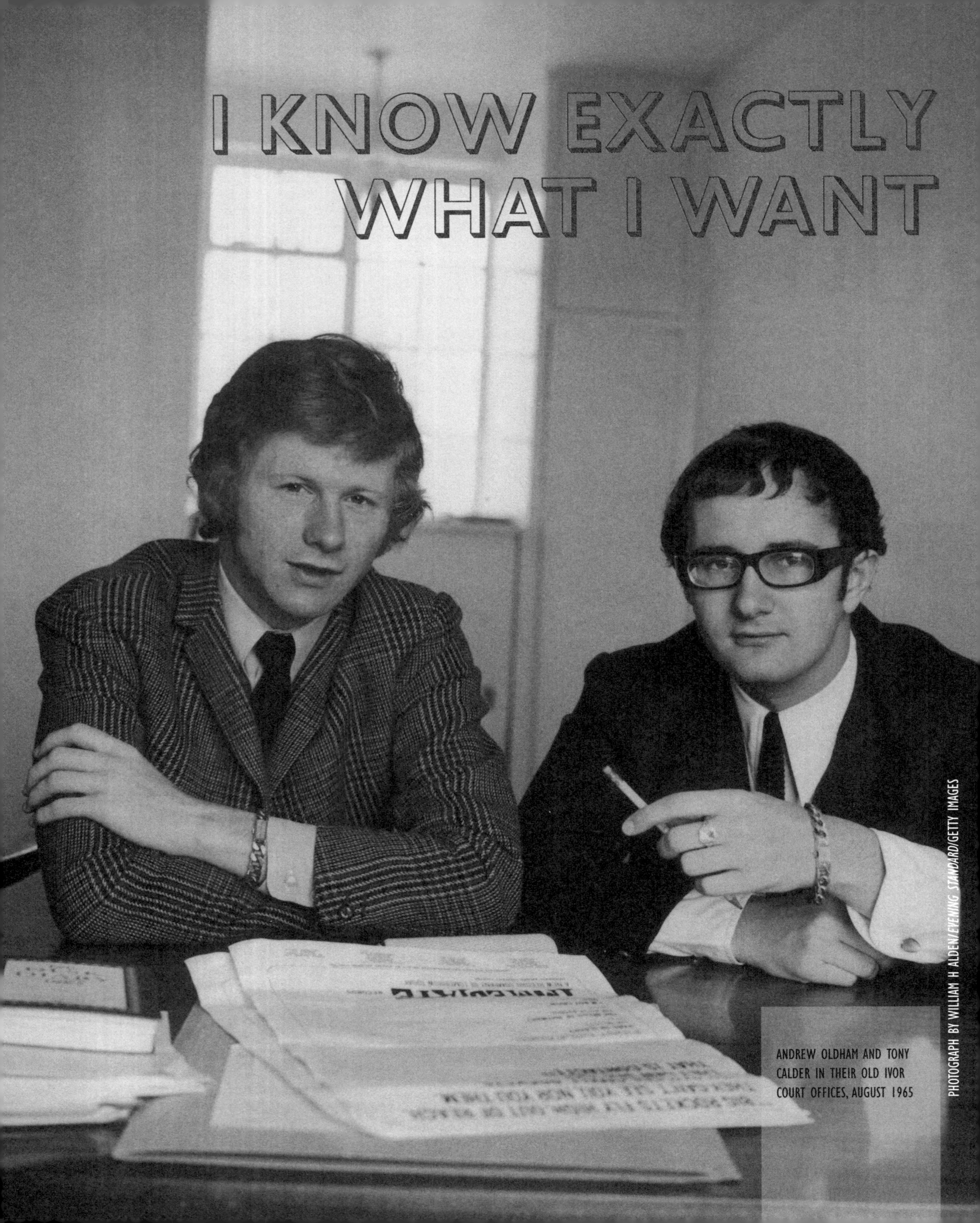

ANDREW OLDHAM AND TONY CALDER IN THEIR OLD IVOR COURT OFFICES, AUGUST 1965

PHOTOGRAPH BY WILLIAM H ALDEN/*EVENING STANDARD*/GETTY IMAGES

At Ivor Court it had all been about, "We're gonna get money", said Oldham. At the new Immediate offices it was all about, "we've got money and we're gonna spend it!", evident by another huge music press advert to announce the change of address.

Immediate celebrated the move and the label's first anniversary by making a documentary about themselves, narrated by top Radio 1 DJ Alan Freeman, called *The Little Bastard Immediate*. The film was photographed, edited and directed by celebrated filmmaker Peter Whitehead. The idea was to use the 20-minute film to pump up the Philips sales and promotions forces around the UK and Europe. It opened with a naked women spread out on a table having her breasts painted to the sound of an exhilarating violin-led version of "Paint It Black" sung by Chris Farlowe. It also featured Mick Jagger thanking everybody for helping promote "Out Of Time" and promising he would be back in the country to produce Farlowe's next hit single.

Oldham employed interior designer, Robin Guild, to refurbish the new Immediate premises, with separate elaborate main offices for himself and Calder; a music room, and various other offices and alcoves for a growing workforce. Oldham had hustled Guild in his weird and wacky Hampstead furniture store, keen at 17 to do PR for him. Then, when Guild got a bigger store in Hampstead, Oldham bought a chair from him. It turned out the chair would need a crane to get it in and the deal ended up leaving the designer out of pocket. Robin Guild remembers:

Oldham said: 'I know exactly what I want, I want a place where I don't know where I am. I don't want to know what time of day it is and I want to be able to walk in wearing a Cecil Beaton hat or a Tibetan robe.' Tony Calder looks at me with his eyes up in the air. They had taken the first floor in New Oxford Street, it was a building called Armward House. I noticed on the letterhead he had got Immediate Records, Immediate House, 63–69 New Oxford Street. I said: 'It's not Immediate House it's Armward House.' Oldham said: 'Oh, I'm changing it.' So one weekend he takes the name off the front of the building and calls it Immediate House, so when everybody comes to work on Monday all the addresses are wrong! He said: 'Oh they'll sue me but by the time they sue me I'll be long gone.'

Tony Calder's office was done very modern for the period—a rosewood and black leather number. Andrew's office door looked like a cupboard from the outside. You opened these orange lacquer doors with big gold handles and stepped onto a marble platform, swung around 45 degrees and then you had to walk down three steps into Andrew's office. He sat himself at a table, famous at the time, designed by the Finish modernist, Eero Saarinen, a tulip base with a white marble top. It was all very avant-garde for its day. It was photographed by *Ideal Home* magazine. It took quite a while to get the job done. The first scheme for Andrew's office, designed by his close friend, Sean Kenny [the celebrated West End and Broadway theatre stage designer who worked closely with Lionel Bart on hits like *Oliver!*], was even weirder. You went through this cupboard into a circular Perspex chamber, like a revolving door, with spiral lines on the inside and outside. In the chamber the floor was gonna look like an album and it would move so you felt as if you were going up, because of the way the spirals were working against each other. You felt like you were going up but in fact you were staying still. All it did was turn you around 45 degrees to face the right direction, to walk into Andrew's office.

Inside Andrew's office you were facing the apex of a triangle; we were going to do it like a church. We were going to put in a pulpit, which was going to be Andrew's sort of desk, and the isle was going to be mauve carpet that was made slightly narrower as it went away from you so that it made you feel the room was longer than it was. There was also bits of alter rail and choir stalls. The idea was that you had gone to heaven to meet Andrew Oldham. Andrew Oldham as God! He loved all this. There was gonna be a huge crucifix behind his desk. But at the time there was The Beatles religious clash when Lennon said the Beatles were bigger than God and Andrew said: 'We can't do it now'.

Andrew asked me: 'Do you do the inside of cars? I know exactly what I want.' The car is black, it's got black windows, standard. We take all the insides out, including the back seat, so now we've got the boot as part of the interior. You put two-winged sort of club chairs back to the driver's bit and where the boot is you put a fireplace. In the fireplace we have one of those kitsch coal affect fires, with fans running to make shadows. Over the fireplace we have a picture frame, one of those baroque Golders Green, Jewish, guilt picture frames but no picture in it, just a white canvas. In the drivers compartment we put a projector and we project movies on the white canvas. 'Imagine', he said, 'I'm going up the M1, I'm facing the wrong way, the windows are dark, I don't know where I am, and I'm round the fireplace looking at the movies. What movies do I run? I run movies of road accidents, so it won't happen to me!' He always had this briefcase with him and alarms used to go off occasionally reminding him to take one concoction of pills or another, he used to carry a Lugar in the briefcase as well.

I remember once in New Oxford Street someone called up to say, 'there's a copper downstairs wants to see Andrew'. Andrew said to Calder, 'Oh you deal with it'. I said: 'You can't bring him in here, the place stinks of marijuana.' He said, 'they don't know anything' and disappeared through the communicating door between his and Calder's office. Calder is sitting there with his feet on the desk and this uniformed cop comes in, holding his helmet, a young cop looking pretty bewildered. The office is pretty palatial and all these sort of strange characters are wandering around. Calder says: 'Yes...' The copper says: 'Are you the owner of the vehicle....' Calder says: 'No.' The communicating door opens and Andrew leaps into the room Nureyev style and shouts: 'I AM ANDREW OLDHAM!' He then proceeds to make this cop really wish he had never come into the office, giving him such a run around.

IMMEDIATE

IS ON THE MOVE
AND AS FROM 1st. AUGUST
WILL BE AT

IMMEDIATE HOUSE
63/69 NEW OXFORD ST.,
LONDON W.C.1.

Telex: 27655
Tel. No: 01 240 3377
Cables: IMMEDCORD LONDON
Telegrams: IMMEDCORD LONDON W.C.1.

THE IDEA WAS THAT YOU HAD GONE TO HEAVEN TO MEET ANDREW OLDHAM AS GOD!

STEPHEN INGLIS

Stephen Inglis, Immediate and Rolling Stones record designer recalls his time at immediate:

I had this new wonderful office at New Oxford Street, a great big art table. Andrew more than tripled my *Ready Steady Go!* Salary when I went to work full-time at Immediate as a designer. It was £10 a week from Immediate and £10 a week from the [Rolling] Stones. I had redesigned *Aftermath for America*, and I did the cover of the [Rolling] Stones live album, *Got Live If You Want It?*, which Oldham liked. On a design level Andrew would just sit and share his ideas and out of it something would emerge and we would use it.

Come three o'clock in the afternoon, Eddie would come and join me and mass-produce joints for Andrew. He would roll 20 or 30 joints and pack them up in cigarette packets and that's what Andrew would go out with for the evening. In those days when you bought a custom Rolls Royce it wasn't uncommon for them to build in a jewel box, a little safe within the car where the lady can put her gems. Andrew had one of those in his Phantom 5 but it was full of drugs.

The windows of the Rolls were all tinted black, except the driver's windows, which were tinted green; it was illegal for the driver to have black windows back then. Andrew would drive along in the Rolls and cops would often stop them, just because they were curious to know who was in the car. Eddie was so fed up of being stopped for this reason that he used to have all his documents ready, he would just wind down his window about half an inch and poke [them] out. As the cops would walk towards the car, the centre divide would go up, sealing off the back, so Andrew was in his little cabin back there smoking a joint looking through the tinted glass at the cops looking at Eddie. In those days they could send you to jail for 15 years for marijuana.

Cynthia was like Andrew's Margaret Thatcher—the office mother. The relationship between Andrew and Tony Calder was like a Jekyll and Hyde partnership. Andrew's up there, everybody loves Andrew, we're following Andrew; meanwhile Tony Calder's telling us to sign this and sign that. Sean Kenny was often around, he would keep Andrew's creative juices flowing.

Artists started signing to Immediate because Andrew had done it with the [Rolling] Stones. Gered Mankowitz was doing all our photography—the [Rolling] Stones and Immediate. Mankowitz lived in Fulham just across the road from the Broadway station. We used to ride into the office together in the morning and stop off at Fortnum and Mason's to have breakfast... we were always working together during the day on different projects at Immediate.

Gered Mankowitz, Rolling Stones photographer, relates:

Everybody loved my pictures of Marianne [Faithfull] and Andrew Oldham and Tony Calder asked if I would like to photograph the [Rolling] Stones. I replaced [David] Bailey. Andrew was open to

OLDHAM: TALENTED, INSULTING, OUTRAGEOUS

OLDHAM LOVED BEING THE SLIGHTLY VILLAINOUS HEAD OF A RECORD COMPANY
GERED MANKOWITZ

OPPOSITE: IMMEDIATE ADVERTISE THEIR CHANGE OF ADDRESS

THE HEADLINE FOR THE ARTICLE "OLDHAM: TALENTED, INSULTING, OUTRAGEOUS", *NME*, AUGUST 1966.

me because he liked the fact that my father was a screenwriter in showbusiness, especially as he had written *Expresso Bongo*. I have an image of Immediate, 1966–68, as being just a glorious time of fantastic creativity. Just mad, fun, extremely creative, a feeling of being very much on top of the tree, top of the pile, the music and energy was fantastic. We were having so much fun. Andrew was just the most fantastic person to be with, we went out quite a lot, he had the cars and the big house.

I was with Immediate most of the time, spending a lot of evenings taking photographs, coming up with ideas, doing designs, adverts, sales presentations, hanging with Andrew, going to recording studios, radio stations, y'know, looning, having a great time. He coaxed performances out of people in the studio, he would say I don't think that's working, try it with a bit more... he used funny language and body movements to communicate in the studio. It was like he was directing traffic. Immediate was the *enfant terrible* of the record business, we were having hits, making great music. A lot of planning and manipulation went into it—this wasn't accident. Andrew loved Immediate, he loved the way of life, and he loved being

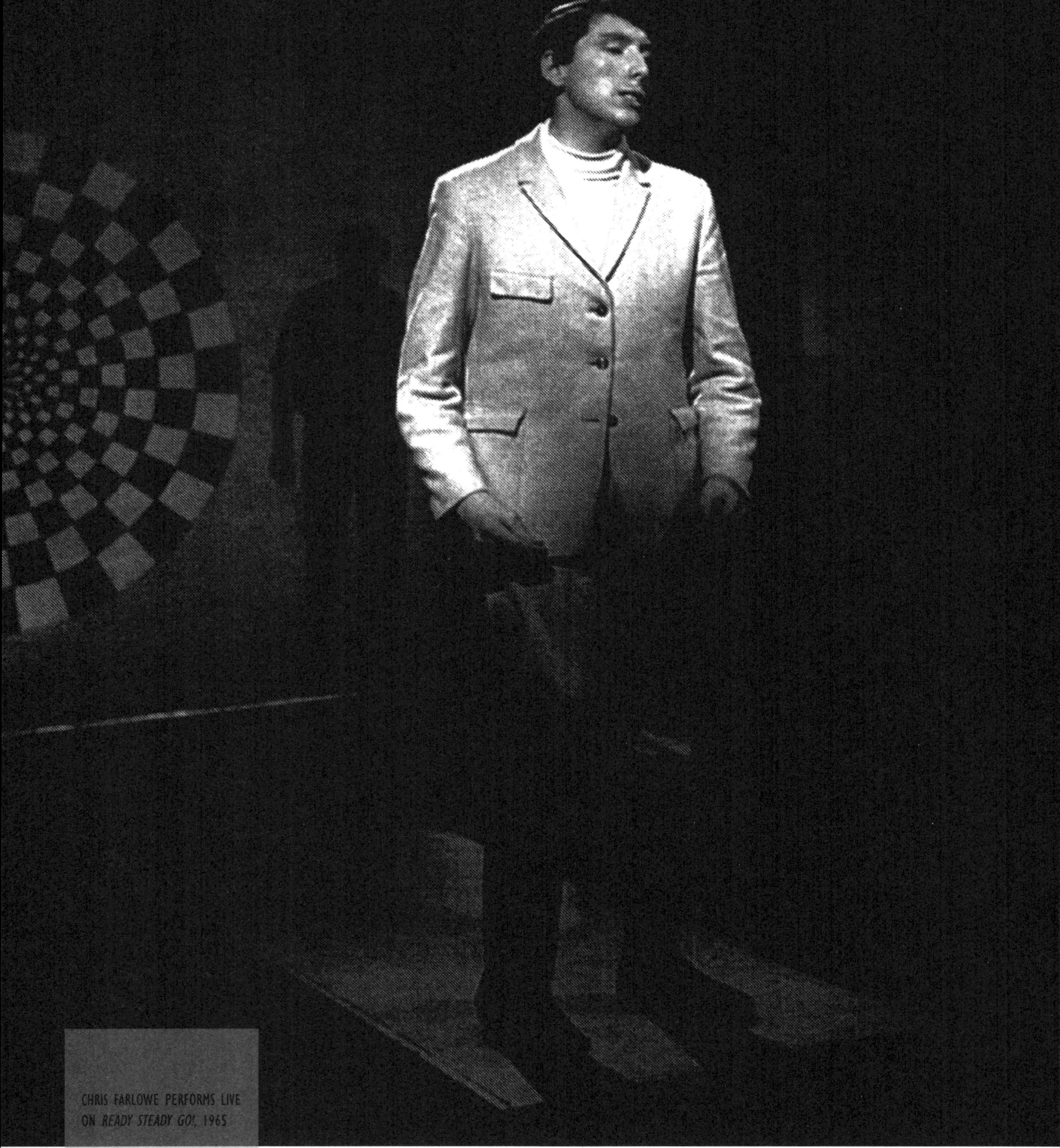

CHRIS FARLOWE PERFORMS LIVE ON *READY STEADY GO!*, 1965

the slightly villainous head of a record company, the whole operation. Andrew used to have a fantastic wardrobe of clothes, all the clothes were arranged by colour, jackets and suits, start with white and end up in black, just an immaculate guy right?

Paul Banes, assistant to Immediate and Rolling Stones accountant Stan Blackbourne remembers:

At the UK office you came into Immediate and on the right hand side you had the reception, on the left there was a little corridor going back. At the end of the corridor was a music room, where we put all out gear and did demo's on a Revox. The first office on the left when you came in was mine and Stan's office, it was next door to Ken Mewis [the new promotions manager] who had an assistant, called Pauline, who went to RCA after Immediate. We had a girl on reception, a very East Anglia, awfully, awfully posh girl. Then there was a big double door that went into what they called New York and LA. New York was Tony on the left who had a wooden panelled office, big leather desk, big leather sofas, outside his office was Jenny. Then in the back, LA, Andrew's office, he had a big fashionable marble topped table, white seats. Their two offices took up 95 per cent of the space really.

I was the third oldest when I started there and I was 20. Immediate were miles in front of everybody else. The whole thing was streets ahead, the attitude, the rapport we had with the artists. The Immediate staff were tight and dedicated, we buckled down to do the work. When a record went in at number one we were all well happy, and it just stuck a couple of fingers up at the people down the road. That's what it was all about!

Oldham gave Keith Altham at *NME* an interview as soon as the new Immediate offices opened—a double-page spread headed "Oldham: Talented, Insulting, Outrageous". Oldham, who was "agitated, bouncing about among the packing cases", had to leave for a flight to New York in 15 minutes and Altham joined him and Calder in the Phantom 5 on the way to the airport. "I'm going to New York then chartering a private plane to Hollywood", he told Altham. "Allen Klein and I are negotiating an outlet for Immediate Records in the US and we also have to discuss plans for the Rolling Stones' film." Oldham also talked about Marianne Faithfull ("Nothing to do with me now"), and the Rolling Stones' girls, Chrissie Shrimpton, Linda Keith and Anita Pallenberg.

The Rolls Royce stopped off at Oldham's Fulham residence and then cruised on to the airport. From the back sear, "with the push of a button", Oldham asked Eddy to drop off a torn suit at Lord Johns for "invisible repair". Oldham told Altham he was moving home too—from the Fulham house into a mansion in Highgate built by Oliver Cromwell's brother. As for Immediate Oldham said he had plans for new artists "but they were still being negotiated... there are lots of egos involved and it depends on something which depends on something else if you see what I mean", he said before talking up newly-signed act Twice As Much. "I would say they have same kind of mass appeal as Cliff Richard"—"worldwide" said Calder finishing his sentence. "Universal simplicity" trumped Oldham.

When asked about Nico—who was used in the photo to accompany the *NME* piece—Oldham said she was now working with the Velvet Underground, earning around £11,000 for eight days in clubs like Hollywood Trips. Altham wrote how he was astonished to hear Oldham compare Scott Walker to Joan Crawford, and declare "The Beach Boys single is not dedicated to me".

Oldham was all business though when discussing the Rolling Stones. Altham brought up a recent New York-based Rolling Stones show, which he said only attracted 11,000 people. "Anyone would think it was bad", Oldham said: "The date was a weekend booking with temperatures in the 1990s. It was the equivalent of playing in Piccadilly Garden on a bank holiday and 11,000 for that ain't bad."

Altham decided Oldham was "going in several directions at once—mostly up". He concluded: "Andrew Oldham is egotistical, talented, insulting, outrageous, and likeable almost in spite of himself. He manages the world's number two group, owns his own record company, produces discs, writes songs, sleeve notes and poetry and publishes the Beach Boys music in Britain. In the hip vocabulary of pop music they say he is happening. Perhaps Mama Cass stressed what is the most overlooked and often unconsidered feature in Oldham's success when she incredulously repeated to me over and over again during a recent interview: "And he's only 22—can you imagine what he'll be doing when he's 30.""

ANDREW OLDHAM IS EGOTISTICAL, TALENTED, INSULTING, OUTRAGEOUS, AND LIKEABLE ALMOST IN SPITE OF HIMSELF

KEITH ALTHAM

GOD ONLY KNOWS

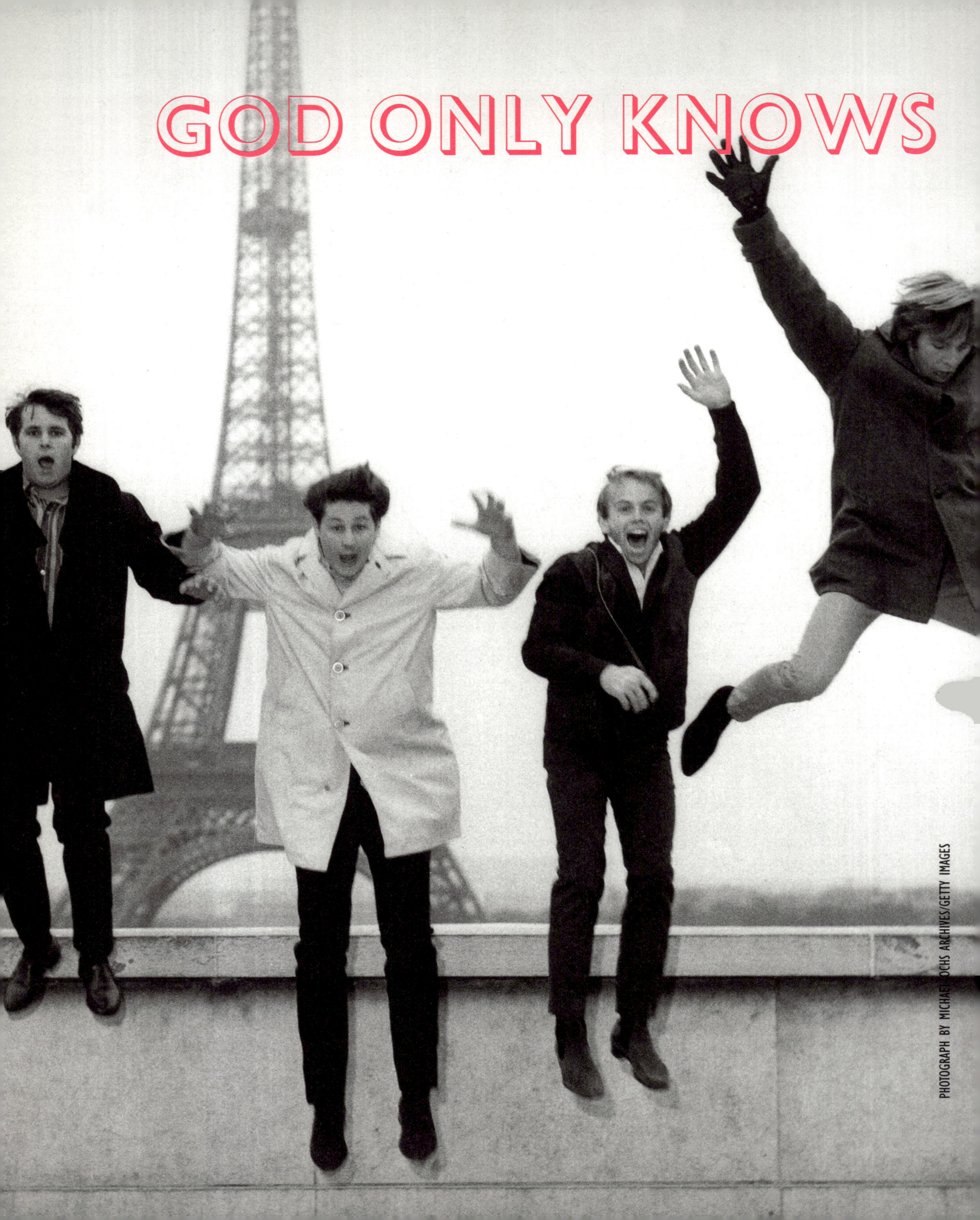

PHOTOGRAPH BY MICHAEL OCHS ARCHIVES/GETTY IMAGES

At New Oxford Street, Immediate established a sister company, Immediate Music, the label's publishing arm. Oldham had got a good publishing deal for Jagger/Richards songs with main London publishing firm, Essex Music, way back in 1963. His cut of the publishing revenues on those 1960s songs still keep him living in style today. As a favour to Essex Music boss, David Platz, who had paid for the recording, Immediate had released the *Who Can I Turn To?* album by Mark Murphy, a Sinatra-era jazz crooner, who both Ella Fitzgerald and Scott Walker adored. Murphy was a star at Ronnie Scott's and landed his own BBC2 television show and sales were relatively brisk but it was nothing more than a passing whim for Immediate. Platz would soon be boss of EMI's Regal Zonophone label, a reactivated old jazz imprint, intended as EMI's version of the "artistically free Immediate".

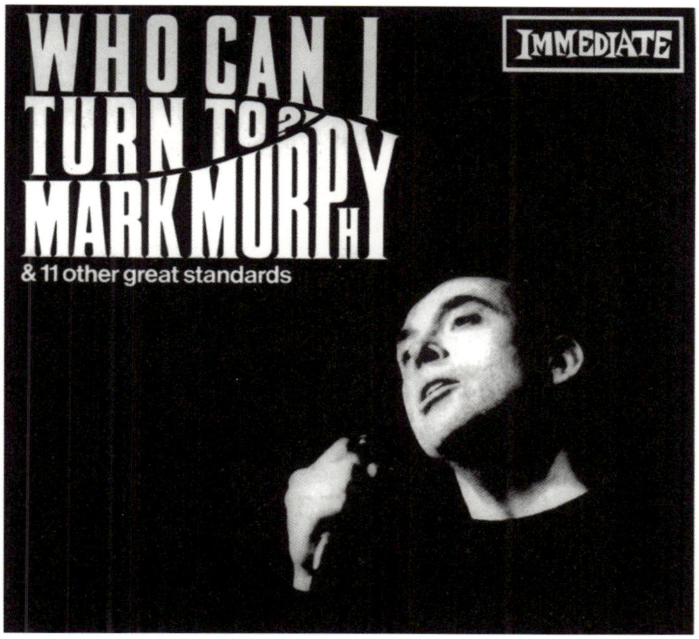
WHO CAN I TURN TO?
MARK MURPHY
& 11 other great standards
IMMEDIATE

The other big London music publishing company, Carlin Music, was run by Oldham's pal, "Viennese" Freddie Bienstock, who had grown hugely wealthy by owning the copyrights to an incredible catalogue of songs. Each time one of Carlin's songs was performed, played or covered—on the radio or stage—Freddie collected a small "performance rights" fee (one play on BBC radio at the time was worth about £2). Publishing revenues were generally split 50/50 with the songwriter. Infamous US music business giant, Morris Levy, said about publishing: "The song works for itself and it never talks back to you." He added: "It's just pennies but it all accumulates to nice money."

Oldham and Calder knew that publishing revenue was a highly lucrative area of the business. They began to sign specialist songwriters to provide songs for their publishing company and to encourage artists releasing records through them to place their songs with Immediate Music, not Essex, Carlin or Dick Rowe, who owned The Beatles song publishing and whose offices were next door to Immediate on New Oxford Street. One of Immediate Music's first signings was Wayne Fontana, who had dropped The Mindbenders and penned the exquisite "Game Of Love", a sure-fire earner. The buzz surrounding the new company was amplified with the press announcement that Immediate Music had secured the UK rights to the publishing on Beach Boys songs. The group's records were released by EMI in the UK but they had not had a UK Top 10 entry for almost two years, since "I Get Around" in 1964. Oldham was a big fan, as witnessed by the 1965 Andrew Loog Oldham Orchestra album, *East Meets West*, which featured one side of Beach Boys covers and one side of Four Season covers. Streamlining Immediate Music and Immediate Records, the songs of Brian Wilson were used for a slew of new releases—the everlasting "You're So Good To Me" by The Factotums which two other Immediate acts, Chris Farlowe and Twice As Much had also cut versions of, "Girl Don't Tell Me" with the Brian Epstein managed act Tony Rivers and The Castaways and The Masterminds' version of "Barbara Ann"—all of which were Beach Boys sound-alikes. The single "Barbara Ann" had to be pulled

OPPOSITE: ROCK'N'ROLL BAND THE BEACH BOYS JUMP OFF A LEDGE IN FRONT OF THE EIFFEL TOWER, CIRCA 1965

"WHO CAN I TURN TO?" BY MARK MURPHY, 1966

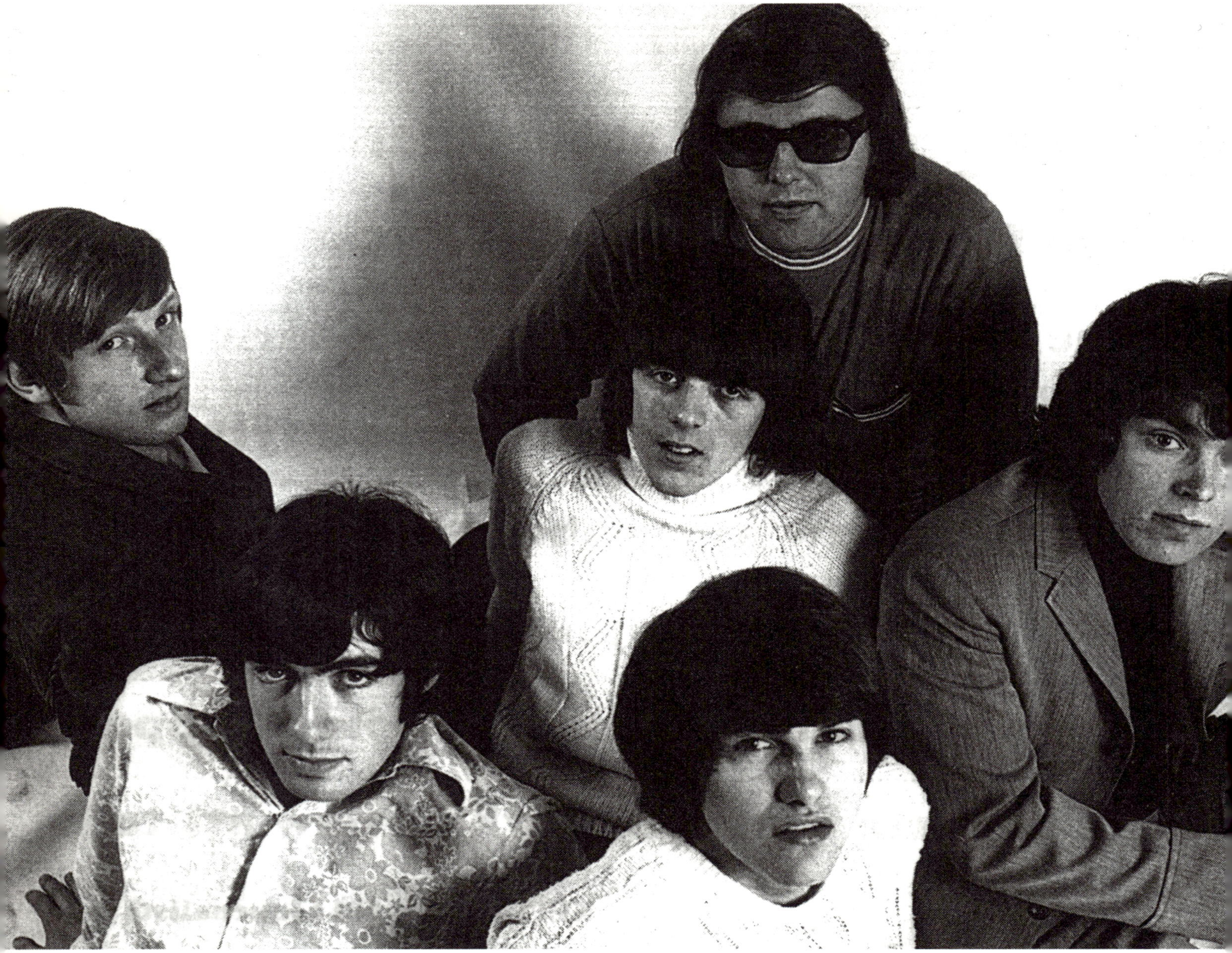

SURF AND SUNSHINE. WHAT DID THAT MEAN IN ENGLAND?

TONY CALDER

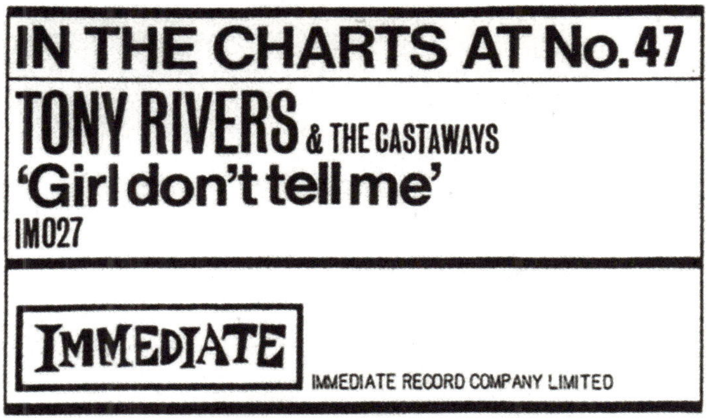
IN THE CHARTS AT No.47
TONY RIVERS & THE CASTAWAYS
'Girl don't tell me'
IM027
IMMEDIATE
IMMEDIATE RECORD COMPANY LIMITED

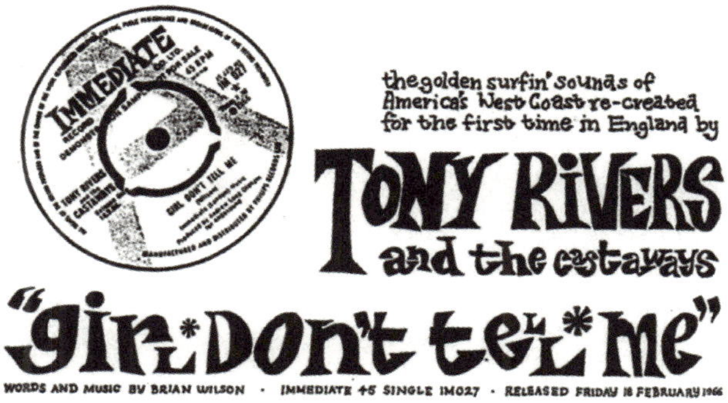
the golden surfin' sounds of America's West Coast re-created for the first time in England by
TONY RIVERS
and the castaways
"girl don't tell me"
WORDS AND MUSIC BY BRIAN WILSON · IMMEDIATE 45 SINGLE IM027 · RELEASED FRIDAY 18 FEBRUARY 1966

when Beach Boys released the same song as a single in UK. "Barbara Ann" was the start of a majestic renaissance for Beach Boys, and five UK Top 5 singles followed in 1966, with songs such as "Sloop John B", "God Only Knows", "Good Vibrations", "Help Me Rhonda", "Heroes and Villains" and "California Girls" all earning Immediate Music more than good money. Tony Calder remembers:

> EMI didn't want to know about Beach Boys, they were just one of those surf bands from the West Coast. EMI didn't want to promote some band that went surfing. Surf and sunshine. What did that mean in England? EMI didn't realise that Brian was a great talent. We broke them in this country. We were doing press on them, getting interviews for them, taking adverts. That's how we got the publishing—as a reward. I remember EMI rang us up and said: 'What have you done with this Beach Boys record?' I said 'we've put it in the charts'. They said: 'Yeah, I can see that but we haven't even manufactured it yet.' I said: 'Well how long do you want?' They said: 'Well it'll be ready next week.' I said 'okay, I'll put it up a place'. So we paid the guy (who fixed the charts at one of the music papers) another hundred quid. The guy from EMI rang up and said, 'we've still got a problem'. I said, 'okay, one more week'.

IT'S JUST PENNIES BUT IT ALL ACCUMULATES TO NICE MONEY

MORRIS LEVY

This was an era when sheet music was still a popular seller and a nice little earner though not as lucrative as it had been a decade previous when gathering round the piano with the family to sing a popular tune had been all the rage. Immediate Music released some sheet music by Beach Boys with colour pictures of the group on the front. From around this time Immediate Music also released sheet music by blues legend, Robert Johnson. Eventually Beach Boys manager, Murray Wilson, used Immediate's tardiness in making publishing payments and the Immediate-fuelled UK hits to land his boys a big advance and better deal for their UK publishing. Before that Oldham took the better part of three weeks to digest an advance copy of the new Beach Boys album, *Pet Sounds*, listening to it intently in hotel rooms from Manchester to Stockholm. He took out adverts in the music press to compare Pet Sounds to Rimsky-Korsakov's Scheherazade and determined himself to record an album, with Twice As Much, that could compete.

OPPOSITE: TONY RIVERS AND THE CASTAWAYS POSE FOR EDITORIAL SHOTS, CIRCA 1965

PROMOTIONAL MATERIAL FOR TONY RIVERS AND THE CASTAWAYS' HIT "GIRL DON'T TELL ME", CIRCA 1965

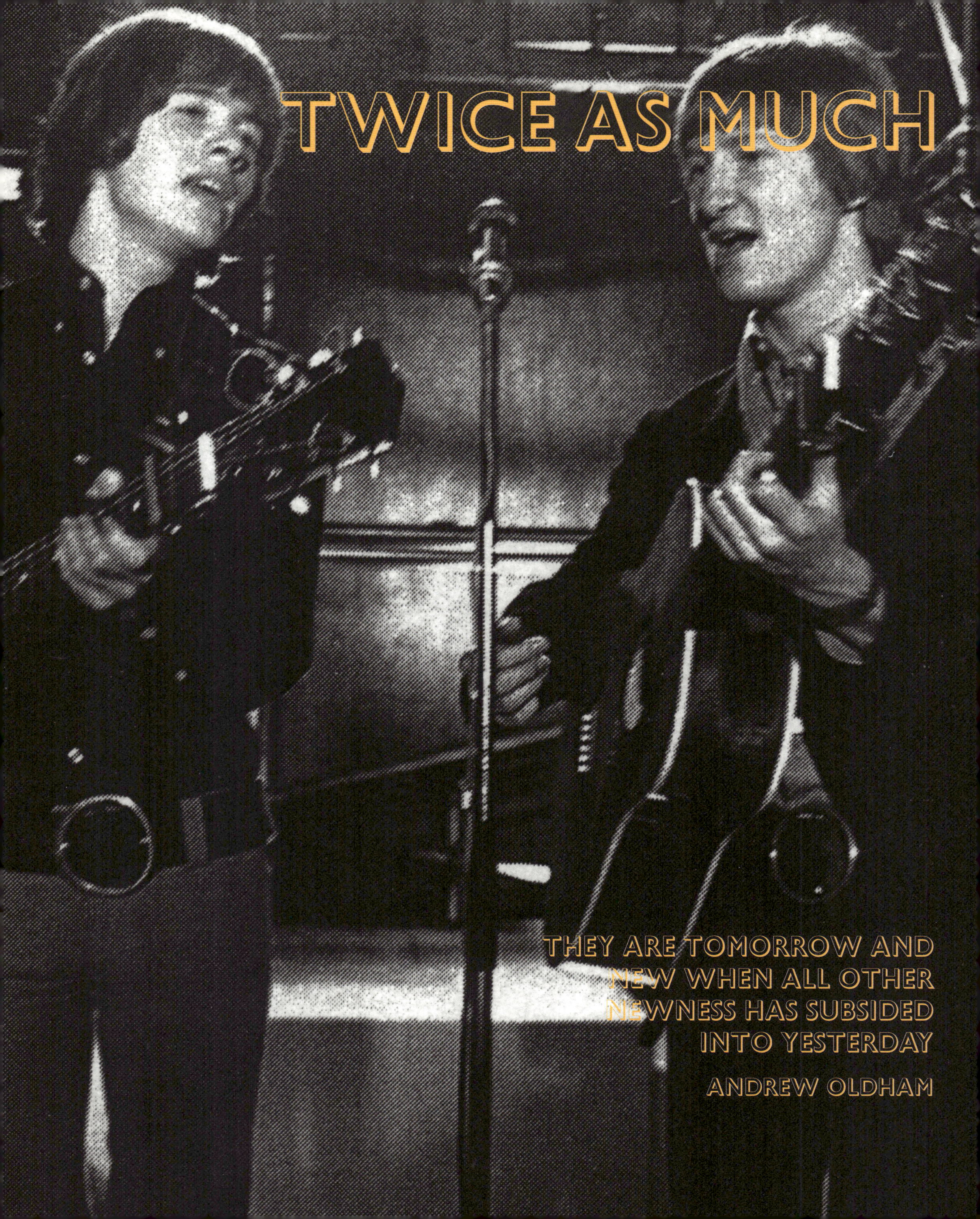

TWICE AS MUCH

THEY ARE TOMORROW AND
NEW WHEN ALL OTHER
NEWNESS HAS SUBSIDED
INTO YESTERDAY

ANDREW OLDHAM

Immediate signed young, green, folky songwriters, Andrew Skinner and David Rose after Oldham started off a week having Cynthia Gainsford play him every tape that had been sent in to Immediate by aspiring acts over the past few months. Oldham spent three days listening to a hundred tapes or more, before choosing Rose and Skinner as winners and arranging for them to make a small budget demo of their songs. Oldham named them Twice As Much and produced them on a Jagger/Richards song "Sittin' on a Fence", while encouraging the duo to develop as songwriters. "He would say, 'here's two or three records, take a bit, listen to that, take a bit out of that,'" said Skinner. "Sittin' on a Fence" was recorded at Pye studios with Art Greenslade and full orchestra. The ornate Elizabethan, harpsichord-heavy backing gave it a kind of quaint feel and it was mixed solid in New York. Apparently Oldham got the name Twice As Much from a *Time* magazine article he read on the flight back from the mixing of the single, after toying with idea of launching them as David and Andrew. Twice As Much were given a big push by Immediate, with adverts touting them as "The Hit Summer Sound of Young England". Oldham introduced them on television show *Thank Your Lucky Stars* and was quoted in the press saying:

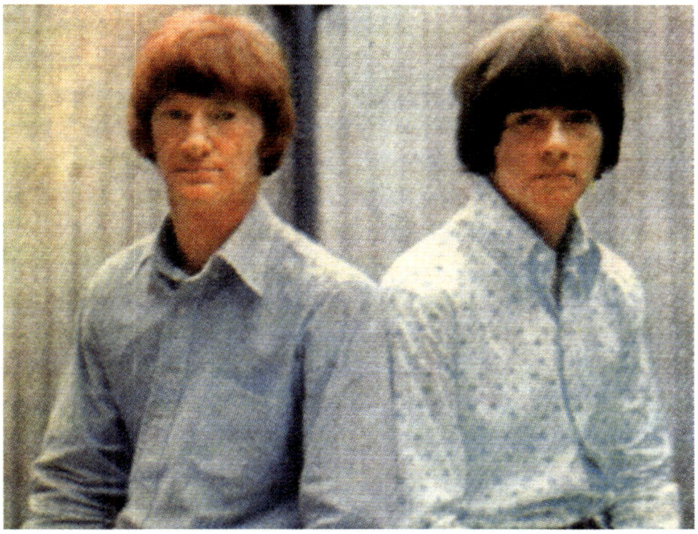

> Not since Marianne Faithful have I gone overboard like this on an act. They are tomorrow and new when all other newness has subsided into yesterday. One is good looking and the other is the sort that people think looks like them. A certain part of the act must be a mirror for the audience to see themselves in.

When "Sitting On A Fence" cracked the Top 20, peaking at number 12, self-congratulatory Immediate adverts went across the press, announcing the single's chart achievement as well as that of Chris Farlowe's number one "Out Of Time" with a special mention for Art Greenslade as arranger on both.

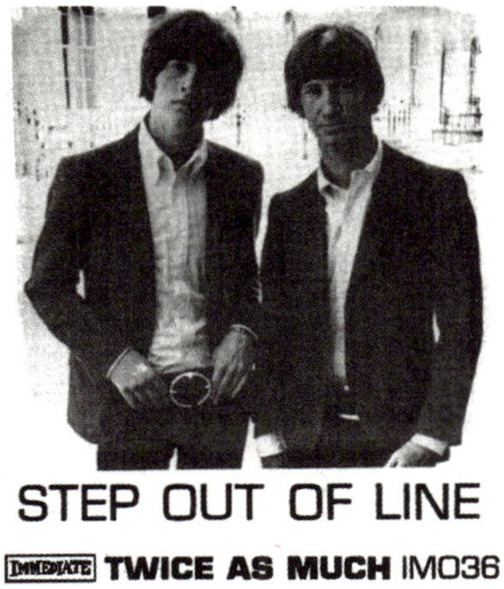
STEP OUT OF LINE
IMMEDIATE TWICE AS MUCH IM036

Twice As Much followed that with two more singles; both original Skinner and Rose compositions. "Step Out Of Line" peaked at number 29 and "True Story" had Billy Fury proclaiming in *Melody Maker*: "It's a great arrangement. I'll bet Andrew Oldham had a hand in that." On both singles Oldham was in total control, skillfully managing the orchestration, allowing the smooth harmonising from the group and sophisticated song themes to shine. Oldham then poured his blood, sweat and tears into the Twice As Much album, *Own Up*; a grand, epic, symphonic, fantasy production, that cost Immediate £26,000 to record (a then benchmark for the cost of making an album). It took about three weeks to complete recording, when the industry standard for albums was three days. Art Greenslade, arranger on Twice As Much's *Own Up* recalls:

> The Twice As Much album was inspired by *Pet Sounds*. It came out before *Sergeant Pepper's Lonely Hearts Club Band* and I thought it was better. Andrew had a lot of strange ideas, and a lot of them came off. We spent a lot of time on that album, damn lot of work went into it. We would finish a session, got the backing track down and Andrew would sit there all night, just keep listening to this backing track played back to him.

OPPOSITE: ANDREW SKINNER AND MIKE ROSE AKA TWICE AS MUCH PERFORM LIVE ON *READY STEADY GO!* CIRCA 1966

TOP: THE DUO STRIKE A POSE, CIRCA 1966

BOTTOM: TWICE AS MUCH ADVERTISING FOR "STEP OUT OF LINE"

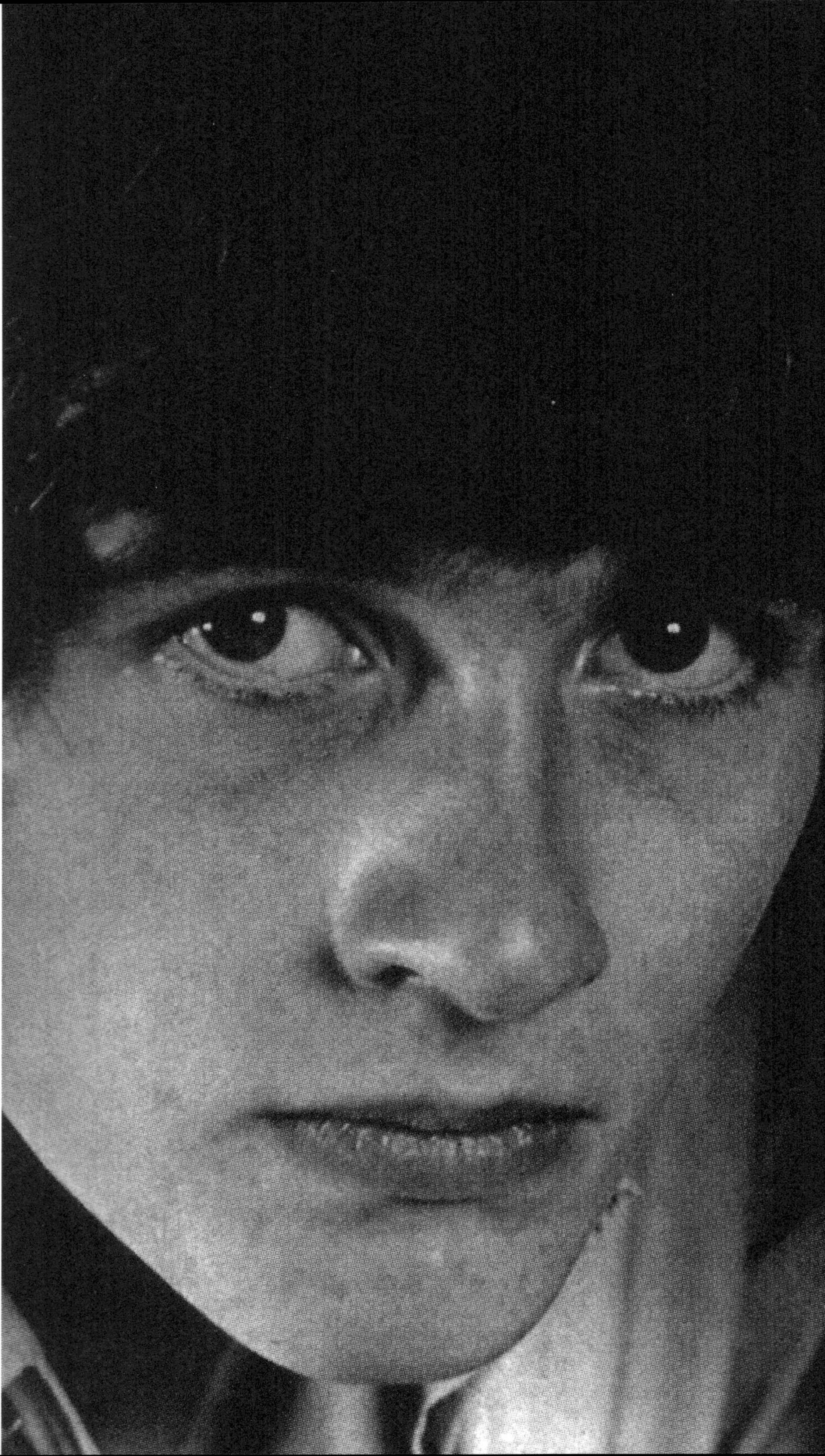

TWICE AS MUCH, APRIL 1967

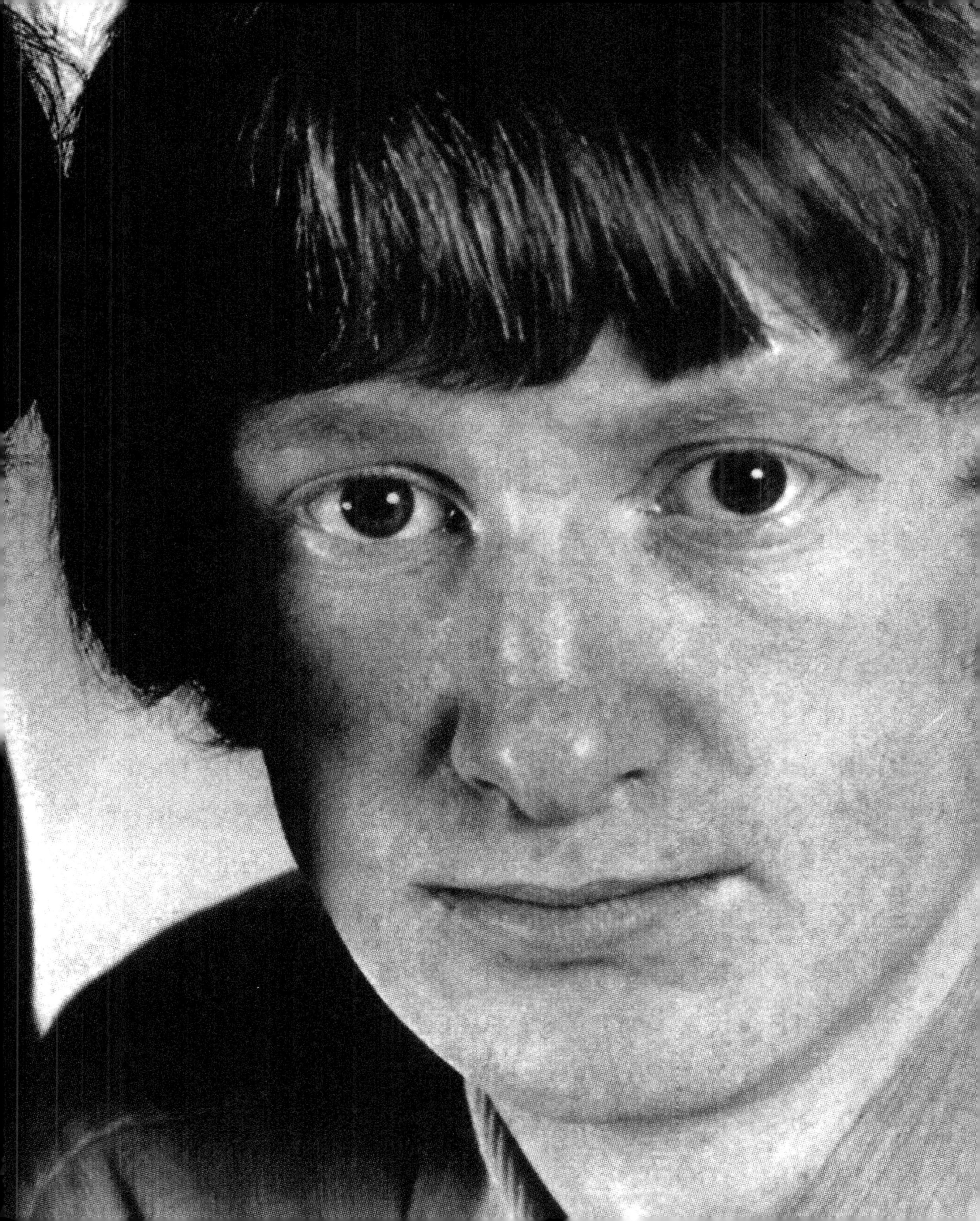

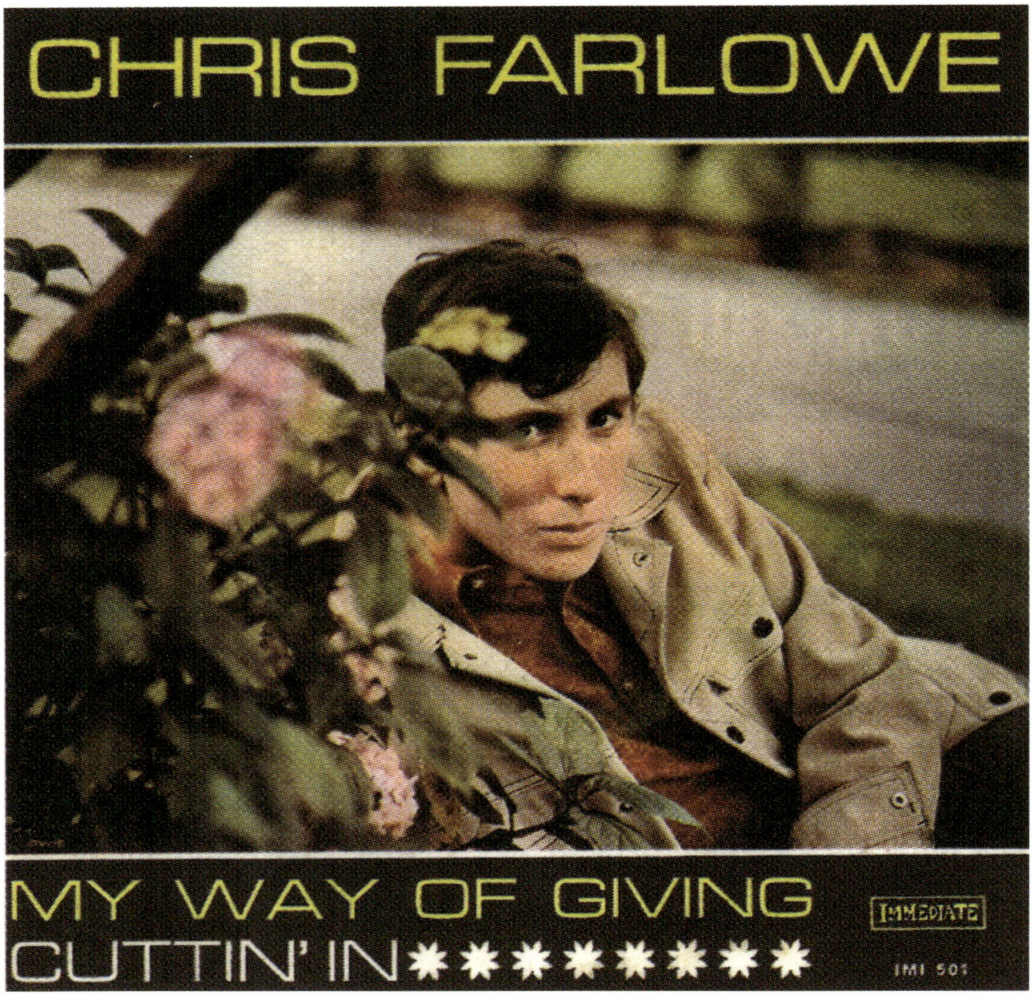
CHRIS FARLOWE
MY WAY OF GIVING
CUTTIN' IN
IMMEDIATE
IMI 501

> Oldham was a very thorough man, a very clever guy. We would get in the studio and he would start kicking it around. Once we had run through it once, he would start changing things, if it were possible to be changed. We had some very good, very clever sessions. Andrew used his favourite musicians. His favourite drummer was Andy White, who had done some sessions with The Beatles. Andrew would go down the stairs, go into the drum booth and spend five minutes just getting this little drum full in, spend the time to get what he wanted, just this stupid little drum fill, you wouldn't bloody know, it wouldn't sell the record, if you blinked your eye it would be gone.

Own Up was recorded at PYE studios, where The Who, The Kinks, Nancy Sinatra, Dionne Warwick, Sammy Davis Junior, The Troggs, The Searchers, Marlene Dietrich and the Spencer Davis Group had all recorded. Oldham booked the cream of session musicians, including Jimmy Page and Jim Sullivan and pianist/keyboardist, Nicky Hopkins. John Paul Jones remembers playing bass along with a stand-up string bass and there was a double rhythm section, three percussionists, two drummers and a full orchestra.

The first woman of rock journalism and the London *Evening Standard*'s young culture writer, Maureen Cleave—she who had got the Jesus quote out of Lennon and was the first to interview Phil Spector in this country—went down to the studio for a feature. "Mr Oldham looks like an impatient world-weary, Little Lord Fauntleroy", Cleave wrote:

> There are golden curls about his ears and dark glasses just as permanently on his nose. He is tall and very skinny and with his bell-bottomed jeans. He sometimes wears ruffled shirts and Tom Jones shoes with buckles. His appearance and manner madden many people. 'They think I'm a rude lout', he says. 'I can't be bothered about being nice—all this hello bit.'

Oldham took Cleave to what she described as a "dark recording studio" to let her on his latest recording: "Four young men sitting on the floor, two more singing 'ooh' into a microphone, another, his chauffeur, leaning against the door, a girl singing behind a screen and a teenage guitarist and pianist playing their heads off." She continued:

Stateside
IMMEDIATE
CHRIS
FARLOWE
MY WAY OF GIVING
YOU'RE SO GOOD FOR ME

AN INVOCATIVE AND INDICATIVE DOCUMENT OF THE 1960s MOMENT AS OPTIMISM, CREATIVITY AND CAREFREE LIVING REACHED CRESCENDO

SIMON SPENCE

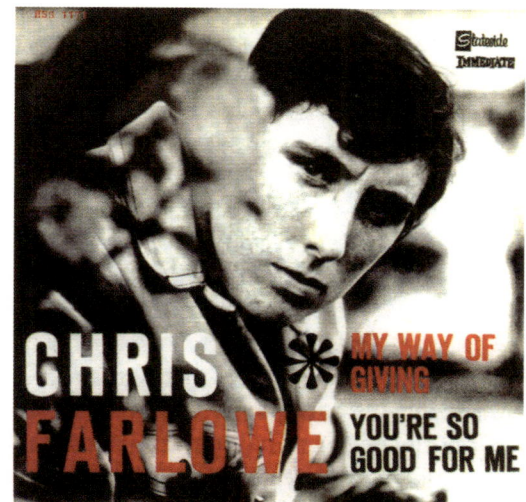

OPPOSITE AND ABOVE: CHRIS FARLOWE'S "MY WAY OF GIVING", JANUARY 1967

> Behind a wall of glass facing them Mr Oldham was soundlessly making the most extraordinary faces and gestures of encouragement to the girl. 'Bah, bah, bah', he appeared to say as he jerked his head back and forth like a hen in time to the music. Occasionally his voice boomed forth, 'I want the ending nice like surf crashing against rocks', or 'I want it very haunting like monks in cassocks'.

Oldham invented his own language in the studio. He would say he wanted "Beethoven goes Latin" and "very wankable, very wankable" after a take that pleased him. When it came to a passage for saxophones, he would assume his saxophone pose. There are film recording of Oldham in the studio producing *Own Up*, as he sings Skinner and Rose through an opening line. Take after take is stopped, being not good enough, before Oldham sings it down to them from the control booth the way he wants it: then they nail it.

There was a session for *Own Up* involving a fairly large string ensemble and in the toilet Oldham overheard some of the players going "God this bloody rubbish, when's it gonna be over". He obtained all the names of the string players on that session and booked them again on a really hot day, turned the air con off and had nothing for them to play. He just sat in front of them for three hours. David Skinner of Twice As Much remembers:

> *Own Up* was his baby, he put a lot of effort into it. He was meticulous with it, he used to go back to New York and remix things. It was incredibly, meticulously made. I certainly didn't see any money out of it, nothing substantial, like you could say, well I earned so much out of that album, everything got absorbed by the living and the making of it.

Own Up featured lavish versions of The Beatles "Help" and "We Can Work It Out", Spector/Goffin/King's "Is This What I Get For Loving You Baby", Jagger/Richards/Oldham's "As Tears Go By" and a slowed down and symphonic version of Small Faces' recent hit "Sha La La La Lee", plus more original contributions from Skinner and Rose, the pick of which, "Life Is But Nothing", would be covered by many Immediate artists to come. Skinner and Rose's sweet harmonies rode on exquisitely layered rhythms with blasts of orchestral punctuations from trombones, chiming bells and tinkling harpsichords, even incorporating cuckoo and raindrop effects. "The sound is absolutely fantastic", said the *NME* review, "teenage angst, street corner Doo-wop, this is an English symphonic look at the theme of Love".

The album never quite got the same recognition as *Pet Sounds*, but the making of it—the gesture at least—awakened many musicians to the way it could be. Small Faces singer, Steve Marriott, brought it up in interviews at the time: "A record like this opens up somebody's mind and makes the way for another record even better. I really dig Andrew Oldham, he's too much. On a scene of his very own and it's great." After reading these comments Oldham called Marriott, who recalls: "He was interested in working with us... did we have any songs?"

Evidently they did. Chris Farlowe's new Immediate single was the Marriott/Lane song "My Way Of Giving" which, despite being "produced by Mick Jagger", failed to make the Top 40. It was recorded at the same time as Rolling Stones were making their album *Between The Buttons* at London's Olympic studios, and Farlowe remembered Marriott and fellow Small Face, Ronnie Lane, taking control in Olympic with assistance from various Rolling Stones. It was "a crazy session", Farlowe said. Small Faces were signed to a friend of Oldham's, Don Arden, who had them on a deal with Decca Records. There was talk of the group recording a Rolling Stones song, while Twice as Much cut another Marriott/Lane track "Green Circles" as a possible single for Immediate.

Drugs, particularly all kinds of speed and marijuana, united the scene as everyone partied on the most effervescent months of the 1960s. *Own Up* is now rarely mentioned when the great albums of all time are listed but it is more of an invocative and indicative document of that 1960s moment than anything else, as optimism, creativity and carefree living reached crescendo.

THE FIRST LADY OF IMMEDIATE

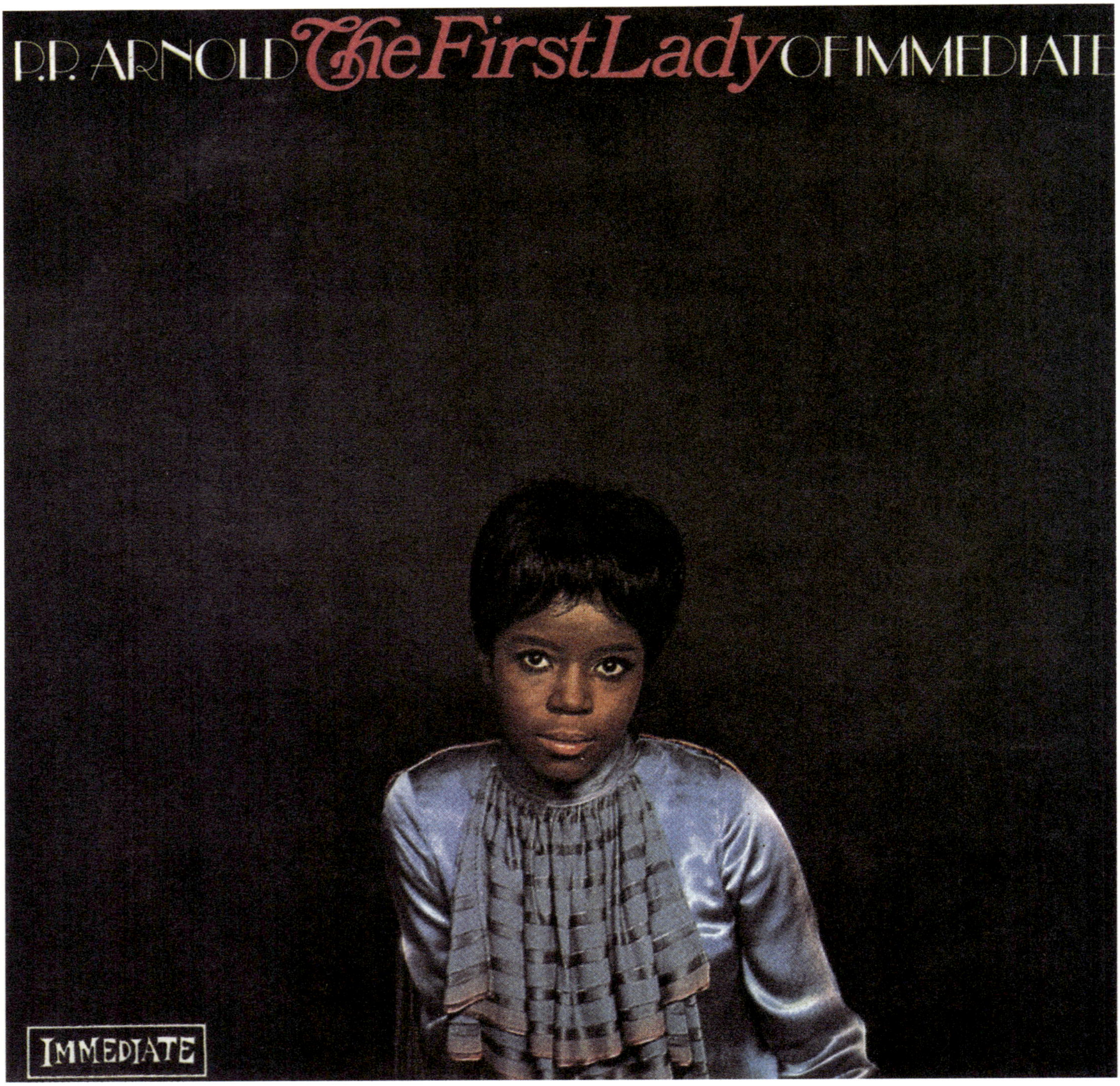
P.P. ARNOLD The First Lady OF IMMEDIATE
IMMEDIATE

It was Mick Jagger who was most knocked out by 21-year-old Pat Arnold. The LA singer had been persuaded to quit her role as an hardworking Ikette in the Ike and Tina Turner Revue. After their September 1966 UK tour with the Rolling Stones she signed a solo deal with Immediate. Since then she had stayed with the label's designer, Steven Inglis, and his girlfriend in their London flat, working with various Immediate musicians in the studio and "waiting for the right track to come along". Gered Mankowitz had christened her PP, and the original plan had been for Jagger to write for and produce her, replicating the process that had brought Chris Farlowe's success.

P-P ARNOLD
Greatest Hits

Instead PP's Immediate debut was a version of "Everything's Gonna Be Alright", which was co-written (with David Skinner) and produced by Oldham and arranged by Art Greenslade. Arnold told the press that Oldham had intended her to record "Is This What I Get For Loving You" by Goffin/King/Spector, the only Ronnettes failure in their run of hits, but the song had been in the wrong key for her voice. Already recorded by Twice As Much on *Own Up*, Oldham used the Art Greenslade arranged backing of "Is This What I Get For Loving You" with a Marianne Faithfull vocal but it was Decca, not Immediate, who released the resulting minor hit. PP's version of "Everything's Gonna Be Alright" backed by Twice As Much's "Life Is But Nothing" sank so fast that many considered PP's Immediate follow-up to be her true debut. Years later, however, the track was repressed and became a Northern Soul favourite.

For her follow-up Immediate single, Arnold got lucky. One door from Immediate on New Oxford Street was the office of The Beatles publisher, Dick James, who—since his incredible stroke of fortune courtesy of Brian Epstein—had built a respectable publishing company with a stable of young writers, among them Elton John and Cat Stevens. Stevens was breaking as a recording artist in his own right with the album *Matthew and Son*, the first release on Deram, Decca's new "contemporary" Immediate-styled label. The young, bearded songwriter was a familiar face at Immediate as his father ran a sandwich bar below the office. Stevens' managers, Mike Hurst (a former member of The Springfields) and Chris Brough (son of 50's *Educating Archie* ventriloquist Peter Brough), thought Arnold had a lot of potential. Hurst, who had produced *Matthew and Son*, was enthusiastic about producing her in the studio and Immediate agreed he take her there with a new Stevens song, "First Cut Is The Deepest". With Greenslade laying on the orchestration and Arnold coming close to the vocal heights of her former lead, Tina Turner, the strength of the song was undeniable and initial response from the radio was positive. Arnold was nothing if not a hard worker and she pushed "First Cut Is The Deepest" with incredible determination and drive. The single went into the Top 20 in the UK and broke across Europe. Arnold performed live and on television in Germany, Switzerland, Greece and Belgium and raved about her Immediate backing group on these dates, "a little four-piece band called The Nice". Arnold was "hoping to add a trumpet and tenor sax' to compliment her own soul revue.

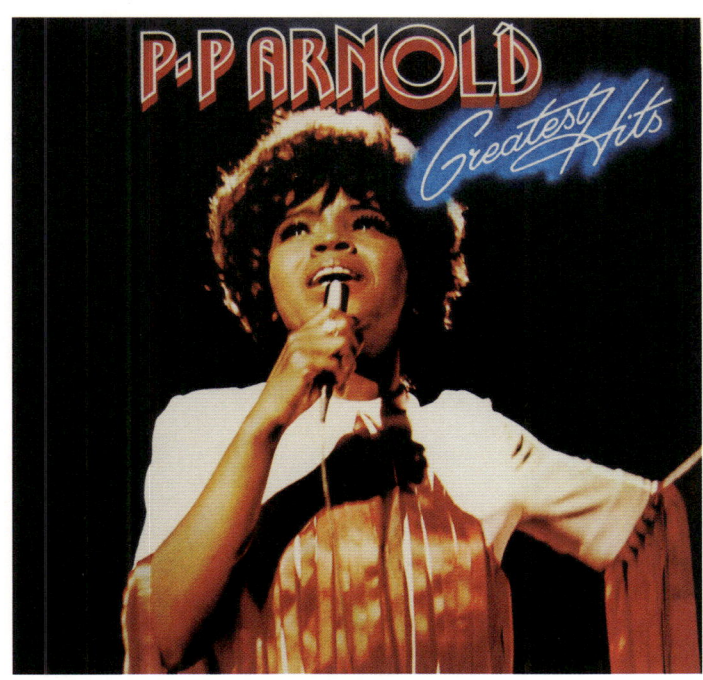

OPPOSITE: ARTWORK FOR PP ARNOLD'S ALBUM, *THE FIRST LADY OF IMMEDIATE*, 1967

PP ARNOLD'S GREATEST HITS PACKAGE, 1977

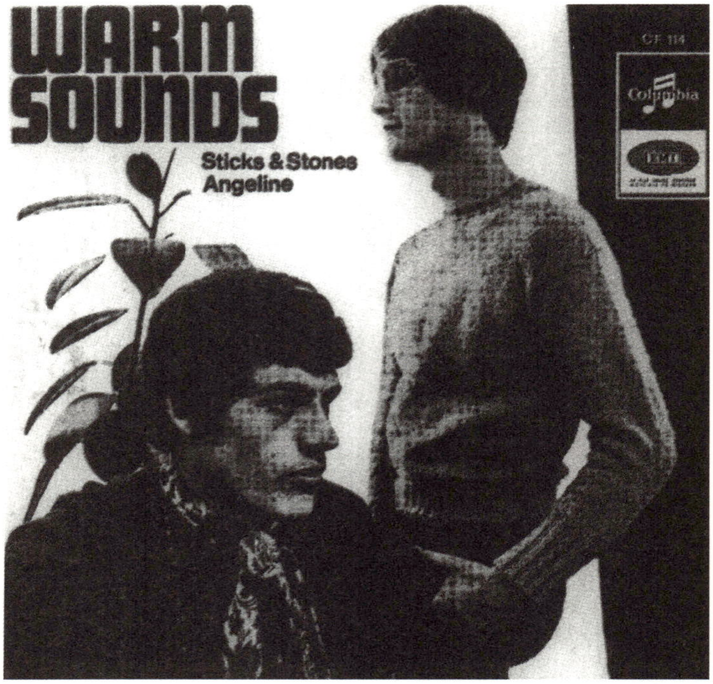
WARM SOUNDS
Sticks & Stones
Angeline
Columbia

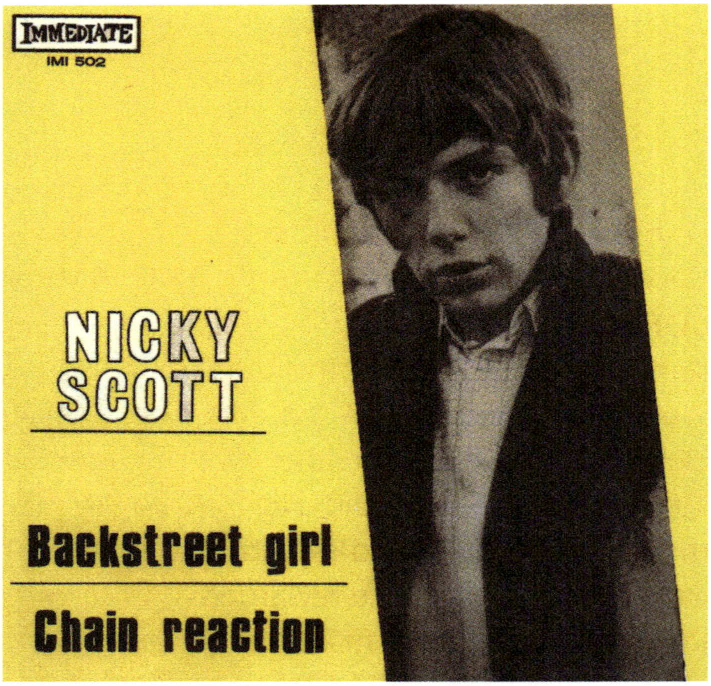
IMMEDIATE
IMI 502
NICKY SCOTT
Backstreet girl
Chain reaction

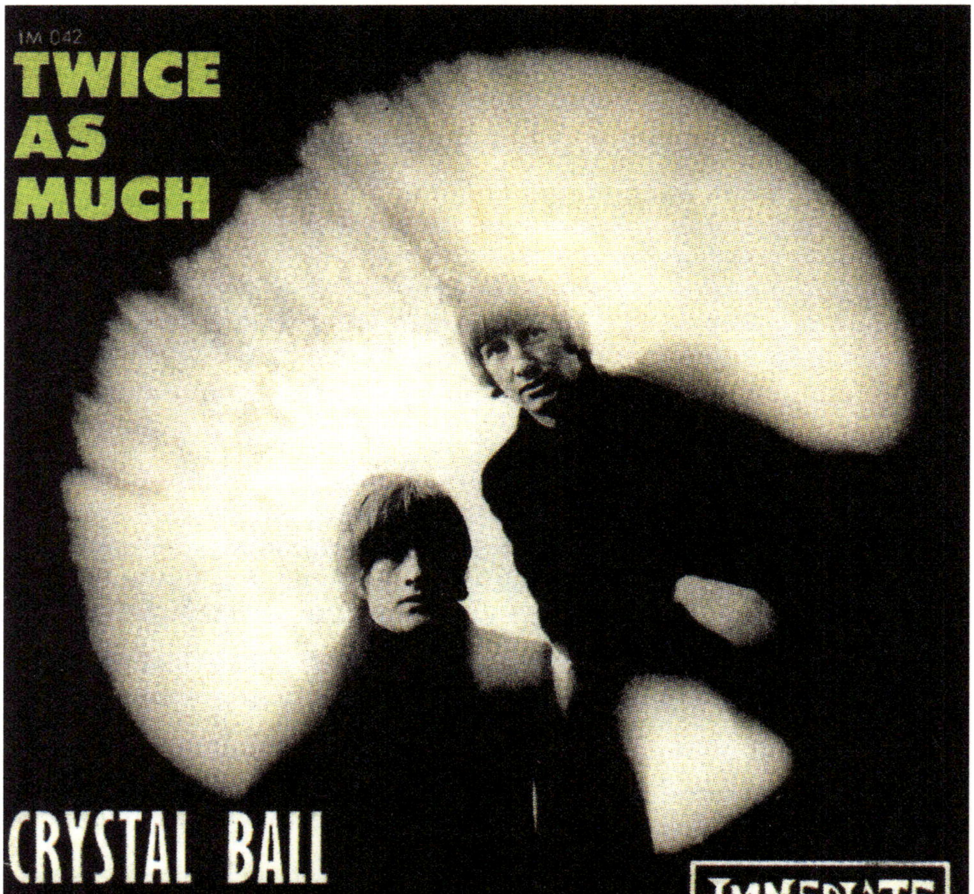
IM 042
TWICE AS MUCH
CRYSTAL BALL
WHY CAN'T THEY ALL GO AND LEAVE ME ALONE
IMMEDIATE

CLOCKWISE FROM LEFT: THE WARM SOUNDS COVER ART FOR "STICKS AND STONES", 1967, NICKY SCOTT'S "BACKSTREET GIRL" (WITH BACKING VOCALS BY MICK JAGGER), JANUARY 1967, AND TWICE AS MUCH PRESENT "CRYSTAL BALL", APRIL 1967

On the back of the success of "First Cut Is The Deepest", Mike Hurst produced a run of awfully crass, Oldham-lite minor singles for Immediate: "Black Sheep RIP" by The Australian Playboys (the nursery rhyme "Baa Baa Black Sheep" set to music), "She Was Perfection" by actor/singer/songwriter Murray Head, "Sticks and Stones" by Warm Sounds, the single "Moanin'" with Chris Farlowe, and PP's third single, "The Time Has Come", by one of his own writers, Paul Korda, which peaked in the UK at number 35 and wasn't all bad.

Chris Farlowe went back to formula with a fantastic Art Greenslade orchestrated, Mick Jagger produced, version of "Yesterday's Papers", a fresh Jagger/Richards track off new Rolling Stones album in the making, *Between The Buttons*. Immediate-arranged versions of the Jagger/Richards tracks often slyly overtook the power of the group's recording by way of dramatic string motifs. Moody-looking Immediate newcomer, Nicky Scott, managed by Yardbird's manager, Simon Napier-Bell, covered another Jagger/Richards track from *Between The Buttons*; "Backstreet Girl". With Jagger on backing vocals, the Scott single was publicised as being produced by Jagger and Oldham, but Jagger's reluctance to help out on promotion in any real terms hindered Scott's chances. A change of tack for his second Immediate single, a limp Oldham-produced version of "Big City", did equally poorly and Scott was dropped from the label. The chart misses piled up but the fun never stopped. "The Changing Of The Guard" by The Marquis of Kensington was a front for The Kinks manager, Robert Wace, whose identity on the track was a poorly kept secret. Wace had originally hired The Kinks to back him at a party, only to come off stage and decide, along with his friend Grenville Collins to manage the "backing band". The single is strong evidence of his influence on Ray Davies' songwriting and the b-side is likely to have featured The Kinks themselves.

Art Greenslade arranged a catchy, upbeat, new Twice As Much single, "Crystal Ball", which also happened to be the name of a prostitute Oldham had invited up the offices with a view to recording. The song was co-written (with Kenny Lynch) by visiting US songwriter, Mort Shuman, who, with his original partner, Doc Pomus, had written classics such as "Teenager In Love", "Can't Get Used To Losing You" and "Save The Last Dance For Me". Shuman had also co-written (with his new songwriting partner Kenny Lynch) "Sha La La La Lee" for Small Faces. Oldham took Shuman into the studio to record an instrumental version of the Mamas and Papas hit "Monday Monday" for Immediate. The songwriter left a more lasting impression by introducing the music of Jacques Brel to the Immediate offices. He would go on to handle the English translations of Brel and the off-Broadway smash *Jacques Brel Is Alive And Well And Living in Paris* made Shuman a star in 1970s and 80s France.

Oldham left London with Shuman, flying to New York to record with one of Allen Klein's clients, Bobby Vinton, (the successful MOR hit balladeer, best remembered for "Blue Velvet"). At CBS studios, with Shuman arranging, Vinton attempted to sing his way through Oldham's symphonic Beach Boys "Good Vibrations" style production of West Side Story's, "I Have A Love". The track was completely unsuitable for Vinton and was never released. Shuman remembered he and Oldham being "Black Russianed to oblivion", while hanging out.

In New York, Oldham ended Immediate's relationship with Bert Berns' record label Bang!. Berns and the label had started the whole ball rolling with "Hang On Sloopy" but subsequent McCoys singles had failed to sell. The group, largely the construct of a back-room production team, had enjoyed a run of Top 20 singles in the US, all issued to little success in the UK by Immediate. The McCoys operated in the slipstream of the prevailing trends, and post "Hang On Sloopy" singles had copied the Rolling Stones' beat or Beach Boys' harmonies with middling results. There was no future for them in the UK but there was no ill feeling and a full-page advert in the music press was dedicated to "Bert Berns, whose music will always be with us".

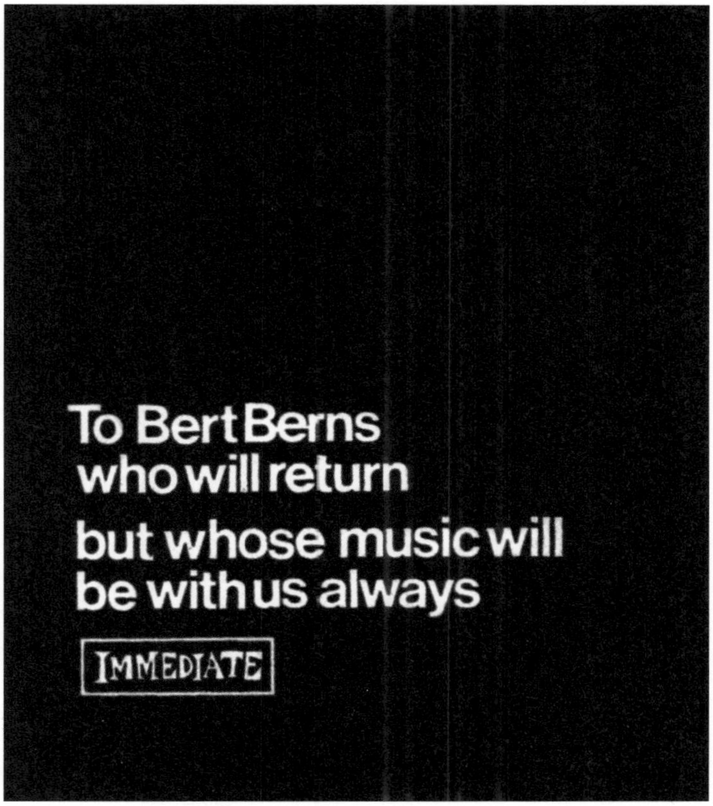
To Bert Berns
who will return
but whose music will
be with us always
IMMEDIATE

A lot of these mid to late 1966 Immediate releases (with rare exceptions) do not stand up to further listening. It was obvious to Immediate that in Arnold they had a great voice, but supplying her with the right material was still hit and miss. Farlowe's take on Rolling Stones tracks was stunningly executed, but seemed inadequate if you could have the original, and Twice As Much seemed to have gone over everyone's head. As for the rest of the releases, novelty was its only redeeming feature. The label needed some grounding before it floated off on a cloud of marijuana smoke.

HERE COME THE NICE

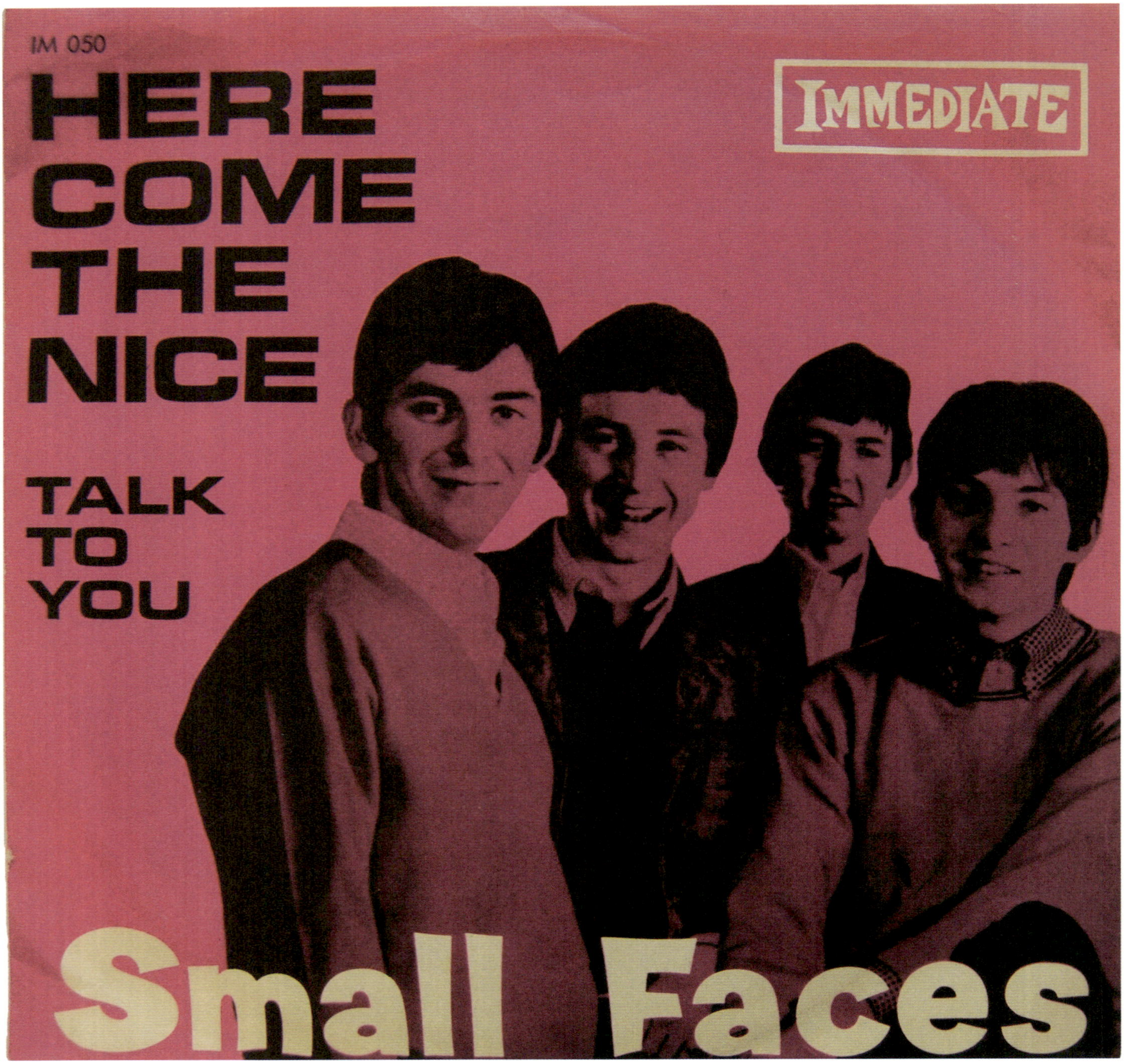
IM 050
HERE COME THE NICE
IMMEDIATE
TALK TO YOU
Small Faces

After massive hits with "Whatcha Gonna Do About It?", "Sha La La La Lee" and "All Or Nothing", Small Faces were riding the UK Top 5 with their latest single, "My Mind's Eye". They were discovered, managed, produced and promoted by the infamous Don Arden who had the band tied to his production company, Contemporary, through which he had an agreement with Decca to release their product. Arden was, by far, the most successful and influential British promoter ever, responsible for bringing over to the UK, the first wave of US talents: Gene Vincent, Sam Cooke, Jerry Lee Lewis, Little Richard, Bo Diddley, Chuck Berry, Ray Charles, Fats Domino, The Everly Brothers and many, many more. He had moved on to developing UK acts after The Beatles slayed their own idols in terms of ticket sales. Arden remembers:

> Small Faces was the first time that I really got stuck in. I found them, recorded them, released their record and got them in the Top 10 in six weeks. That's all it took, six weeks. The song I had on my shelf, a couple of the guys that worked for me, for £25 a week, Brian Potter and Ian 'Sammy' Samwell wrote "Whatcha Gonna Do About It?" I used to phone up *Ready Steady Go!* and *Top of the Pops* and get artists on television, just bosh like that, through the fact that I was the number one promoter in Europe. If I phoned them up they were on. After the first smash hit Small Faces said they didn't wanna work with Sammy anymore because they were ungrateful bastards. He cried his fucking eyes out and there was nothing I could do about it. I offered them to Immediate when they first started. Stevie [Steve Marriott] knew Tony Calder, but he never did anything for them. Andrew didn't see the commerciality in them, he turned them down, and he didn't want to know. To me they had an image of their own, they looked like four little Oliver Twists—street urchins. When they came out they looked like four half grown kids, and when they opened up the sound was so powerful— that was the impact. That's the way it hit me the first time I saw them at this concert I put on at Margate, they walked out and the impact, I thought 'they can't fail'.

Oldham had now changed his tune about Small Faces. After the rave-up at Olympic studios with Rolling Stones and Chris Farlowe, the Small Faces writing team, Marriott and Lane, had supplied a couple of songs for Immediate artists. Their run of hits to date was undeniable and Oldham sounded out the group on a possible deal. The previous time anyone tried to steal the Small Faces from Arden they ended up being dangled by their ankles from a fifth floor balcony. Now, though, the nation's undisputed number one mod outfit were giving Arden enough of a headache for him to take a more prosaic approach. The 'ungrateful bastards' refused to play "Sha La La La Lee" on any of their lives dates and were bitching about their new single "My Mind's Eye", claiming Arden had arranged it's release without consulting them and had just gotten themselves banned from *Top Of The Pops* after laying a massive strop on the show's producer. Arden had a new act

OPPOSITE: SMALL FACES' "HERE COME THE NICE" WITH THE CATCHY B-SIDE "TALK TO YOU", JUNE 1967

SMALL FACES, CIRCA 1967

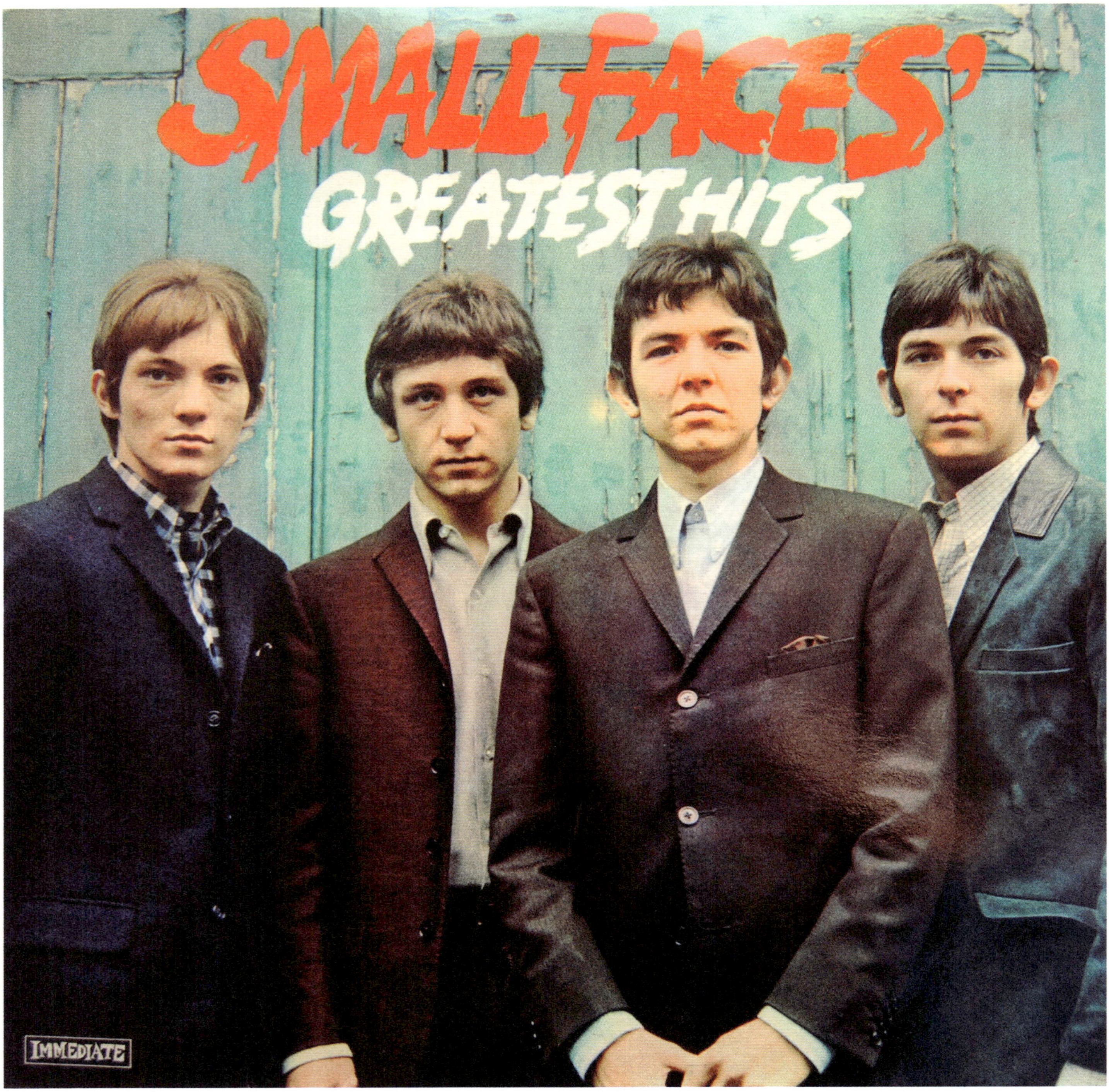
SMALL FACES'
GREATEST HITS
IMMEDIATE

I NEVER LIKED [TONY CALDER] AND I NEVER TRUSTED HIM

DON ARDEN

SMALL FACES' *GREATEST HITS*, CIRCA 1966

breaking, Amen Corner. Andrew Loog Oldham was a friend of Arden's from way back and the £25,000 Immediate were offering was some pay-off. Don Arden recounts:

> It's a funny thing, how people like Calder talk: 'Oh yes I bought Small Faces from Don Arden.' Tony Calder is full of shit. First of all if he ever bought anything, it was on behalf of Immediate, if he ever did anything it was on behalf of Oldham really. He was a bullshitter, all the time. I never liked him and I never trusted him. I sold the Small Faces recording contract to Harold Davison [an agent/impresario] then he sold it on to Immediate. Calder saying, 'oh yeah, we bought the record contract for £25,000 from Don, delivered it to him in a brown paper bag because he needed the cash at the time'. Calder would always put something like that in to try and bring me down. Deep down looking back I think I always hated Calder and he hated me. We hated each other.

Oldham recollects Allen Klein wiring him the Small Faces money, apparently putting £25,000 in a brown paper bag and giving it to Arden, who was then happy to induce a breach of contract with Decca, allowing Small Faces to sign with Immediate. The money was a colossal amount to pay for a group—Philips, for instance, had never paid a group a more than £10,000 advance. The £25,000 figure equalled the industry's largest ever advance for a group, which EMI—the UK's most powerful major label—had recently put up to sign The Yardbirds in a hotly contested bidding war. It is safe to assume that the EMI advance for The Yardbirds did not come in cash or a brown paper bag. Soon after Jimmy Page was persuaded to join The Yardbirds and quit Immediate. He gave the reason that he was amazed by a demo from songwriter Cliff Ward. He had gone "rushing in to see Tony Calder really excited but Calder just wasn't interested. Not because he didn't like it but just because he wasn't into singing unknowns. Apart from the Small Faces—for obvious reasons—he just wasn't interested in newcomers."

In industry terms the much-publicised Small Faces deal established Immediate as more than just a hobbyhorse for the Rolling Stones manager and all but destroyed Decca (the UK's second biggest label) as contemporary force. A *Melody Maker* article "Small Faces in Big Record Tie-Up" talked about a lucrative long-term deal for the group "who will in future produce all their own records". Oldham was keen to stress that he would be in no way involved in the production of Small Faces recordings which were "solely the group's responsibility", adding: "The group is embarking on a joint publishing venture with Immediate Music, getting songwriter's contracts." It was "one of the most important label changes this year", reported *NME*. Decca released a Small Faces single they had previously recorded, "I Can't Make It", but with no backing from the group it peaked at number 26. In *NME*, Steve Marriott of Small Faces claimed:

> We wanted to go to Immediate because Oldham offered us every freedom besides being a management company. Their interests were selling records and nothing more than being a record label. They knew that if they let us loose and gave us the reins then we could write better material and last longer. Oldham knew we could and would write stuff that lasted forever which, quite frankly, a lot of it has and still will. They were very shrewd people in that sense. It was a good move. It was such a big family thing up at Immediate, all helping out at each other's recording sessions. There were only about four or five acts on the label, admittedly all charting, but only a handful of people were responsible for it all, so everyone got to know each other very well.

Small Faces debut on Immediate, the label's 50th single—"Here Come The Nice"—had originally been called "Here Come The Nazz", from the title of a white magic book Steve Marriott had been reading. Recorded at Olympic Studios, produced and written by Marriott/Lane, it was the label's biggest hit for over a year, spending ten weeks in the Top 40, peaking at number 12. It seemed incredible that this blatant tribute to a well turned out drug dealer, had escaped BBC censure, a fantastic return to form for both Small Faces and Immediate.

Decca attempted to cash in by releasing a collection of early Small Faces material on the LP *From The Beginning—The Small Faces At Their Best Yet!*. Immediate sought an injunction against *From The Beginning*, alleging they owned four of the tracks on the album. They then hurriedly completed basic recordings of fourteen new Marriott/Lane tracks, and, within a week, rush-released their own Small Faces album, *Small Faces*, an understandably patchy affair that nonetheless showed great potential. Immediate then splashed out on an advertising campaign for the album to eclipse that of Decca's, announcing: "Whichever way you look at it, there are only four Small Faces. But there is just one Small Faces LP. It's on Immediate." Innovative promotional copies of the album, featuring hook exerts from the songs, intercut with DJ John Peel spieling great hype about the band, was sent to DJs, journalists and record shops. Thanks to all the commotion and smart promotion, *Small Faces* became Immediate's best-selling album to date, cruising in to the Top 10, easily outselling Decca's effort.

Immediate would spare Small Faces from their usual gruelling live schedule that had seen them play every toilet up and down the country under Arden, and encouraged them just to live, create and be who they wanted to be. The label granted the band their heads, believing they could be made responsible enough to create something special on their own. As much as Immediate promoted itself as a young maverick company, this was almost a brave new adult world—it being unheard of at the time for a record company to give an act a block of hash and allow them "to go off for six weeks and come back with masterpiece they had in them" with the only proviso being "have fun getting it done". Small Faces had previously been in a world where three days was the norm to create an album. Marriott and Lane handed over a new song to Immediate, "(Tell Me) Have You Ever Seen Me", and Marriott went into the studio to produce it for Immediate with a new band, The Apostolic Intervention, whose drummer (Jerry Shirley) he was friends with. Marriott featured heavily on backing vocals on the single.

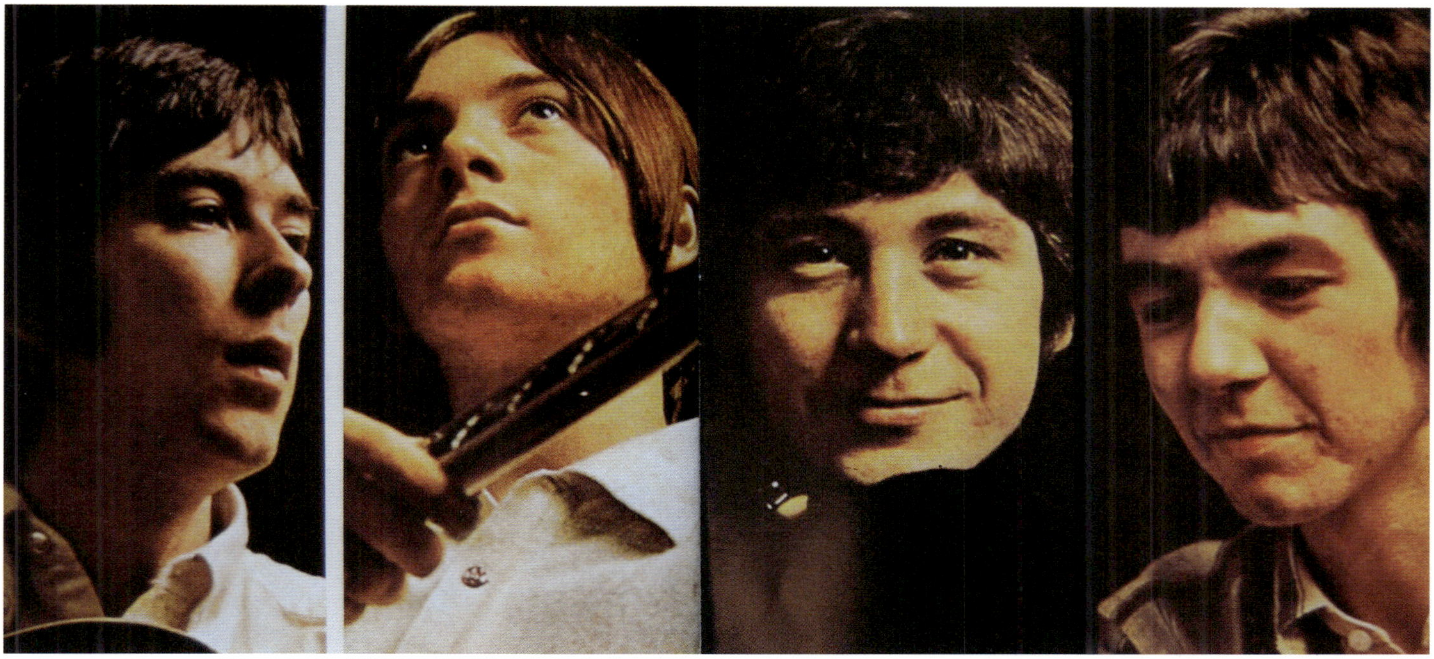

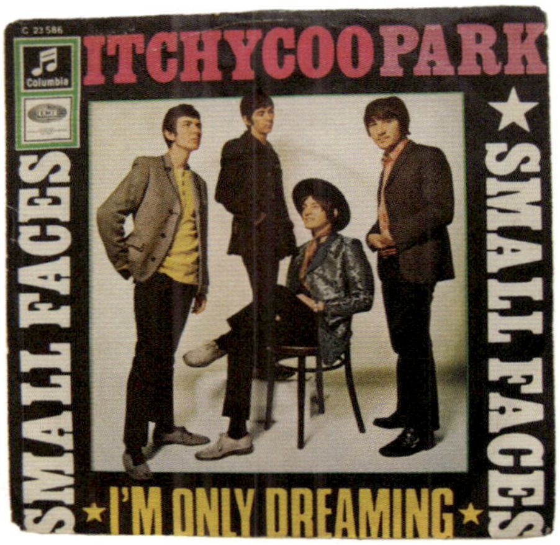
Columbia
ITCHYCOO PARK
SMALL FACES
SMALL FACES
I'M ONLY DREAMING

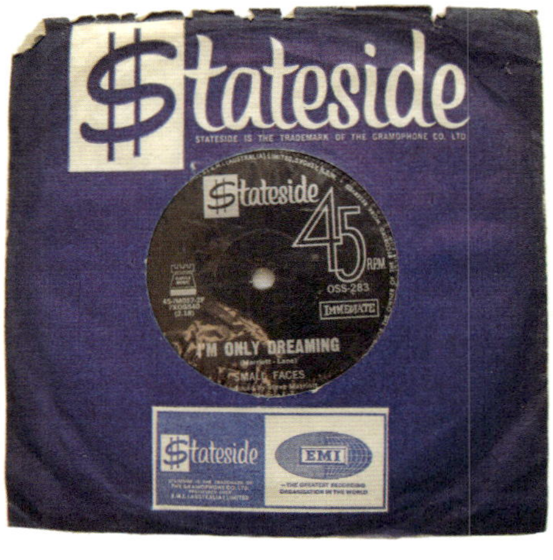
Stateside
STATESIDE IS THE TRADEMARK OF THE GRAMOPHONE CO. LTD
Stateside
45 RPM
OSS-283
IMMEDIATE
I'M ONLY DREAMING
SMALL FACES
Stateside
EMI

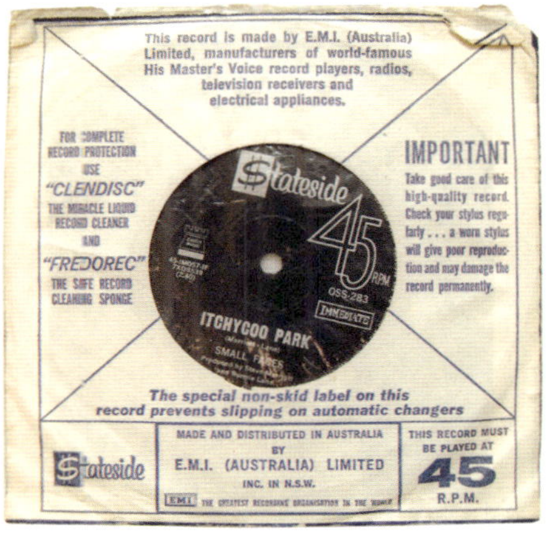
This record is made by E.M.I. (Australia) Limited, manufacturers of world-famous His Master's Voice record players, radios, television receivers and electrical appliances.
FOR COMPLETE RECORD PROTECTION USE "CLENDISC" THE MIRACLE LIQUID RECORD CLEANER AND "FREDOREC" THE SAFE RECORD CLEANING SPONGE
IMPORTANT
Take good care of this high-quality record. Check your stylus regularly . . . a worn stylus will give poor reproduction and may damage the record permanently.
Stateside
45 RPM
OSS-283
IMMEDIATE
ITCHYCOO PARK
SMALL FACES
The special non-skid label on this record prevents slipping on automatic changers
Stateside
MADE AND DISTRIBUTED IN AUSTRALIA BY E.M.I. (AUSTRALIA) LIMITED INC. IN N.S.W.
THIS RECORD MUST BE PLAYED AT 45 R.P.M.

OPPOSITE TOP: SMALL FACES PERFORMING LIVE

OPPOSITE BOTTOM: DURING A ROUTINE EDITORIAL SHOOT, CIRCA 1966

TOP: A DETAIL FROM THE SINGLE, "ITCHYCOO PARK", DEPICTING THE BAND, 1965

BOTTOM: THE OFFICIAL VERSIONS OF SMALL FACES' "ITCHYCOO PARK", AUGUST 1967

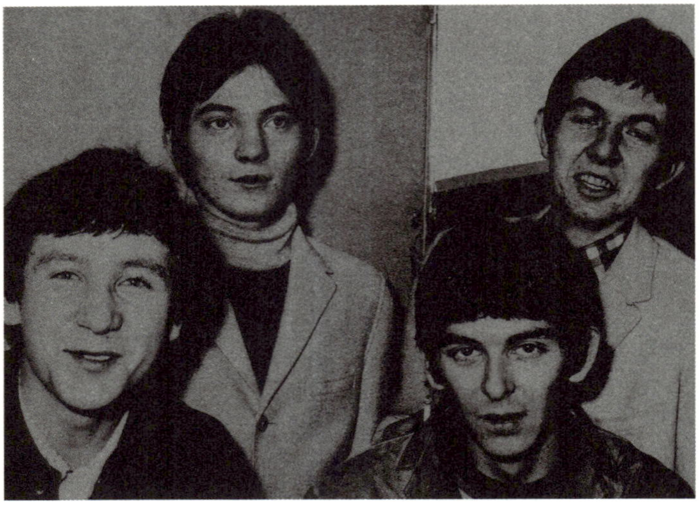

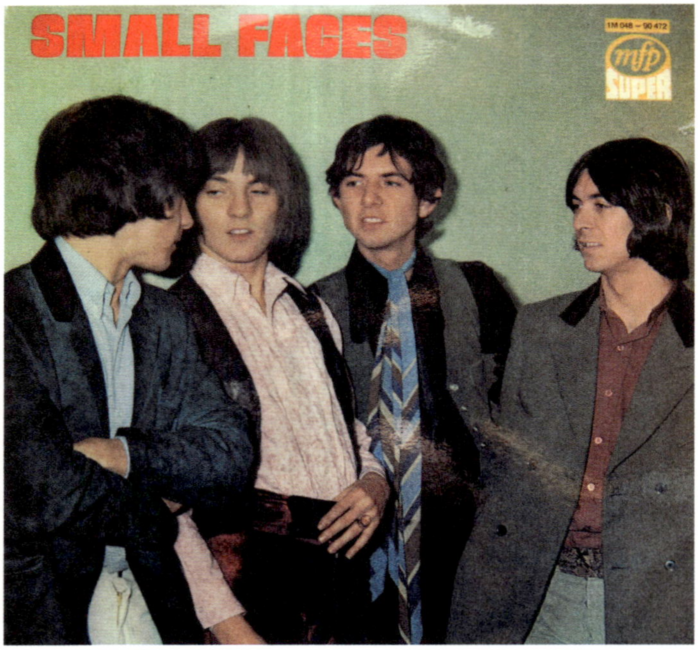
SMALL FACES
mfp
SUPER

DEEP DOWN LOOKING BACK I THINK I ALWAYS HATED CALDER AND HE HATED ME. WE HATED EACH OTHER

DON ARDEN

TOP: A VERY YOUNG SMALL FACES, SHOWN IN AN ALBUM DETAIL, CIRCA 1965

BOTTOM: COVER ART FOR *SMALL FACES*, CIRCA 1965

Jerry Shirley recounts:

> I was playing in a band with my brother on guitar called The Little People. Steve had sung our praises to Andrew who was interested but didn't like our name. Steve suggested The Nice. He was always saying 'nice, which usually meant nice gear [marijuana], you know. Anyway we all thought what a great name but Andrew had other ideas. He announced in mock dramatic voice, 'I think you should be The Apostolic Intervention'. We though uuugghh, what's that? But reluctantly we said okay and then five minutes later, he decided to call PP Arnold's backing band, The Nice. Oldham brought us into his office, sat us down, gave us a huge stack of black [US] records and said, 'here, snag some of this and come back when you've learnt it'. I was only 14 years old; mouth open, going 'Wow!'. On a daily basis I sat in the Immediate office watching all these astonishing people coming and going; Andrew, Mick, Brian... it was nothing short of remarkable. There was a stack of Brian Jones' guitars in the music room at Immediate, Gibson Firebirds, all rusted with blood all over them. I remember Andrew running through the office one day with this great big pressure gun, firing water at everyone. I was down at Olympic Studios, doing some things with Steve as part of a possible Andrew Loog Oldham Orchestra thing, I look up and there's Jimi Hendrix staring at me. Steve was like showing me off, like: 'Here y'are, check this guy out.' Steve was by far a better keyboard and guitar player than Keith Richards, he was one of the most often underrated talents, it was scary to be around him sometimes, he was that good. His singing, his keyboard playing was amazing, his rhythm playing second to none. Later in life his lead playing got real good too. Hendrix said the guitar solo on "Whatcha Gonna Do About It?" was one of his favourite solos. At that point Steve had been playing the guitar for eight weeks or something, how he grabbed that great big old Gretsch and made it feed back and used the wang-bar, no one had done that. The Gretsch was taller than he was.

With the Small Faces on board, and now that their initial two-year distribution deal with Philips had expired, Oldham and Calder took the opportunity to sign a more lucrative European distribution deal with EMI, who paid £50,000 for a three-year tie-up. Philips would soon after be taken over by the Dutch company PolyGram and the German light bulb firm Siemens, with a new UK record label, Polydor, created to 'compete with'—but ultimately supersede—the old Philips imprint. It was hoped that the deal with EMI would allow Immediate to capitalise on its UK success in Europe, something the label had been unable to do with any consistency via Philips. Immediate were "going international" and "getting our own logo throughout Europe" as Calder put it. Oldham said: "Frankly Philips were very good to us. They gave us our break and without Leslie Gould's help we would never have got started. If they had not given us the break that got us off the ground we would never have got the deal we have today with EMI." The relationship was off to a sensational start before a record had even been released when, at an EMI sales convention, Oldham put sleeping pills in the soup and became so out of it he ended up chasing an EMI executive down the stairs with a gun and a wooden plank with nails in it.

Tony Calder remembers:

> We opened up our first sales conference with a slide of EMI building with a lump of shit against it. We said: 'We're not a company that throws shit against the wall.' We did all that but what did you expect us to do. Ken East was the Managing Director of EMI UK and Oldham had a good relationship with him.

Ken East remembers:

> [Immediate] were the first major independent, they had huge success. The company had an aura about them, Immediate was the independent company of the day and they wanted to do funny things, which of course they did. The dog shit thing? Oldham was ahead of his time in that sense wasn't he? Shock marketing, this was 1967. Things were a lot more straight up and down than they are today. Oldham was certainly different, some people loved him, and some people thought he was nutcase but they had good records and we were in the record business. EMI were competing for Immediate. They were new, very new, they were at Philips but we were able to persuade them they had do better with EMI. At EMI Immediate had their own stock risk out of necessity because they created the record. They should know better than anybody, how many they needed to press and how many were gonna be sold. If they said press 5,000 of this, they were responsible for the manufacturing costs and they were kept in our warehouse. When they were sold, we shipped them and we would collect payment from the retailer. If the record was £1, we would collect the £1 from the dealer, keep 20 per cent for ourselves and give the rest to Immediate. If the record didn't sell they were still Immediate's records, they took the stock risk. You got crazy things from Oldham and Calder, one big spender was bad enough but the two of them together was just dynamite.

To celebrate the deal there was a new Immediate slogan to be printed on all record sleeves, "Happy To Be A Part Of Industry Of Human Happiness" replacing the old "A New Record Company of Tomorrow Today". New Immediate head of promotions, Ken Mewis, a former hairdresser, reported monthly to EMI's Manchester Square offices, presenting new product to the main 50 EMI sales reps throughout the UK.

The staff list at Immediate continued to grow. There was another publicist, Ray Tolliday, and new receptionist, Mick Jagger's recent ex-girlfriend Chrissie Shrimpton. Oldham's personal assistant, Cynthia, had left Immediate, pregnant, but there was a new staff lawyer, Timothy Hardacre, to keep things tight. Hardacre parodied his pin-striped profession to perfection and the press photo of him, Oldham (still disguised in exquisite Irving Thalberg-style Last Tycoon attire) and Calder, to announce Hardacre's appointment made for a great image. Timothy Hardacre, Immediate Solicitor remembers:

I first met Tony Calder when he had TR Ltd—a press relations company that had one room in the top of a building in Poland Street. Two guys ran it, one was Tony Calder, who was DJing at the Lyceum and other Mecca ballrooms and was doing press for The Mojos, Swinging Blue Jeans, Searchers and The Undertakers. I became company secretary. Tony introduced me to Oldham after Oldham had fallen out with David Jacobs, who was the most famous showbusiness layer in London, he later committed suicide or was murdered, and nobody knows which. Oldham was highly unstable.

Mick Jagger came into my office at Immediate saying, 'Get with it, you've got to have flashing lights, you've gotta have machines'. I said "You don't know what you're talking about." I had a drinks cabinet, table, bronze statue and French antique clock, then someone came in and put up a big abstract painting. Immediate had a very simple contract with EMI, two pages, I went up to the boardroom to meet with the chairman, before Ken East. His first words were "How much money do you want?" I asked for £30,000, he said "Right" and wrote the cheque.

Oldham thought he was immortal, they all did. I once went to serve a writ on Don Arden for Immediate, he said 'writs!, this is what they mean to me' and he threw them in a cabinet on top of a great pile of other writs. He said, 'now I'm gonna throw you outta the window'. Then he said, 'sit down and have a drink.'

OLDHAM GOT SO OUT OF IT HE ENDED UP CHASING AN EMI EXECUTIVE DOWN THE STAIRS WITH A GUN AND A WOODEN PLANK WITH NAILS IN IT

SIMON SPENCE

EURO VISION

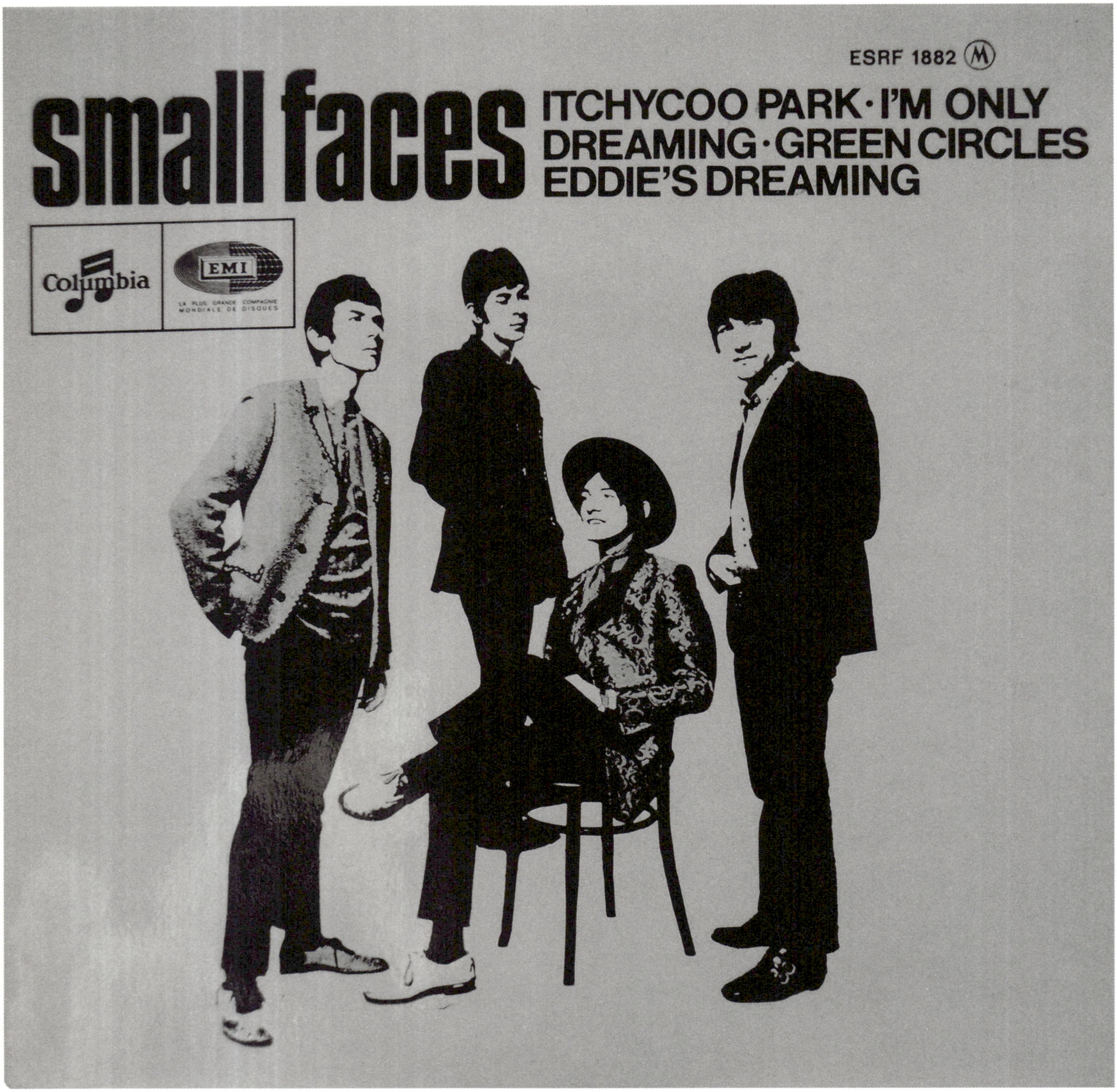
ESRF 1882 M
small faces
ITCHYCOO PARK · I'M ONLY DREAMING · GREEN CIRCLES EDDIE'S DREAMING
Columbia
EMI
LA PLUS GRANDE COMPAGNIE MONDIALE DE DISQUES

Immediate had made "enormous strides" in its second year according to *Record Mirror* "despite the mushrooming of dozens of new independent labels Immediate still ranks as the pace-setting independent which other breakaway operators envy and try to emulate".

Oldham and Calder were interviewed at length, revealing how they were currently shooting an Immediate film to be screened at their new distributor EMI's autumn sales conference. The "creative, impulsive" Oldham and the "quieter, calculated" Calder said they were undaunted by the loss of the recently outlawed pirate radio stations in the UK that had played such a huge role in breaking many Immediate hits.

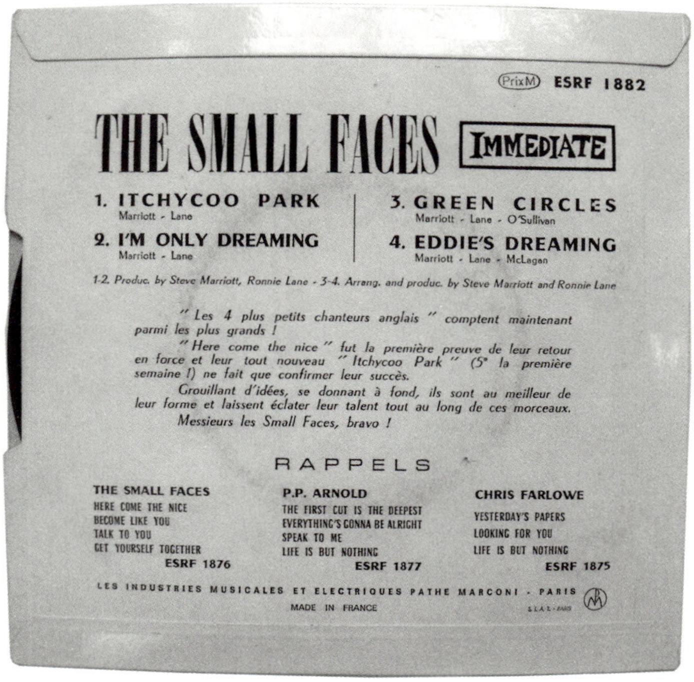
PrixM ESRF 1882
THE SMALL FACES
IMMEDIATE
1. ITCHYCOO PARK
Marriott - Lane
2. I'M ONLY DREAMING
Marriott - Lane
3. GREEN CIRCLES
Marriott - Lane - O'Sullivan
4. EDDIE'S DREAMING
Marriott - Lane - McLagan
1-2. Produc. by Steve Marriott, Ronnie Lane - 3-4. Arrang. and produc. by Steve Marriott and Ronnie Lane
" Les 4 plus petits chanteurs anglais " comptent maintenant parmi les plus grands !
" Here come the nice " fut la première preuve de leur retour en force et leur tout nouveau " Itchycoo Park " (5° la première semaine !) ne fait que confirmer leur succès.
Grouillant d'idées, se donnant à fond, ils sont au meilleur de leur forme et laissent éclater leur talent tout au long de ces morceaux.
Messieurs les Small Faces, bravo !
RAPPELS
THE SMALL FACES
HERE COME THE NICE
BECOME LIKE YOU
TALK TO YOU
GET YOURSELF TOGETHER
ESRF 1876
P.P. ARNOLD
THE FIRST CUT IS THE DEEPEST
EVERYTHING'S GONNA BE ALRIGHT
SPEAK TO ME
LIFE IS BUT NOTHING
ESRF 1877
CHRIS FARLOWE
YESTERDAY'S PAPERS
LOOKING FOR YOU
LIFE IS BUT NOTHING
ESRF 1875
LES INDUSTRIES MUSICALES ET ELECTRIQUES PATHE MARCONI - PARIS
MADE IN FRANCE

"We rely just as much on the BBC" says Calder "and we feel that good product will get away even without the pirates". "Personally I think the whole recording field is wide open in Britain right now" commented a newly bearded Oldham. "We give our acts total freedom because this is the only environment in which people can create properly", said Calder, attempting to explain the Immediate philosophy. "Steve Marriott of the Faces likes our set-up so much he says it's like being back at school again." Calder continued: "It really took us 18 months to find out exactly what we wanted to do and where we were going wrong." "I suppose our biggest failure was in not consolidating Chris Farlowe's success after his number one hit with "Out Of Time"", admitted Oldham. "But we still don't feel we've lost him. He can get into the charts with the right material at any time as was proved with "Out Of Time"". Neither of the "two latter day tycoons" would admit to having made massive money out of Immediate and its associated publishing, production and management companies. "We had ploughed a great deal back into the company to build it up", insisted Calder.

The coming months—Oldham and Calder told *Record Mirror*—would see Immediate focus more on albums and the two were "very pleased" with a new policy of packaging LPs in sealed polythene which they were convinced would "give the consumer greater faith in purchase". They also planned to continue their innovation of sending out "sampler LPs" to main dealers—as first witnessed with the Small Faces' debut album on the label—and explained how, ten days before any of their artists appeared in a town, they would be sending publicity material for displays in dance halls and record shops, another of their innovations which is widely imitated to this day. They also revealed they were lining up a major European tour for Immediate artists to "consolidate the label on the continent". Their next big goal, they said, was film and "the book business", planning to publish five titles in October, including a paperback, *The Immediate Success Story*. "We are dealing with artists and writers not just records and we feel that this is the only way to operate—trying to encourage people to use their own ideas", concluded Calder.

Peter Whitehead, who had shot the promotional film *The Little Bastard Immediate*, was a partner in the Immediate book company. He was also at work editing the new Immediate promo:

OPPOSITE AND TOP:
SMALL FACES EP ARTWORK
AUGUST 1967

For *The Little Bastard Immediate*, I remember Oldham asked, 'how much?' I said '£2,000' and Cynthia wrote a cheque out there and then. For the next one it was just Andrew saying: 'Hey listen Peter, we're having these sales conferences, I want you to string a load of film together, bung all the various group's together.' I didn't say I wanted contracts, 'I want this, and I want that'—I just said in the spirit of the thing: 'Let's go out and do it.'

Immediate was now; addiction, the present; it was actually a deliberate attempt to snub the institutions, even though Andrew very surreptitiously used the big companies to make all his money, he still didn't really tow the line.

We called the film, *Here Come The Nice*. Oldham said: 'Listen the guys wanna film in Camber Sands, we're all leaving on Friday at five in the morning; Small Faces, PP Arnold, Twice As Much.' We just set off. I was sitting in the back of Andrew's Rolls Royce with him and Tony, by the time we got to Camber Sands we were stoned. I was so stoned I couldn't see through the fucking camera. I think the idea was to film the new Small Faces single "Itchycoo Park" as the dawn was breaking. There was no time at seven in the morning to get the instruments together, so we just stuck them all in the sand and started filming. The whole thing, as far as I was concerned, was a total catastrophe. I didn't think I had shot a single foot of film that was usable. By the time I got back and stuck it all together none of us thought it was terribly good, it was never properly finished. A rough cut was shown to all the salesmen.

When I started my publishing company, Lorimer Publications, we did screenplays, bought a load of rights off various film directors, did something on Che Guevara, made *Benefit Of The Doubt* with the Royal Shakespeare Company about Vietnam, Andrew distributed them and everything; he put up the money. For a year and a half they financed it all and it became Immediate Publishing. We even published some books together, all based on cinema. Then I took it back because somebody came along and offered me a better deal. I went back to Andrew and Tony and said: 'Listen guys I think I've got a good deal with Andrew Sinclair, I wanna go off and do it as Lorimer again.' They said: 'Okay, whatever.'

I found both Andrew and Tony extremely easy to deal with, we never had a single piece of paper between us. We just understood each other and got on very well. He and Tony were the odd couple, like Laurel and Hardy, they complimented each other very well. I don't think you could have got two more madder people than Andrew or Tony at the time. The offices were near to where I lived in Soho and I think Andrew saw himself as an Arab prince surrounded by a harem or something.

Immediate set about exploiting the EMI deal with a major European package tour. The tour with PP Arnold, Small Faces, Twice As Much and Chris Farlowe, lasted 20 days, travelling through Germany, France, Holland, Belgium, Luxembourg, Sweden, Austria, Switzerland and Italy. EMI had offices in each territory and Oldham and Calder worked diligently to bring them all on board, knowing their support would determine whether future Immediate releases in each country would get a proper servicing. They also made a strong links with television, radio and press in each territory, with Europe's top pop television show, Germany's *The Beat Club*, coming out in total support and featuring at least one Immediate artist on a weekly basis. Further support came from Emperor Rosko's Radio Luxembourg show, recorded in Paris and broadcast across Europe. Tony Calder remembers:

We made EMI's whole European operation come alive. It made EMI, who had all these companies in every territory acting independently, suddenly start to operate as a unit. EMI knew what we had done, they did appreciate it and they let us get on with it. They never said, 'you've gone too far'. We would do these junkets of Immediate acts around Europe and as we were coming into land, Oldham would stand up and say: 'We're in Italy, the only words you need to know are Fuck off in Italian.' We would come off the plane everywhere, any country, shouting 'Fuck off'. There was a guy in Germany at EMI, English guy, Ian Groves, Oldham comes up and says 'hey nice to meet you', and starts taking a piss against the fucking guy's limousine. The name of the game was if you don't promote nothing happens. We promoted. We taught everyone how to promote artists, not just the records but also the artists. Even then we were making television promo films, short videos of artists miming to songs. We took new acts like The Nice and started breaking them around Europe, for us it was the natural thing to do at the time but nobody else thought so.

Ken East, Managing Director at EMI UK recalls:

It's true. When I first came into the overseas division, they wouldn't even talk to each other. The people in Belgium wouldn't talk to the French and the Germans wouldn't talk to the Dutch and it was part of my job to make them do so. I used to have to almost bash their heads together. When we got Immediate for Europe, it became a huge success and success binds people together and Immediate definitely contributed to the unity of EMI's European music companies.

Mike Leckenbush, the producer and director of *The Beat Club*, was introduced to illegal substances by Immediate and, subsequently, Leckenbush wanted a monthly drug delivery. Ken Mewis would take an Immediate act and his delivery over once a month. Then David Skinner, of Twice as Much, began a liaison with Leckenbush's personal assistant, so Twice As Much probably appeared on *The Beat Club* more than any other Immediate act—if there was no single they would do an album track. As a result their "True Story" single was a Top 10 hit in Germany, Holland and Switzerland. In Milan, Oldham was fed up with answering the same questions from the same reporters so chauffeur Eddie and Mewis took turns at playing Oldham while he slept. According to a source it was always risky taking Chris Farlowe to Germany for television radio

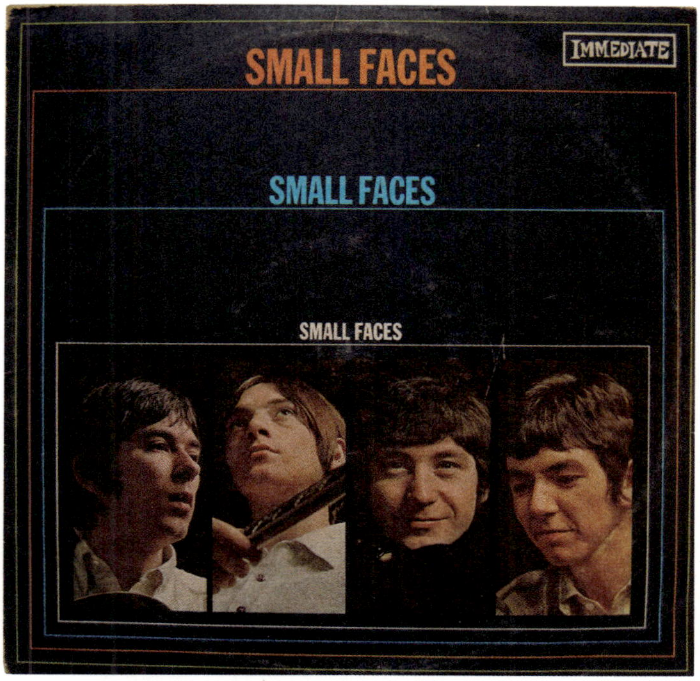
SMALL FACES
IMMEDIATE
SMALL FACES
SMALL FACES

IMMEDIATE THE *ENFANT TERRIBLE* OF THE BRITISH RECORD INDUSTRY IS NOW TWO YEARS OLD AND NOT REALLY A BABY ANYMORE

RECORD MIRROR FEATURE

ANOTHER SMALL FACES' COMPILATION, REISSUED IN JUNE 1967

and press, as you would turn your back and he was off to buy Nazi memorabilia (Farlowe's collection of wartime mementoes would grow over the years and he would end up opening a shop in Islington called Out Of Time to sell it). David Skinner of Twice As Much remembers:

> I remember with Plonk [Ronnie Lane] of Small Faces we went through a craze of painting our boots with eyes and cottages with smoke going up yer ankle. It was just one big binge, just this sort of drug and alcohol ridden haze of music and great times. You used to do a lot of miming, you basically mimed to your single or your hit. That was it, you were on for about three minutes. So people tended to be very out of it on those occasions, you didn't have to sing or do anything, just sort of look alright. As long as you could un-stick your mouth it was alright. We did take a lot of medication. There were very powerful forces at work in terms of creativity. The drugs helped. Oldham was like a walking clinic and the acts on Immediate obviously dug him a lot. I remember having some really good times in the studio with Steve Marriott and Ronnie Lane, coming in and doing backing vocals and everybody really grooving and having a great time together, there was a lot of laughter. Tony was more like the guy in the tie, with the button-down shirt and the haircut, and he seemed to be more New York, whereas Andrew was more LA. I think a lot people found Andrew very encouraging, he was very supportive to his acts. Chris Farlowe used to have this irritating habit of ad-libbing just about between every line, 'yeah baby', shit like that, we used to laugh about that. Andrew had a knack of having him laugh at it too, it was very funny.

After the European tour, Small Faces put the finishing touches to their new single, "Itchycoo Park", at Olympic studios in the leafy London outskirts of Barnes. Olympic, having started life behind Selfridges on Oxford Street in an old disused Synagogue, was now considered the premier independent studio in the country. Olympic housed two recording studios, Olympic Studio One and Two, and they were both booked around the clock by Oldham, at an expensive £25 an hour. The studios were available for Immediate acts and the slow beginnings of a new Rolling Stones album. George Chiantz, engineer at Olympic studios remembers:

> There was great excitement when [Rolling] Stones showed up at the studios. Small Faces were in at the same time, I think Bill sang on one of their tracks or they sang on some of the Rolling Stones stuff. Steve said Keith wanted him to replace Brian Jones in the band. Andrew was in and out of Olympic all the time, with the Small Faces and PP Arnold, doing demos for a panoply of Immediate artists. The one thing that was characteristic of Steve Marriott was he would always push you that 20 minutes beyond which you could not go. So you wound up hating him. You just couldn't stay awake any longer and he would say just do a backing vocal or another mix. If you had an all night session with Marriott you were not going to get out until they had already set up the studio for the next batch of musicians. You could not get him out of the studio, he just loved it in there.

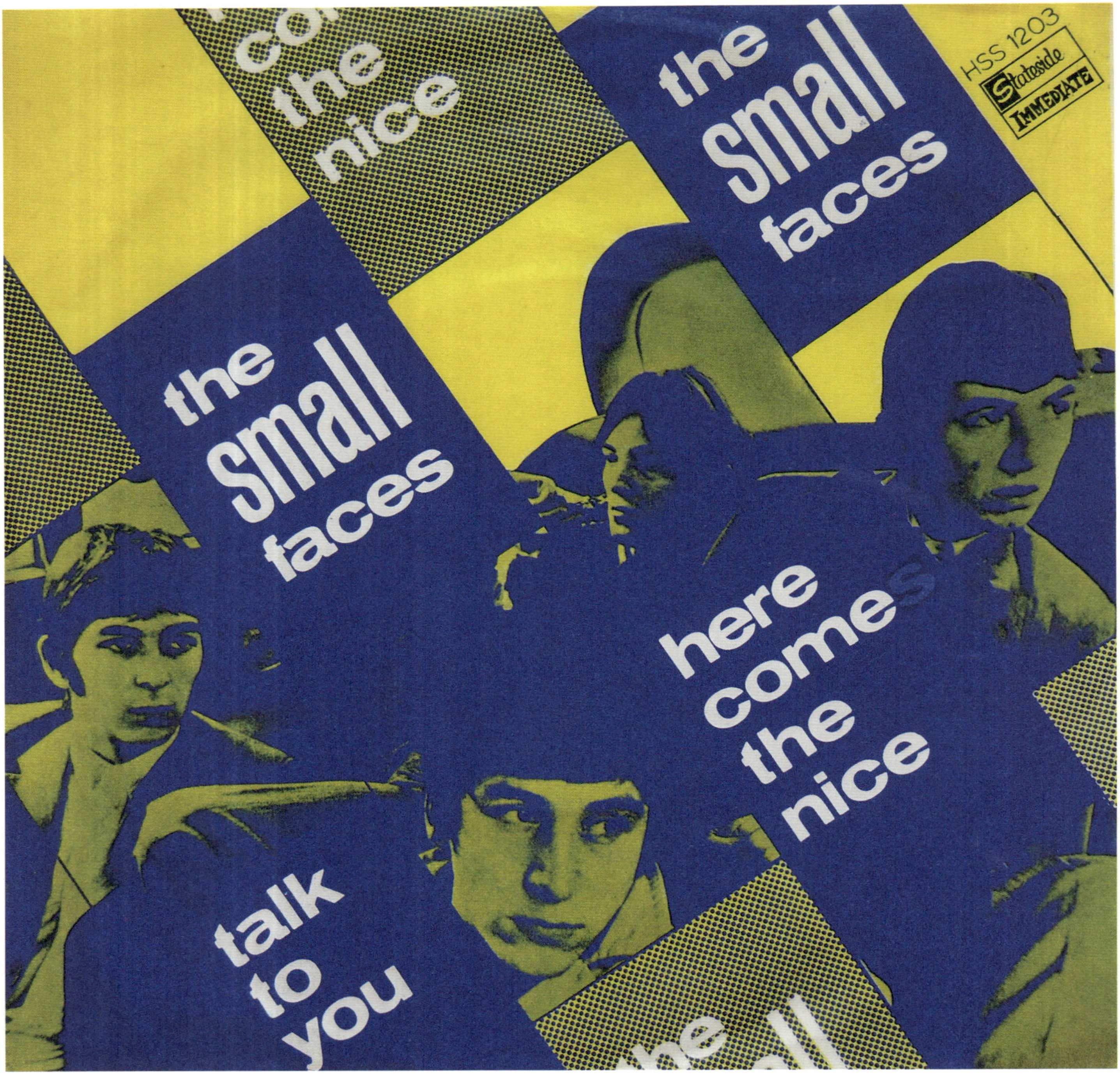
HSS 1203
Stateside
IMMEDIATE
the small faces
the small faces
here comes the nice
talk to you

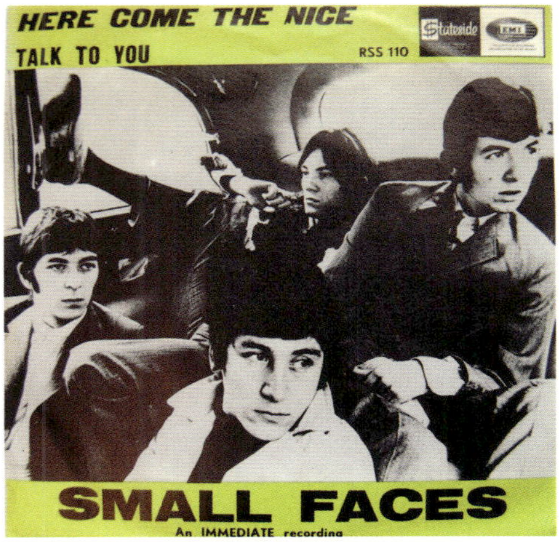
HERE COME THE NICE
TALK TO YOU
RSS 110
Stateside
EMI
SMALL FACES
An IMMEDIATE recording

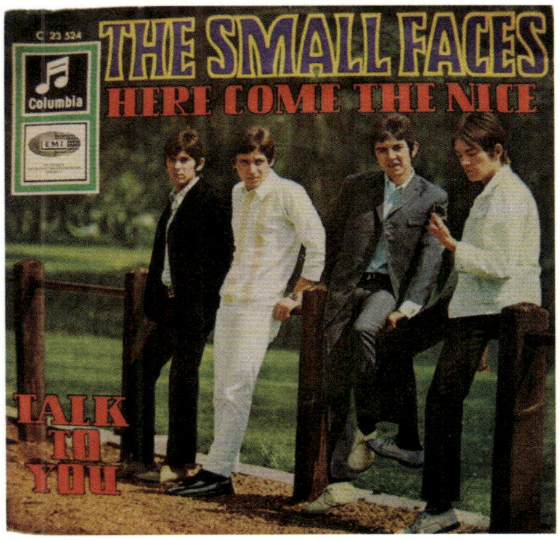
C 23 524
Columbia
EMI
THE SMALL FACES
HERE COME THE NICE
TALK TO YOU

IMMEDIATE STAFF RECALL OLDHAM FLYING BACK FROM MONTEREY IN A KAFTAN, SCATTERING FLOWERS ALL AROUND AS HE FLOATED INTO HIS OFFICE

SIMON SPENCE

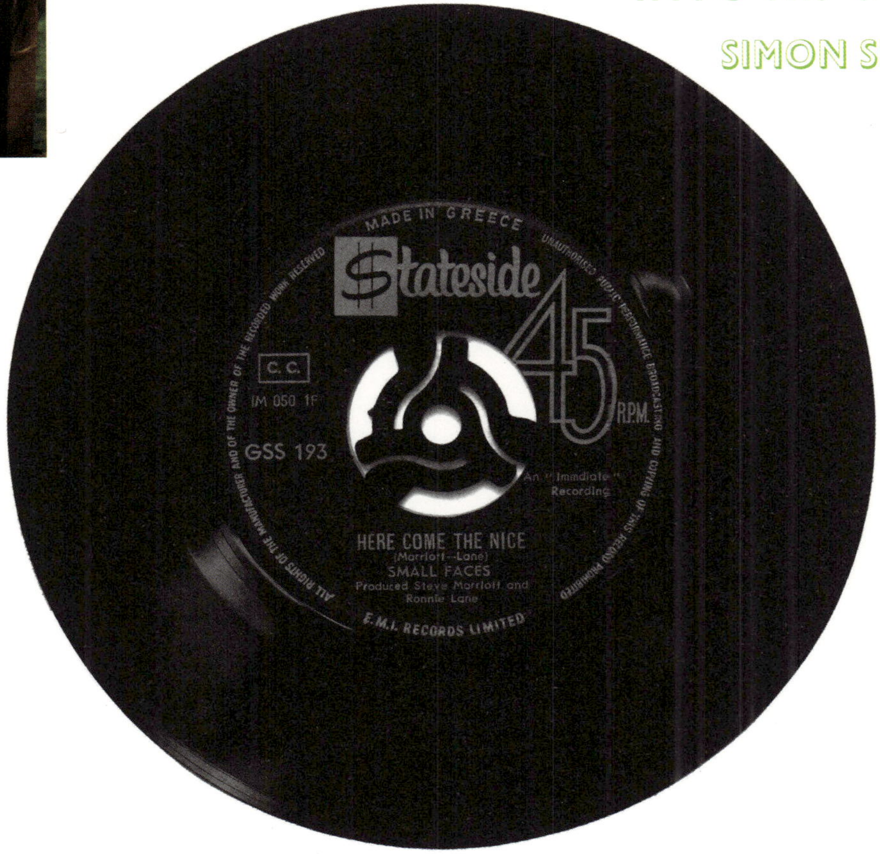
MADE IN GREECE
Stateside
45
R.P.M.
C.C.
GSS 193
HERE COME THE NICE
SMALL FACES
E.M.I. RECORDS LIMITED

A SELECTION OF THE SMALL FACES' US, UK AND EUROPEAN RELEASES FOR THEIR IMMEDIATE DEBUT "HERE COME THE NICE"/"TALK TO YOU", JUNE 1967

Immediate to EMI after Philips split; new labels

EMI has signed a deal with Andrew Oldham and Tony Calder under which it will now distribute the Immediate label. The first two releases on the new outlet are set for March 31—"Green Circles" by Twice As Much, and a debut disc from the Apostolic Intervention titled "Tell Me Have You Ever Seen Me." This follows last week's report of Immediate's split with Philips, who formerly distributed the label.

Oldham and Calder were expected back in London today (Friday) after visiting New York to negotiate a U.S. outlet for Immediate.

Roulette is the latest American recording company to be issued under its own label in this country. It will be distributed in Britain by Philip Solomon's Major Minor company, under a deal clinched between Solomon and Morris Levy, president of Roulette.

First British release will be Tommy James and the Shondelles' current U.S. hit "I Think We're Alone Now," on April 15. Agreement has also been reached for Roulette to distribute the Major Minor output in the States.

The Stardust label, mainly devoted to Irish showbands, is to be launched next month by impresario Arthur Frewin in conjunction with Melodisc Records.

Decca is to launch the LHI label—owned by U.S. composer and record producer Lee Hazelwood—in the spring.

Philips Records will market the CBS catalogue on musicassettes under a deal signed this week. First release of these CBS tapes will be in early May and will include recordings by Tony Bennett, Barbra Streisand, Bob Dylan and Andy Williams, plus the "West Side Story" and "My Fair Lady" soundtracks.

I WAS SO STONED I COULDN'T SEE THROUGH THE FUCKING CAMERA
PETER WHITEHEAD

ANNOUNCEMENT STATING THAT PHILIPS WILL BE TAKING OVER THE IMMEDIATE DISTRIBUTION FROM EMI

Tony Calder remembers:

I got a phone call from Stevie one night from Olympic, two in the morning, he says: 'You've got to hear this, it's a smash. Where's Andy?' Steve always called him Andy. Steve said: 'Do yourself a favour, get hold of him, this track's got phasing on it.' I said: 'What the fuck's that?'

"Itchycoo Park"—utilising the new studio technique of 'phasing' and written and produced by Marriott/Lane—met with initial resistance from the BBC, who considered banning the record because of it's "I got high" lyric. Immediate issued an official statement:

"Itchycoo Park" is a story about a park in the east end of London. It's a slum area similar to the slums of Brooklyn. There isn't any green grass in this park. It's just a strip of wasteland with swings, a sand pit and a hill. At the bottom of the hill there are loads of stinging nettles (thorns). Kids used to ride their soapboxes off the hills into the stinging nettles and get all itchy. Hence the name Itchycoo Park. There is also a little pond where the ducks land, where the kids feed the ducks.

The BBC backed down and adverts for the single were plastered on the *NME* front page and featured four small children in overgrown parkland scrub holding an upside down Itchycoo Park street sign: the only clue to the record being advertised. Ronnie Lane would later explain his thinking behind the track:

Andrew had a lot of influence over us because we were very impressionable and he was very moody. He would swan around in his shades and his limousine and he was quite amusing really. He had this camp humour and that's when we started to do these little cameos like "Itchycoo Park". Had Andrew known it at the time, of course, he would have probably have demanded a royalty payment.

The single became Small Faces' biggest UK hit for a year, peaking at number three in the UK, and going on to surpass all previous chart achievements for the group throughout Europe and the world. It was number one in Sydney and in the top five in Holland and Belgium. In interviews to promote the hit, Marriott praised Immediate:

Unlike previous deals, where the band had no control over the music and were even considering breaking up, Andrew gave us a sense of direction and freedom. Along he came and the whole sky seemed to clear up. Immediate is a young company run by young people. I can go to the offices in new Oxford Street and just sit and smoke and drink tea—chatting the afternoon away. Andrew digs the people he works with, and he people he works with dig him, that's how it should be everywhere.

In an *NME* interview Marriott also revealed Small Faces were planning to go off to the US, to make that well-deserved and long-awaited breakthrough:

We've got a new label in the States, CBS. That's a good label to be on out there and we're very hopeful. That's where Andrew comes in again. You know what happened to us previously in the States? They released "All Or Nothing", "Sha La La La Lee" and "Whatcha Gonna Do About It" and decided we were an R&B group, so we got restricted airplay. I mean R&B? We're more a Walt Disney sound.

Oldham was helping out pals Lou Adler and Mamas and Papas star, John Phillips, in the US with the organisation of the Summer of Love 1967 Monterey Festival when he struck a new distribution deal for Immediate in the US with CBS for an advance of $100,000. It was a massive deal that reflected Oldham's stature in the US. Trade magazine *Cashbox* called Oldham "a musical giant", and for *Billboard* he was one of the top five record producers in the world. Lou Adler also made a deal with CBS around Monterey time for his label, Ode, and he had introduced CBS President, Clive Davis, to Oldham. Oldham inked the deal in New York at the CBS head office on 77th Street, allowing CBS exclusive US rights on Immediate product for two years with a third year option. Prior to this only a few Immediate singles had come out in the US. Farlowe's "Out Of Time" and Twice As Much's "Sittin' on a Fence" had been released via MGM, in deals made by Allen Klein.

At Monterey, Oldham had recommended booking The Who and Jimi Hendrix for the three-day festival, which attracted 100,000 people to a small coastal town between San Francisco and LA, to celebrate "music, love and flowers". Flowers being the symbol of the festival, a hundred thousand orchids were distributed amongst the crowd, and a poem called Flowers written by Oldham in the festival programme.

Brian Jones was the only Rolling Stone to attend the festival, accompanied by Nico, and the two stayed with Oldham and his wife, Sheila, at a rented house in Monterey. Brian was supposed to introduce a few acts with fellow MC, Monkee, Mickey Dolenz, who dressed as an Indian for the occasion. Mamas and Papas, The Animals (whose singer Eric Burden had relocated to San Francisco), and Simon and Garfunkel were the major draws of the festival, with support from unsigned San Francisco band the Big Brother Holding Company, featuring Janis Joplin, plus The Byrds, Jefferson Airplane, Otis Redding, Ravi Shanker, the Grateful Dead, Hendrix and The Who (whose awesome auto-destruction antics at the festival launched them in the US). Four months later The Who scored their first US hit "I Can See For Miles".

CBS Records' President, Clive Davis, said he had "an awakening at Monterey" and paid an astounding $250,000 for Janis Joplin and the Big Brother Holding Company in a deal brokered by Dylan manager, Albert Grossman. CBS was the Tiffany network in the US and already had Bob Dylan, Simon and Garfunkel, The Byrds and Barbara Streisand. Davis was intent on turning the label into a rock powerhouse and alongside Janis Joplin he signed up Blood Sweat And Tears, Santana, and Chicago.

Oldham stayed on in LA after Monterey to work on a "Summer of Love" offering from Rolling Stones for the US market, *Flowers*, their ninth US album, cobbled together a compendium of mostly previously unavailable (in the US) 1966 Rolling Stones material and a few hit singles. Oldham used the LA graphics team, Tom Wilkes and Guy Webster (who had been responsible for the Monterey Pop Festival packaging), for the cover art. The album peaked at number two, staying on the charts for an incredible 35 weeks.

Immediate staff recall Oldham flying back from Monterey in a kaftan and a cowboy hat stuffed with flowers and scattering flowers all around as he floated in to his office. He put out an *NME* advert to promote Scott McKenzie's "San Francisco (Be Sure To Wear Flowers In Your Hair)", which became the talk of the trade and Immediate staff plugged and promoted the record faster and better than EMI (whose record it was in the UK).

Immediate's entire creative team was flown to New York to meet with CBS department representatives. Clive Davis told *Billboard* he wanted to "further Oldham's career as a record entrepreneur", guaranteeing "CBS could sell more albums than any other company in the US for Immediate".

Under the new deal, CBS went to work on making the Small Face Immediate's first US hit act. After issuing "Here Come The Nice" as a taster, they went all out promoting "Itchycoo Park" and it shot up the billboard charts, selling 329,4300 copies to peak at number 16 (the single sold about 250,00 in the UK and about 268,000 in the rest of Europe). It was swiftly followed by the release of the Small Faces debut US LP, *There Are But Four Small Faces*, as an Immediate 'special'. Bruce Hinton, the newly appointed manager of sales and promotion at CBS, who now handled both Immediate and Adler's Ode records, thought it imperative Small Faces start promoting themselves in the US and wanted the group to tour there as soon as possible to capitalise on the hit.

Instead Immediate sent CBS a video of Small Faces miming to "Itchycoo Park", shot in Chiswick Park, with the group dressed in "cartoonish" kaftans and "painted plimsolls". For some reason the real thing couldn't make it to the US and much momentum was lost.

IT'S ALL OVER NOW

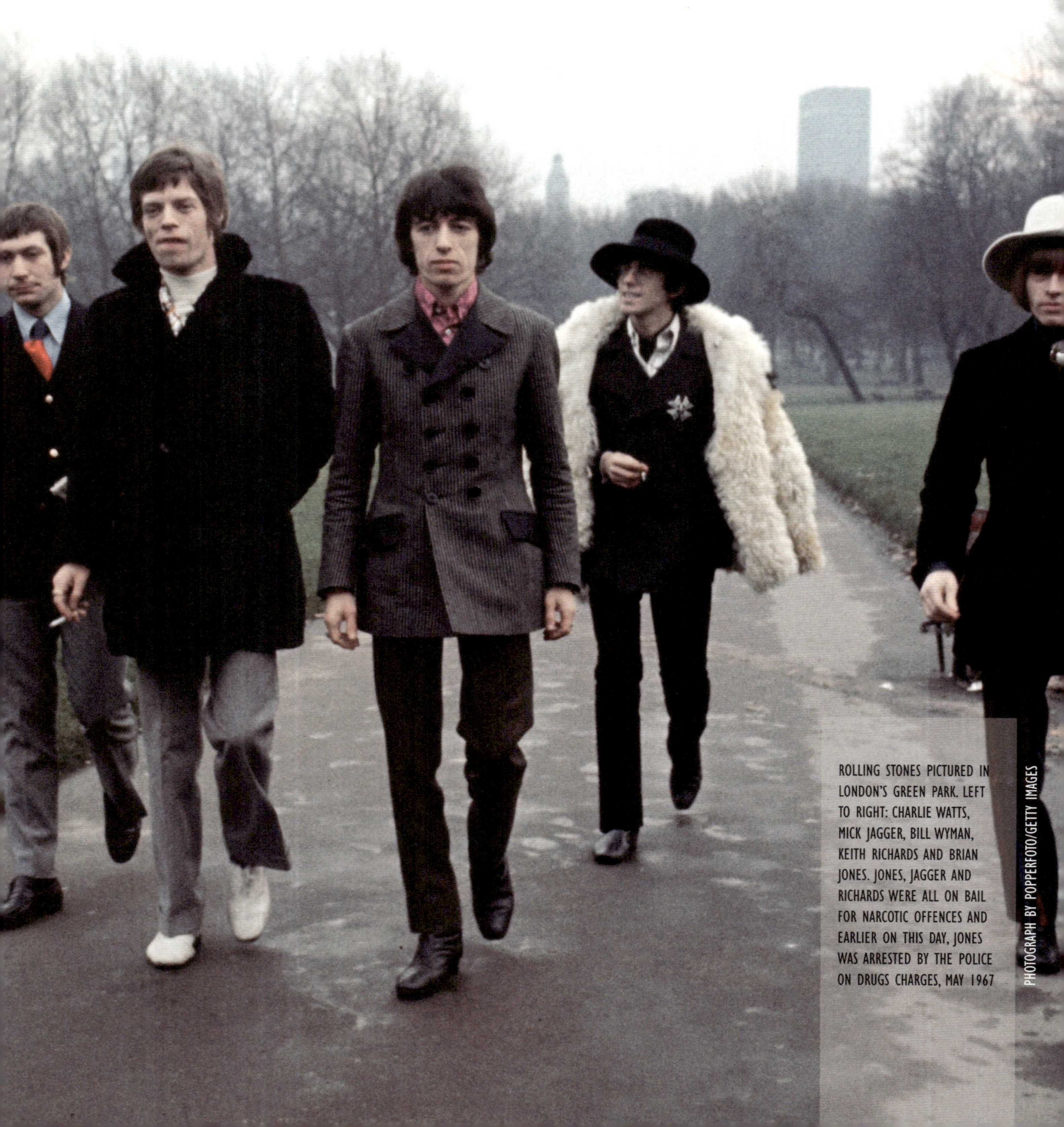

ROLLING STONES PICTURED IN LONDON'S GREEN PARK. LEFT TO RIGHT: CHARLIE WATTS, MICK JAGGER, BILL WYMAN, KEITH RICHARDS AND BRIAN JONES. JONES, JAGGER AND RICHARDS WERE ALL ON BAIL FOR NARCOTIC OFFENCES AND EARLIER ON THIS DAY, JONES WAS ARRESTED BY THE POLICE ON DRUGS CHARGES, MAY 1967

PHOTOGRAPH BY POPPERFOTO/GETTY IMAGES

ony Calder remembers: "Rolling Stones got resentful of Monterey. Andrew was in a world of his own. He was happy, he was working, doing the press calls with Lou. He was out of his box but for the first time away from the fucking pressure of the UK police, not knowing where to sleep at night. He was like the person I first met".

There had been discontent brewing between Oldham and the Rolling Stones since the end of 1966 when the single "Have You Seen Your Mother Baby, Standing In The Shadows" performed disappointingly in the US, spending only four weeks in the charts and peaking at number nine. Keith Richards broke rank first to insist that the wrong mix of it had been released. "The original track was fat and fantastic", he told the New York Times. In the UK after seven consecutive number ones, the single peaked at number three.

Oldham told the press "Have You Seen Your Mother Baby, Standing In The Shadows" was "about the attitude that exists between parents and their children. The shadow is the uncertainty of the future. The uncertainty is whether we slide into a vast depression or universal war." Later in an interview with music monthly Rolling Stone Jagger stated:

> "Have You Seen Your Mother?" was like the ultimate freak-out. We came to a full stop after that. I just couldn't make it with that anymore; what more could we possible say? We couldn't possible have kept it up like that. You just drain out totally. It's just the end of a certain period and we had to stop. We had done it, there was nothing more we could do. We just had to wait until we had organised ourselves, and you know, things had changed.

Looking back Keith Richards said: "Suddenly in late 1966 we were so exhausted that we couldn't go on the road. We were wiped. It was a pressure cooker."

With the unwieldy title, feedback-drenched backing and impenetrable lyrics, "Have You Seen You're Mother Baby, Standing In The Shadows" heralded headlines in the UK, "Have The Stones Gone Too Far?" and "Stones: What Went Wrong?" Allen Klein had predicted the group would gross an astonishing $20 million in 1967. Since a start of 1967 with the release of single "Let's Spend The Night Together" and album Between The Buttons there had been a six-month silence for the Rolling Stones with no gigs and no releases.

The single "Let's Spend The Night Together" should have been a major triumph for Oldham. The basis of the track had been recorded in Hollywood, at RCA studios, before further work in London, at Pye and Olympic studios. Oldham had overseen a beautifully blended, perfectly balanced mix of piano and guitar, with Charlie's drums leading the charge and was justly proud at having successfully steered the Rolling Stones toward a fuller, smoother, more mature sound, after the over-the-edge sonic assault that fans had found difficult to swallow. "Even the backing harmonies were smooth", Oldham joked. However, during a star turn on the Sunday Night At The London Palladium—ITV's premier family entertainment show—Rolling Stones had done the unthinkable by refusing to appear with the rest of the show's entertainment at the end of the programme on a revolving stage. The stage wave was a long-standing tradition and having previously told the band the show was too establishment for them, Oldham had persuaded the group it was a good idea to appear this once and thought it well worth the effort to go all the way and wave goodbye. There was a very public, violent, stand-up row between Jagger and Oldham on stage at the Palladium over the issue. Oldham felt it wrong to so blatantly disrespect their record-buying public. Eventually comedians, Dudley Moore and Peter Cooke, held up a Gerard Scharfe painted impression of the group for the spinning finale but by then, Oldham, close to tears, had turned his back and walked.

"Let's Spend The Night Together" peaked at number three in the UK and the Rolling Stones flew to New York to promote the single on The Ed Sullivan Show, another massive Sunday evening television event. Here the sexual demands laid down in the lyric caused the show's producers to insist that the chorus line of the single be altered. Years later Jagger would claim he did not comply and mumbled his way through the line rather than sing altered lyrics (but it's clear he sung the alterations, rolling his eyes and singing "Let's spend *some time* together"). There was also a danger—Klein told Oldham— that the single would be banned by radio stations in the US over the lyric. Loathe to let go of the controversy and fantastic feel of "Let's Spend The Night Together", he allowed himself to be persuaded by Klein that the single's flip side, "Ruby Tuesday", was the best song for US radio and it became another huge number one there.

The album Between The Buttons went to number two in both the US and UK in its first week, kept off both top spots by the latest pop craze, The Monkees. A result of cumulative recording in Hollywood, Pye and Olympic Studios, the NME review praised Oldham, who had produced 'an album richer than ever before in terms of variation of pace, sound and excitement".

It seemed as if Rolling Stones—with a new sound, and through a policy of saying no to all interviews (via a newly appointed PR, Les Perrin, an old-school king who had looked after Count Basie, Duke Ellington and Frank Sinatra)—had ridden out the first hints of a backlash in the UK. Then News of the World printed a sensational pop star drug exposé claiming Mick Jagger had admitted to taking LSD, Benzedrine and marijuana. The story was written by Mike Gabbert, the same journalist who had broken a big football betting scandal in 1962 and would go on in the 1990s to edit The Sunday Sport. Hell-bent on exposing Rolling Stones, Gabbert, in his haste to do so, had in fact cornered the fast disintegrating Brian Jones in a nightclub, and it was he who had openly confessed to taking the drugs cocktail. Jagger made matters worse by announcing on The Eamonn Andrews Show: Live

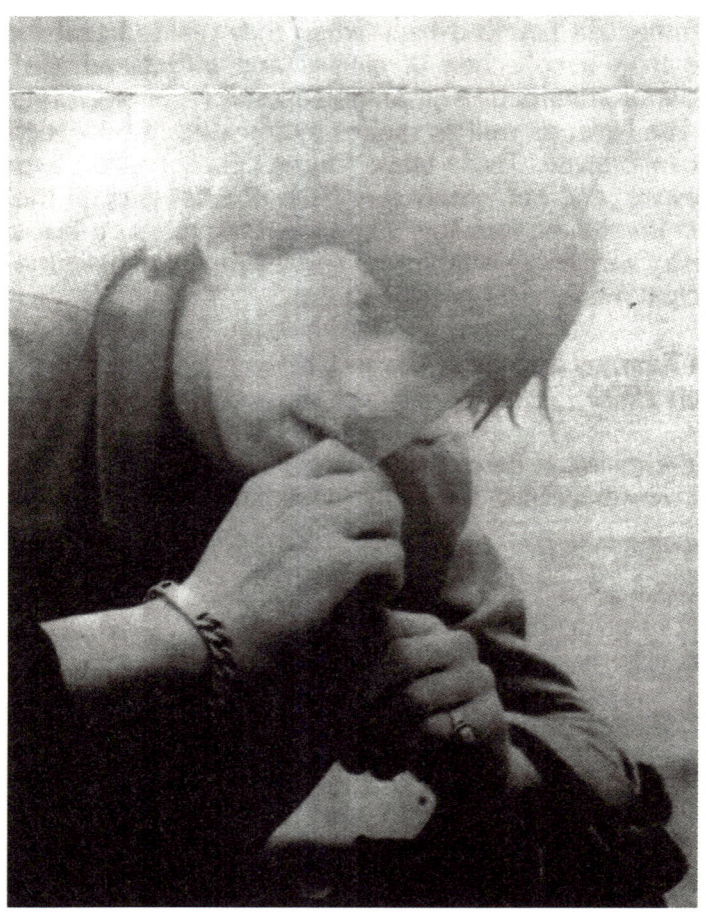

SUDDENLY IN LATE 1966 WE WERE SO EXHAUSTED THAT WE COULDN'T GO ON THE ROAD. IT WAS A PRESSURE COOKER

KEITH RICHARDS

From London, that he intended to sue *News of the World*. In time-honoured gutter press tradition, reporters from the paper vowed to hound him and the Rolling Stones until they had further sordid revelations that would kill off the libel action. The paper had the advantage of working in conjunction with the police who were now forming special drug squads especially to crack down on the pop music scene and, despite The Beatles singing the praises of LSD on their single "Strawberry Fields", the police had marked the Rolling Stones down as top of the hit list: public enemy number one for real now.

Oldham had warned Jagger, Richards and Jones that strutting about in outlandish "druggy" clothes (from the new King's Road boutiques) and flaunting their wealthy degenerate lifestyle, sent out the wrong message. He knew a drugs conviction would mean the withdrawal of visas to the US; a huge money-spinner. In early February, tipped off by *News of the World*, the Sussex police swooped on a party at Richards' Redlands country retreat in West Wittering. A quantity of heroin, amphetamine and marijuana was found and Jagger and Richards were arrested and charged for possession. "Drug Squad Raids Pop Stars' Party", claimed the *News of the World* spread merrily. On one level their arrest befitted the image Oldham had so assiduously created for the Rolling Stones and maybe he should have been delighted: evidently he wasn't. Whispers started coming back from friendly policemen, via Les Perrin, warning Oldham to watch out, because the police were after him too.

Allen Klein took centre stage in the Jagger/Richards court cases, making a big splash by flying into London and telling *The Daily Mirror* "Their problems are mine. I'm working my ass off to get them the best lawyers and will be in the front row of the trial every day." Klein had pointed out to Oldham that, should Jagger or Richards get jail time, there needed to be enough Rolling Stones product to tide them over, or at least a single to ride on the back of public sympathy should that happen. Oldham had been having terrible problems getting all five Rolling Stones to show at Olympic studios to record. When they had, the sessions had produced nothing of worth, and at times it seemed as if they were playing deliberately badly to wind him up. Oldham persevered, managing to finally get the basics of a new single, "We Love You", together. Tony Calder recounts:

> I remember the [Rolling] Stones came in to Olympic one night, when they were out on bail they were doing "We Love You" and it was a dog. [John] Lennon came in and said, 'set the mic up' and he goes in and puts the falsetto voice on. I had tears in my eyes, it was magic; that made the record. It was phenomenal.

Oldham added prison doors clanking shut to tag onto the end of the single if the two Rolling Stones were convicted and organised a video to be ready for *Top of the Pops* if that happened. Filmed by Peter Whitehead, the video was shot in a church in Essex and featured Marianne Faithfull, Richards, Jones and Jagger acting out the trial of Oscar Wilde. When the sensational news came that the verdict on Jagger and

THE ONE AND ONLY
KEITH RICHARDS, CIRCA 1965

Richards was not guilty, everyone presumed "We Love You" was a guaranteed number one but the BBC banned Whitehead's film and the Rolling Stones were unprepared for television or concerts. The single peaked at a disappointing number eight and the Rolling Stones album sessions at Olympic were still going nowhere.

The situation at Immediate only served to exacerbate the growing rift between Oldham and Jagger. Having been refused a third of the label, Jagger was reluctant to produce or promote Immediate in any way. Then there was Steve Marriott, a talent who could be considered a serious rival to Jagger, who had started to get under Jagger's skin in every way. Since Jimmy Page had left the label, Marriott was the new great hope at Immediate. Just turned 20, he had pipes that shred the soul, an iconic mod look and impudence that bordered on the indecent. He was working in the studio with one-time Jagger preserve, PP Arnold, and had been sleeping with Jagger's ex-girlfriend, Chrissie Shrimpton. While the two Rolling Stones were on trial for drugs, Marriott had sneaked a hit with a song blatantly trumpeting a speed dealer, "Here Come The Nice", and the massive acid and marijuana anthem, "Itchycoo Park". Jagger, now 24, didn't need telling twice that the competition from Marriott makes him look a little long in the tooth. Although he gives his reasons as multitude, Marriott's magnificence hastens Jagger's exit from Immediate and contributes to the ending of Oldham's management of Rolling Stones.

Oldham was still just 23 when it was announced he and the Rolling Stones were going their separate ways. Les Perrin delivered the official statement: "The [Rolling] Stones have parted from their recording manager because the band have taken over more and more of the production of their own music. Andrew Oldham no longer has any connection whatsoever with the Rolling Stones." Mick Jagger added in *NME*:

> I felt we were doing practically everything ourselves anyway. And we just didn't think along the same lines. But I don't want to have a go at Andrew. Allen Klein is just a financial scene. We'll really be managing ourselves. We'll be producing our own records too. I shan't continue to produce for Immediate, it was all so draggy, the biggest disappointment is not doing Pat Arnold's records.

In retrospect, Jagger more recently admitted that, "the reason Andrew left was because he thought we weren't concentrating and that we were being childish". Oldham told *NME* at the time:

> Everything the [Rolling] Stones have done has been natural. They were not puppets, they were people. Whatever else is said about them they were as close to professional as any five artists can get. We split because we had no need of each other anymore. As people we went in different directions. There was no definite decision. It was just over. We just weren't on the same wavelength anymore. We had gone as far as we could together. It was time to move on.

The divorce was messy. Having decided to let Allen Klein sort out the legal ramifications, Oldham's original co-manager in the group, Eric Easton, sued for half the Rolling Stones income to date in a £1 million High Court litigation. Easton, who had done nothing for the group of much note, especially over the past couple of years, pursued a prison committal order against Oldham "for failing to comply with an undertaking to produce a list of documents or to pay into an account money he received in respect of their three years of joint management of the [Rolling] Stones".

When Easton's lawyers came knocking, the Immediate staff arranged for a man called Bruce to be dressed as Oldham. As soon as the word would come that the writ men were on their way to the second floor, Oldham nipped out on the roof, diving next door through Dick James' office window, while Bruce, happily accepted the paperwork. The dispute over the three-year Oldham/Easton co-management agreement on the Rolling Stones—signed when Oldham was just 19 and Easton was in his 40s—was settled when Allen Klein took control of everything, paying Oldham and Easton both an estimated £700,000.

JOHN LENNON CAME IN AND SAID 'SET THE MIC UP' I HAD TEARS IN MY EYES, IT WAS MAGIC

TONY CALDER

WOULD YOU BELIEVE

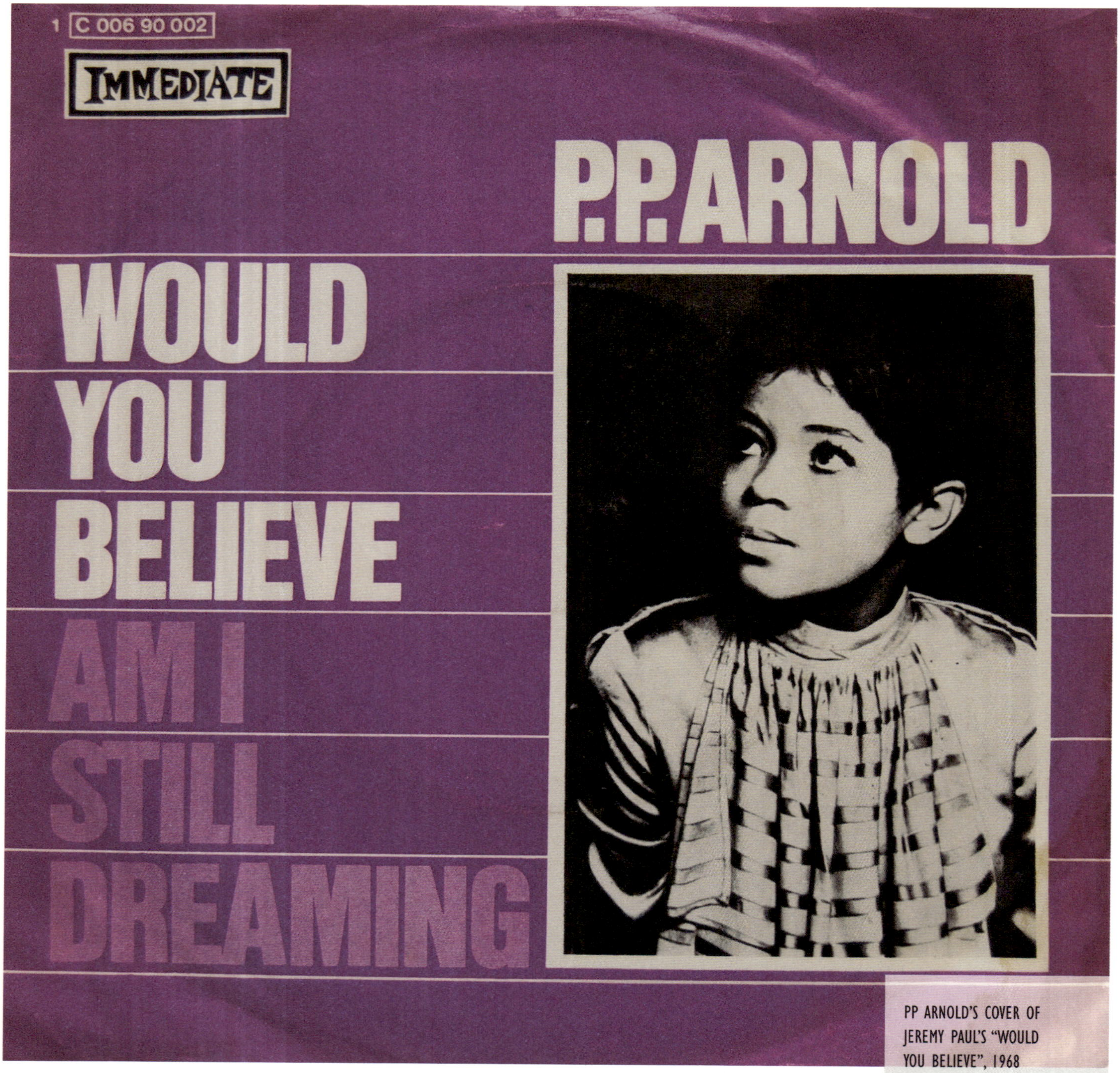
1 C 006 90 002
IMMEDIATE
P.P. ARNOLD
WOULD YOU BELIEVE
AM I STILL DREAMING

PP ARNOLD'S COVER OF JEREMY PAUL'S "WOULD YOU BELIEVE", 1968

In the aftermath of the split with the Rolling Stones, Oldham suffered further violent mood swings. He displayed outrageous indulgence one minute (when a junior member of staff at Immediate admired his jacket Oldham made a present of it) and psychopathic cruelty the next (sackings involved a quick upturning of the desk). Oldham was in the office more often now, casting a half opened eye on administration with Calder, waiting until the normal stream of talent trooped into offices just before lunch and camped there for the rest of the day as lunch turned into tea. There were wild nights out for Oldham with theatre designer Sean Kenny who, with his down-to-earth Irish wit and sage, entertained and educated with the possibility of new worlds and adventures he was always exploring. They often drank together at Fulham Road's Trencherman (sometimes seen hurling trash cans across the road), and together they came up with a plan for Kenny to design the stage and set for a "Love-In". Their Love-In would be the UK's answer to Monterey, featuring PP Arnold, new Immediate group, The Nice, Donovan and Pink Floyd.

Oldham had been an atypical manager since he had discovered Rolling Stones, aged 19, and devoted his life to them. Now that life was over. £700,000 was a handsome pay-off, and he still held a sizeable interest in the publishing on Jagger/Richards songs, but it had become about more than just the money. He had confessed to Kenny he often felt suicidal and had been suffering from recurring bouts of depression. A similarly "redundant to requirements" Brian Epstein had recently committed suicide, at the age of 32, from an overdose of barbiturates. Kenny recommended his psychiatrist Dr Mac (Doctor Luke McLoughlin) who also treated Tony Hancock (before the comedian committed suicide), The Shadows, Hank B Marvin and the hallowed Jet Harris. Dr Mac diagnosed Oldham as suffering from manic depression and put him through a treatment of electric convulsive therapy, with electrodes attached to his temples and a device placed in his mouth so that he could not shatter his teeth or bite off his own tongue. Then 180 to 460 volts of electricity would be sent through his brain, often rendering him unconscious. Oldham also spent weekends at Hampstead's Bethanie Nursing Home, where Dr Mac would administer a Deep Sleep Treatment, putting him into a sort of coma for days, held down with a combination of barbiturates, sedatives and the latest psychotropic drugs on the market.

If Dr Mac hadn't knocked Oldham out and there was nothing on television, chauffeur Eddie would take doctor and patient in the Phantom 5, up the M1 to nightclubs out of town to see comics such as Bob Monkhouse and Frankie Howerd or acts such as Shirley Bassey. Sometimes Oldham would fall asleep before he got there and later ask Eddie if he had had a good time. Eddie would reply "yes it was okay" or "you were totally out of order". The show went on at Immediate and acts that got to see Oldham always left happily stoned on whatever was the flavour of the day, usually having forgotten the reason for their visit; artistic discussions, money or just to chat. There were more new staff at New Oxford Street now; Steve the messenger, a cockney likely lad, would run errands and deliveries on his moped. Jim Watson was recruited from EMI and promptly dismissed by Oldham, who said he looked like a dummy from a Burton's window. Keith Lewis was recruited from EMI for a marketing position, but was far too straight to cope with Immediate for longer than a couple of months and joined A&M as general manager.

There were other diversions: one afternoon three new E-Type Jaguars pulled up outside the Immediate offices and Oldham leant out of a window to chose a colour. Oldham eventually got back to work in the studio, excited about producing his new favourite Immediate act, Del Shannon, whose early 1960s rock'n'roll chain of hits—"Runaway", "Hats Off To Larry", "Little Town Flirt", "I Go To Pieces"—spoke of loneliness, despair, failure and broken promises. Oldham had recently met Shannon, who was now recording for Liberty Records in the US but going nowhere with current producer, Tommy 'Snuff' Garrett, in London at a BBC show. Del Shannon remembers:

Al Bennett was the president of Liberty. When he was in London, I called him and said: 'Andrew Loog Oldham wants to produce me, he's expensive, he goes into the studio with top cats.' We had 25, 30 musicians. So for three or four weeks I had the time of my life with Andrew. He had let us use his Rolls [Royce]. I liked him because he was very adventurous. He wasn't in a good place in those days, 'cause of the break-up with the [Rolling] Stones, but I liked him and I liked working with him musically. He did it all. I just said 'take over', and that's a dangerous thing for an artist to do, unless the guy really knows what you're doing and knows your style.

Oldham recorded Shannon at Olympic Studios utilising the talents of John Paul Jones, Nicky Hopkins, PP Arnold and many more Immediate regulars on songs he had selected from the growing Immediate Music song catalogue. Jeremy Paul, one of Immediate Music's songwriters remembers:

I wrote a song called "Mind Over Matter" and played it to Andrew. He said it was wicked. At that second he phoned up Del Shannon and played it to Del over the phone. Del flipped, he said: 'I'm coming over right away to record it.' They took him to Olympic Studios. I got a call about one in the morning, 'Jeremy it's Andrew, get down to Barnes now, Del can't sing the top note'. They had got Del Shannon high as a kite. I went out on the floor, I write in falsetto, I write for females, this was a girl's song. I screamed at the top of my voice. Del got the note. I think they speeded up the track. I wrote this song "Would You Believe". PP Arnold recorded a version of the song that went Top 10 in Italy. I met Andrew in the South of France when he was 16 and I was 15, we used to mess about on this little £10 Woolworth's harmonium at my parent's place down there. I kept it and used it on some of my demos. When Small Faces were doing Ogden's [Nut Gone Flake] they insisted on using this Harmonium.

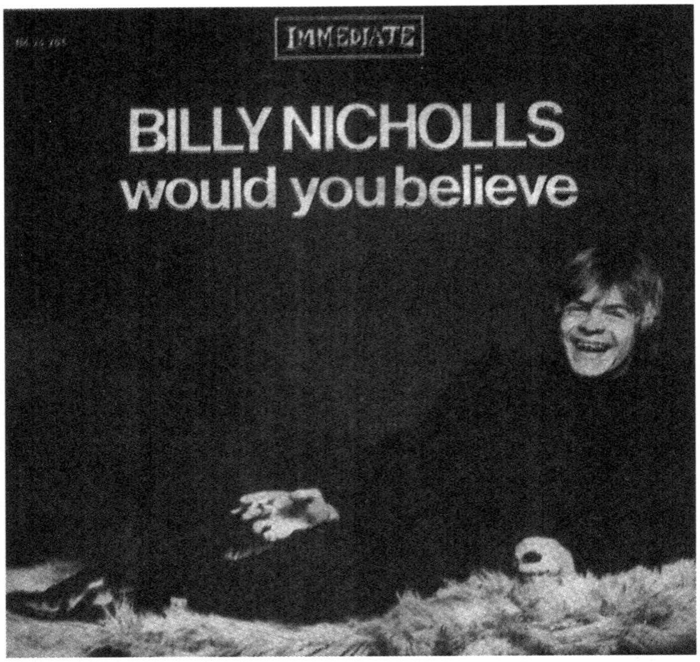
IMMEDIATE
BILLY NICHOLLS
would you believe

Contractual details prevented Immediate releasing the Shannon material in the UK and in the US Liberty did not consider it in keeping with his image and shelved it. The tracks Oldham cut with Shannon, were re-appraised, to great acclaim, 20 years later when the album was issued on CD.

In these chaotic, drug-fuelled times, also rumoured to be recording for Immediate were acts such as Manfred Mann's Paul Jones, Madeline Bell, *Hair* star Linda Kendrick, Buffalo Springfield member Neil Young (who was said to have cut a track for the label, produced in London by Oldham/Jack Nitzsche), David Bowie, Jethro Tull and the Chris Brough managed Aisha, but none released any official product on the label.

Small Faces were keeping themselves busy, in the studio working with Billy Nicholls, a new good-looking teenage signing to Immediate. He recorded Jeremy Paul's "Would You Believe" as a single (produced by Marriott and Lane) and used the same name as a title for the album. Nicholls was friends with Cat Stevens, having worked alongside him and Elton John as a songwriter in Dick James' office. At Immediate Nicholls, like all the acts, was put on a weekly wage. He was on £20 a week, with "my own room full of Revoxes, mellotrons and the [Rolling] Stones' guitars". The *Would You Believe* album featured heavy involvement from Marriott on guitar and vocals, Stevens on piano with Jerry Shirley from Apolostolic Intervention on drums, and all the regular Immediate session crew: Nicky Hopkins, John Paul Jones and Art Greenslade. Despite a great advertising campaign and an astonishing sound, there was little demand for the album and a follow-up single, the Nicholls penned "It Brings Me Down", with a video shot in Piccadilly Square, London, was axed. The album is now one of the most sought after rarities on Immediate, an original vinyl pressing of the album reportedly worth £1,600.

OLDHAM DISPLAYED OUTRAGEOUS INDULGENCE ONE MINUTE AND PSYCHOPATHIC CRUELTY THE NEXT

SIMON SPENCE

Mike d'Abo was more new blood at the label; another teenage songwriter, freshly signed to Immediate Music. He was the lead singer in Manfred Mann, having replaced Paul Jones who had retired from group after a run of eight Top 10 hits such as "Do Wah Diddy Diddy" and "5-4-3-2-1". With d'Abo on vocals the group had cut more adventurous material such as "Semi-Detached Suburban Mr Jones" and "Pretty Flamingo" and just scored a number one smash in the UK with "Mighty Quinn". Despite the group being signed to Fontana, there was nothing in the contract to stop d'Abo from writing his own songs for Immediate. Soon after signing to Immediate Music he wrote "Build Me Up Buttercup" for The Foundations, which sold in excess of three million worldwide. Oldham and Calder were happily convinced that they had in d'Abo their very own Jimmy Webb, the new hot writer in the US who had scored with "Go Where You Wanna Go" and "Up, Up and Away". "They gave me the names of two other singers they wanted me to work with", remembered d'Abo: "Rod Stewart and Chris Farlowe. I had never actually heard of Rod Stewart until they mentioned him to me." Stewart had been signed up at Immediate since early 1967 and, like PP Arnold before him, had been waiting for the right song to record. He had already cut a single for Decca, "Good Morning

OLDHAM CONFESSED TO KENNY HE OFTEN FELT SUICIDAL AND HAD BEEN SUFFERING FROM RECURRING BOUTS OF DEPRESSION

SIMON SPENCE

OPPOSITE: BILLY NICHOLLS ON A SHEEPSKIN RUG ON THE COVER OF HIS SONG "WOULD YOU BELIEVE", JANUARY 1968

TOP: PP ARNOLD AND MIKE D'ABO, CIRCA 1965

BOTTOM: THE NICE IN THE STUDIO, 1967

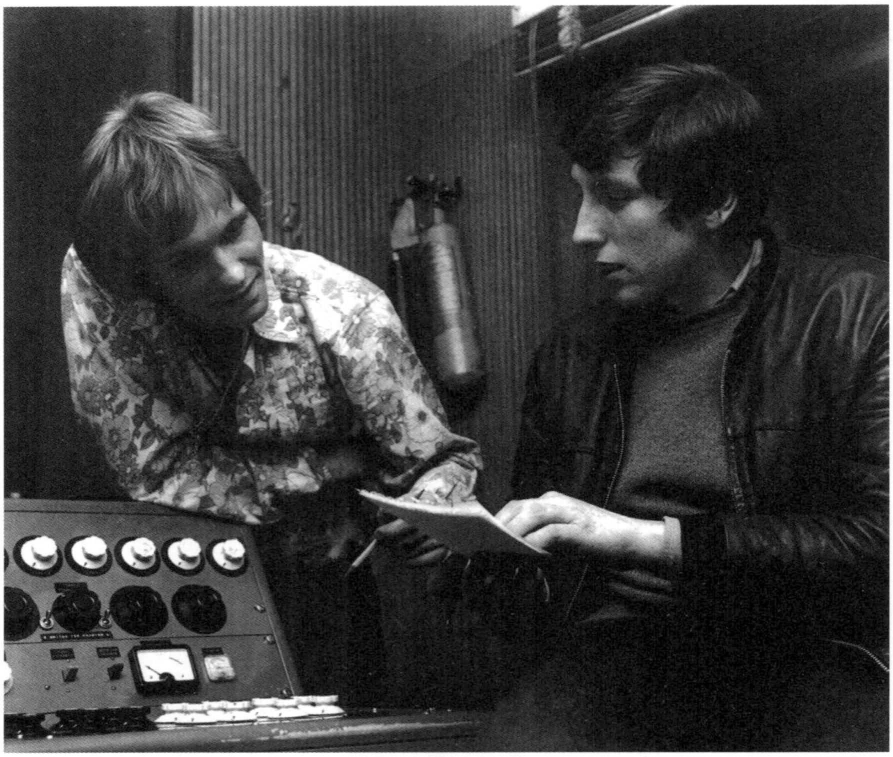

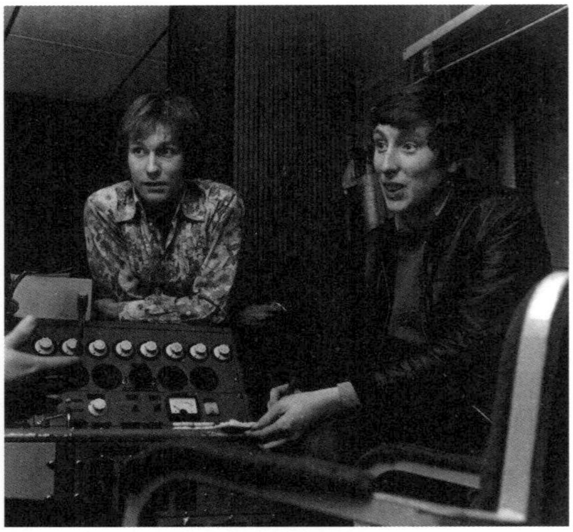

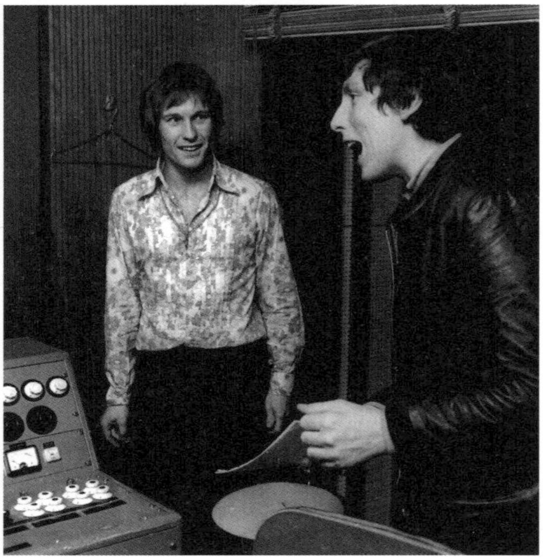

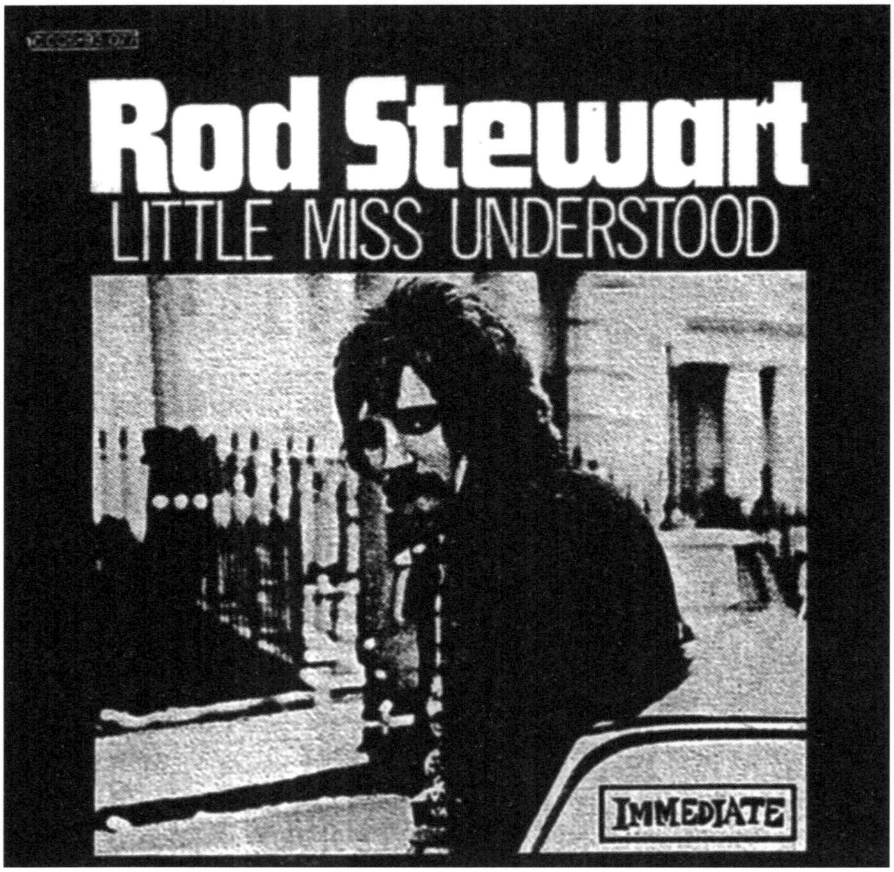

Rod Stewart
LITTLE MISS UNDERSTOOD
IMMEDIATE

TOP: MIKE D'ABO AND CHRIS FARLOWE RECORD "HANDBAGS AND GLADRAGS" IN THE STUDIO, 1967

BOTTOM: ROD STEWART LOOKS MOODY ON "LITTLE MISS UNDERSTOOD", MARCH 1968

OPPOSITE: PROMOTION FOR CHRIS FARLOWE'S "HANDBAGS AND GLADRAGS", NOVEMBER 1967

Little Schoolgirl", and recorded a version of Sam Cooke's "Shake" for EMI. Now, after a brief stint with Long John Baldry's Steampacket, he was occasionally singing with London blues outfit, Shotgun Express. Tony Calder remembers:

> I remember Rod first coming into my office and feeling: 'This guy's got it!' I actually saw a star in front of me. Andrew and I loved him. But at the time Mick [Jagger] was jealous. Rod was pretty and younger. Jagger said: 'You like him don't you?' Andrew and I replied: 'Of course we do. He's going to be a superstar.' Before Oldham broke up with the [Rolling] Stones, we talked Mick round and persuaded him to produce Rod's debut single for Immediate but, as the time neared, he pulled out. There were also plans to have PP Arnold and Rod record an album with Jagger producing but they were scotched when Mick threw a tantrum and said he was not going into the studio.

Jagger had, in fact, made it to the studio for a session with Rod earlier in the year, with Keith Richards, Nicky Hopkins and PP Arnold, among others. They cut a cover of "Working In A Coalmine". Stewart's early manager, Geoff Wright, recalled a row in the studio, "with Mick saying Rod could not hit the high notes, and that his voice wasn't right for the song". In the end d'Abo wrote and produced Stewart's sumptuous piano-driven Immediate debut, "Little Miss Understood", with Small Faces helping out in the studio. Stewart had a colour sleeve, himself in a moody pose and his name emblazoned across top; but sales-wise in the UK the record was not a success, with only 263 copies sold. Nonetheless Rod's new style received exceptional reviews and heavy airplay. Immediate regarded him as a long-term policy act and intended to continue recording and promoting him. Stewart said he liked the Immediate family and recorded a duet with PP Arnold on the Barry Mann/Cynthia Weil song "Come Home Baby". One of Rod's old girlfriends, Jenny Rylands, was now married to Steve Marriott and she urged her new husband to write a hit for Stewart. "Marriott wrote some incredibly commercial things for me to record", Rod said later. Immediate tried to convince their US distributor, CBS, of Stewart's potential but "Little Miss Understood" was never released in the US. Six months later, Stewart joined The Jeff Beck Group as did Immediate session man Nicky Hopkins. They both enjoyed considerable success in the US with the Jeff Beck album, *Truth*—released on the CBS-owned Epic label—which sold approximately 160,000 copies. Stewart said later about his single on Immediate: "I came very near to selling out when I released that."

D'Abo also provided the song for Chris Farlowe's next single, the plaintive "Handbags and Gladrags", a cut that put the singer back up and around the Top 20, peaking at number 23 and, after "Out Of Time", would become his most celebrated Immediate outing. "Handbags and Gladrags" was later resurrected by Stereophonics as the theme tune to BBC television comedy *The Office*.

PP Arnold's former backing band, The Nice, released their debut Immediate single "The Thoughts of Emerlist Davjack", written and produced by Emerlist Davjack; a name made up of segments of the four band members' surnames. Compared with what was

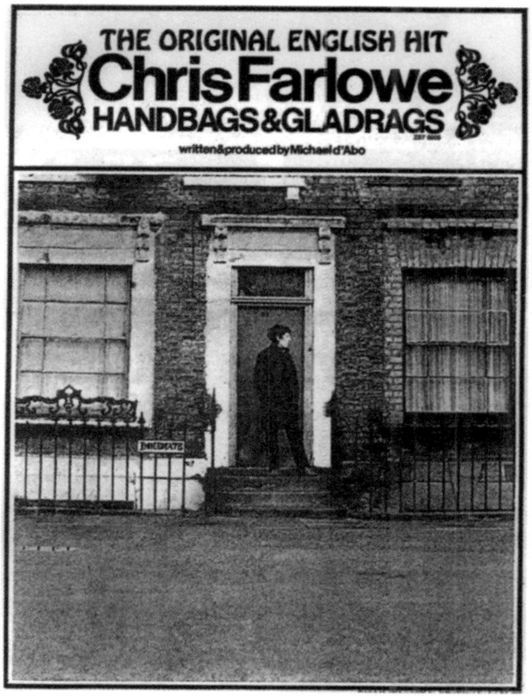
THE ORIGINAL ENGLISH HIT
Chris Farlowe
HANDBAGS&GLADRAGS
written&producedbyMichaeld'Abo

to come from The Nice, the single was fairly straight psychedelic pop and showed plenty of promise. The group had debuted live in front of a 60,000 strong crowd at The National Jazz and Blues Festival in Windsor Great Park and followed that with a residency at the Marquee Club, wrestling the house records from such luminaries as The Jimi Hendrix Experience, The Who and Rolling Stones. The group had developed a great live show, sounding like a more aggressive, punky, Pink Floyd, with extended organ led outbreaks of freeform madness. *Melody Maker* hailed The Nice as successors to Eric Clapton's Cream: "Their music is wholly unlike any being played by another modern pop group—in Britain or America", the paper reckoned, "It is violent, often neurotic, yet rich in chords, harmonies and melodies. They improvise as spontaneously as a jazz group, they are as free as a psychedelic group, but with vastly superior instrumental ability." On a UK package tour with Jimi Hendrix, Pink Floyd, Outer Limits, Amen Corner and The Move, The Nice proved a huge success and the group's organist, Keith Emerson, was on his way to being an unlikely star. The Nice were also the first Immediate act to visit the US—to support the release of their debut single over there—where they garnered much critical acclaim on a short club tour of The Scene in New York, Whiskey A-Go-Go in LA and the Fillmore Auditorium in San Francisco. Yet, after the brief manic production of Del Shannon, all these promising developments at Immediate left Oldham feeling strangely flat, as he struggled to find anything that could give him the same buzz as Rolling Stones.

OGDEN'S NUT GONE FLAKE

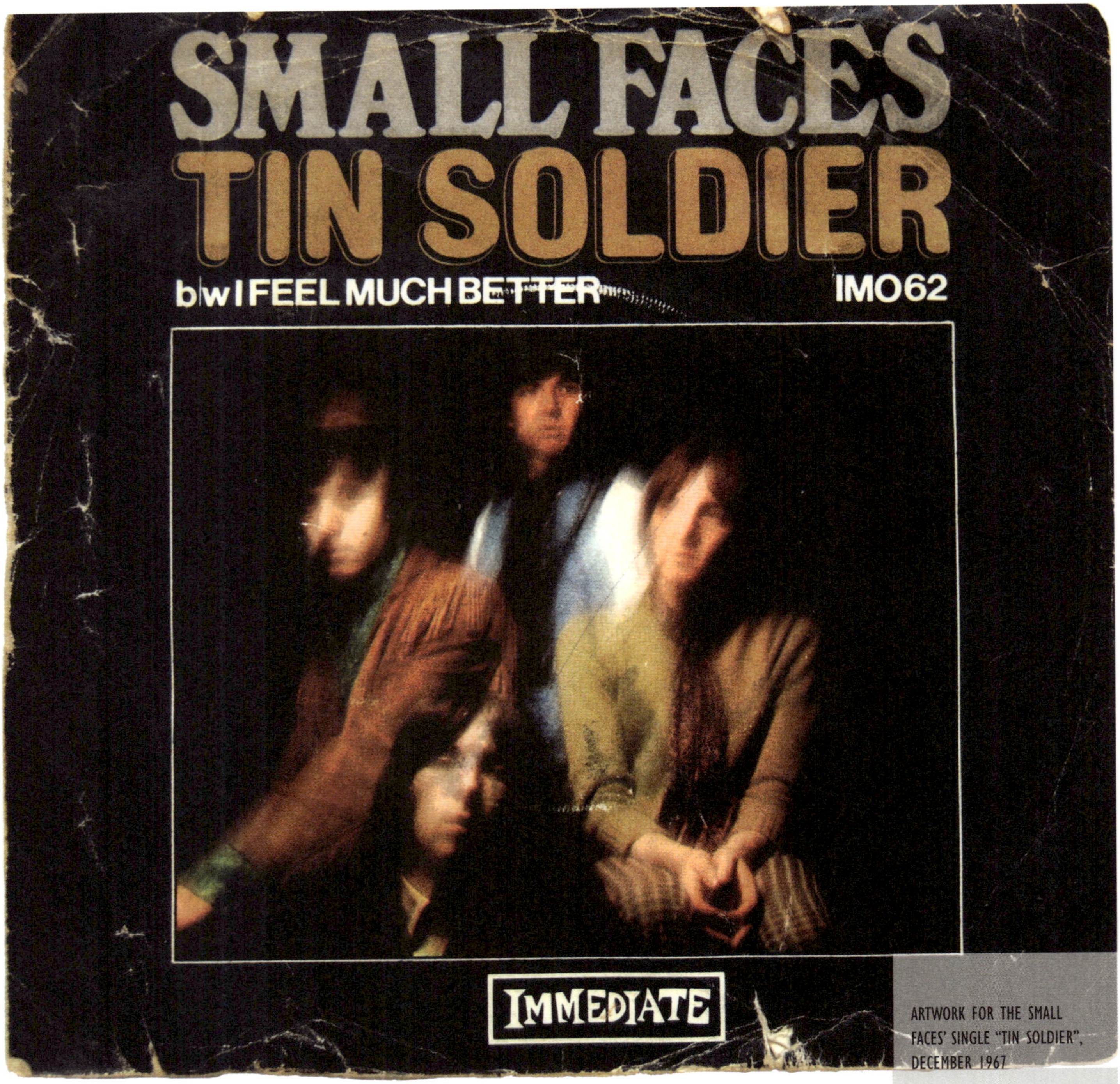
SMALL FACES
TIN SOLDIER
b/w I FEEL MUCH BETTER
IMO62
IMMEDIATE

ARTWORK FOR THE SMALL FACES' SINGLE "TIN SOLDIER", DECEMBER 1967

he unstoppable enthusiasm of Steve Marriott—who Oldham described as "the best of Mick and Keith in one vibrant soul"—played a significant part in rekindling Oldham's love affair with life, Immediate and the UK chart. Having lost interest in the Top 10 since his Rolling Stones split he was pleasantly surprised to hear the UK had never had it so good with songs such as "Heard It Through Grapevine", "Your Precious Love", "You Make Me Feel Like A Natural Woman", "Higher and Higher", "Never My Love" by The Association and "The Letter" by The Box Tops (led by 16-year-old Alex Chilton), all riding high. Marriott delighted in leading Oldham to enjoy a different rhythm of life, forcing US soul and Stax onto the playlist in the Immediate offices; a selection of Bobby Bland, Rufus Thomas, Larry Williams, James Brown and Solomon Burke. Inspired Oldham, who had purposely kept a low public profile since the Rolling Stones split (not wanting to be pointed out as "the ex-Rolling Stones manager"), decided he had had enough of playing Howard Hughes. He got his hair styled in a Carmen-rollered afro, matched with a new beard, make-up, eyeliner and shades. His wealth was apparent in the handmade suits, glittering rings, cuff links, bracelets and watches he flaunted. Oldham would spend 45 minutes on his new hairstyle each morning, while Eddie rolled the first joint of the day. Oldham would then look out of the window, select a car from his fleet, and be in town at Immediate's office by ten. Again he was happy to be a part if the industry of human happiness.

NME feature writer, Keith Altham, who had handled so many Rolling Stones features in the past, was one of the journalists summoned to the Immediate offices to listen to Oldham's new groove, an advance hearing of Small Faces new single "Tin Soldier", the first record ever to be released on coloured vinyl. Written and produced by Marriott/Lane, the song had originally been heading for PP Arnold—but she had been so blown away by it, Small Faces had had second thoughts and kept it for themselves. Arnold had sung backing vocals on the track and did the same on the many television appearances undertaken by the group to promote it. ""Tin Soldier" is the real us", Marriott told Altham, adding that "Itchycoo Park" was really just "a nice kind of send-up. We wanted to make a record that was really us... We can play this one live but we could never get the same effects on "Itchycoo Park"." Marriott also talked of a UK tour in the Spring and spoke of his continued desire to go to the US if "Tin Solider" followed "Itchycoo Park" into the charts. Small Faces had disappointed all by being unable to promote themselves in person in the US on the back of the huge success of "Itchycoo Park" over there. Calder even bluffed to CBS that it was due to "unbelievable demand in Europe". It was, however, rumoured the band were having trouble getting working visas for the US as keyboardist Ian McLagan had been busted for possession of dope. McLagan remembered the situation differently in his memoirs: "We should have gone over to the US when "Itchycoo Park" was in the charts. The problem was we weren't tight on stage. Once we had the freedom in the studio, we just cut out most of our live playing."

Altham, who would go on to be the Rolling Stones 1970s PR, wrote:

Once more unto Andrew Oldham's inner sanctum off Oxford Street to interview his group Small Faces and discuss the fate of "Tin Soldier" with songsmiths Steve Marriott and Ronnie Lane. It was just like old times when music, laughter and sarcasm were the hallmark of many a colourful interview with another known group which Andrew managed. When I made my entrance (one cannot simply enter Andrew's office as you walk through and onto a raised balcony) I was not totally prepared for the *Alice In Wonderland* tea party scene that unfolded before me. Gambolling about the office were two lanky Afghan hounds and a black and white collie of doubtful pedigree. While seated around the table were Steve Ronnie, Andrew and a journalist left from a previous interview. He [the journalist] was apparently asleep and remained affixed to his chair throughout the interview. In beautiful green tumblers on the table was Black Russian a delightful drink.

Altham later explained:

Immediate was intuitively very clever. Andrew had enormous flair and he did know talent when he heard it. He knew a face when he saw one. David Bowie was doing stuff for Immediate around that time. Oldham was terrible, he was rude, obnoxious, bad-tempered, he humiliated people, he was dreadful. Andrew and Tony used to sit in this white office behind this double desk painted white with all these white phones. The two would whisper into each others ears. It was rather disconcerting to say the least, you would wonder what the hell they were talking about. You would ask a question and they would start mumbling to each other. I asked Tony about this years later and he said it wasn't about anything at all, they used to do it deliberately just to put people off.

The harder, more heartfelt "Tin Soldier" hit the Top 10 in the UK and blazed up the charts around Europe, and the world. In Australia and New Zealand, where "Itchycoo Park" had been a massive number one, the single raced in to the Top 10. Oldham, Calder, Small Faces and co-headliners, The Who, jetted out to Australia for a two-week, 20-date tour (dubbed The Big Show) in January 1968. The tour was arranged by the Rolling Stones' Australian promoter, Harry Miller. The Who had just released their *Sell Out* album and Pete Townshend had begun work on an ambitious rock opera but Small Faces were the bigger pull and closed the shows. Small Faces were badly under-rehearsed, a subplot of the visit was to tighten them up for live UK dates, and at Sydney Stadium Marriott walked off stage in a strop, kicking off about the low-quality gear the band were playing with. He was disconcerted when the venue's famous revolving stage got stuck mid-way through the group's set. The Who, who had been touring since their triumph at Monterey, were a much tighter unit on stage, if just as volatile, and it was agreed that from now on they would close the shows.

SMALL FACES
TIN SOLDIER
b/w I FEEL MUCH BETTER
IMO62
IMMEDIATE

C23672
Columbia
SMALL FACES
TIN SOLDIER
I Feel Much Better
An IMMEDIATE Rec.

IMMEDIATE
IMF 503
SMALL FACES
TiN SOLDiER
I FEEL MUCH BETTER

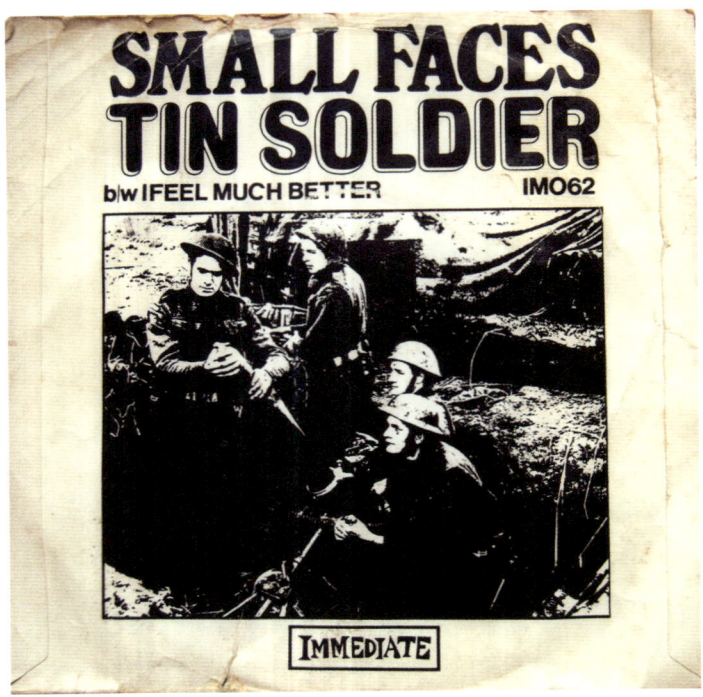

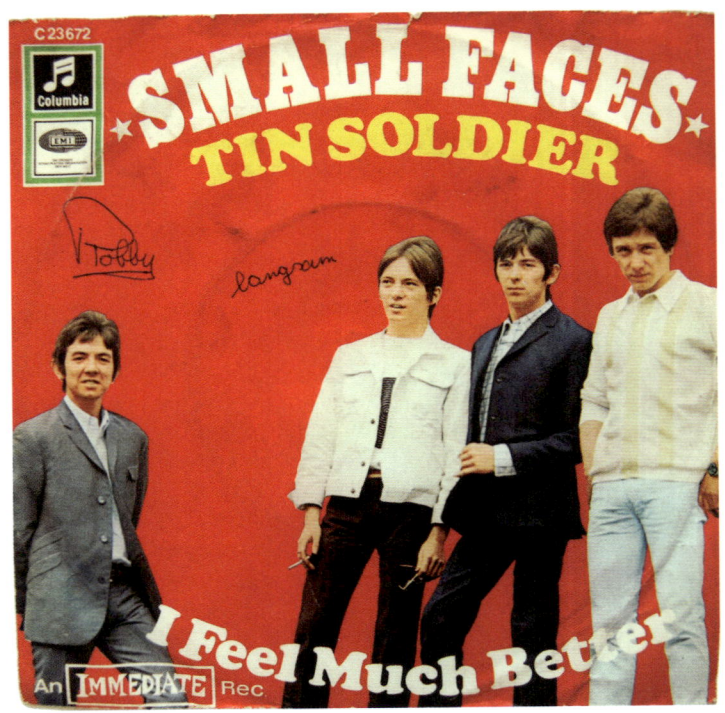

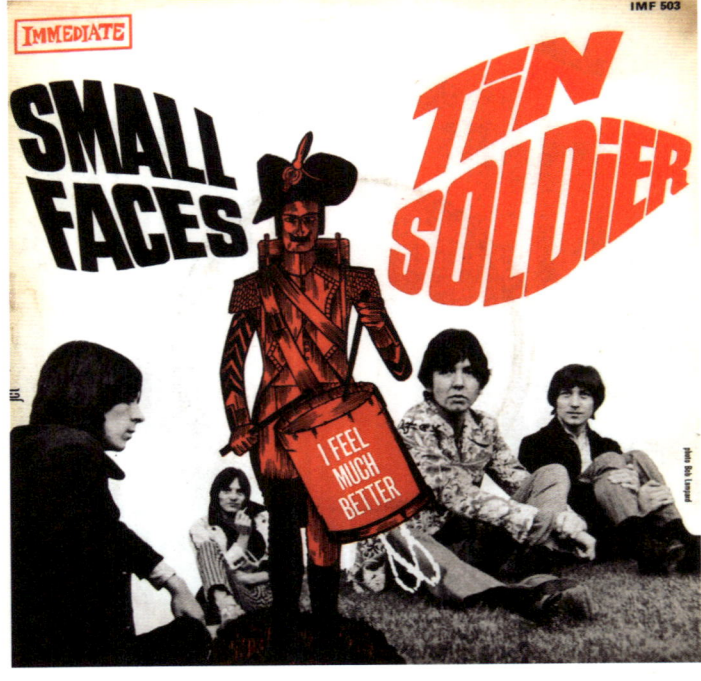

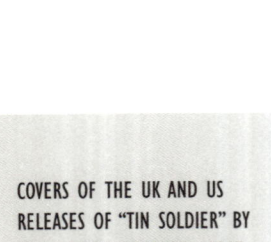

COVERS OF THE UK AND US RELEASES OF "TIN SOLDIER" BY SMALL FACES, DECEMBER 1967

THE NEXT THING THAT WENT OUT WAS THE TELLY

STEVE MARRIOTT

A conservative Australian press ridiculed both The Who and Small Faces in venomous newspaper attacks, particular offence taken at the "screaming of obscene four letter words on stage". Townshend had to be held back from punching one reporter who dubbed *The Big Show* "The Pig Show". One daily newspaper urged fans to boycott concerts, describing Small Faces as "weedy, bumptious, arrogant, sulking, sneering ambassadors for Britain", accusing them of inciting riots, adding "the 8,000 fans who had bought tickets at $3.60 (AUS) a head" were being ripped off by the "scruffiest bunch of pohms that ever milked money from this country's kids". The newspaper attacks, reminiscent of Rolling Stones' first visit there, amused Oldham, as he recovered from a two-day stay in a Melbourne hospital. He had had an altercation with a security guard, who had stopped him going backstage and questioned his status. When Oldham announced he was about to show the crowd the "greatest lighting show Melbourne had ever seen", the guard said "no you're not", and knocked him out.

On an internal flight to Sydney, via Melbourne, before transferring to a connecting flight to New Zealand, the entire touring entourage were greeted off the flight by an armed squad of police. The captain of the plane had radioed ahead complaining of "beer swilling" and abuse. Although the air stewardess who had made these complaints later admitted to exaggerating her story (and was sacked) the incident set a precedent for a week of madness in New Zealand, typified by the party organised by Harry Miller and EMI (who distributed Immediate down under) for Steve Marriott's twenty-first birthday in Wellington. Presented with a portable record player and a stack of records, Marriott (stoned and drunk) threw another of his tantrums:

> I still remember the track, "Baby Don't Do It", a Marvin Gaye track that Stevie Wonder did a great version of. Then the record player started to feed back on itself. So I bunged it out of the window and off the balcony, it was a mad moment. It was the highest building in Wellington, one of the high-rise hotels. So Wiggy (a roadie for the The Who) ran down, brought it back up, all in bits and throws it off again. Well, it was the wrong thing to do in front of Keith Moon, because the next thing that went out was the telly, armchairs, the whole lot went out of the window, the whole room. It wasn't sort of the hip thing to do then, it was just mad. It was dumb because the groups didn't do that then. I don't think anyone had done it. There was an audience watching us down below, so we thought 'What can we do?' So I said, I know, let's ring up and say someone's got in our room and destroyed it, say they've nicked a couple of guitars to give the story a bit of credibility. Because we thought, 'fucking hell, we can't own up to this'. So we rang down and the police and management came up and incredibly we got away with it. Then EMI presented me with a proper stereo and the hotel spent all day putting new French windows and doors on this suite and new furniture gets put in.
>
> Come the evening, Keith came up again and he said: 'They've done a good job haven't they?' Then dosh! He's done it again, put another chair through the French window, he's going, 'yes yes yes,' bunging things out and smashing things. The whole room was fucking wrecked again. Now we can't get away with it and it also makes us look like right liars from the time before. The management are banging the door; Keith looked at him and said: 'I fucking did it!' So they brought in the police but we got them pissed. Instead of doing their job and keeping us under control they ended up going mad, drinking all the brandy. We were all wearing their big white helmets, dancing about. Well, they brought in the army after that. They had these geezers outside each one of our doors in short trousers with bolt loaders like fucking big Lee Enfield muskets. You would open the door and they would go, 'get back in there', at gunpoint and that's a fact. So New Zealand was glad to see the back of us as well.

It cost Immediate a small fortune not only to compensate for hotel damages but also to stop any further action being taken by New Zealand authorities (Oldham ended up losing around £10,000 on the tour). But nothing could be done to stop Marriott's increasingly temperamental behaviour, and he walked off stage again in Auckland, screaming "this fucking piano's out of tune". He was also becoming hostile toward the rest of the group, particularly his songwriting partner Ronnie Lane. At the time, Lane was said to be on Marriott's back over his predilection for handing out their songs to other Immediate artists when he felt they could be better used for the band. Tony Calder remembers: "Steve says to me: 'I'm not going on with that arsehole [Ronnie Lane] again. I'm not having that cunt nick my money anymore. He's never written a fucking song, he's a fucking arsehole, he treats me like a piece of shit, and I'm not finishing this fucking tour.'" Later, in a more sober mood, Marriott would explain:

> To be honest me and Ronnie didn't write an awful lot together. We wrote apart, just like McCartney and Lennon, Jagger and Richards: they didn't write together they just heaped it together. "Renee the Docker's Delight" is probably the one me and Ronnie laughed at the most and a thing called "Happy Town Toy Days" on Ogden's Nut Gone Flake LP, we wrote that together and "Itchycoo Park". Maybe them three sums me and Ronnie up. We actually wrote those together. I wrote "Tin Soldier", "Lazy Sunday", "All Or Nothing", stuff like that. Ronnie wrote the more obscure stuff, really good songs, great songs. I tended to write the hits as it were.

The touring party flew back to London with leaders in Australian newspapers baying good riddance: "Both bands are unwashed, foul-smelling booze-swilling no-hopers and we don't want them back again!" Pete Townshend made a pledge never to return down under and—despite massive financial incentives over the years—has kept his word.

Oldham had turned 24 in Australia. It was a cold January in London when they had all set off and, despite the chaos of the tour, he'd enjoyed the sunshine break in Australia, topping up his tan and running water-skiing classes at every opportunity. The Who drummer Keith Moon's idea of a joke had been to cut the rope as soon as the boat skipper announced there may be crocodiles in area. Moon and Oldham together were a recipe for madness and in their rich, flower power gear, they'd give over-the-top Nazi-style addresses and salutes from hotel balconies as the booze, sun, drugs and sea went to their heads.

Back feeling comfortable with himself, Oldham attempted to exert some control over business at Immediate. The bills on Small Faces' eagerly-anticipated album had been allowed to pile up and it was long overdue. The six-week countryside retreat had given way to almost six months of on and off recording at Olympic studios. Now boats were being hired to ferry the group up and down the Thames for lyric writing sessions in an effort to get the album completed. Of the material Oldham had heard, he particularly rated a track Small Faces were not considering including on the album, with Marriott branding it just 'a joke'. Oldham urged Marriott to reconsider, reminding him of how many number one records had been thought of as a joke by their recorders. "Blatant commercialism often scares the act", he told me, just as Rolling Stones had initially regarded "Satisfaction" as a "bit of a gimmick". Small Faces decided to listen to their manager, worked a little more on finishing the track, adding toward the finish—as a tribute to

Oldham's belief that the song was a national anthem—a take off of the "Satisfaction" riff. Acetates were sent out to radio DJs to gauge response. It was suggested that the track was missing something so Oldham added bells from the Square in Barnes, where Marriott lived, and other atmospherics. Four weeks later "Lazy Sunday" was at number two in the UK, Steve Marriott's yell of "Fuck the neighbours" managing to sneak by radio censors. For many "Lazy Sunday" was the perfect marriage of hallucinogenics and the musical vaudevillian roots of working class England, creating one of the greatest tracks ever recorded in the 1960s.

Immediate adverts for the single, placed prominently on the front page of NME, featured a violent confrontation between students and police. The image was a snapshot of the recent Left Bank Riots in Paris, when 10,000 students took the streets to march against university conditions in an explosion of grenades, street-fires, tear gas guns, water cannons, paving stones and firecrackers.

NME writer Keith Altham was up at Immediate again for a Small Faces interview to promote "Lazy Sunday" and an exclusive preview of the Small Faces album in progress. He noted Oldham lounged along his black leather sofa looking magnificent, "like some eastern potentate, in a black and gold embroidered silk robe". "Beautiful blue crystal goblets were produced and filled with sparkling liquid" and, Altham wrote:

> For half an hour they bombarded my senses with sounds from the completed side of their next album—and what an album it is. I am sworn to secrecy about the format but can tell you that they have come up with a fantastic narrator to link the tracks and every track I heard was brimful of good fun, excitement and happy music.

The band's keyboard player, Ian McLagan, told Altham about "Lazy Sunday:

> When we first cut the record everyone thought it was a laugh, Steve started singing it in the studio and began to laugh at the song. Then we all began laughing at it. It was really quite a straight song to begin with until Steve began chucking in 'rinky dinky doos' for a giggle. When we finished it we all thought it was very funny but had no intention of releasing it. None of us wanted to release this record at first. Humour is such a strange thing. You never know whether other people will see it the same way and we felt "Tin Soldier" was much more the kind of thing we wanted to do. It was really the enthusiasm of people like Andrew and Michael d'Abo which won us round and we began to think, well maybe everyone else will see it as a giggle too.

"Lazy Sunday" made number one in Holland, Singapore, New Zealand and Switzerland (where "Tin Soldier" was also at number nine). It was number two in Germany and breaking in Italy. On their first live dates since Australia, Small Faces toured Italy, Scandinavia and Germany, where a series of concerts broke all previously established attendance records. In the UK, praise for the single came from every quarter. Daily Express said "I don't think Immediate has released a bad disc" and Daily Mail reckoned: "Small Faces, once the rowdiest beat group, have matured since their association with Immediate into one of the most creative groups in Britain today."

Immediate's Head of Promotions, Ken Mewis, was handed the job of delivering "Lazy Sunday" to the US where, after the massive sales of "Itchycoo Park", "Tin Soldier" had sold a disappointing 35,000 copies. He reported back that CBS were not convinced of the potential of "Lazy Sunday" and was unsure when or if it would be released, especially as he group were still prevaricating over touring the country. This drove Oldham and Calder in to a frenzy. Oldham recounts in his legal defense:

> After the first six months of our relationship with CBS, not only were Tony Calder, myself and our then general manager Ken Mewis having problems keeping CBS to their promises regarding advertising, promotion, time-buys etc. We were becoming increasingly suspect of their word and version of exactly what was happening to our product in the US. As there was no way of checking their reports of activity, efforts, response to product via reviews and radio stations, we only had their word to go on. Unfortunately, it had been impossible to maintain the outside promotion men we had hired independently to promote "Itchycoo Park" by Small Faces [at a cost of £5,000]. It was a matter of sheer economics, the cost of maintaining these people who CBS thought unnecessary and would not consider making any contributions to their fees; in fact they considered the hiring of them as an insult to their company. Thus, after "Itchycoo Park" we had only the word of CBS's personnel handling Immediate regarding activity.

Ken Mewis recounts:

> I was in a meeting in New York at CBS with [president] Clive Davis who was talking about the launch of "Lazy Sunday" and the new Small Faces album, when we were interrupted by an urgent telex from London: 'Ken go to Bloomingdales and get me two tubes of Braggi Bronzer, message end. ALO.'

The failure to translate the European success of "Lazy Sunday" in to major US sales was a major setback, but the disappointment was buried beneath the unveiling of the much-anticipated Small Faces album, Ogden's Nut Gone Flake, in the UK. Keith Altham wrote in NME that apart from being encased in the first circular sleeve he had ever seen, the album was a landmark for the group: "A storm-braining elctrilode of the highest Tudeimagns as their narrator on side two, Stanley Unwin might put it and almost certain to put the group in the same smash album selling bracket as Beach Boys, Rolling Stones and Jimi Hendrix." It was a gloriously conceived and executed conceptual album that fused Small Faces at their most organic and playful. "Lazy Sunday" had been a fine taster but tracks such as "Afterglow", "Song Of A Baker", and "Rollin' Over" showed the band developing a far more contemporary, heavier, warmer rock sound.

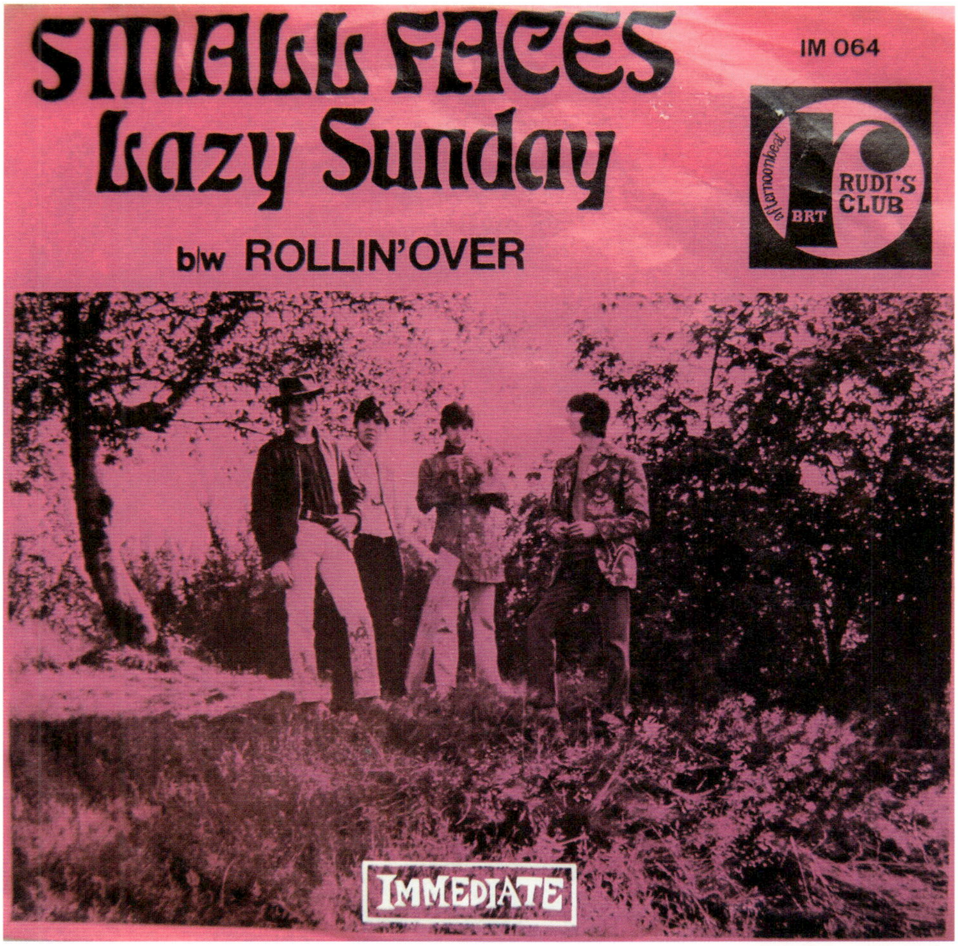
SMALL FACES
Lazy Sunday
IM 064
b/w ROLLIN'OVER
RUDI'S CLUB
BRT
IMMEDIATE

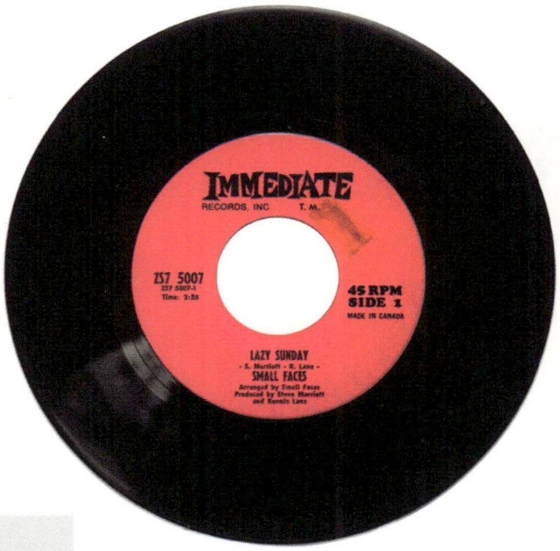
IMMEDIATE
RECORDS, INC T.M.
ZS7 5007
Time: 2:55
45 RPM
SIDE 1
MADE IN CANADA
LAZY SUNDAY
- S. Marriott - R. Lane -
SMALL FACES
Arranged by Small Faces
Produced by Steve Marriott
and Ronnie Lane

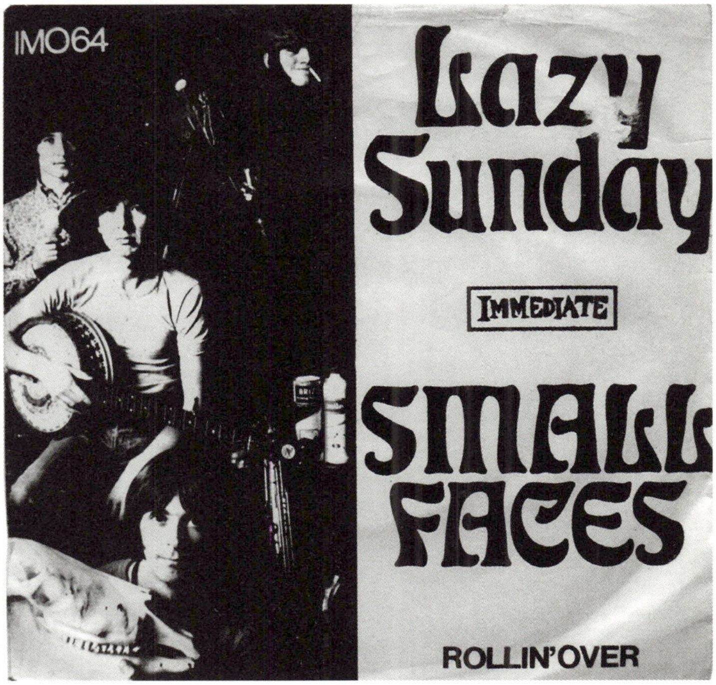
IMO64
Lazy Sunday
IMMEDIATE
SMALL FACES
ROLLIN'OVER

"LAZY SUNDAY" BY SMALL FACES. "WHEN WE FINISHED IT WE ALL THOUGHT IT WAS VERY FUNNY BUT HAD NO INTENTION OF RELEASING IT" SAID IAN MCLAGAN, APRIL 1968

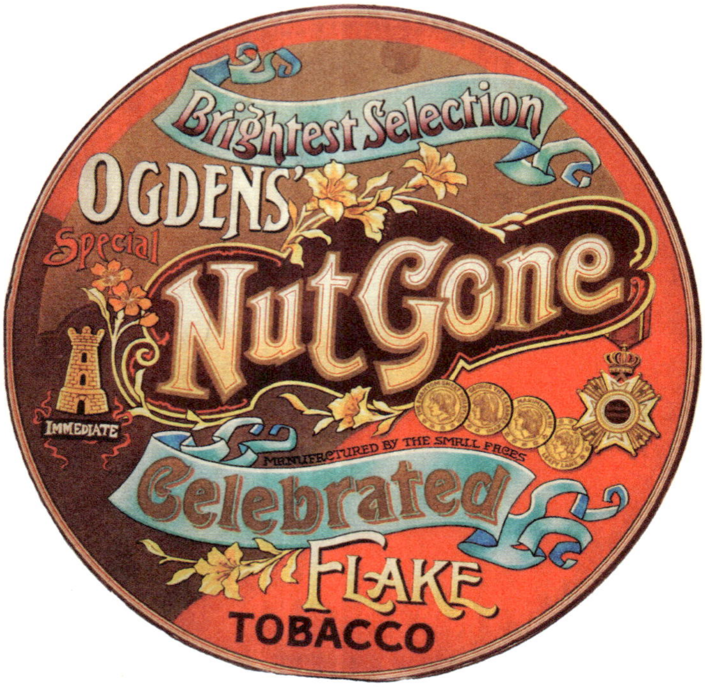
Brightest Selection
OGDENS'
Special
Nut Gone
IMMEDIATE
MANUFACTURED BY THE SMALL FACES
Celebrated
FLAKE
TOBACCO

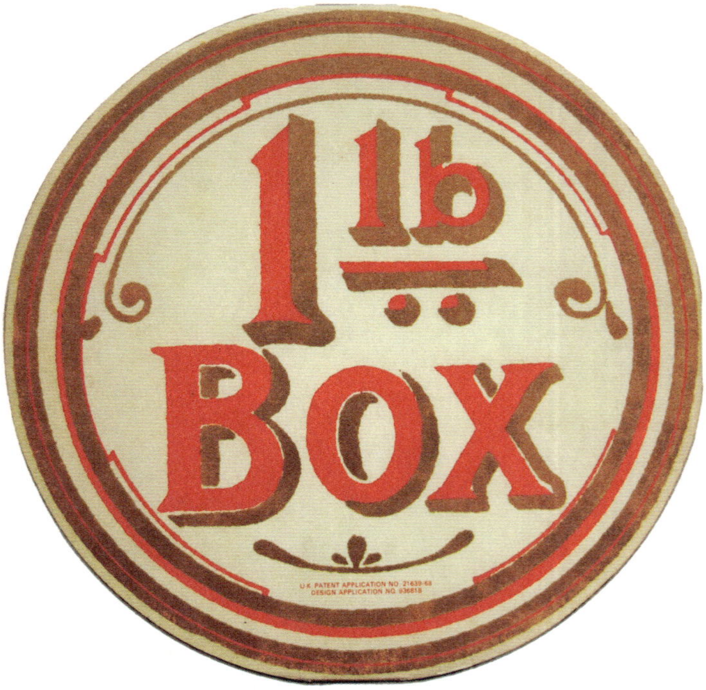
1 lb
BOX

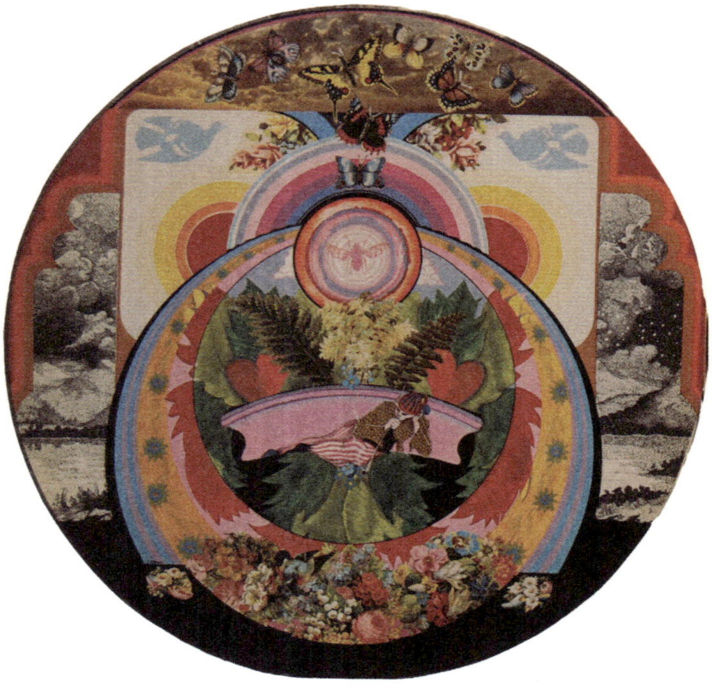

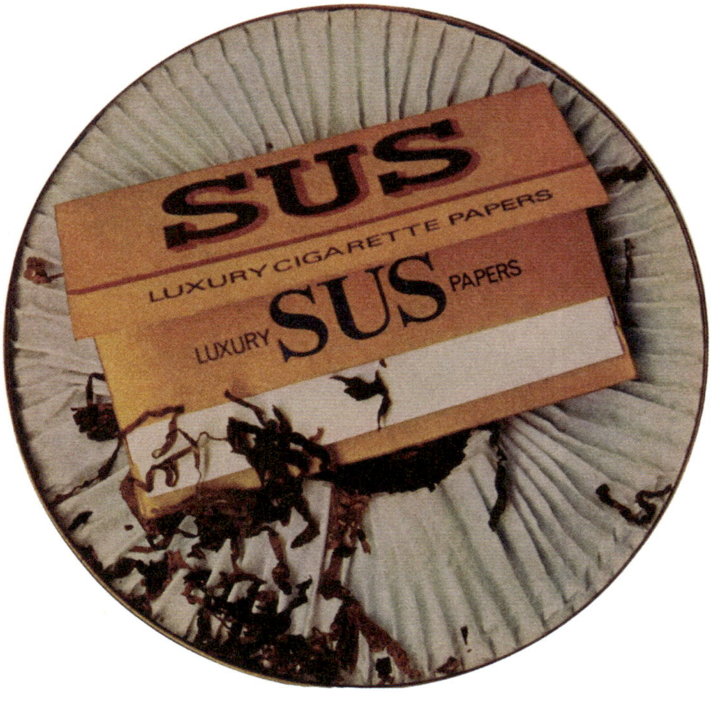
SUS
LUXURY CIGARETTE PAPERS
LUXURY SUS PAPERS

THE INNARDS OF CRITICALLY ACCLAIMED SMALL FACES ALBUM *OGDEN'S NUT GONE FLAKE*, JUNE 1968

The concept came in the second half of the album—it being the story of fictional character, Happiness Stan, searching for the other half of the moon. Here the band's love of strong arm instrumentals and their skill with quirky, child-like, almost nursery rhyme, lighter touches (including songs such as "Happy Day Toys Town"), plus actor Stanley Unwin's narration linking the tracks, showed that Small Faces were in a unique headspace.

The packaging of the album was a huge triumph, it came in a round tobacco-style tin, with a multilayered sleeve ingeniously unfolding to reveal pictures of king size 'rolling papers' and blurry Mankowitz shots of the group. The album's title and the package was mischievously adapted from a popular branding of rolling tobacco, Ogden's Nut Brown Flake.

The sleeve idea was concocted by Immediate one night in Bremen, Germany, after Small Faces had appeared on television show *The Beat Club*. Gaining authorisation from different tobacco companies was a problem but the outrageous packaging really sold the album. Immediate promoted *Ogden's Nut Gone Flake* with an advert parodying the Lord's Prayer that proved further good publicity, with certain vicars and members of Parliament up in arms about the Bible's word being abused for 'pop' promotion. The label issued a flip statement: "There has been a lot of comment about it. But we didn't write it. We borrowed it from God. We merely changed the words a bit."

> Small Faces
> Which were in the studios
> Hallowed be thy name
> They music come
> Thy songs be sung
> On this album as they came from your heads
> We give you this day our daily bread
> Give us thy album in a round cover
> As we give thee 37/9d
> Lead us into the record stores
> And deliver us Ogden's Nut Gone Flake
> For nice is the music, the sleeve and the story
> For ever and ever

A more sedate Immediate advert told: "*Ogden's Nut Gone Flake* manufactured by Small Faces. Cool, clean satisfying. Firmly packed. Luxury strength. In the unique round packet."

The glowing reviews, advertising and excitement over the package, in addition to this being the band's first album for over a year, meant *Ogden's Nut Gone Flake*, on the first day of release in the UK, sold 20,000 copies and the LP smashed into the charts at number nine. Seven days later it was at number one and stayed there for six weeks. *Ogden's Nut Gone Flake* stayed in the Top 10 for 19 weeks in total, going on to break the 100,000 mark in the UK to become Immediate's biggest album to date. In Europe *Ogden's Nut Gone Flake* sold 110,000 copies in Germany alone. In a year that saw the release of Rolling Stones' *Beggars Banquet*, The Beatles *White Album* and Jimi Hendrix's *Electric Ladyland*, *Ogden's Nut Gone Flake* would be voted "the album of the year" by *NME* with many other critics concurring. Steve Marriott recounts:

> We cleaned up every award in the book for it and Oldham collected them. We caught him on the stairs of Immediate's office, his arms full of bits of plastic—Best Artwork, Best Design, Best Album.

Pete Townshend remembers:

> *Ogden's Nut Gone Flake* was a world-shaking record. When they first played it to me the only material I had heard to which it could be compared to were concept pieces, like Pet Sounds or *Sergeant Pepper*. I was jealous of Small Faces' sound, they were becoming a real extraordinary sonic force to be reckoned with.

"It made us laugh", Marriott said in *Melody Maker* of *Ogden's Nut Gone Flake*, and continued:

> Anything that made us laugh we liked. God knows how it worked but it did and I'm very proud of it, and the other Small Faces are too. It was worth the year's work. We didn't know a thing about the Lord's Prayer advert until we saw it in the music papers and frankly we got the horrors at first. We realised that it could be taken as a serious knock against religion but on thinking it over, we didn't feel it was particularly good or bad it was just another form of advertising.

Small Faces' drummer, Kenny Jones, told *NME*:

> Really this album is just the beginning of things. Before we were with Immediate our albums used to turn out like sausages. They had stuck us against the nearest brick wall and take a photo for the cover. We never really could work up much pride into what we were putting in it with that kind of system. We are getting better lyrics together and better ideas. On stage we use six brass players: trumpets, saxophone and trombones. When we go in to the studio now we don't have to worry about wasting half an hour and we recorded some of the tracks on *Ogden's [Nut Gone Flake]* perhaps ten times.

Glowing with refreshed optimism, Immediate delivered *Ogden's Nut Gone Flake* to CBS at the US label's annual record convention in Puerto Rico. They showed a short film, narrated by John Peel, talking up the album, a success in every major market outside Japan and US (although in Japan a massive campaign had just been launched). Also showcased on film were PP Arnold's track, "Angel Of The Morning", a new The Nice single, an adaptation of Leonard Bernstein's "America" from *West Side Story*, and a newly signed Immediate act Duncan Browne; "a composer/arranger/singer about to enter the area of music creativity shared by such talent as Bob Dylan, Paul Simon, Jim Webb". The footage of The Nice performing live at the Marquee club, a PP Arnold video for "Angel Of The Morning" and a BBC2 documentary about Small Faces and the making of *Ogden's Nut Gone Flake*, was well received.

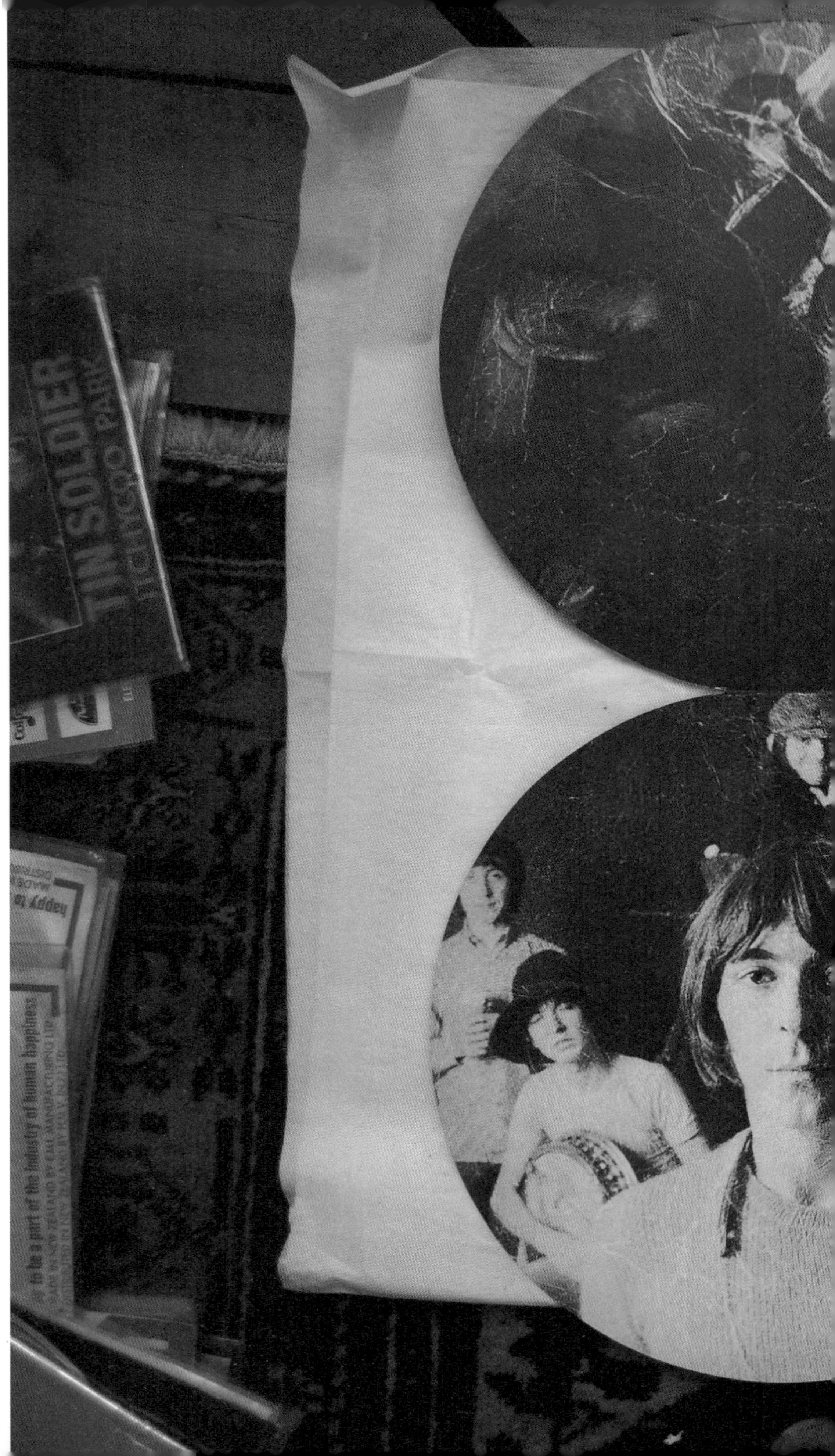
TIN SOLDIER
ITCHYCOO PARK
to be a part of the industry of human happiness

OGDEN'S NUT GONE FLAKE
PULLOUTS FEATURING EACH MEMBER OF SMALL FACES ON A CIRCULAR DISC, JUNE 1968

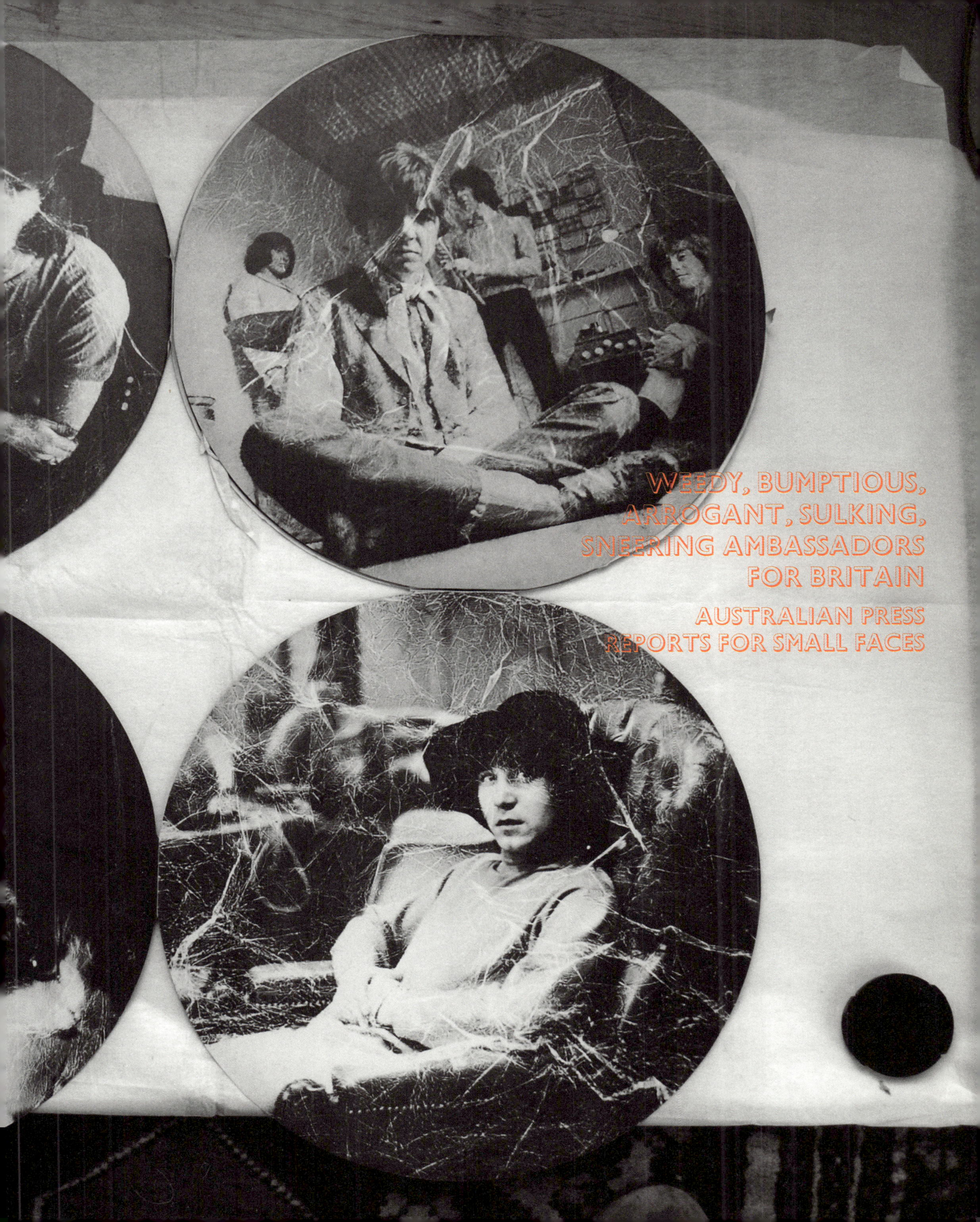

WEEDY, BUMPTIOUS, ARROGANT, SULKING, SNEERING AMBASSADORS FOR BRITAIN

AUSTRALIAN PRESS REPORTS FOR SMALL FACES

The Greatest Story Ever Told

The Old Testament

I   In the beginning God created the heaven and the earth

II   And the earth was without form and void, and darkness was upon the face of the deep

III   And God said, Let there be light: and there was light

IV   And God saw the light: and it was good: and God divided the light from the darkness: And the evening and the morning were the first day

V   On the second day God made the firmament and called the firmament Heaven: and saw that it was good

VI   And God called the dry land Earth and the waters called He Seas: and the land brought forth grass after its own kind: and the evening and the morning were the third day

VII   And God called forth light to rule over the day and darkness to rule over the night and the evening and the morning was the fourth day

VIII   And God created fowl that may fly and every living creature that moved: and God saw that it was good: and the evening and the morning were the fifth day

IX   So God created man in his own image: and male and female created He them: and God saw everything He had made and behold it was good: and the evening and the morning were the sixth day

X   And God rested on the seventh day and saw that this was a good place to create a record industry: and saw that it was alright

XI   And from then the record industry rested

The New Testament

I   And it came to pass that the record industry begat a little bastard called Immediate and Andrew Loog Oldham and Tony Calder were Immediate: amidst all the shepherds and their sheep

II   In the land at that time rested a great hatred for independents and many died as they were begat: but Immediate made their first record Number One and caused bigger companies to listen

III   And Immediate went straightway into the charts with the records that followed and once again begat a Number One with 'Out Of Time' Chris Farlowe: so it came to pass that the music of Immediate spread across the lands and seas as did the label: and Immediate saw that it was good

IV   Then did Immediate lead Immediate Artistes into the Continent for 40 days and 40 nights to appear on television and before the multitudes that gathered thereof to hear of the little illigit. indie that was getting bigger

V   And there were many who heard the songs of P. P. Arnold, Chris Farlowe, Small Faces and The Nice for Immediate created miracles in the eyes of the disbelievers and all who heard marvelled at the success

VI   Now, with a label that crossed the world and 'Itchycoo Park' in their charts, the time came to walk across the water to America, the land of milk and money so that people who dwelt therein could hear of what had come to pass

VII   And the people heard 'Itchycoo Park' at least, but there came a great silence from America to Immediate Records

VIII   And in all the lands of the world except the promised land of milk and money did 'Lazy Sunday' rise higher and sell more than any record that went before: and it came to be written in every chart that was written

IX   The America heard: Immediate rose from the quiet with 'Ogdens' Nut Gone Flake' and sitteth on the right hand of the record industry: and from that day forth everyone knew of Immediate

HERE ENDETH THE FIRST LESSON

Certain content herein has been adapted with very special permission and no intent to offend.

LEFT: IMMEDIATE'S BIOGRAPHY DIVIDED INTO OLD AND NEW TESTAMENTS, CIRCA 1968

RIGHT: DUNCAN BROWNE, LEFT, WITH LYRICIST DAVID BRETTON, 1968

The presentation concluded: "In ending this our first Epistle to the American, Immediate looks forward to CBS Records repeating the success in the States that the Immediate label has scored with every Immediate artist throughout the rest of the world." There was also an Immediate biography handed out, based on *The Bible* and split into the New and Old Testaments. Before flying on to the Bahamas and Antigua in the Immediate-hired Lear Jet, Calder and Oldham spoke briefly from the rostrum, presenting their US sales and marketing manager Bruce Hilton, on his retirement, with a gold disc for his work with Herman's Hermits.

Soon after, Ron Alexenburg, Immediate's new promotion manager at CBS, redesigned the award-winning *Ogden's Nut Gone Flake* package, and pulled the song "Mad John" off the album as a single. "We agreed to this", said Oldham, "although we felt that were the track strong enough we would have released it as a single in the UK. The result—another flop." "Mad John" not only failed to get the airplay CBS promised, but it received no advertising of any importance. *Ogden's Nut Gone Flake*, Europe's biggest selling and most critically acclaimed album of 1968, suffered the same fate—no advertising, no airplay—and only managed to shift a pathetic 25,326 copies in the US, plus a further 5,000 on import, with many retailers finding it easier to get hold of the original UK version than the CBS pressing. The reverberations of this failure to capitalise on the European success of *Ogden's Nut Gone Flake* in the US market shook not just the confidence of all at Immediate in CBS's handling of the product, but also the band's belief in themselves.

Steve Marriott, who saw many of his contemporaries gaining rich reward in the US, hastily delivered a new Small Faces single he felt would be more in tune with the long-haired, folk-tinged, heavy-rock scene dominating the US. At home, in his mansion set in fives acres of leafy Buckinghamshire, he recorded "The Universal". He was sat in the garden when he recorded a strum-along on a tape cassette. This version, despite several attempts at Olympic, could not be bettered in the studio, where only a gentle trombone and clarinet hook could be suitably added to his garden guitar and vocal. It meant the sound of his dogs barking, and his wife Jenny greeting him as she came back from shopping, stayed on the recording. "Recorded in 30 minutes", Marriott boasted of the single:

> The dog was barking because my roadie had just turned up to go to a gig. What I done was; I got up, had a boiled egg in the garden, I had my 12 string and I was writing this song and I thought this sounds good I'll slap it down on my tape recorder. We tried to do it in the studio but it didn't work. Because obviously the way I sung it, it was right off the fucking cuff and when I come to do it in the studio you've got red lights, microphones and it's not the same. So we kept the cassette version and dubbed on the trombone and all we kept was my voice and 12 string and all the noises that went with it, the cars and the dog. It's a great song.

However, "The Universal" peaked at a lowly number 16 in the UK charts and, worse, it was not even considered fit for release in the US. Marriott took it hard. "When it wasn't a hit in a big way it was considered a mistake and it killed me", he said. "I didn't write again for a long while. The disenchantment that comes, even from the rest of the guys, when things ain't a hit, is a crippler. I just went apart in the head."

Marriott proved unwilling to take the hit album *Ogden's Nut Gone Flake* on the road in Europe and the few UK live shows the group had done to support "The Universal" were disappointing affairs. Even if they could get working visas for the US, the band were in no fit state to endure the long months touring now required to break the country. Marriott's nut really had gone flake. He told the press:

> Pop audiences have changed. Once it was screaming all the time when we were on stage. There's nothing we like better than a crowd of kids rioting, punching bouncers, pulling down walls and hitting each other. Kids come now and expect to sit and hear the sounds on our records, and of course they don't. We can't do it on stage. We've been doing college gigs in Britain and the audience here are all so way above it. They only like you because you happen to be 'in' at the moment—they don't understand what the hell it's all about. It's sad. Bring Back Violence!

> **RONNIE LANE'S NEVER WRITTEN A FUCKING SONG, HE'S A FUCKING ARSEHOLE, HE TREATS ME LIKE A PIECE OF SHIT AND I'M NOT FINISHING THIS FUCKING TOUR**
> — STEVE MARRIOTT

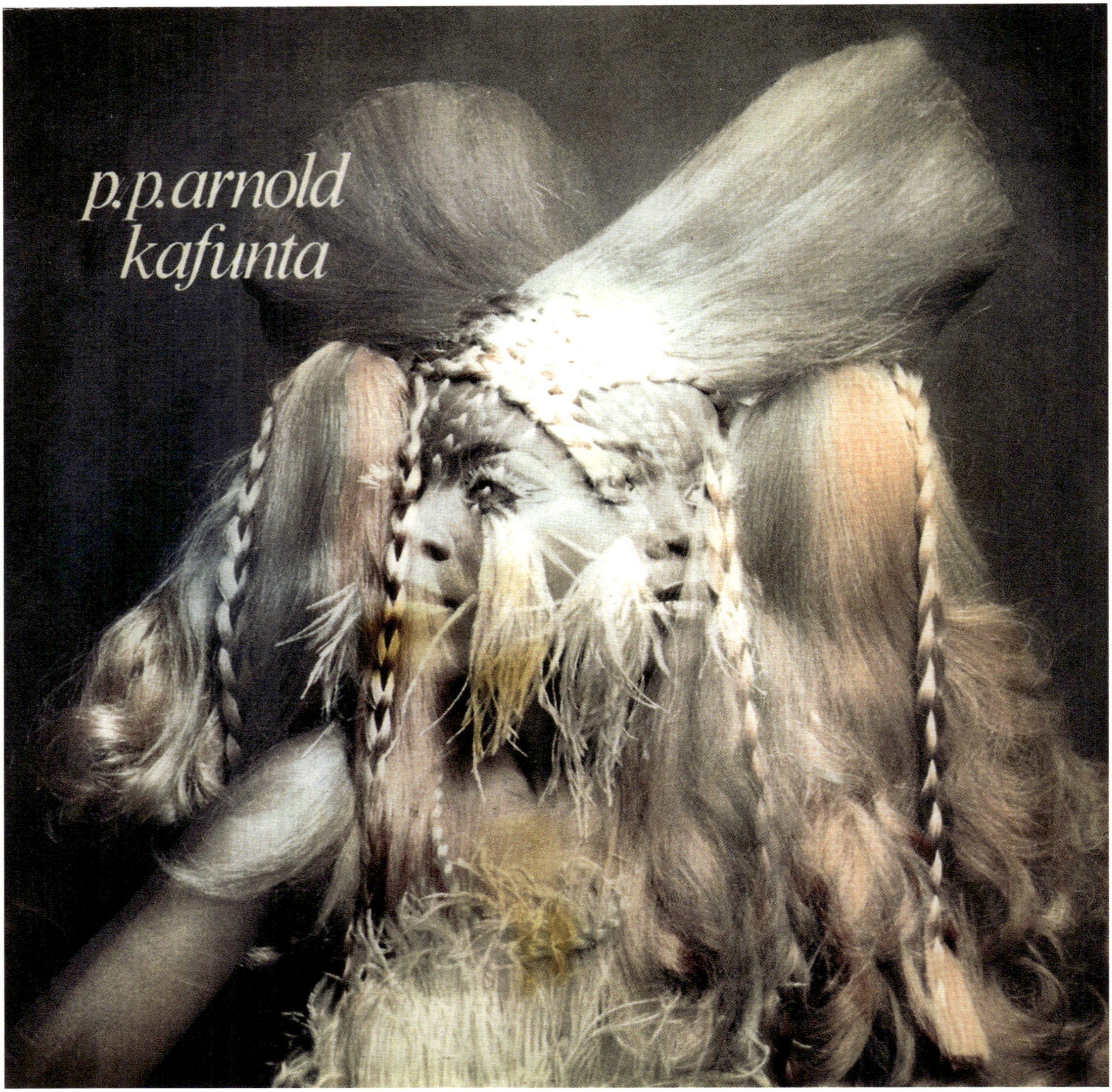
p.p.arnold
kafunta

To the casual observer all at Immediate seemed golden still, basking in the afterglow of *Ogden's Nut Gone Flake*'s European success, with a fine array of young songwriters on board. The Nice were beginning to make a name for themselves and there was promise of great things to come from PP Arnold and Chris Farlowe. For Calder and Oldham the label's abject failure in the US was reaching a critical stage and they couldn't hide the fact much longer.

After the success of "First Cut Is The Deepest", which had sold approximately 40,000 in the UK to go Top 20, PP Arnold had been working in Europe consistently. Her UK follow-up "The Times Has Come", sold a respectable 20,000 on the continent. Now she was breaking out again with a song Marriott and Lane wrote and produced for her. "If You Think You're Groovy". The b-side of the single was a track from the Immediate vaults, "Though It Hurts Me Badly", which she had written herself and was produced by Mick Jagger. With the soul epic "If You Think You're Groovy" climbing the UK charts, Arnold was eager to promote it, and herself, in the US. CBS said not to bother, they had been unable to rouse any interest in the single nor her debut Immediate album, *The First Lady Of Immediate*. Beautifully packaged, the album was compiled from recordings made in 1967, with Mike Hurst or Mick Jagger producing. Oldham had contributed a more recent, monumental production of Spector/ Mann/Weill's epic "Born To Be Together" and promised Arnold he would be taking a more hands on approach with her career in the future, telling her he was going to make her a cross between Ronnie Spector and Aretha Franklin. Oldham more than lived up to that promise, producing a scintillatingly sentimental version of "Angel Of The Morning"; Small Faces' solid backing of past outings replaced by fragile but immaculate, understated orchestration. The track was arranged by John Paul Jones and written by Chip Taylor, who had also written "Wild Thing". It was another huge hit in the UK, staying on the charts for 11 weeks. The single did get a US release but sold no more than 800 to 1,000 copies and received no promotional push aside from "bulk product adverts".

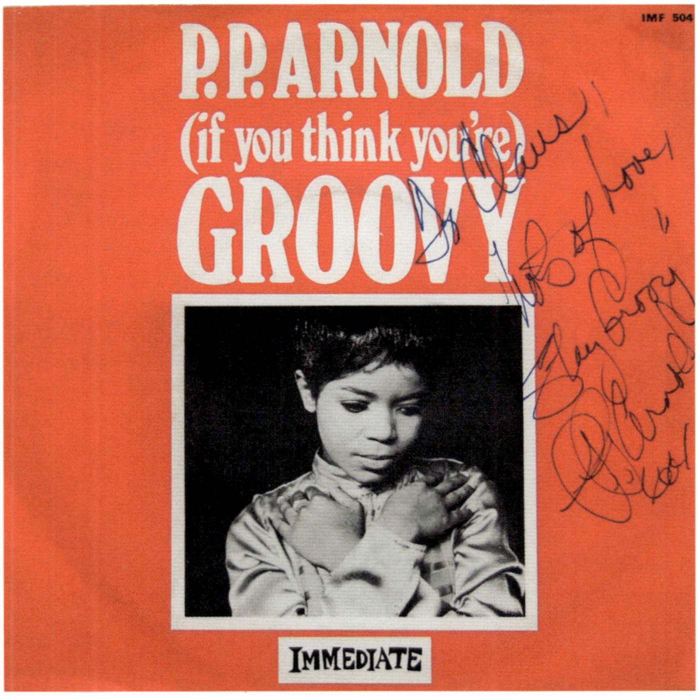
IMF 504
P.P. ARNOLD
(if you think you're)
GROOVY
IMMEDIATE

At Olympic studios, recording a new PP Arnold album, Oldham had stood in front of her like a conductor, dragging the words out of her and really bringing out her performance. She would go over the songs bar by bar until Oldham was completely happy and *Kafunta* was complete. Tracks on the album fell into four linked parts: Kafunta One ("God Only Knows", "Yesterday", "Eleanor Rigby" and "Angel Of The Morning"), Kafunta Two ("As Tears Go By") Kafunta Three ("To Love Somebody") and Kafunta Four ("Welcome Home"). Oldham also rerecorded her on a far superior performance of "The First Cut Is The Deepest" for a forthcoming single. "Kafunta is Swahili for Soul", Oldham told *NME* as Immediate's packaging of the album came in for special praise, "worth buying for the cover alone" wrote *NME* of a Gered Mankowitz shot of Arnold with her hair styled to look like a red Indian headdress.

OPPOSITE: *KAFUNTA* BY PP ARNOLD, JANUARY 1970

"IF YOU THINK YOU'RE GROOVY" BY PP ARNOLD, JANUARY 1968

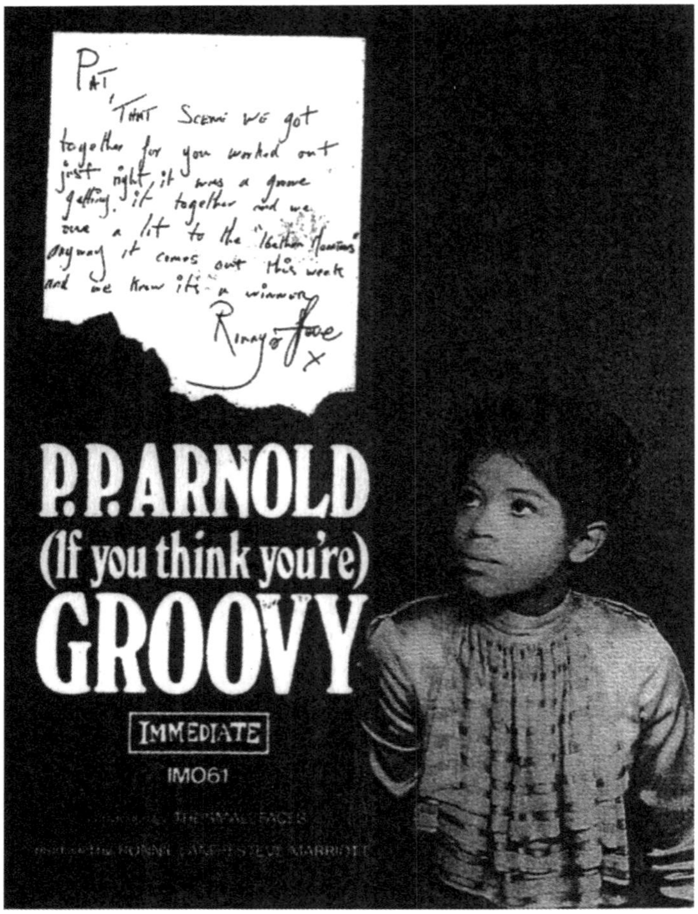
P.P. ARNOLD
(If you think you're)
GROOVY
IMMEDIATE
IMO61

PROMOTION FOR "IF YOU THINK YOU'RE GROOVY" BY PP ARNOLD, JANUARY 1968

OPPOSITE: TOP: "STEP OUT OF LINE" TWICE AS MUCH, AUGUST 1966

BOTTOM: CHRIS FARLOWE'S "DAWN", NOVEMBER 1968

However, when the word came back that CBS were refusing to release *Kafunta* in the US, the whole Arnold project deflated and Immediate bit the bullet and released her from her contract, allowing her a better shot at making it in the US. She quickly signed to Atlantic Records there and switched to Polydor in the UK. Her first single in the US on Atlantic was Oldham's version of "First Cut Is The Deepest", complete with full-page music press adverts. In *Cashbox* magazine, Arnold was named "West Coast Girl of the Week", describing "First Cut Is The Deepest" as "a near classic". In short, Atlantic made a big impact with Arnold on the US scene, something CBS had showed no interest in doing.

Twice As Much were also released from their Immediate contract after getting the thumbs down from CBS. Their debut single, "Sittin' on a Fence", had sold 55,000 copies in Europe and 35,000 in the US, via Allen Klein's short-lived deal with MGM. Their three subsequent singles, "Step Out Of Line", "True Story" and "Crystal Ball", had in total sold about 65,000 copies in Europe and the UK, but CBS hadn't considered any "right" for a US release. Twice as Much's final statement, *That's All* (a greatest hits package)—which included a version of Mann/Weill's classic "Coldest Night Of The Year", a duet with Oldham's early 1965 discovery, Vashti—proved a hit in Europe and sold 10,000 in the UK.

Another Immediate greatest hits album, *The Best Of Chris Farlowe*, hit the Top 20 but a recent single, "The Last Goodbye"—from the film of the same name and written and produced by Mike d'Abo—hadn't capitalised on the success he'd had with "Handbags and Gladrags", and Farlowe was another artist who was stiffing in the US.

CBS had released Farlowe's version of "Paint It Black" as a single, promising full advertising and promotion (which did not materialise) and sales were just 1,674. A US album, *Paint It Farlowe* (made up from cuts off the UK *Art Of Chris Farlowe* album), packaged at the request of CBS, sold a total of 1,596 copies. Despite having sold 21,417 copies in the UK, the US figures for "Handbags and Gladrags" suggested it had sold minus 1,187 copies. "An achievement unique in the recording business, ie selling a negative number of records", said Oldham. Farlowe had sold well over half a million singles and 100,000 albums in Europe and, like Arnold, was getting itchy feet over his failure to make inroads in to the US market. Several of his old UK 'blues' friends, such as Eric Clapton, were having huge success in the US. "I'm tired of banging my head against a brick wall", Farlowe told the press.

After the release of two more UK singles, the violin-drenched Oldham production of "Paint It Black" and "Dawn"—with his old backing band The Thunderbirds and produced by 'Staff'—Immediate released Farlowe from his contract. Like PP, he signed up to Polydor in the UK and to Atlantic Records in the US. "We had no alternative but to give Chris Farlowe a release from his contract worldwide", Oldham would later claim in a

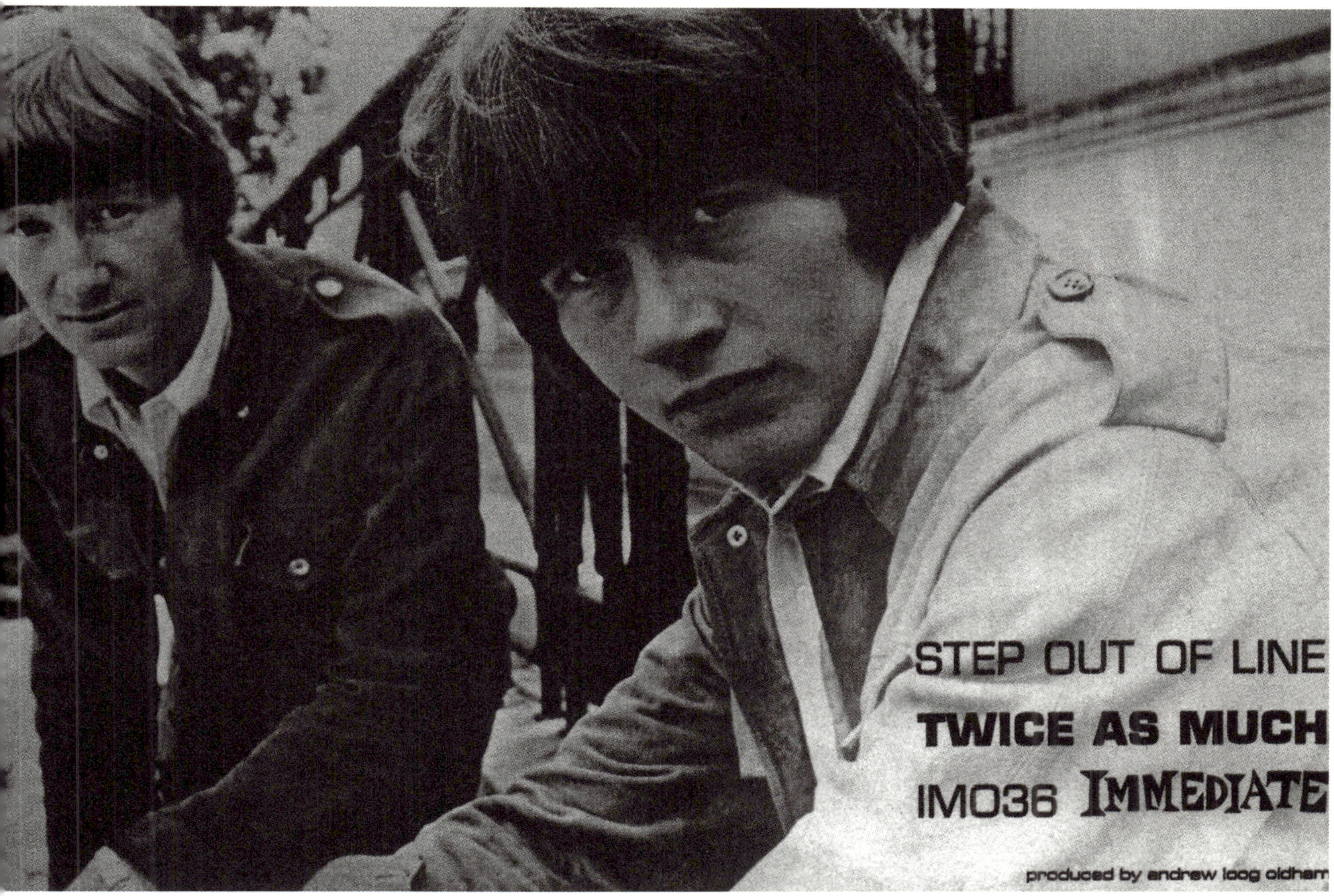
STEP OUT OF LINE
TWICE AS MUCH
IM036 IMMEDIATE
produced by andrew loog oldham

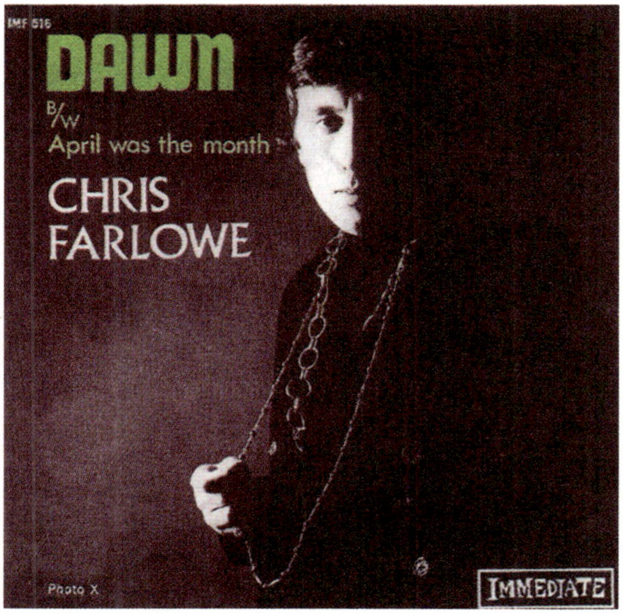
IMF 516
DAWN
B/W
April was the month
CHRIS
FARLOWE
Photo X
IMMEDIATE

court affidavit: "CBS' agreement and attitude allowed us no way possible to change Farlowe's label in the US to a company satisfactory to Farlowe's management/agency and thus allowing us to retain him through our usual channels outside of the US."

With three major artists gone, and gossip in the industry growing, Immediate needed, more than ever, for The Nice to continue on their upward trajectory. The group's debut Immediate LP, *The Thoughts Of Emerlist Davjack*, had followed the single of the same name and featured on the cover a great Gered Mankowitz shot of the group huddled together topless and wrapped up in cellophane though which you couldn't be quite sure if organ maestro, Keith Emerson, had his penis peeping out of his zip. The album deviated wildly—from organ-driven prog-rock to overblown takes on classical (Bach) and jazz (Dave Brubeck's "Blue Rhondo A La Turk"). It was considered a "mind shattering" album, by *Melody Maker*. The group were further buoyed by more good reviews applauding their mix of "free-form experimental pyschedelia with classically-influenced jazz art-rock". Radio DJs such as Radio 1's John Peel and a burgeoning underground press were giving them a big push.

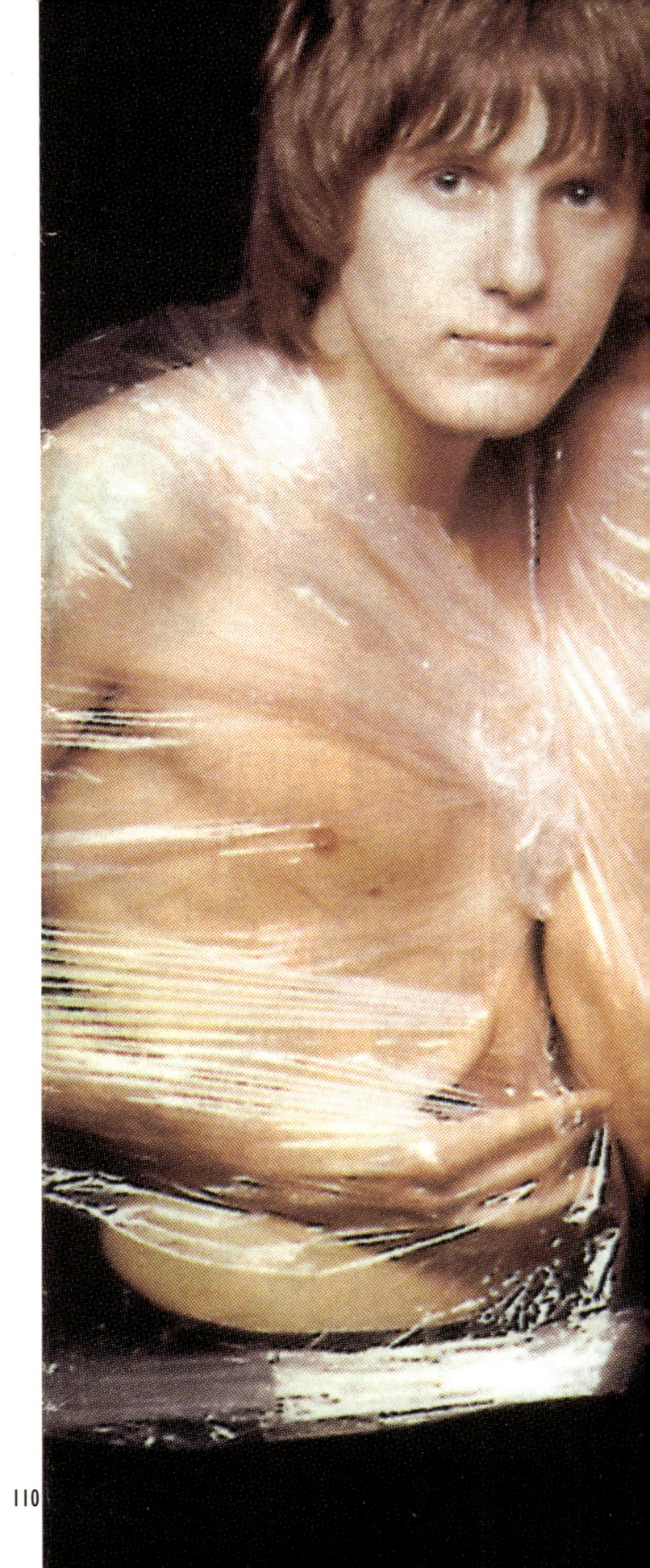

THE NICE, CIRCA 1968

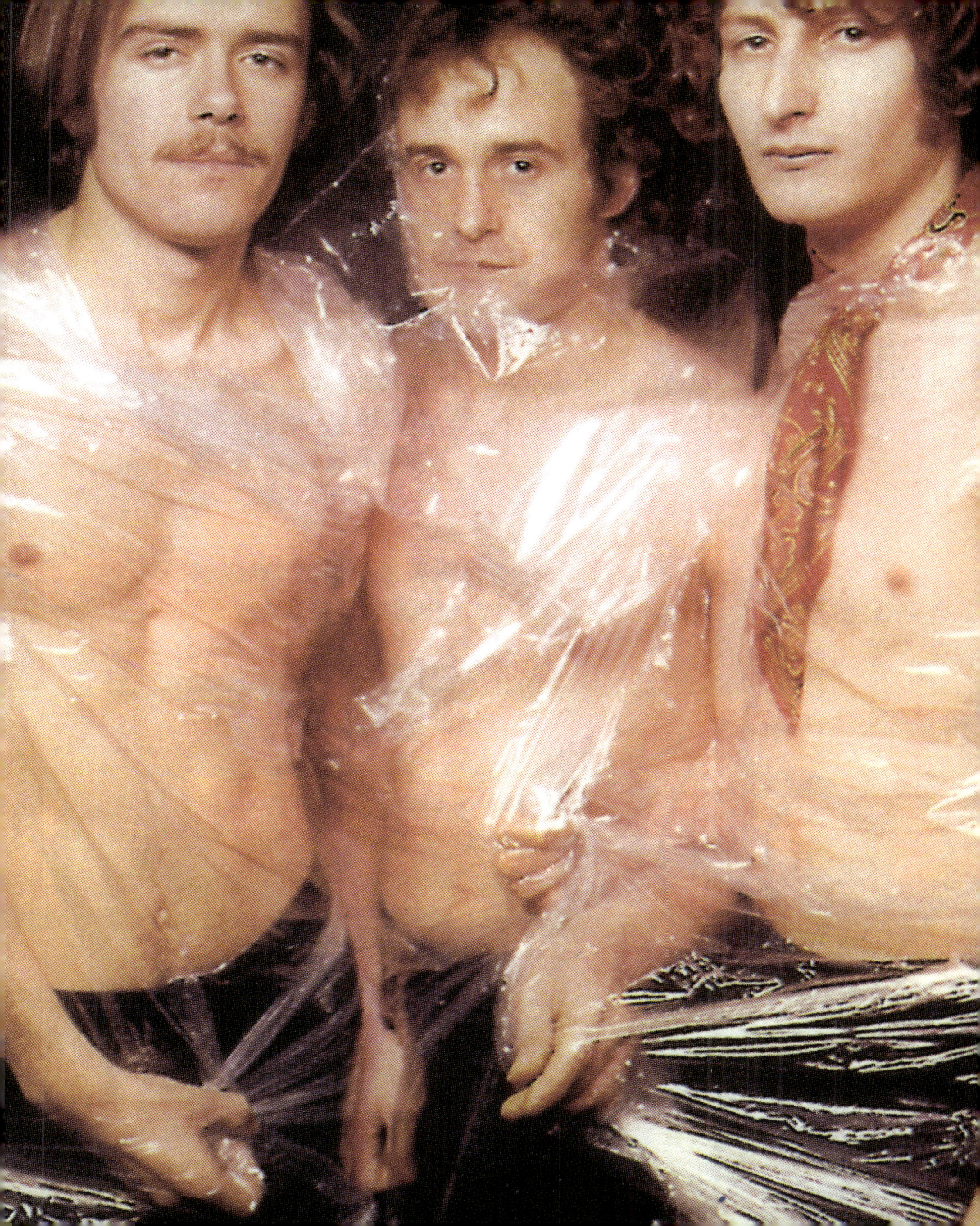

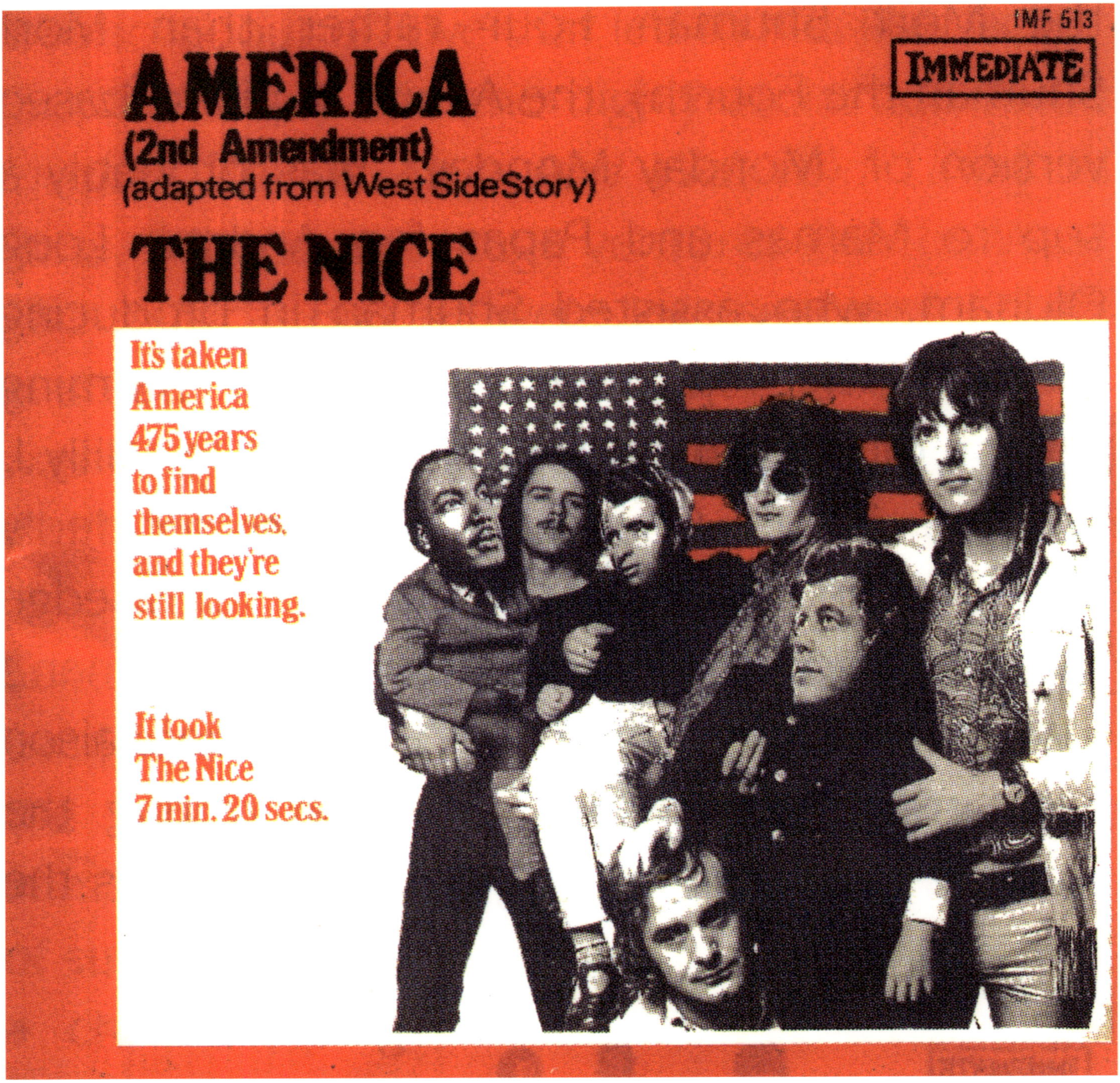
IMF 513
IMMEDIATE
AMERICA
(2nd Amendment)
(adapted from West Side Story)
THE NICE
It's taken
America
475 years
to find
themselves.
and they're
still looking.
It took
The Nice
7 min. 20 secs.

The Nice

The group had cemented their underground reputation with a headline grabbing performance at the Festival of Light show at Alexandra Palace, an event that also featured The Who and Pink Floyd. Live, The Nice had developed a stage show that never failed to impress, with organist Keith Emerson making a regular feature of attacking his keyboards with knives. Oldham who had had little to do with the group thus far, beyond naming them, decided to take a more hands on approach, cutting a crazed seven minute instrumental based on "America", the Bernstein/Sondheim written anthem from *West Side Story*. Production was again credited to the group, as Emerlist Davjack, but Oldham was heavily involved with it. Arnold's young daughter delivering the spoken climax: "America's Government with promise and anticipation is murdered by the hands of the inevitable."

The US was undergoing a period of huge cultural, political and social upheaval and Oldham was looking to make a considerable statement. The nation was still in shock over a second Kennedy assassination. Californian Senator Robert Kennedy, who was running for president and had frequently expressed support for an Israeli gunned down on the anniversary of the Arab-Israeli six day war. The Vietnam War was bloodier than ever with Viet Cong suicide squads besieging the US Embassy in Saigon and the US' largest air base in Da Nang. On the streets conflict between anti-Vietnam protestors and the police forced the National Guard into action. Martin Luther King had also recently been assassinated: shot dead on a hotel balcony in Memphis Tennessee. In the Watts district of LA 'racial violence' had erupted and 2,000 police had left three dead and 45 injured, evoking memories of the 1965 Watts Riots in which 34 lives were lost. "The two sides of America—it's violence and it's attempt at maintaining calm—are represented on "America"", was *NME*'s interpretation of The Nice's new single, under the headline, "American violence inspired The Nice".

The Immediate advert campaign, shot by Gered Mankowitz, featured three small boys wearing masks of the now three famous assassinated US heroes: John F Kennedy, his brother Bobby Kennedy and Martin Luther King. Each small boy sat on a knee of the group members, with a strapline that read, "It's taken America 475 years to find themselves, and they're still looking. It took The Nice seven minutes 20 seconds". The advert featured prominently on the *NME* cover, in many national newspapers and in an extensive poster campaign countrywide. It was broadly attacked for being distasteful, but Immediate remained unrepentant via press release:

> All forms of communication are an art form and those unable to respect others expression must condemn themselves. People throughout the world have felt the necessity to express their emotions and thoughts of American tragedies and each person must use the medium of expression that is within his ability. The posters that show everyone the end product of violence will continue to be displayed. The Nice are sincere in their compassion with Americans and will continue to express their emotions through any medium they choose.

OPPOSITE: THE NICE'S CONTROVERSIAL COVER FOR "AMERICA" FEATURING CHILDREN DRESSED AS JOHN F KENNEDY, BOBBY KENNEDY AND MARTIN LUTHER KING, JUNE 1968

THE NICE, CIRCA 1968

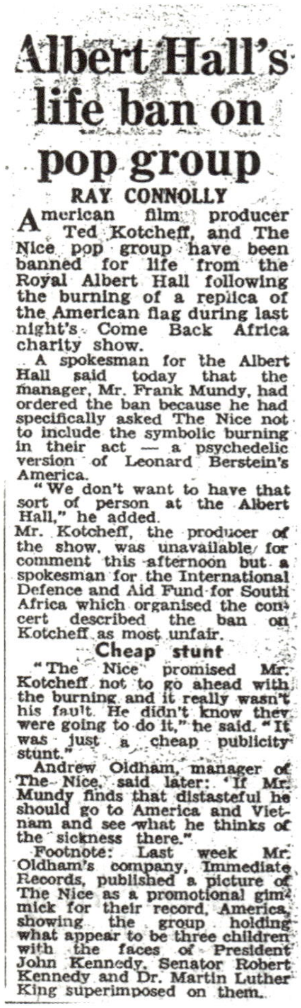

Albert Hall's life ban on pop group

RAY CONNOLLY

American film producer Ted Kotcheff, and The Nice pop group have been banned for life from the Royal Albert Hall following the burning of a replica of the American flag during last night's Come Back Africa charity show.

A spokesman for the Albert Hall said today that the manager, Mr. Frank Mundy, had ordered the ban because he had specifically asked The Nice not to include the symbolic burning in their act — a psychedelic version of Leonard Berstein's America.

"We don't want to have that sort of person at the Albert Hall," he added.

Mr. Kotcheff, the producer of the show, was unavailable for comment this afternoon but a spokesman for the International Defence and Aid Fund for South Africa which organised the concert described the ban on Kotcheff as most unfair.

Cheap stunt

"The Nice promised Mr. Kotcheff not to go ahead with the burning and it really wasn't his fault. He didn't know they were going to do it," he said. "It was just a cheap publicity stunt."

Andrew Oldham, manager of The Nice, said later: 'If Mr. Mundy finds that distasteful he should go to America and Vietnam and see what he thinks of the sickness there."

Footnote: Last week Mr. Oldham's company, Immediate Records, published a picture of The Nice as a promotional gimmick for their record, America, showing the group holding what appear to be three children with the faces of President John Kennedy, Senator Robert Kennedy and Dr. Martin Luther King superimposed on them.

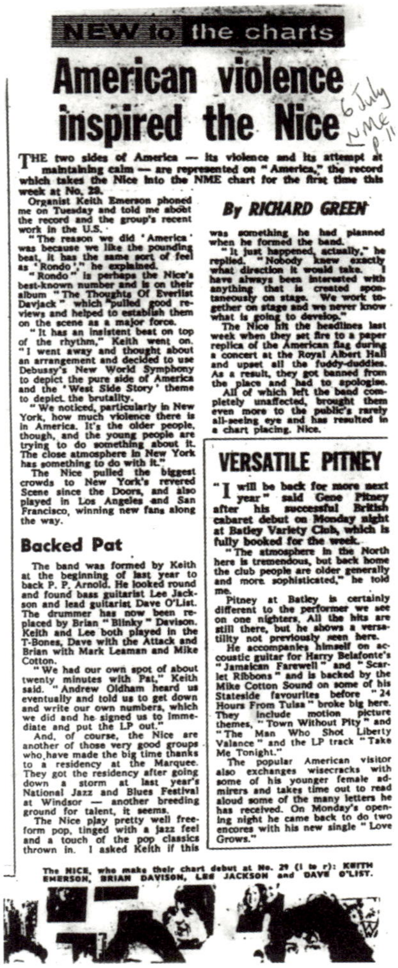

NEW to the charts

American violence inspired the Nice

6 July NME p 11

THE two sides of America — its violence and its attempt at maintaining calm — are represented on "America," the record which takes the Nice into the NME chart for the first time this week at No. 29.

By RICHARD GREEN

Organist Keith Emerson phoned me on Tuesday and told me about the record and the group's recent work in the U.S.

"The reason we did 'America' was because we like the pounding beat, it has the same sort of feel as 'Rondo'," he explained.

"Rondo" is perhaps the Nice's best-known number and is on their album "The Thoughts Of Everlist Davjack" which pulled good reviews and helped to establish them on the scene as a major force.

"It has an insistent beat on top of the rhythm," Keith went on. "I went away and thought about an arrangement and decided to use Debussy's New World Symphony to depict the pure side of America and the 'West Side Story' theme to depict the brutality.

"We noticed, particularly in New York, how much violence there is in America. It's the older people, though, and the young people are trying to do something about it. The close atmosphere in New York has something to do with it."

The Nice pulled the biggest crowds to New York's revered Scene since the Doors, and also played in Los Angeles and San Francisco, winning new fans along the way.

Backed Pat

The band was formed by Keith at the beginning of last year to back P. P. Arnold. He looked round and found bass guitarist Lee Jackson and lead guitarist Dave O'List. The drummer has now been replaced by Brian "Blinky" Davison. Keith and Lee both played in the T-Bones, Dave with the Attack and Brian with Mark Leaman and Mike Cotton.

"We had our own spot of about twenty minutes with Pat," Keith said. "Andrew Oldham heard us eventually and told us to get down and write our own numbers, which we did and he signed us to Immediate and put the LP out."

And, of course, the Nice are another of those very good groups who have made the big time thanks to a residency at the Marquee. They got the residency after going down a storm at last year's National Jazz and Blues Festival at Windsor — another breeding ground for talent, it seems.

The Nice play pretty well free-form pop, tinged with a jazz feel and a touch of the pop classics thrown in. I asked Keith if this was something he had planned when he formed the band.

"It just happened, actually," he replied. "Nobody knew exactly what direction it would take. I have always been interested with anything that is created spontaneously on stage. We work together on stage and we never know what is going to develop."

The Nice hit the headlines last week when they set fire to a paper replica of the American flag during a concert at the Royal Albert Hall and upset all the fuddy-duddies. As a result, they got banned from the place and had to apologise.

All of which left the band completely unaffected, brought them even more to the public's rarely all-seeing eye and has resulted in a chart placing. Nice.

VERSATILE PITNEY

"I will be back for more next year" said Gene Pitney after his successful British cabaret debut on Monday night at Batley Variety Club, which is fully booked for the week.

"The atmosphere in the North here is tremendous, but back home the club people are older generally and more sophisticated," he told me.

Pitney at Batley is certainly different to the performer we see on one nighters. All the hits are still there, but he shows a versatility not previously seen here.

He accompanies himself on acoustic guitar for Harry Belafonte's "Jamaican Farewell" and "Scarlet Ribbons" and is backed by the Mike Cotton Sound on some of his Stateside favourites before "24 Hours From Tulsa" broke big here. They include motion picture themes, "Town Without Pity" and "The Man Who Shot Liberty Valance" and the LP track "Take Me Tonight."

The popular American visitor also exchanges wisecracks with some of his younger female admirers and takes time out to read aloud some of the many letters he has received. On Monday's opening night he came back to do two encores with his new single "Love Grows."

The NICE, who make their chart debut at No. 29 (l to r): KEITH EMERSON, BRIAN DAVISON, LEE JACKSON and DAVE O'LIST.

The single became the longest ever to make the Top 20, and stayed on the UK charts for 16 weeks, defying all the normal rules of promotion and airplay. But Tony Stratton-Smith, The Nice's manager, was not happy. He was demanding "a written undertaking that in future no more of the controversial posters will be distributed", claiming that the group's bookings and even record sales were suffering as a result of the poster's adverse affects on the public. He told the press: "The Nice feels that if the posters are issued in America, they will do considerable harm. The group has been offered a US college and television tour in September and we have no wish to create ill will from the outset."

The controversy surrounding the group grew more inflamed when Oldham persuaded The Nice to burn US army draft cards at a gig at the Marquee club in London and then a large US flag at a charity concert at the Royal Albert Hall in aid of the International Defence and Aid Fund for South Africa, an event part-organised by Sean Kenny. The US flag burning stunt went through the roof, with coverage across the tabloids. Frank Mundy, manager of the Royal Albert Hall, was reported as saying he had specifically asked The Nice not to include any symbolic burning in their act during his "Come Back Africa" production. A spokesman for the International defence and Aid Fund for South Africa said: "I didn't know they were going to do it. It was just a cheap publicity stunt." Oldham responded in the press by saying: "If Mr Mundy finds that distasteful he should go to the US and Vietnam and see what he thinks of the sickness there." Afterwards Emerson said in the papers that he was forced into burning the flag. Stratton-Smith told the press: "The Nice are the last group to need this sort of publicity. The boys don't like it and perhaps Immediate will wake up to the fact that they are something more than a stunt group." Tony Stratton-Smith later recalled:

> Oldham's Immediate was brilliant. They had a marvellous A&R policy. They developed some great artists. We had the absurd situation where Oldham appointed his personal barber as a general manager. This poor chap was paid to sit there listening to managers' gripes and say he would look into it. But I learned a lot of good things creatively from Immediate. With respect to Andrew I don't think he really had any faith in The Nice. I think he totally underestimated what they were about. That's why they brought me in.

THE CONTROVERSY SURROUNDING THE GROUP GREW MORE INFLAMED WHEN OLDHAM PERSUADED THE NICE TO BURN A US FLAG AT THE ROYAL ALBERT HALL

SIMON SPENCE

"THE TWO SIDES OF AMERICA—IT'S VIOLENCE AND IT'S ATTEMPT AT MAINTAINING CALM—ARE REPRESENTED ON "AMERICA"" *NME*'S INTERPRETATION OF THE NICE'S "AMERICA", CIRCA 1968

OPPOSITE: THE NICE, 1968

Oldham's handling of the "America" single had elevated the group to new levels of notoriety, but Stratton-Smith's constant moaning had drained much of the fun from the process. For the cover of *Ars Longa Vita Brevis* (Latin for Art Lives Long and Life is Short), The Nice's second Immediate album, which was to feature an x-ray of the group with harmless coloured dyes in their veins, Oldham wanted to substitute the dye for a slow working poison. Although Oldham lost interest, Immediate worked hard to promote *Ars Longa Vita Brevis*. It featured a 19-minute translation of Bach's "Brandenburg Concerto" and the minor hit single, the lyrically punky and musically punchy, "Brandenburger".

The group benefited from a BBC2 documentary devoted to them (Immediate had reputedly bought off the same guy who made the Small Faces' BBC2 documentary) and an avalanche of praise from the UK media. *Melody Maker* wrote: "A major breakthrough in pop group experimentation. The Nice are swathed in great majesty, improvisation and discovery." Elsewhere Keith Emerson was being hailed as the "Jimi Hendrix of the Hammond Organ".

Nik Cohn wrote in *Queen* magazine: "Keith Emerson is the best pop organist in the country, and one of the best in the world." Both *Record Mirror* and *NME* named The Nice as the world's second-best instrumental group of 1968 and Emerson won the Keyboard Player of the Year award from *Beat Instrumentalist* magazine. US reviews for the album were even more effusive, calling The Nice the "most significant British group since The Beatles". US shows in San Francisco, LA and New York, further enhanced their status. At the Scene Club in New York they beat previous entrance records that had been set by The Doors. But when it came to turning that goodwill and grassroots support into record sales in the US, CBS were less responsive than expected. Lee Jackson, the group's bassist and lyricist, said:

CBS got it into their heads that they would trail release the single, "America", and they picked of all places Miami, Florida. Now why on earth release a thing like that there in a millionaire's playground, I can't imagine. In fact Andrew was completely amazed: 'What the fuck... Why Miami?' It sold quite well, it did about 25,000 in Miami. I think it just got moved slightly on the underground stations in New York.

Both of The Nice's album were released in the US but neither sold in any significant numbers. After the CBS knock backs with PP Arnold, Chris Farlowe and Twice As Much, the failure of The Nice to make any serious dents in the US market (especially with all the praise heaped on the group's shoulders), was hard to take.

A final episode in this seemingly endless struggle with their US distributors pushed Oldham over the edge. Duncan Browne was a 21-year-old singer songwriter newly signed to Immediate, one specifically tailored toward the US market. Oldham produced Browne's album, *Give Me Take You*, "A very good and poetic LP with a pervading air of melancholy", wrote John Peel in a *Record Mirror* review. Initially the LP seemed to work, with CBS

NEW SINGLE
RELEASED JULY 12th

DUNCAN BROWNE

On The Bombsite

from the album "Give Me Take You" IMSP 018

B/W

ALFRED BELL

IM070

IMMEDIATE

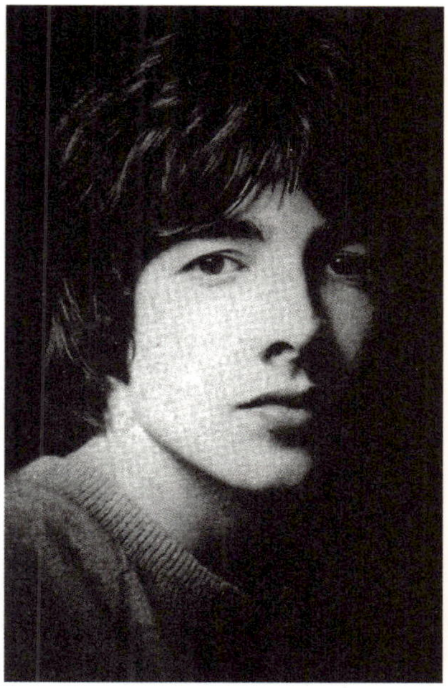

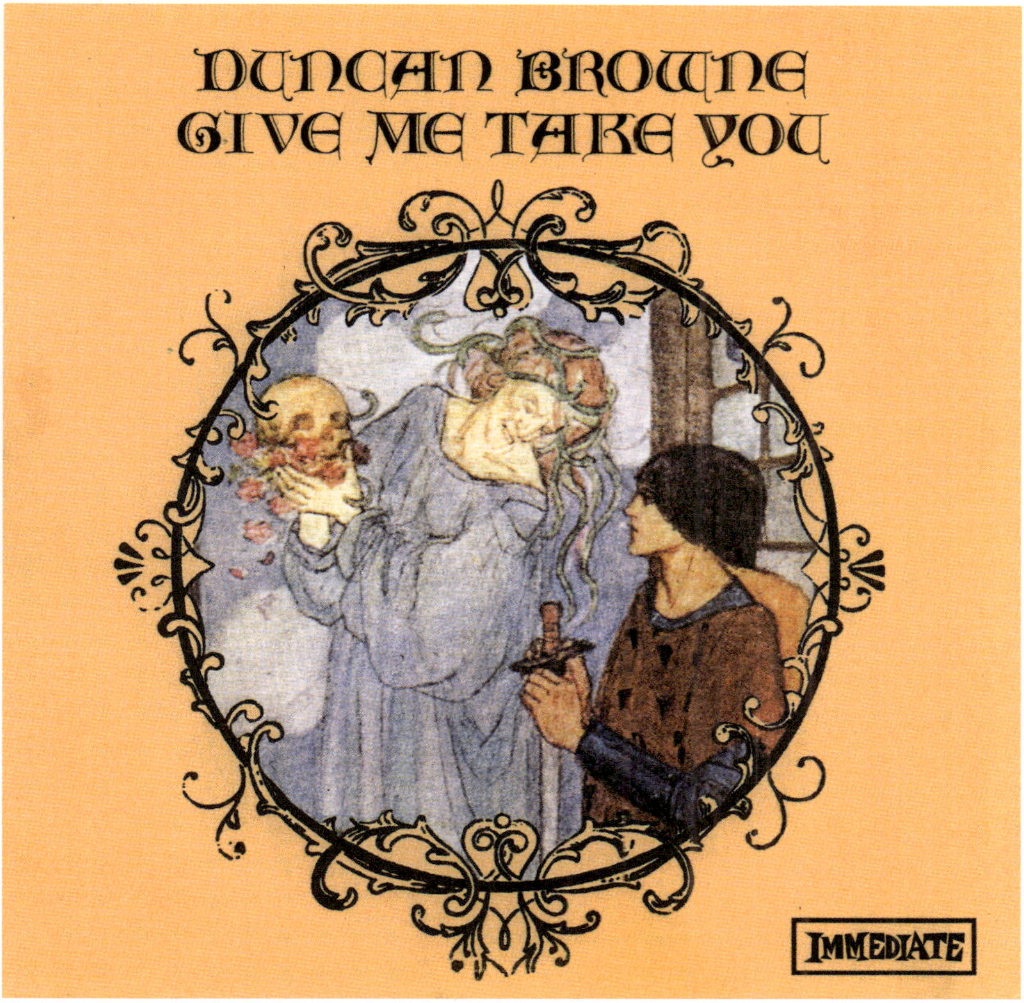
DUNCAN BROWNE
GIVE ME TAKE YOU
IMMEDIATE

THE NICE'S MUSIC WAS A MAJOR BREAKTHROUGH IN POP GROUP EXPERIMENTATION

MELODY MAKER

comparing Browne to their own acts Bob Dylan, Paul Simon and Leonard Cohen. However the label failed to follow though with any real support and a single from the album "On The Bombsite" sold 38 copies in the US; the album not doing much better, (selling 985 copies). This terrible showing in the US brought a swift end to Browne's contract at Immediate. Oldham had geared Browne for the US market but if CBS weren't playing ball, forget it—and fuck them. Maybe in the past he would have used his charm and contacts to bring CBS onside. Now the disappointment just festered as he sought refuge in more of Dr Mac's sleep treatment and electric shock therapy or simply by ingesting colossal amounts of drugs and booze.

OPPOSITE: "ON THE BOMBSITE" ADVERTISING, 1968

DUNCAN BROWNE AND HIS ALBUM *GIVE ME TAKE YOU*, JULY 1968

TONY AND THE HAMBURGERS

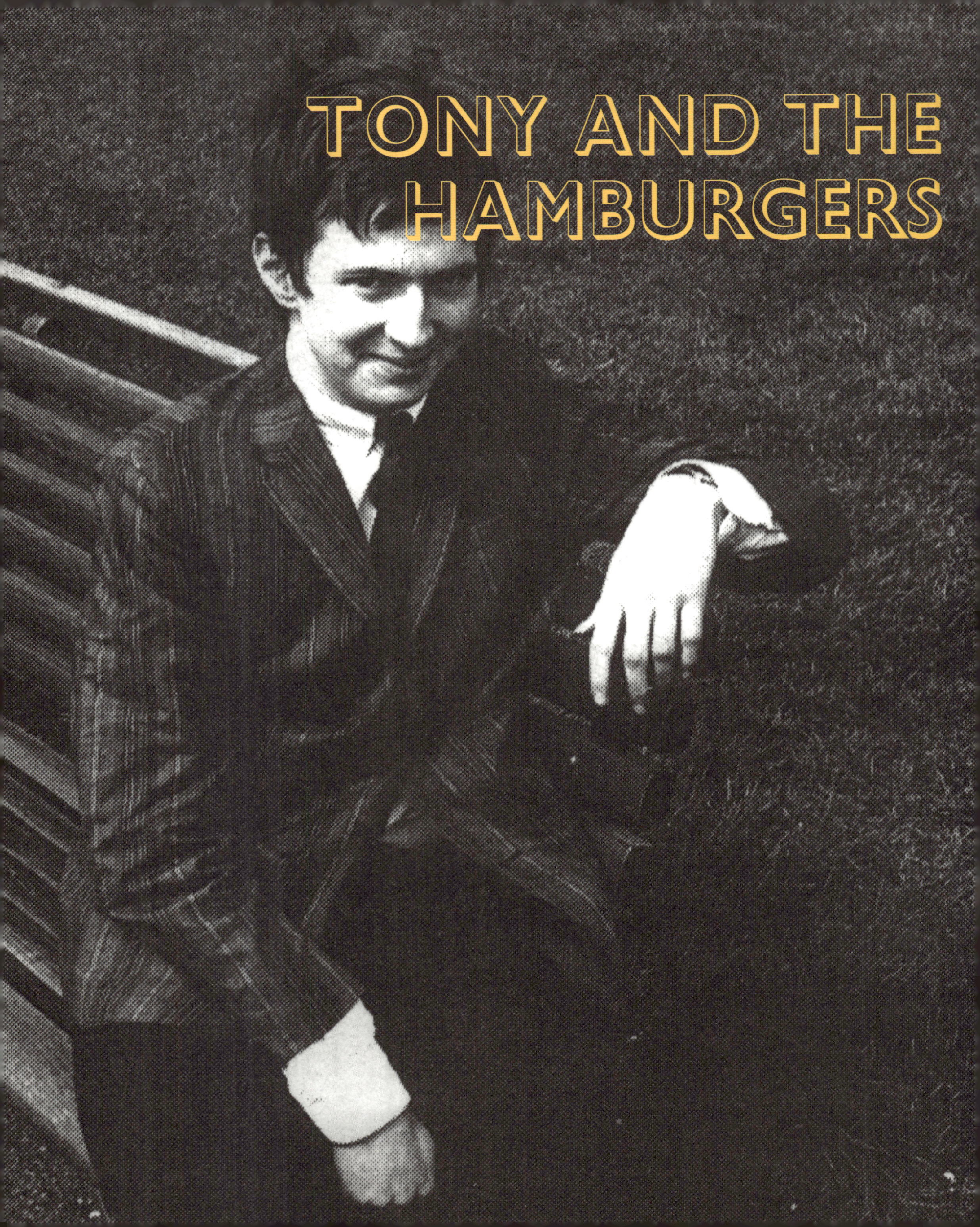

While Oldham licked his wounds, Tony Calder was left to come up with his own solutions on to how best bolster Immediate's reputation in the UK. With PP Arnold, Chris Farlowe and Twice As Much gone, rumours were now circulating in the music business that the Small Faces were breaking up. Oldham had made no secret of his dislike for the post-psychedelic wave of "scuzzy blues" groups making hay in the US—the homegrown Crosby, Stills and Nash, Janis Joplin, Grateful Dead, Jefferson Airplane, Creedence Clearwater Revival and their UK counterparts, Blind Faith, Fleetwood Mac and other such 'heavy' artists. The scene was becoming more and more successful and millions of pounds were being made. Where Oldham saw the death of pop, Calder saw only the money Immediate could be making if they went down that road. He sounded out a deal to license the whole of US label A&M's product for the UK and gave Immediate's European distributor EMI six new A&M albums to listen to by artists such as Joni Mitchell, Joe Cocker, Procol Harum, Spooky Tooth, hoping they would put up some of the cash needed to complete the deal. It came to nothing. Calder also negotiated the UK licensing on "Bad Moon Rising" by Creedence Clearwater Revival but that too went astray, the hit single ending up on the Fantasy label in the UK. Crosby, Stills and Nash were also interested in being on Immediate in the UK but again this deal failed to materialise. It's safe to assume Calder couldn't get the final okay out of Oldham to make any of the deals a reality.

So Calder took an ingeniously different approach. A lot of the new UK groups making it big in the US featured guys who had recorded for Immediate in the past such as Jimmy Page, John Mayall and Eric Clapton. Clapton had gone massive with Cream and bigger still with his new group Blind Faith. So Immediate re-issued "I'm Your Witchdoctor", the 1965 John Mayall And The Bluesbreakers single, advertising it as featuring Eric Clapton, who had then been a Bluesbreaker. Sales were encouraging in the UK and even CBS couldn't deny Clapton had sales potential and released the single in the US to promising response. Encouraged, Calder cobbled together an album from the Immediate vaults for the US market, *An Anthology of British Blues*. It was the label's best seller in the US for over a year. The press release explained why:

> The idea of Mick Jagger and Bill Wyman of the [Rolling] Stones, Jimmy Page of The Yardbirds and Blind Faith guitarist Eric Clapton together on one record may sound somewhat unlikely. However, on the Immediate album, *An Anthology Of British Blues*, there are several tracks featuring this very line-up. The British blues scene grows stronger every day and for an understanding of the growth and power of the Movement this Immediate album is essential. John Mayall's Bluesbreakers have recently scored great successes in the US

JOHN MAYALL'S
BLUESBREAKERS
I'm Your Witch Doctor
b/w Telephone Blues
IMMEDIATE IM 012
released Oct. 22nd

OPPOSITE: ERIC CLAPTON, 1966, FEATURED HEAVILY AND CONTROVERSIALLY ON THE IMMEDIATE *BLUES SERIES*

JOHN MAYALL'S BLUESBREAKERS PROMOTION, OCTOBER 1965

BLUES
ANYTIME
VOL.1
AN ANTHOLOGY OF
BRITISH BLUES
featuring
JOHN MAYALL & THE
BLUESBREAKERS
ERIC CLAPTON
SAVOY BROWN
BLUES BAND
T.S. MC. PHEE
JO-ANN KELLY
STONE'S MASONRY
IMMEDIATE

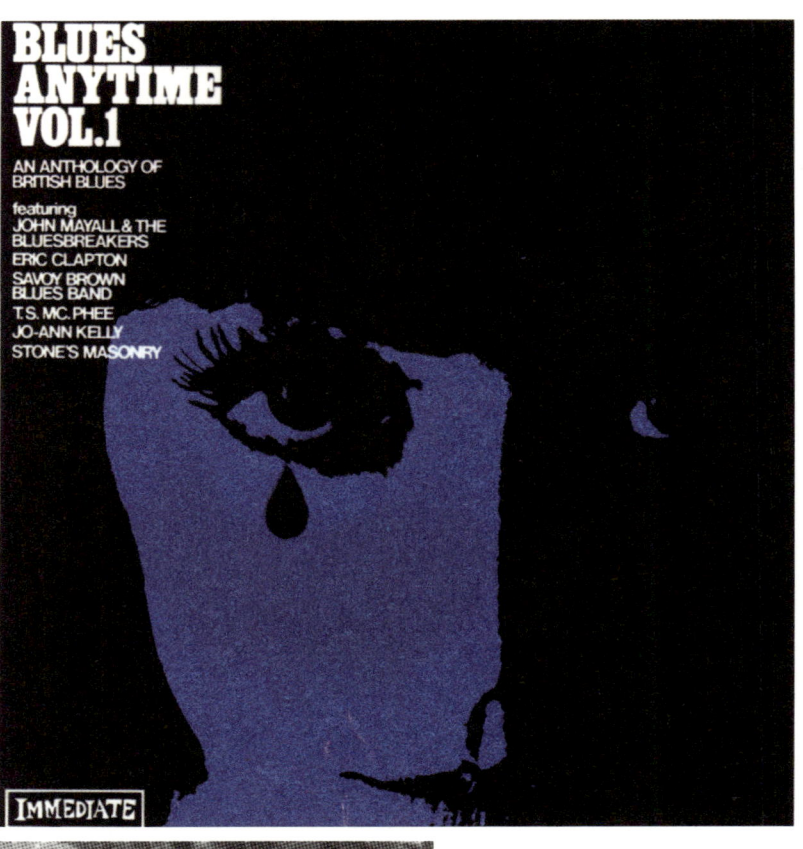

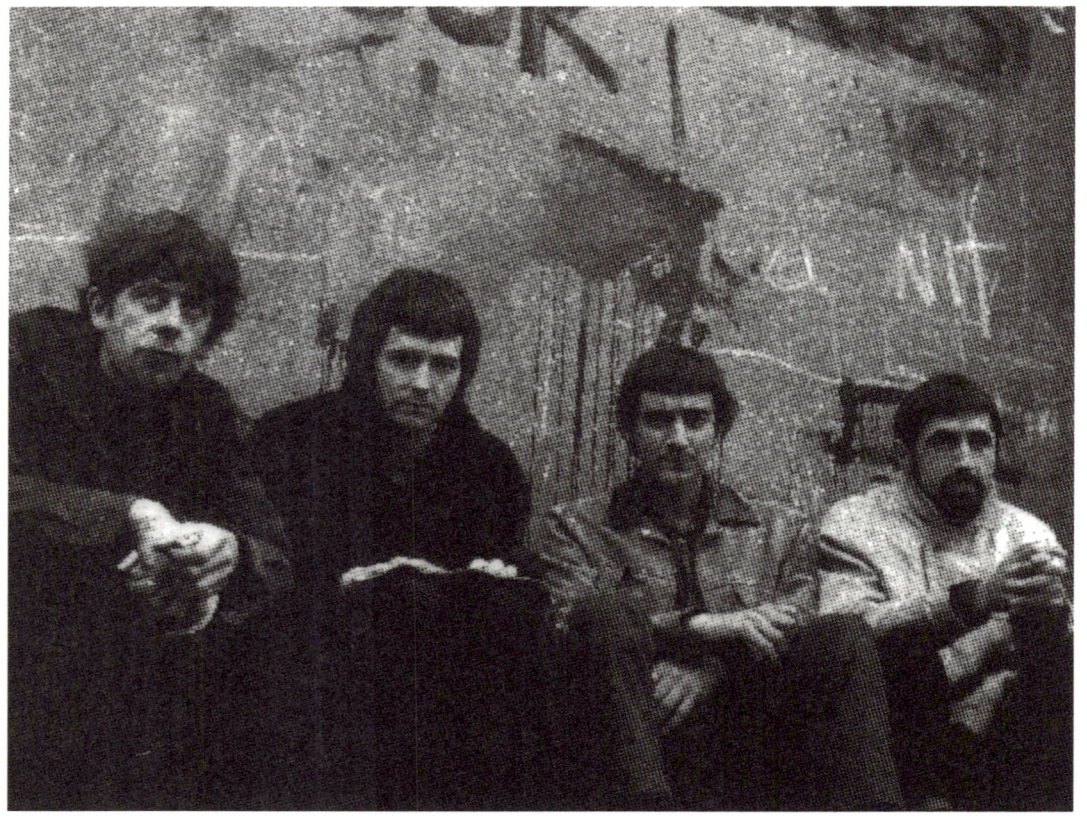

TOP: THE ALBUM ARTWORK FOR *BLUES ANYTIME VOL. 1*, 1968

BOTTOM: JOHN MAYALL'S BLUESBREAKERS FEATURING ERIC CLAPTON (SECOND LEFT), 1968 and have been an institution in Europe for many years. They also contribute several tracks, again featuring the man Clapton who had become a model for guitarists everywhere. The album boasts further tracks by lesser known, but nonetheless vital, Blues groups who contain musicians who have since become deservedly famed throughout Europe. Immediate have earned the public's gratitude with these historic recordings.

In the UK two lavishly packaged compilations appeared, *Blues Anytime Vol. 1* and *Blues Anytime Vol. 2*. Released in conjunction with Mike Vernon's Blue Horizon Records (home to Fleetwood Mac and Chicken Shack), the albums again featured the early work of the best and biggest names in British blues: Jeff Beck, Cyril Davies, Long John Baldry, Nicky Hopkins, John Mayall and The Bluesbreakers, Jimmy Page, John Paul Jones, Mick Jagger, Bill Wyman and Ian Stewart and Fleetwood Mac's Jeremy Spencer. The standout track, "On Top Of The World" by John Mayall's Bluesbreakers, was again heavily advertised as featuring Clapton. In fact, Clapton featured on both albums, solely credited with tracks such as "Snake Drive", "Miles Road", "West Coast Idea" and "Tribute To Elmore" and, with Jimmy Page, on "Freight Loader", "Choker and Draggin' My Tail".

How Calder and Immediate came by these Clapton recordings remains a mystery. The songs were secretly recorded on a two-track, reel-to-reel deck hidden behind a sofa at Clapton's house as he jammed with Jimmy Page is compounded by Led Zeppelin trivia. Whatever the story, these Immediate releases destroyed Page and Clapton's once close relationship. Clapton apparently didn't buy Page's claims that he had to hand over the tapes or he would be sued by Immediate. Tony Calder remembers:

> Jimmy Page would wander in, saying: 'Hey man, I've recorded Eric.' The tape-recorder was never hidden. They used the bathroom to get the echo effect. Jimmy would say 'come on Eric we'll go into the bathroom and record these'. I didn't even know what the blues were! I just knew it was something from over there that you put over here and if you put a proper package on it and had these names like Eric Clapton, who were credible, it would sell.

Ken Mewis remembers:

> When we needed another name or two to help fill out an album of obscure blues tracks we would call Jimmy Page. He would get an 'out of it' Eric Clapton round to his house and just jam away with a Revox [recorder] running behind the sofa. The next day Jimmy would come into Immediate with the tape and collect £100 cash, saying, 'call it anything, forget about royalties, just don't let Eric know, if you need a name, use my street address Miles Road'.

Calder looked at the British Blues series as a classical line, a way of adding depth to the company and both albums were big hits in the UK selling in total close to 50,000. In the US *An Anthology of British Blues Vol. 2* was released, followed by *Blues Anytime Vol. 3* in the UK. The link up with Blue Horizon records also resulted in Malcolm Forrester becoming the new head of Immediate Music. Forrester had vast experience in publishing, having worked for Freddie Bienstock's publishing company Carlin (the top firm of the era), and for David Platz at Essex Music (the other main London publishing company). Forester had set up his own publishing company, Getaway Music, which held the Fleetwood Mac publishing rights, hence his involvement with the Blue Horizon label. Forrester pooled his lot with Immediate Music and the Immediate staff went to work on the new Fleetwood Mac single, "Albatross", helping make it a UK number one hit, even though the group remained on Blue Horizons records. Malcom Forrester, remembers:

> Tony Calder phoned me and said: 'You've got to run our publishing house, Immediate Music.' I went round there and they had the publishing on so many good things. They had the Beach Boys stuff, Small Faces, all these songs that they owned, all these good writers, stuff by Jagger/Richards, Marriott/Lane, Cat Stevens, Billy Nicholls, Mike d'Abo, who had just written "Build Me Up Buttercup" for them. They had all the blues stuff, Jimmy Page, Eric Clapton, John Mayall. We decided if we pooled our stuff we would have one of the best publishing houses in the UK.
>
> I found Tony Calder to be stunningly bright, quite sensational. My office at New Oxford Street, was up the far end, right away from Tony and Andrew, it was like my own little department, much more low-key. At the time a play on BBC radio was most probably about three or four pounds on performance income. I remember all the staff being in mohair suits, made to fit, shirts made to fit, there were no jeans in the Immediate offices.
>
> Everyone worked on the legend of Andrew. It was always a very gentlemanly company, not bloke-ish, none of that, 'whoo! Check her out', which was unusual in that period. When the whole company car thing started in this country, Andrew was waiting on New Oxford Street for a cab to take him somewhere and I came by in my Zephyr Ford with tail fins. I said I would take him. It was on my way home, he's got in and he's gone, quite disgusted, 'it's all plastic inside'. When he got out the car he said 'tell Tony he's got to get you a new car'. I was offended. A few weeks later Calder says 'you got to go down to Norman's in Mayfair, we just chose a Mercedes for you'. All my young publishing friends in those days were gob-smacked. Immediate, as a whole, was stunningly hard working, grafting all the time. It wasn't a lapsidazical place, the reason it was successful was hard work, you could go to the Immediate offices nine o'clock at night and see the whole office packing records for mail shots. Calder would send out for hamburgers before it was even fashionable. An early night was eight o'clock finish. Hard-work but good fun. I have to say I always thought Chris Farlowe was a lucky bastard, they bought the number one spot with "Out Of Time", there were loads of better singers around, Georgie Fame, Zoot Money, Geno Washington. One time I was sitting in a booth with Andrew in the Rainbow on Sunset Boulevard.

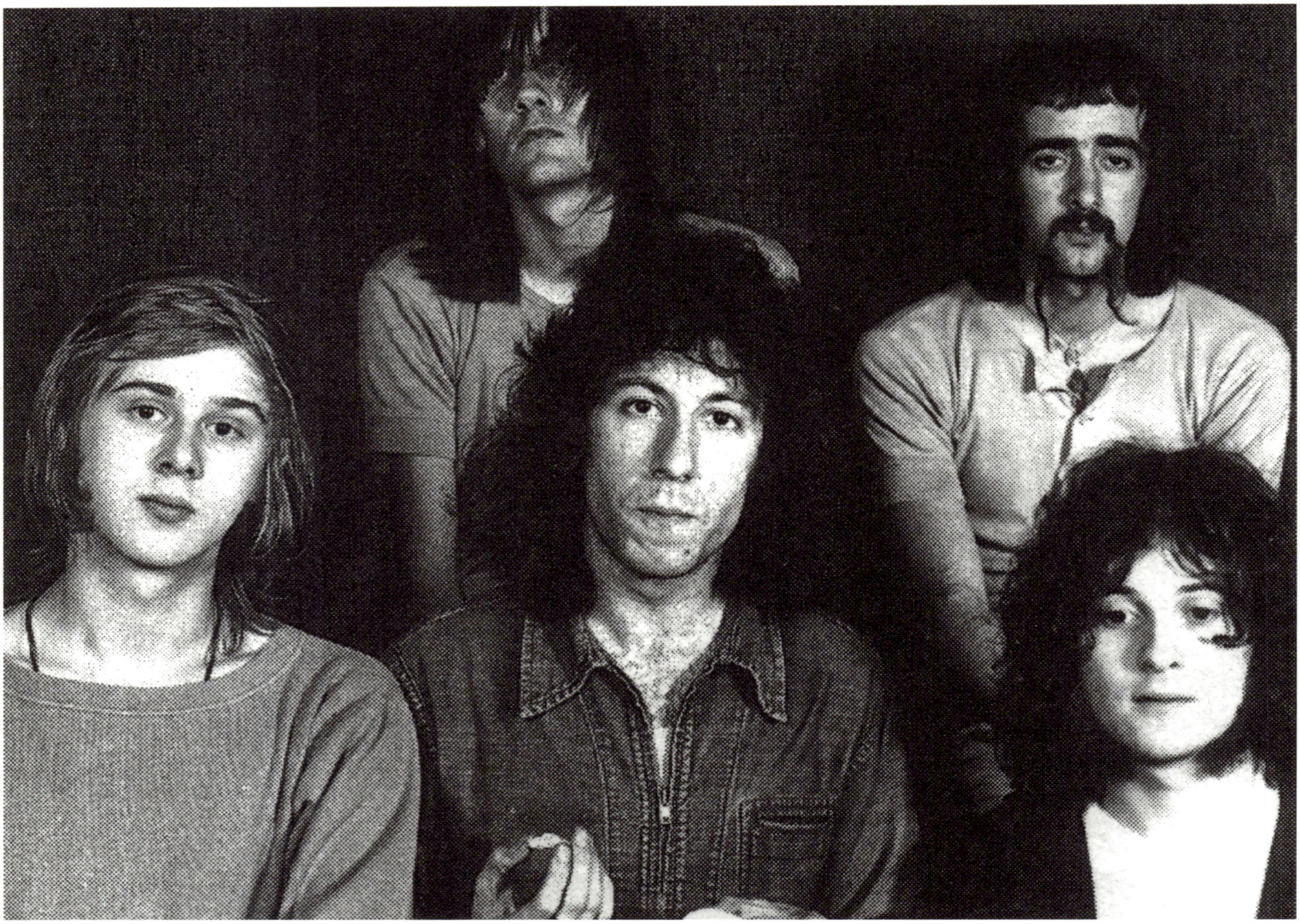

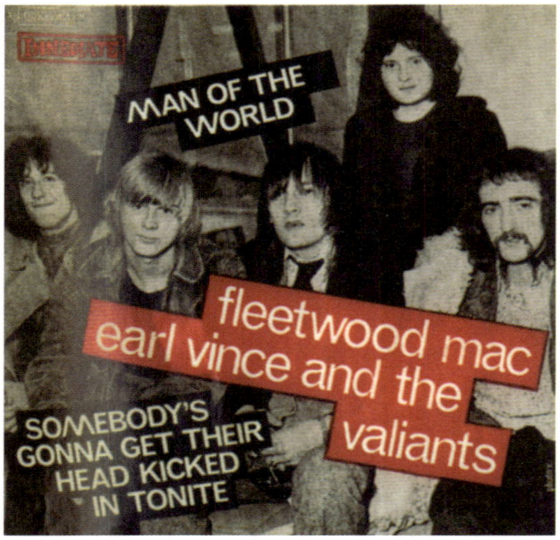
MAN OF THE WORLD
fleetwood mac
earl vince and the valiants
SOMEBODY'S GONNA GET THEIR HEAD KICKED IN TONITE

OLDHAM CONSIDERED FLEETWOOD MAC AS JUST ANOTHER SCUZZY BLUES GROUP

SIMON SPENCE

TOP: FLEETWOOD MAC WHO WERE FRONTED BY JEREMY SPENCER, 1969

BOTTOM: FLEETWOOD MAC'S "MAN OF THE WORLD", 1969

There was two guys with us, when they went I said 'who was that?'. Jerry Goffin and Jimmy Webb—enormous writers at the height of their careers—just sitting there having a beer, chatting.

Paul Banes remembers:

> When Malcolm joined I went to work for him. On the publishing side we looked after *Sea Of Tunes* for the Beach Boys, they would have sold over half a million. We looked after Childy Singleton, a big producer in Nashville. The biggest song I had with Immediate Music was a cover we got with Val Doonican. We sold so many records, 50,000 a day every day before Christmas. 700,000 copies. We had "Build Me Up Buttercup" by Mike d'Abo that was a huge hit, we had Long John Baldry.
>
> If we were looking at immediate Music in terms of Music Week, we would have been a top five publishing company at the time. All the songwriters were home produced more or less. We had "Albatross" by Fleetwood Mac and Chicken Shack, acts the Malcolm introduced. The publishing with Small Faces, we set up a publishing company for them called it Avakak, a 50/50 deal. Mike d'abo had a company called Michael d'Abo Music. Status Quo came in. Their manager Bob Young came in. They were getting two per cent record royalty with Pye and he wanted to know if we could give them four, five or six per cent, like we were giving our other acts. All these bands were in the same boat, the majors were still taking liberties. [At Immediate Small Faces were on UK artist royalty of five per cent on 90 per cent UK and 4.5 per cent world from July 1 1968.]
>
> We were very close with Donovan and he was working with Small Faces in the studio. The staff weren't making a fortune. Everybody used to chip in. We would systematically do a mail-out to the fan clubs, Small Faces, whatever, letting them know what was available. Everybody would be there until midnight, sticking bits of paper into envelopes. Tony would nip round the Wimpy bar and buy us all Wimpy and Chips.

With Forrester on board, Calder zoned in on Fleetwood Mac. Not content with owning the group's publishing, he wanted to release the follow up to "Albatross" on Immediate. He moved fast and Peter Green's achingly maudlin "Man Of The World" backed by the glam rock "Somebody's Gonna Get Their Head Kicked In Tonite" (credited to Earl Vince and The Valiants who were really Fleetwood Mac fronted by Jeremy Spencer) was quickly in the shops. The advert for "Man Of The World" was another Immediate special taking over the entire *NME* front cover. It depicted a reclining policeman smoking a joint, backed by four golden Labradors and a Andy Warhol flower painting. Immediate wanted the 'police officer' to look as stoned as possible, and David Bailey's bill for the photos read: "Fee £500, Props £500 (for authenticity)." For a while Immediate and Fleetwood Mac seemed a good fit. Both Fleetwood Mac founder members Green and Mick Fleetwood had played with former Immediate act John Mayall And The Bluesbreakers, and they had a good relationship with Forrester. The group were coming straight from a massive number one single with "Albatross" and 150,000 sales took "Man Of The World" straight to number two in the UK charts, unable to shake "Get Back" by The Beatles.

It was announced in the press that Fleetwood Mac planned to record an orchestral-choral LP telling the story of Christ for Immediate, who began arranging continental gigs for the group. Oldham had not paid particularly close attention to the Fleetwood Mac deal and considered the group (pre-Buckingham and Nicks) just another scuzzy blues group and nothing to get worked up about. Calder had handled the negotiations, persuading Immediate's European distributor EMI to bankroll a massive advance for the group—but somehow things didn't work out as planned. Tony Calder remembers:

> I got all the money lined up from EMI. Quarter of a million quid we lined up, highest UK deal ever done at the time and we're sitting at number two. Oldham comes out of the treatment centre and has lunch with Fleetwood Mac's manager Clifford Davis, calls me and says: 'The deal's off. He cut his roll with the wrong knife. I won't sign the cheque.'

As Andrew Oldham recounts:

> Malcolm Forrester calls me and says I've got to meet him at this lawyer's office in Holborn. I alight from the Roller, see Malcolm on the pavement and ask him what's up. He says, 'you remember Fleetwood Mac'. I say, 'yeah, I met them twice'. He says, 'well we forgot to sign them'.

Malcom Forrester recalls:

> I had the publishing of Fleetwood Mac and that's how Immediate got them. What went wrong is we had a conflict with Clifford Davis. It's a load of old tosh about forgetting to sign them. Ted Oldman was our lawyer at Immediate and he was Clifford Davis' lawyer. That's a conflict of interest. They were telling us we could not continue with my publishing agreement with the writers of Fleetwood Mac at Immediate Music. Calder was good in these situations; aggressive, sharp and quick. Oldham wouldn't have known what was going on.

Conclusively Fleetwood Mac's manager Clifford Davis announced the group were leaving Immediate, telling *NME*: "There has been many problems and we have accordingly decided not to sign with Immediate." Davis used the success of "Man Of The World" to negotiate a deal with the US label, Warner Bros Reprise, for Fleetwood Mac; taking with them the tracks they had recorded for Immediate.

A BOMB ON THE BUS

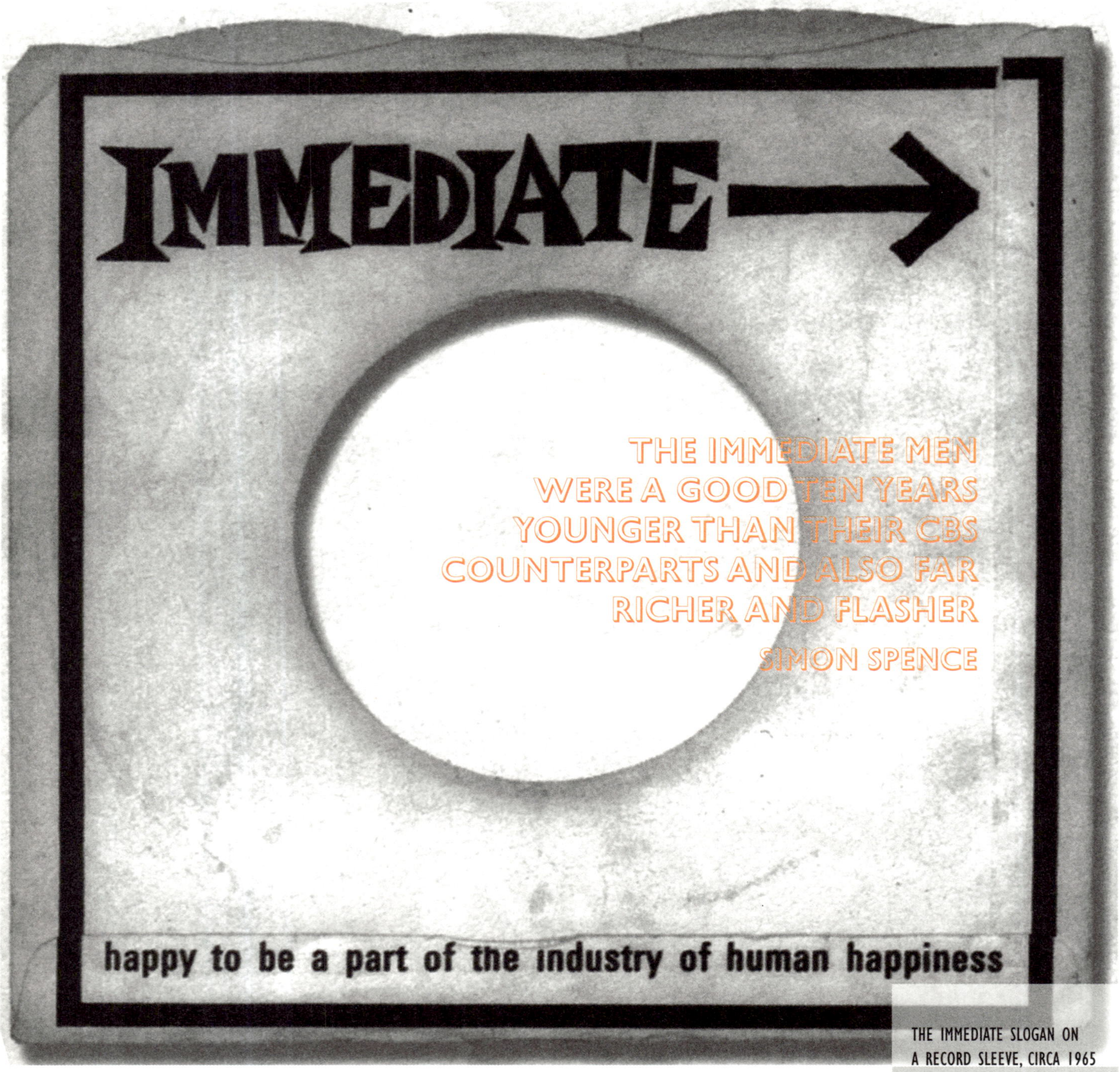
IMMEDIATE
happy to be a part of the industry of human happiness

THE IMMEDIATE MEN WERE A GOOD TEN YEARS YOUNGER THAN THEIR CBS COUNTERPARTS AND ALSO FAR RICHER AND FLASHER

SIMON SPENCE

THE IMMEDIATE SLOGAN ON A RECORD SLEEVE, CIRCA 1965

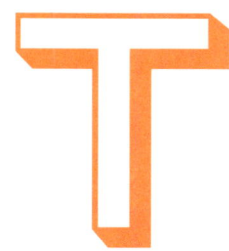

The President of CBS records, Clive Davis, worked 18 hour days and knew every detail of his operation, right down to the daily sales figures. It seemed inconceivable that such a man would have pissed away the potential of Immediate in the US. A recent CBS album, *The Rock Machine Turns You On*, released to promote the label's contemporary acts, featured Bob Dylan, Laura Nyro, Janis Joplin (all three of whom were managed by Albert Grossman), Moby Grape, Blood, Sweat and Tears, The Byrds, Simon and Garfunkel, Taj Mahal, Big Brother and The Holding Company, Leonard Cohen, Johnny Cash, Roy Harper, Tim Rose, The Zombies, The Electric Flag The Peanut Butter Conspiracy, Spirit (produced by Lou Adler), The United States Of America and Grace Slick. Surely, Oldham felt there was room on this compilation for at least one track by an Immediate artist, even if was The Nice.

Ever since Oldham had inked the CBS/Immediate deal with Davis, the relationship between the two men had faltered. For Immediate, the whole thing had been a catastrophe, while for Davis it was an easy thing for him to write-off. Over the past couple of years, Davis had overseen a doubling of CBS' annual record profits to a figure around the $10 million mark, with his post-Monterey rock signing leading the way. He was a Harvard educated lawyer, a middle class Brooklyn Jew who, under the old President, Goddard Lieberson, had quickly risen from assistant consul to administrative vice president overseeing A&R. He then became general manager and ultimately president of CBS. Alongside their new rock roster, CBS had deals with leading black labels Philadelphia International and Stax, plus reliable stalwarts such as Bob Dylan, Simon and Garfunkel and Barbara Streisand doing well. Davis was also closing in on the signing of Bruce Springsteen and Billy Joel. Davis was not a man to take kindly to criticism, having surrounded himself with a formidable clique of 'yes' men.

Oldham told me:

> When we were having all the hits with Small Faces, we weren't able to capitalise on it in the US. One hit in the US, then CBS pulled the plug and didn't promote *Ogden's [Nut Gone Flake]* because Small Faces wouldn't tour. Anyway it became apparent the CBS policy was recoup and bury. CBS slogan for the time, should have been 'We want it and we'll bury it!' It was criminal.

The lack of success Immediate was having in the US had severely dented the reputation of the label in the UK—it was not a good position from which to be looking to sign new talent or to keep those already on board from looking at their options.

Perhaps having Ken Mewis, the former hairdresser, liaise with CBS had been a mistake. Maybe the situation could be resolved with a good old fashioned head-to-head between the bosses themselves. Oldham and Calder flew out to New York and rented an apartment in the same residential block where Clive Davis lived, the expensive Suite 24B, 80 Central Park West, overlooking Central Park. Tony Calder recounts:

> Clive rang up one morning and said: 'Have you got an appointment with me today at ten? Well meet me downstairs in 15 minutes, we'll go down to the office together.' So we get downstairs, and the bus comes along and we get on the bus and he puts the money in. We thought it was hysterical that he travelled to work on a bus. Clive got the record to number one ["Itchycoo Park"], he didn't bother to sell the album [Ogden's Nut Gone Flake]. I think Oldham upset him somehow. CBS were sitting on that record, still do it today. If a US record label decides to work the record they'll work the record. They can also go through the motions of making out they're working the record. If the President of the company doesn't call it a priority you're dead. You needed to know where their marketing was being spent, we didn't know at the time.

Lou Adler recounts:

> Oldham and I had similar situations at CBS. For me, it wasn't so much Clive Davis, it was the maze of departments and people you had to deal with. If you were like Oldham and myself, and were involved in all aspects of your artists' career and the records they made—producing, managing, art directing, marketing—you were naturally frustrated by the big company machine. I left less than a year after making my deal.

The meeting between Davis, newly named CBS Vice-President Walter Yetnikoff, Oldham and Calder did not go well. The Immediate men were a good ten years younger than their CBS counterparts and also far richer and flasher; a fact that irked the salaried CBS company men. They discussed Led Zeppelin, Oldham and Calder having been told by the group's founders, both Immediate stalwarts—Jimmy Page (who had recently left The Yardbirds), and John Paul Jones—that Led Zeppelin were available at $250,000 for a five year deal. Calder and Oldham wanted the CBS men to put up half the cash and were flatly told they should be able to secure the deal themselves and, anyway, such a deal would not be valid because Page, as one of the Yardbirds—who had racked up four giant albums and several Top 20 singles in the US on the CBS owned Epic label—was still under contract to CBS. This proved untrue, as no action was taken when Led Zeppelin signed to Atlantic at Page's asking price. Led Zeppelin would be one of the biggest groups of the coming year in the US, their first album selling over 700,000 copies.

Oldham and Calder brought up the debacle of the Small Faces situation in the US, outright accusing the CBS pair of not knowing their arses from their elbows. Davis and Yetnikoff had heard about the Fleetwood Mac fiasco and accused the pair of talking rubbish. Calder was keen to talk about the British Blues albums. *Vol. 2* in the series had recently sold 18,406 in the US but many shops found it easier to get hold of the product straight from the UK and a further 5,000 albums had been sold

OLDHAM ACCUSED THE CBS PAIR OF NOT KNOWING THEIR ARSES FROM THEIR ELBOWS

SIMON SPENCE

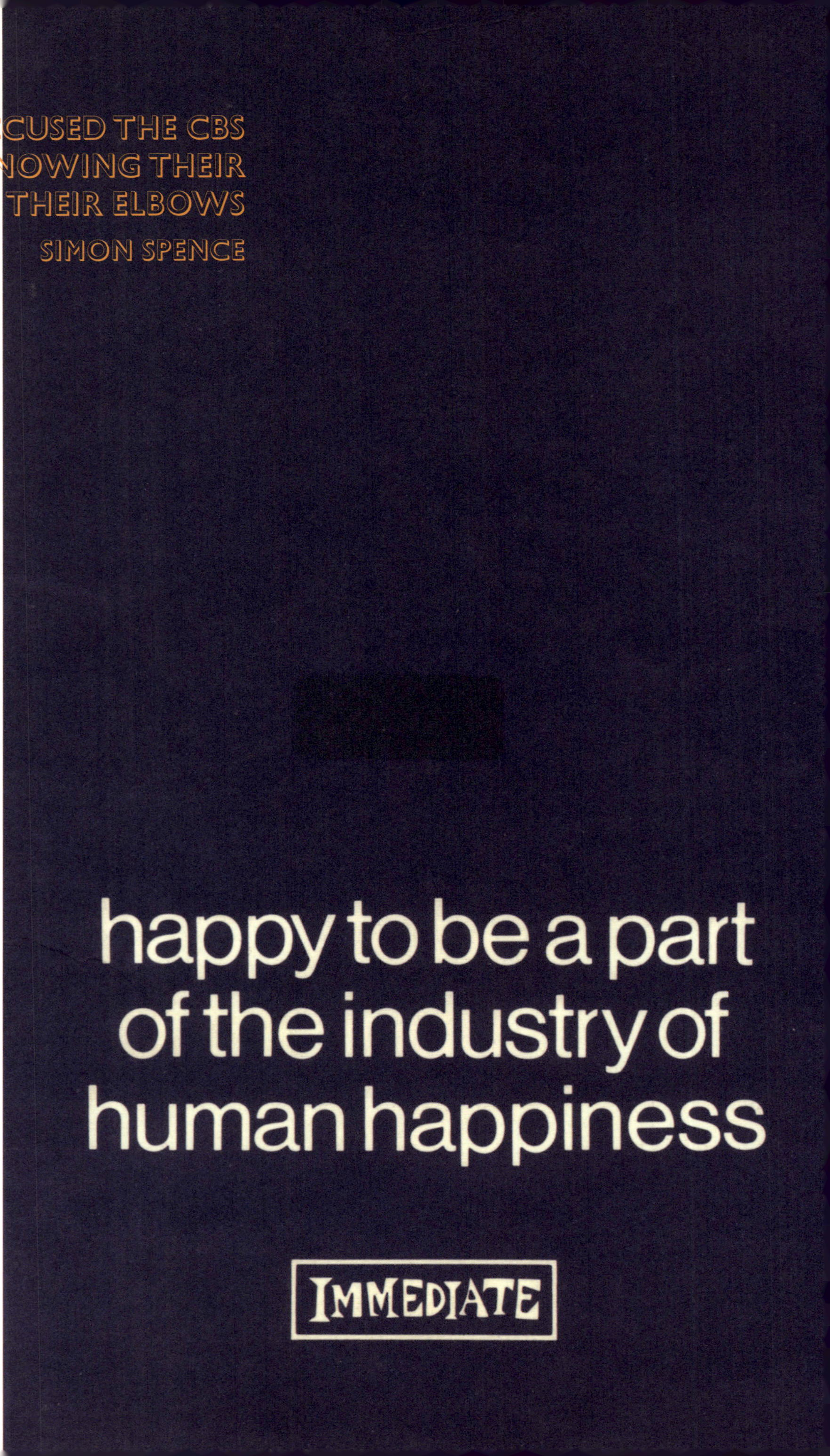
happy to be a part of the industry of human happiness
IMMEDIATE

IMMEDIATE PRESS KIT FOLDER COVER, CIRCA 1967

on import. The meeting degenerated and it was obvious to all nothing productive would come of it. Later that day, Oldham heard from Allen Klein that Davis had been on the phone and told him: "Oldham and Immediate have no knowledge or understanding of the US market."

In frustration Oldham confronted Davis at his home and threatened to blow up the bus Davis travelled to work on. Davis responded by having a restraining order issued, forbidding Oldham from going within a hundred feet of the CBS offices or his private residence.

That was the end as far as Immediate were concerned. The label's two-year distribution deal with CBS was due to expire in a few months and Oldham and Calder planned to keep on the New York apartment as permanent base for Immediate operations in the US. Once the CBS deal expired they expected to be able to attract new distributors for the label and start afresh. Paul Banes was transferred from the UK to run the New York office. He had been with Immediate for 16 months, starting out as an assistant to in-house accountant Stan Blackbourne and working his way up to a senior position on the publishing side at Immediate Music before recently replacing Ken Mewis as promotions manager. In US music trade magazine, *Record World*, under the headline, "Immediate Steps Up Stateside Activities", Banes said optimistically: "In England we have an identity and they tell us when we get it over here we'll really go places." Banes later recollected:

> I went into the office in London one morning, there was one stage where nobody knew what was going to be happening. Tony introduced me to Frank Chalmers who was our international person at EMI. I was gonna be leaving and maybe going to work for EMI in France because it was a territory where EMI was not getting very far, our worst territory in Europe. I spoke to Frank about going to live in Paris, then suddenly outta the blue Tony said to me on Monday: 'whattaya doing next week?' Basically I was off to [the US]. On the Saturday I had gone. They had found the apartment in New York, Jenny [Calder's wife] had already been out there buying furniture. She was there when I got there. We went to set up the office and everything outside of the UK was gonna be rooted through New York, ie. all the royalties, all the statements, all the paperwork everything. I went out there and set up the bank accountants in New York, we set up two publishing companies, Nice Songs and Lovely Music and I was basically left to get on with it. Except initially it was sorting out the paperwork.

> The CBS situation was unfortunate. We had done 400,000 with "Itchycoo Park", but CBS couldn't follow it up. In the US there had been a big fuss because Ogden's [Nut Gone Flake] was in a round sleeve. There was bad blood over Led Zeppelin. It was all bollocks and it all got out of hand. If you look at the repertoire we took into CBS, what we had in the UK, what we put up on the table, and us saying, "we can get Led Zeppelin, all we need is $150,000", then you get a fax back from Clive Davis saying Jimmy Page is under contract to us, which more or less means fuck off.

Oldham had fallen out big style with Clive. We needed to do consistent sales in the US, that's where the money was. The company could have easily run on the back of what we were selling everywhere else. Andrew and Lou Adler met Clive Davis at Monterey Festival. Clive actually saw the two biggest producers either side of the water, Andrew with the Rolling Stones and Lou with the Mamas and Papas, figures if he gets the two producers he gets the two acts. Unfortunately that didn't happen and CBS in New York was too fucking corporate. Dealing with them had been horrendous and we were all looking forward to the end of the deal with them and just moving on.

> **IN FRUSTRATION OLDHAM CONFRONTED DAVIS AT HIS HOME AND THREATENED TO BLOW UP THE BUS DAVIS TRAVELLED TO WORK ON**
> SIMON SPENCE

STILL A TWINKLE

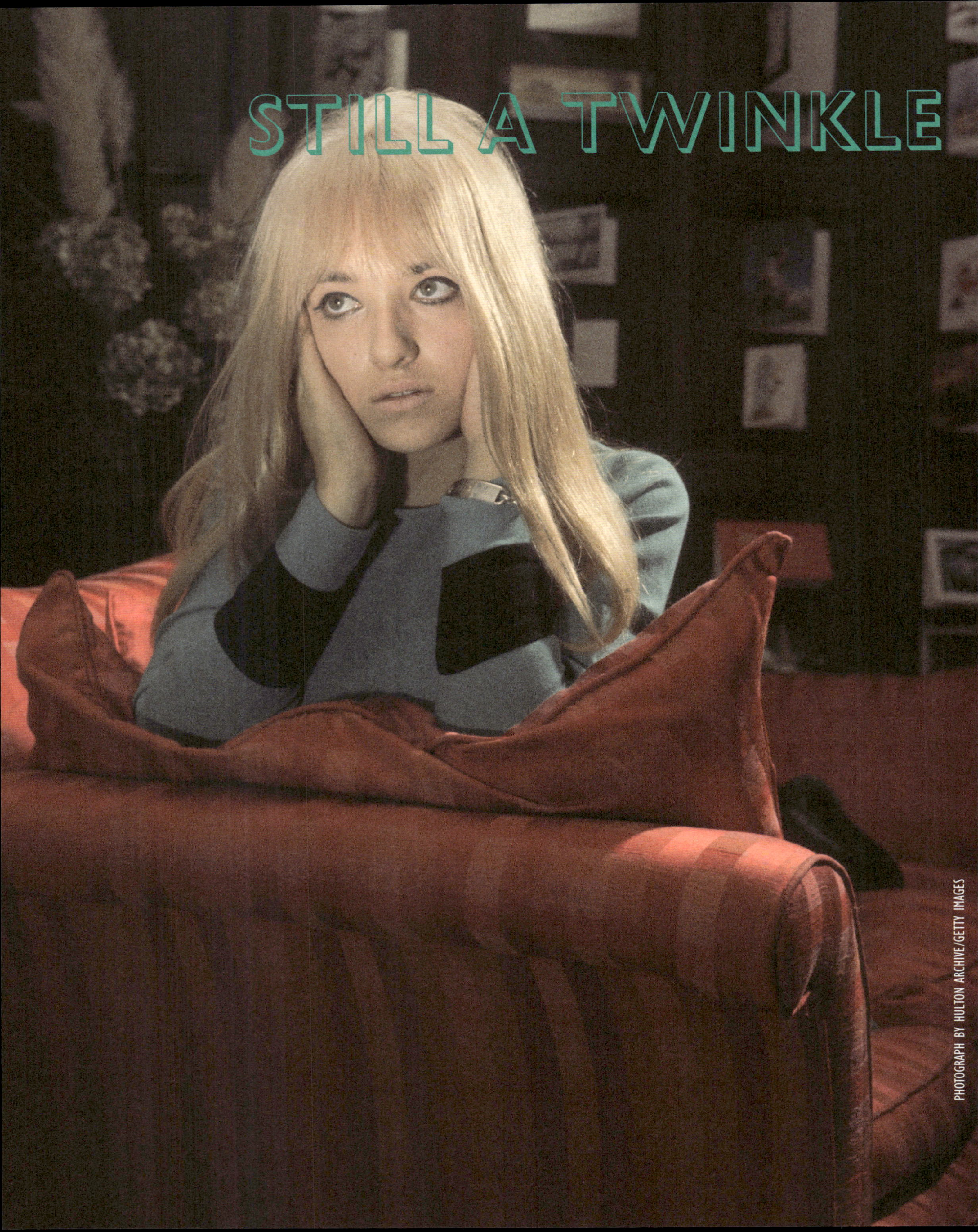

PHOTOGRAPH BY HULTON ARCHIVE/GETTY IMAGES

Oldham spent extended periods at the new Immediate offices in New York, partying hard. There was cocaine and musicals *Hair* and *Oh Calcutta* to enjoy. He hit the town with Sean Kenny, occasionally Kenneth Tynan, and new movie star pal Richard Harris. The 37-year-old Irish actor had scored a huge screen hit with a musical *Camelot* and then taken the lengthy, melodramatic Jimmy Webb written "MacArthur Park" to number one on the US singles chart. Harris had followed that up with "The Yard Went On Forever", again written by Jimmy Webb, an anti-Vietnam song based on a speech by the late Robert Kennedy. Oldham enjoyed egging on Harris at various gigs on the actor's US concert tour. Old friend Phil Spector was also up for a laugh again. It had been a few years now since his swansong with Ike and Tina Turner's "River Deep, Mountain High" and he had newly signed a deal with A&M Records and come back strong with a Ronnettes single "You Came, You Saw, You Conquered". A lounge act he discovered while hanging out in Las Vegas, The Checkmates Ltd, had also been successful. Another old pal, Art Kass, was in charge at the latest hot New York independent label, Buddha Records. Kass had started out running the infamous Kama Sutra label and now together with former Cameo Parkway player Neil Bogart (later famed for his Casablanca label), were instigating a huge bubblegum pop revival with Buddha. After all the serious heavy rock posturing at CBS, this really tickled Oldham. Buddha was scoring huge hits thanks to production team Jerry Kasenetz and Jeff Katz. They were on a stupendous run in the US chart and former Immediate recordee Joey Levine was the voice for a string of made-up groups such as 1910 Fruitgum Company, fronting songs such as "Simon Says", "Chewy Chewy" and "Yummy Yummy (Yummy I Got Love In My Tummy)". "Sugar Sugar" by The Archies, the latest from Monkees creator Don Kirshner was another big bubblegum hit at the time.

Inspired, Immediate decided to go back to their roots—their love of the three-minute thrill—and set up a similar bubblegum hit factory in London. They created a new company as a front and called it Instant, Oldham and Calder having decided against diluting the more mature image Immediate had garnered since delivering serious hit albums from Small Faces, The Nice and with the Blues Series. Kenny's restaurant napkin scribble was used as the new imprint's logo, and Instant was up and running, signing up writers to write and produce bubblegum pop—such as Mike Finesilver and Peter Kerr, who had written and produced "Fire" for The Crazy World Of Arthur Brown. Early releases on Instant included Oldham's production of Leeds outfit, The Outer Limits, who had previously recorded for Deram, with a sumptuously arranged, harmony-driven, pop sing-along "The Great Train Robbery", based on the Ronnie Biggs tale, written by the group's Jeff Christie. While Finesilver and Kerr came up with a bouncing bit of London bubblegum, "Happy Miranda" for the made-up group Excelsior Spring.

Telex No. 27665
Telephone 01-486 4931
Cables Immedcord London W1

INSTANT RECORDS LIMITED
111 GLOUCESTER PLACE
LONDON W1

25th April, 1969

INSTANT - ANOTHER QUALITY LABEL FROM IMMEDIATE

Albums:

'EUROPEAN CUP FINAL 1968' INLP001

Manchester re-attracted public attention to their achievements by another victory in the F.A. Cup Final, the first victory for Manchester since Manchester United won The European Cup Final against Benfica.
Now is the time to get extra sales from this unusually packaged souvenir album.

'TONITE LETS ALL MAKE LOVE IN LONDON' INLP002

The automatic sales which follow the films release throughout Britain are not attracting sufficient attention to this sound-track album featuring Chris Farlowe, Mick Jagger, Pink Floyd, Michael Caine, Julie Christie, Edna O'Brien etc.

ANY OFFER CONTAINED IN THIS LETTER DOES NOT CONSTITUTE A CONTRACT
S.S.Oldham J.R.Calder

OPPOSITE: IMMEDIATE SINGER TWINKLE (LYNN ANNETTE RIPLEY), CIRCA 1965

ONE OF THE NUMEROUS IMMEDIATE RELEASE FORMS SIGNIFYING THE CURRENT RELEASES ON NEW INSTANT LABEL, 1969

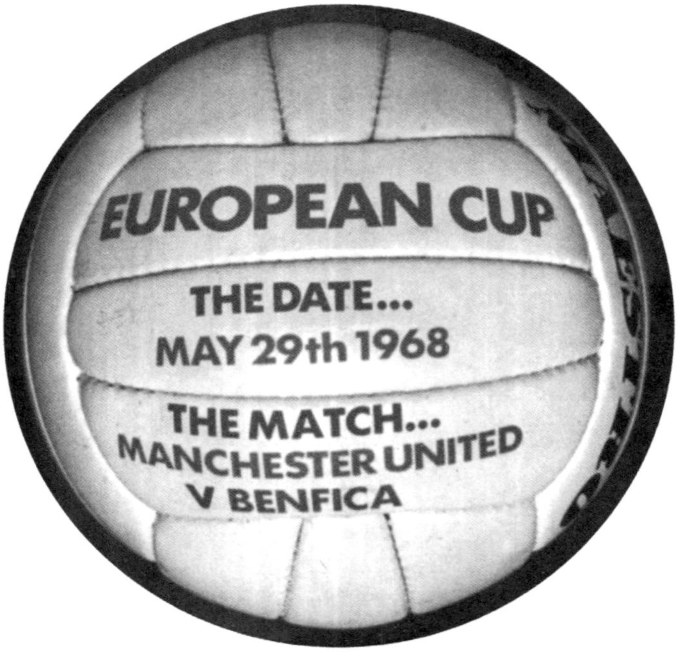
EUROPEAN CUP
THE DATE...
MAY 29th 1968
THE MATCH...
MANCHESTER UNITED
V BENFICA

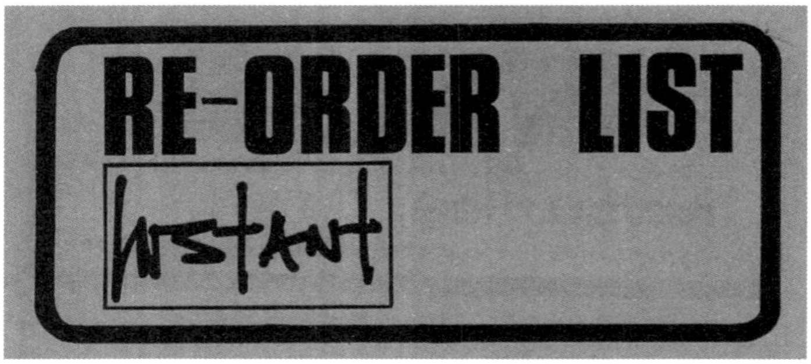
RE-ORDER LIST
Instant

Twinkle seemed to personify the Instant ideal. She was a great-looking, hard-nosed 22-year-old mod girl, who had had a huge hit in the UK with biker anthem "Terry", a song on par with the Shangri-La's "Leader Of The Pack". She was part of a trio of Don Arden managed acts to record for Instant, one who Don remembered as having a number one in Japan. Twinkle wrote her own songs and Immediate producer/songwriter Michael d'Abo was put to work producing her. They came up with a sensational track "Soldier's Dream", but decided it would follow-up her debut "Mickey". When "Mickey" was not a hit, "Soldier's Dream" was shelved and Twinkle was lost. Arden's other two artists at Instant, Copperfield, with the bubblegum-on-rote of "Any Time That Your Sad And Lonely" and an eponymous heavy rock album by Samson, faired no better. The short-lived labels bestselling release was a football album, *Highlights of the 1968 European Cup Final*. The album was literally a BBC commentary at a Manchester United verses Benfica match at Wembley. United won making them the first English club to win the European Cup. *Highlights of the 1968 European Cup Final* featured an all-star line-up of Eusebio, Charlton and Best and came in another round sleeve, this time in the image of a football.

Instant also branched out into soundtracks, releasing of the music from Peter Whitehead's new documentary film, *Tonite Let's All Make Love In London*, which had won acclaim at both the London and New York film festivals. The album featured the music of Pink Floyd, The Animals, Small Faces, Vashti, Twice As Much, Chris Farlowe and snippets of chat from Julie Christie, Lee Marvin, Mick Jagger, Michael Caine, Allan Ginsberg, David Hockney, Vanessa Redgrave and Edna O'Brien.

There were also plans for Instant to release the cast album for a new musical Oldham was involved in. He had been spending relaxed afternoons in rehearsals at London's Mermaid Theatre with Sean Kenny, heavily involved in a production based on Jonathan Swift's *Gulliver's Travels*. Oldham was producing music for the show with d'Abo, who had also got the lead role in the production. Despite having received an Ivor Novello songwriting award for "Build Me Up Buttercup" and producing and writing an array of hits for Immediate, d'Abo was still holding down his day job as singer in Manfred Mann. He was now being feted as "one of the first pop stars to cross over into theatre work". Of his own move in to the theatre, Oldham told *Daily Telegraph*: "At the moment I'm just amused by it, I don't know whether it's the novelty or not. There's a lot more bread [money] in it than I actually thought. I originally started doing this just for fun." d'Abo told the press:

> Andrew encouraged me to be creative by producing and writing for Immediate. I had always felt awkward bringing my songs to the Manfreds but now I had free reign in my ideas. It was through my involvement with Immediate that Andrew set up a meeting with theatre director Sean Kenny. Bernard Miles [Mermaid Theatre's owner] had had a successful annual run with *Treasure Island* but for this particular Christmas they wanted to put on Sean's adaptation of *Gulliver's Travels* for the

TOP: INSTANT ALBUM *HIGHLIGHTS OF THE 1968 EUROPEAN CUP FINAL*, MAY 1968

BOTTOM: THE INSTANT LOGO, 1968

OPPOSITE: TWINKLE'S SEMINAL RELEASE, "MICKY"

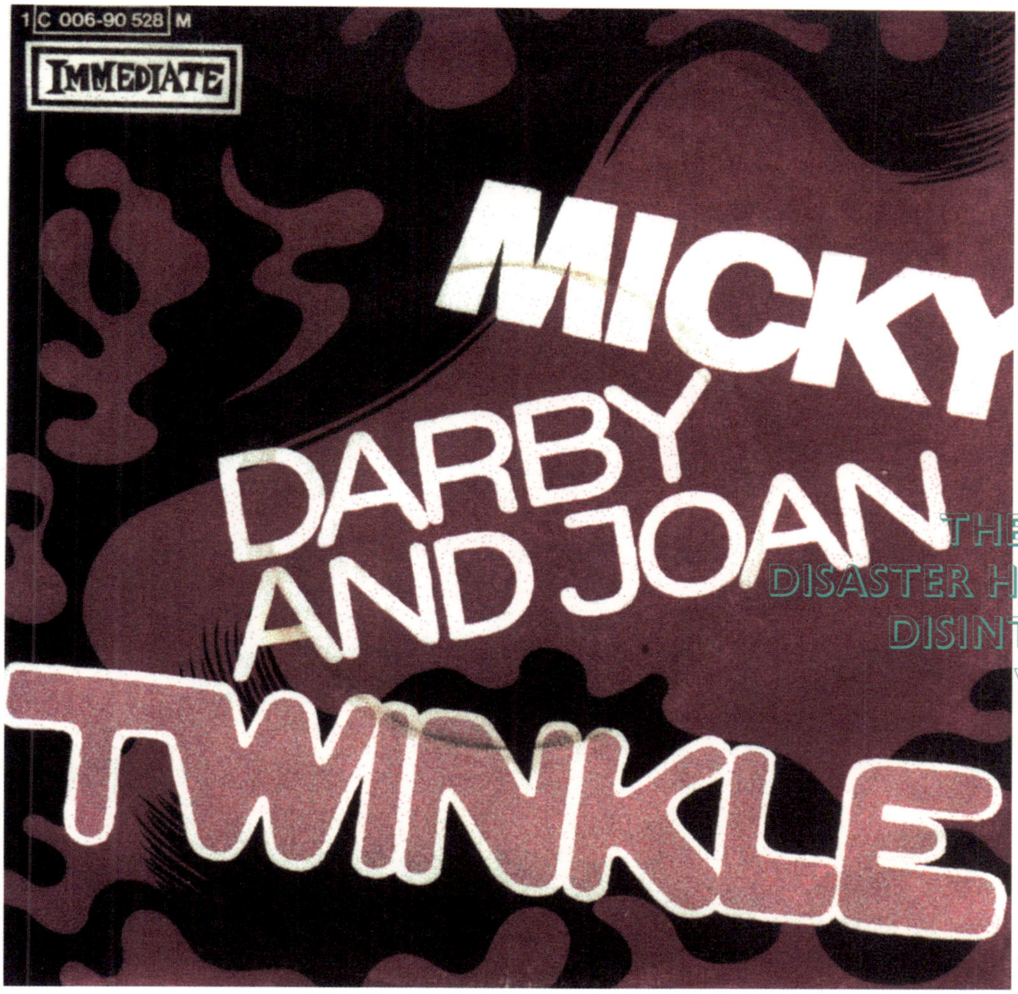
1 C 006-90 528 M
IMMEDIATE
MICKY
DARBY AND JOAN
TWINKLE

THE FLEETWOOD MAC DISASTER HAD EXPOSED HOW DISINTERESTED OLDHAM WAS IN IMMEDIATE

SIMON SPENCE

> first time. I auditioned for the lead by reading the prologue and found they were already seriously considering me for the role. I was terribly excited.

Gulliver's Travels was a sell-out show and a single was planned for release—an Oldham produced, d'Abo-written song, "(See The Little People) Gulliver's Travels", on which Small Faces had helped out in the studio. But Manfred Mann, having put up with d'Abo writing and producing for Immediate, objected to their singer fronting the single, essentially going solo. D'Abo claimed group leader, South African Manfred Man, was "paranoid the single would be a hit and I would leave the group the same as [previous singer] Paul Jones had".

"Our lawyers have told us not to comment", Calder told the press. Manfred Mann successfully prevented d'Abo releasing the single and Oldham heavily remixed the entire soundtrack to *Gulliver's Travel's* and released it as an Instant album. "I took it home and listened to it and thought, 'my God, what is this cacophony", said d'Abo. Oldham had cut up songs from the musical, looping and running them backwards over samples from The Lovin' Spoonful, Small Faces, The Nice, Little Richard and more. D'Abo left both Immediate and Manfred Mann soon after and would go on to star in the Broadway version of *Gulliver's Travels* with a new score written by Lionel Bart.

While Oldham indulged himself at the theatre, Calder also followed his passions and hooked up with Maximum Sound studios and started a low-key rock steady and dub offshoot of Instant called Revolution. Singles were released from legendary reggae star Owen Gray (who had previously cut for ska-friendly labels such as Bluebeat and Trojan) and Jimmy Scott, a Georgie Fame band member, who came up with "Ob La Di Ob La Da Story", a notable adjunct to The Beatles hit. Paul McCartney explained:

> I had a friend called Jimmy Scott who was a Nigerian conga player, a real cool guy. He had a few expressions, one of them was: 'Ob la di, ob la da, life goes on bra.' I said to him I really like that expression, and I'm thinking of using it, and I sent him a check in recognition of that fact later because, even though I had written the song and he didn't help me, it was his expression.

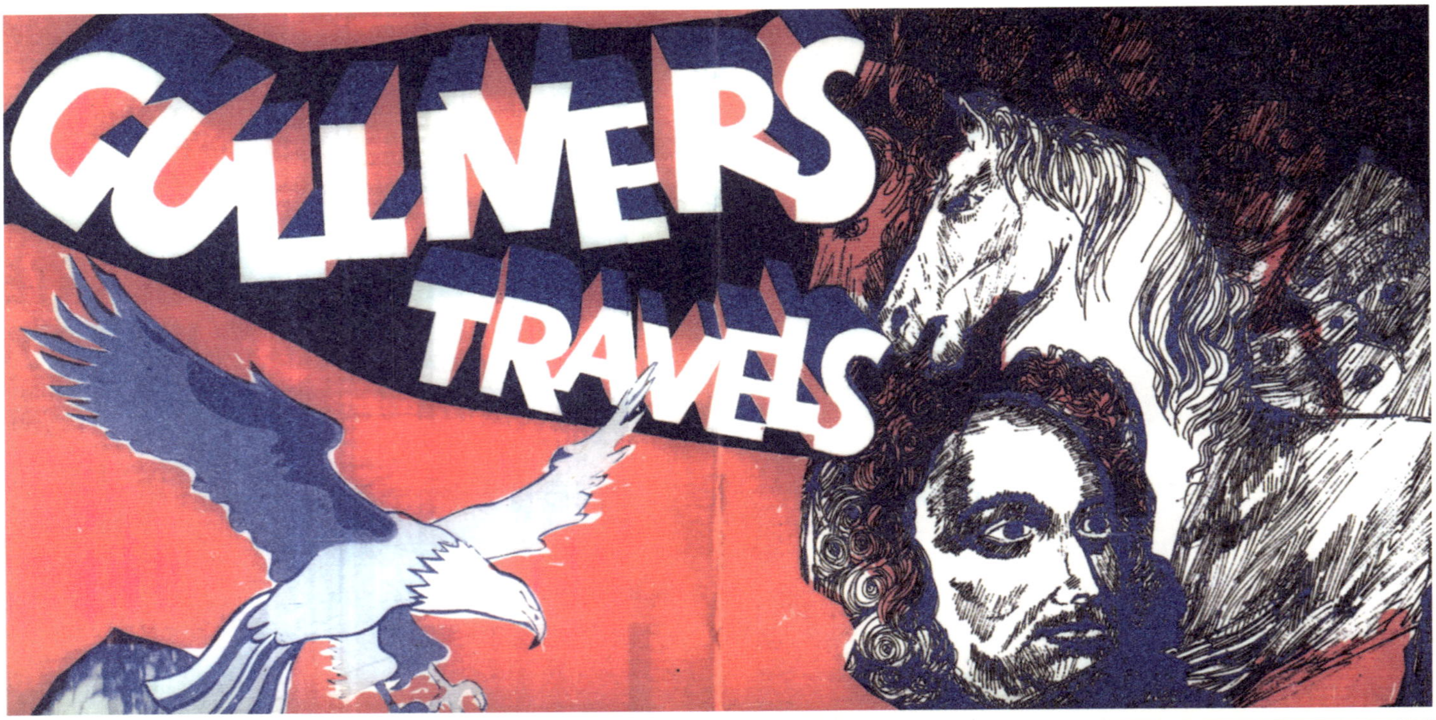
GULLIVER'S
TRAVELS

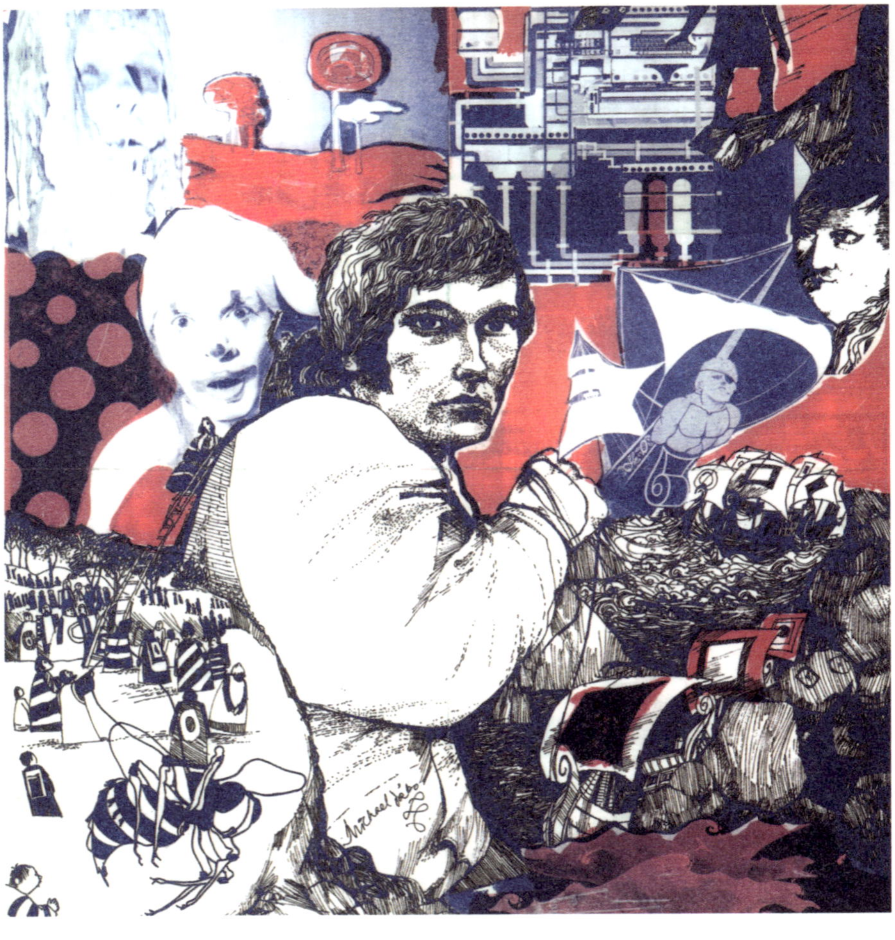

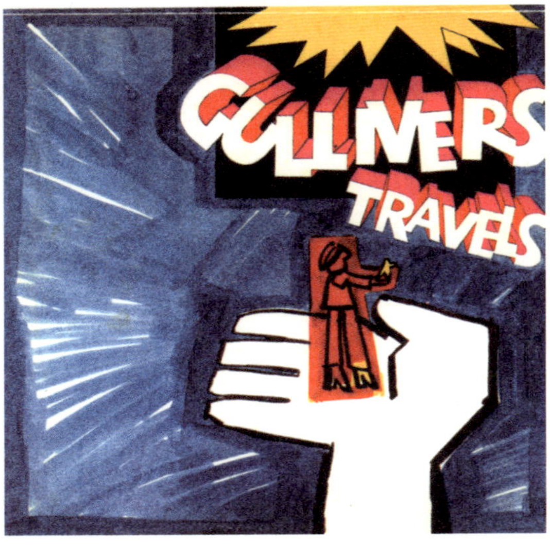
GULLIVERS
TRAVELS

THE ALBUM ARTWORK *GULLIVER'S TRAVELS* WHICH SHOWCASED THE TALENTS OF MIKE D'ABO (OPPOSITE), 1969

After these two singles, Revolution dovetailed with Instant to release a double a-side from reggae act Sonny Burke (who had recorded for Island, Bluebeat and Black Swan), and the Eddie Thornton Outfit (the brass section who had played on *Ogden's Nut Gone Flake*) who were now working with Georgie Fame.

Calder had also tried to sign The Equals, featuring Eddie Grant. The band's UK number one "Baby Come Back" sounded like it should have been on Instant. The group's manager Eddie Kassner half-jokingly agreed to sell the band for "£25,000 cash in brown paper bag" but when the cash was delivered, Kassner sent it back asking for double. The Equals stayed on President Records but Tony Calder would end up managing Eddy Grant in the 1980s during his second run at fame, including the singles "Electric Avenue" and "I Don't Wanna Dance".

Instant product kept the staff at New Oxford Street busy while Immediate went through an undeniably fallow period. The Fleetwood Mac disaster had exposed how disinterested Oldham was in Immediate, there had been no good news from Small Faces for the longest time and The Nice were out of circulation, working on new material. Now d'Abo had quit there was a real paucity of talent at Immediate. The company was no longer the only maverick in town either. The major labels all had their own "happening" imprints for new talent, such as Deram, Regal Zonophone and Polydor. There had been a gallop for US labels to set up bases in the UK, such as A&M and Warner Bros, and a swathe of young British entrepreneurs had been inspired by Immediate to try their own hand at creating something similar, such as The Who's Track records. It meant that, even worse than being perceived as on the skids, Immediate was almost considered part of the (new) music business establishment. This would not do, and to cheekily remind the rest of the UK industry what Immediate was all about Oldham and Calder pressed, packaged and sent out a limited edition Christmas 1968 UK album (200 copies) entitled the "Meditation Con", a "comment on the state of the industry". It was sent to every managing director of every record and publishing company in the UK.

Oldham, having gotten hold of some unreleased Mamas and Papas tapes, got Gered Mankowitz to take photos of eight 'hippie looking people' (the current vogue group look in the US) and sent a friend of his chauffeur Eddie round to new US label in London, MCA, with the package, claiming to be the manager of a band called The Gurus. A series of meetings were held, and taped, between the Immediate stool and MCA head Mike Sloman, Oldham edited together snippets where Sloman was caught declaring "people like me make important decision about what the public will or will not hear" and instructions to his secretary to "tell Mickie Most to fuck off". Tony Calder recounts:

> We wired and taped everything. Sloman said the vocal harmonies in the mix weren't quite right, so could you get it re-done. The following week we sent in the guy in with exactly the same acetate and Sloman said, 'ah that's much better' and he agreed to sign them. That's when we had to call it off. But we released this 12" double-sided acetate of the conversation edited together and sent it to key people in the business. I think it destroyed Mike Sloman, which is quite sad, he was the head of MCA in the UK, and died of pneumonia a few years later. But it started to show the hypocrisy of how the industry was working and that we weren't prepared to be hypocritical.

IF PARADISE IS HALF AS NICE

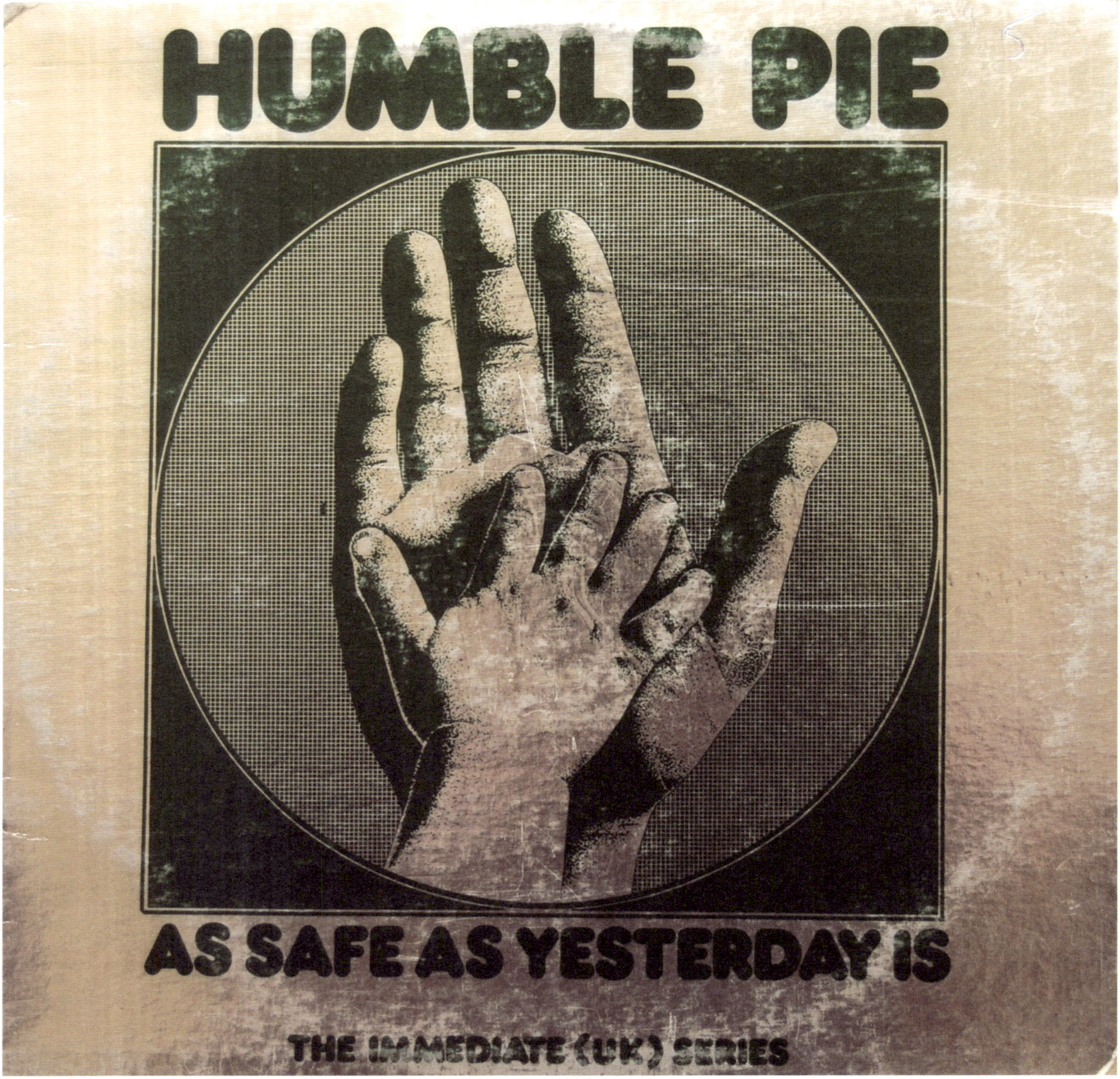
HUMBLE PIE
AS SAFE AS YESTERDAY IS
THE IMMEDIATE (UK) SERIES

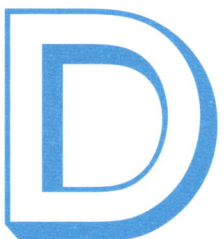

Don Arden had supplied Instant with Twinkle, Copperfield and Samson to little success. After selling Small Faces to Immediate, Arden had built himself a useful stable of 1960s stars, scoring major hits such as "Bend Me, Shape Me" and "High In The Sky" with lightweight pop act Amen Corner. Arden told a hilarious story about Amen Corner I hope we can print, that saw him arriving early to collect the group for a television recording and—finding them all out—alarmed they'd miss the show, he climbed in through the lead singer Andy Fairweather-Low's bedroom window to be confronted by posters of an extreme political nature covering the walls. "At that stage," said Arden, "I said, 'Go fuck yourself'. I just said goodbye and I did another sale. To me it meant nothing. My attitude was next please. You didn't have to die for Amen Corner."

IF PARADISE IS HALF AS NICE
(IL PARADISO DELLA VITA)
AMEN CORNER
ON IMMEDIATE RECORDS
CYRIL SHANE MUSIC LIMITED,
3/-

Arden already had The Move as ready made replacements and visited Immediate with Amen Corner's next single, "If Paradise Is Half As Nice". He told Calder he could arrange for the group to switch from Decca-owned Deram to Immediate for £17,500. Calder wishfully telexed CBS to request $60,000 to sign the group and was turned down flat. He called Oldham, who was seen less and less about the offices nowadays, to convince him the track was a major hit in the making. "Was there enough money in the Immediate kitty to sign the group?", Oldham asked. Calder said not. The cash was eventually put up out of Oldham's own pocket, supplied via Allen Klein—a forward against Oldham's Rolling Stones earnings. Fairweather-Low recalled the label switch:

> As far as we knew we were managed by Ron King/Galaxy Productions. Following the Hendrix tour we turned up at the office to discover Arden sitting in King's chair. He informed us we were now on the Immediate label. It sounds strange but that's how it came about, although it seemed cool to be on the same label as Small Faces

Two weeks later, in early 1969, Immediate released "If Paradise Is Half As Nice", which had been produced by the feted Kinks/Who producer Shel Talmy. The advert for the single, taking up a whole front page of *NME*, featured a starving African child with begging bowl.

1968 had been a boom year for the UK record industry with revenue topping £30 million. A hundred million records had been sold, the highest number since 1964 when singles accounted for the bulk of the sales. Now albums accounted for that bulk and the singles market was soft. From a dead start 150,000 sales took "If Paradise Is Half As Nice" straight to number one, replacing "Blackberry Way" by Arden's act The Move. Calder had gambled on spending heavily to get "If Paradise Is Half As Nice" to number one, an illegal swindle he had also used to hype Fleetwood Mac up the charts, expecting to recoup and profit from the guaranteed three months of continuous radio play and

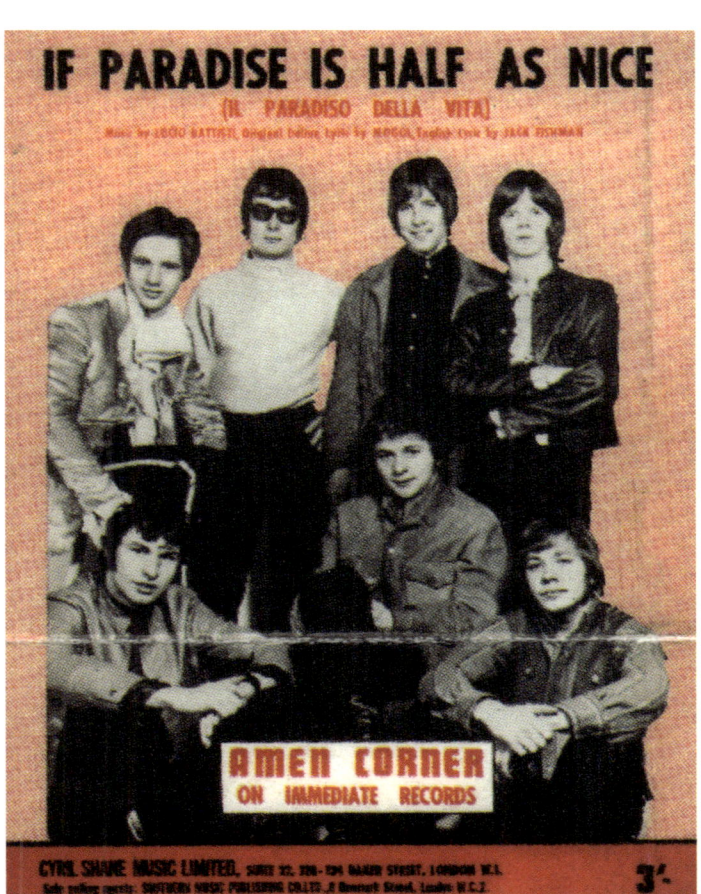

OPPOSITE: *AS SAFE AS YESTERDAY IS*, HUMBLE PIE, CIRCA 1968

AN ARTICLE DESCRIBING THE MUCH NEEDED CHANGE OF SCENE FOR AMEN CORNER, 1969

AMEN'S FAST NEW SINGLE

IT all started with "Gin House" and this week that record is released once more by Decca in their new "Demand Performance" series. The same time as "(If Paradise Were) Half As Nice" is released on the Immediate label starting it all again with a change of scene for Amen Corner.

Why a change of scene?

"We were beginning to feel a bit stale, so we decided to have a big change-round all over," explained Andy Fairweather-Low famed one-time owner of a pink Marcos sports car ("I'm fed up with it now. Know anyone who wants to buy it?").

MANAGEMENT

"We didn't change our recording label — we had a change of management, and we're with Harold Davison for agency. As a group I think we'd reached a point where we wanted to go in a particular direction, musically, and that needed a different set-up. As we were progressing we felt we wanted to go with a more progressive record company. So we chose Immediate—they may be a small company compared with someone like Decca, but they're very big in ideas and they're very go-ahead.

"There's nothing wrong with Decca — we have nothing against them. It was purely time for a change and we felt we needed the more personal touch that you get from a smaller company. And I'm glad we went to Immediate — everything just seems to click into place. The recording session for our new single was ridiculous — it went so fast. We just went straight through the number and it came out as we wanted it. And it isn't only the musical side of things that's worked out well — so far everything seems just right for us.

"It's not that Amen Corner are becoming a so-called progressive group — we're still out-and-out commercial and I think we'll stay that way, even though individually we may have more serious musical ideas. Now we feel a bit freer to work on new ideas for the group — it's like starting again, but on a different rung of the ladder."

"Gin House" was the first step on the first rung and "Half As Nice" the second on the second — and comparing both these new releases mirrors the way Amen Corner have moved. And that's one of their main appeals — while always insisting on remaining strictly commercial they have managed to develop their music, to change while still retaining their very own sound.

Has Andy changed much personally during that time?

"Obviously I'm still the same basically — though a lot of little things are different. For example at one time if I'd bought a jacket and then taken it home and decided I didn't like it, I'd have put it in the wardrobe and forgotten it. But now if I don't like something I've bought, then I take it back and change it. That car of mine is another example — at one time it was something I really wanted. I had visions of how it would be, especially the interior with the stereo record player and the television set and the fitted cigarette box — in fact everything. But when I got the car I was so disappointed with the way it had been done — the leather didn't fit, the television fell off its supports, the record player kept jumping about — that now I've lost interest completely. I'd put it on a pedestal and it just didn't come up to expectations.

PUSHED AROUND

"One way I've noticed in how I've changed is that now I put up with a lot less than I used to — when we were new in the business I used to let myself be pushed around a lot because I felt, well, they know what they're doing. Now, though, if I feel that what I'm being asked to do is a bit unreasonable, then I don't do it. It's not a matter of being big-time — I used to worry about that a lot more — but I'm sure a lot of people who aren't in a pop group, in the public eye, wouldn't put up with some of the treatment we're expected to.

"The thing is that you're bound to change anyway, leave alone after a couple of years in the pop business. You get more used to things, and so your attitude changes.

"One thing that I don't like though is the way that some people think that because they're in the public eye it entitles them to make statements and give opinions about anything, whether they know what they're talking about or not. I couldn't do that. If I don't know about a particular subject, then I don't talk about it—if I were to make some statement just for the sake of being controversial and someone who knew what he was talking about were to take me up on it, I wouldn't be able to defend what I'd said. The one thing I do know about is music, and I'll argue for hours on that subject with people who disagree with me. But something like politics I know nothing about at all—and I'm just not interested anyway—so I never argue about it."

In March Andy and Amen Corner are off to America for a few weeks. And I'm sure they'll do very well there—in fact I know it. Their brand of music and their stage act can't fail in the States. But Andy isn't looking forward to going at all. His opinion of America and the majority of Americans is almost unprintable. "The only way I'll survive a month over there," laughed Andy, "is by being continually drunk."

I can't see that happening—but I hope there's enough good in America to dispel Andy's fears and doubts of that country and its inhabitants

AMEN'S ANDY FAIRWEATHER-LOW

---

genuine sales that would follow. The scam went to plan and, after a week at number one, the sing-a-long single slowly glided on down over 11 weeks through the Top 40 and went on to sell 250,000 in the UK.

Fairweather-Low, told *NME*: "Immediate, our new record label, are excellent at promoting groups. Look what they have done for Small Faces and The Nice. Well maybe the The Nice's flag-burning thing was a mistake but we won't go in for anything commercial like that."

Immediate swiftly followed the massive "If Paradise Is Half As Nice" with another Amen Corner single, "Hello Susie", written by The Move's Roy Wood. Produced by Shel Talmy "Hello Susie" was another massive hit, peaking at number four. Talmy remembers:

I think I produced "If Paradise Is Half As Nice" at Olympic Studios; good record, good band. Andy Fairweather-Low certainly had a most unique voice. The fact of the matter is I wanted a different record than "Hello Susie", which I think would had made them humongously big called "At Last I've Got Somebody To Love". Oldham turned it down. They wanted "Hello Susie". I had feel a lot better if someone paid me for them.

It is thought that Talmy never got paid at the time because Calder did not like him—the same thing, incidentally, had happened to Duncan Browne. "Hello Susie" was followed into the UK charts by Amen Corner's debut album on Immediate, *The National Welsh Coast Live Explosion Company*, recorded live at the Royal, Tottenham. The album was a screaming teenybopper-fest that featured covers of Lennon/McCartney's "Penny Lane", Jim Webb's "MacArthur Park", and their previous big hit singles "Gin House", "Bend Me, Shape Me", "High In The Sky", "If Paradise Is Half As Nice" and "Hello Susie". Despite problems producing enough of the double album sleeve jackets (a further sign of Immediate's ailing finances), *The National Welsh Coast Live Explosion Company* made a decent showing in the UK Top 20. Immediate promoted the band, against the prevailing trend, as the UK's most "overground group". "Underground means a group with a single that doesn't make the charts", Oldham told *NME*.

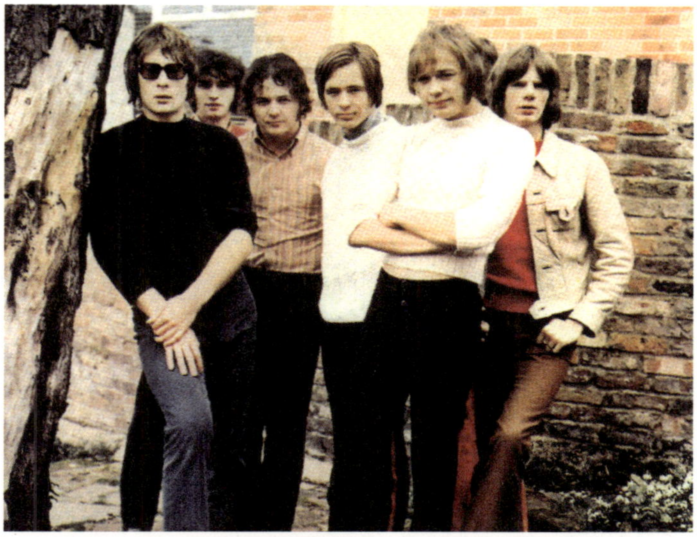

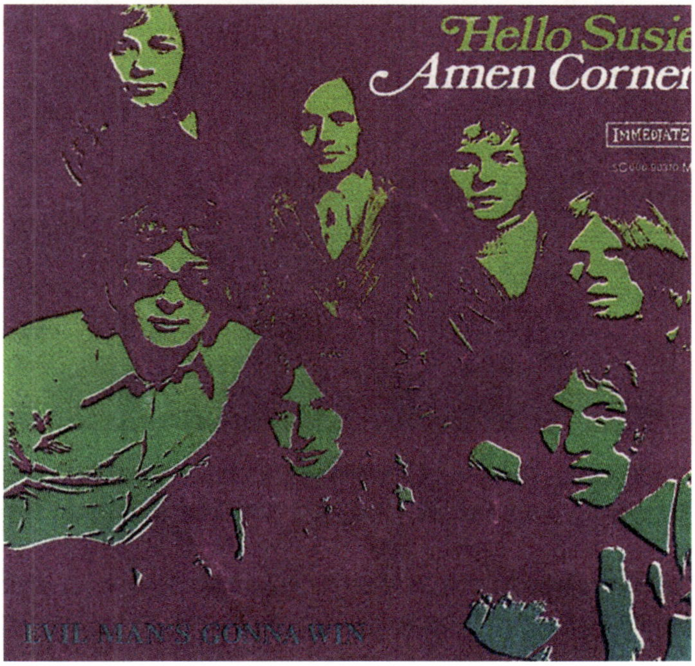
Hello Susie
Amen Corner
IMMEDIATE
EVIL MAN'S GONNA WIN

OPPOSITE: AN ARTICLE DESCRIBING THE MUCH NEEDED CHANGE OF SCENE FOR AMEN CORNER, 1969

TOP: AMEN CORNER PROMOTIONAL SHOT, 1969

BOTTOM: "HELLO SUSIE", 1969

Privately, Oldham admitted Amen Corner did not excite him. Aside from Fairweather-Low he couldn't name another member of the group. "I went to see Amen Corner live in Cardiff after the hit", Oldham told me, "and thought to myself if this is showbusiness what the fuck am I still doing in here".

The issue over having to front the cash himself to sign the group also brought home to him how negligent Immediate had become over finances. Over the years he had constantly bailed out and propped up the label with money from his Rolling Stones earnings, the £25,000 he had laid out to sign Small Faces being the most substantial amount. Now though he knew he would soon be facing a large tax bill on all those Rolling Stones earnings, a bill he was told to expect to be in the region of a half a million pounds. He warned Calder that from now on he expected the label to be self-sufficient and the two agreed to downsize their offices (much of the Immediate paperwork was now going through the New York office anyway), closing down their New Oxford Street offices and moving to 111 Gloucester Place, W1. The new tenants at the old Immediate head quarters were a US label starting up in London; Warner Bros. Evident of the amount of drugs Oldham was taking and a sign of his aberrant leadership at Immediate, he splashed out lavishly to have the wife of his movie star friend Richard Harris, acquire huge wooden Church doors from the set of her husband's film *Camelot*, and used them to separate his and Calder's new offices. Calder responded in kind, having his wife Jenny fly out to Paris to buy expensive chandeliers for the new office.

One of Calder's cash-generating ideas involved a company house and disco in Antigua, the popular Caribbean tourist destination. He planned to launch a travel company called Instant Travel to take people there. He also oversaw re-releases of "Hang On Sloopy", "Out Of Time", and "First Cut Is The Deepest" and a hastily hashed together Chris Farlowe compilation album made up of studio odd and ends; *The Last Goodbye*. There were also two more Blues albums, *British Blues From The Beginning* for the US market and a half-hearted *Blues Leftovers* for the UK market. None of these releases made much capital and Calder's hope that Amen Corner would come good in the long-term was looking suspect. Calder had laid out plenty of cash to hype them into the charts but seemed to have over-estimated their longevity as an act, especially in a climate where heavy rock dominated the most lucrative albums market.

Fairweather-Low (dubbed "one of Britain's most photographed and popular teenage faces") was asked by *Melody Maker*: "Did Andy—idol of the teenyboppers—feel the Amen Corner's scene was losing way to the underground groups?" There had been many empty seats at Amen Corner's recent concert at the Royal Albert Hall's Pop Proms. Was it an indication that the nation's "fave rave" group was beginning to wane? He said:

> It's only [the US] that doesn't take too kindly to Amen Corner. We've never yet had a hit there. In [the UK], we can get across to the kids with our stage performances. But the Americans

IM 24 007
IMMEDIATE
AMEN CORNER
IF PARADISE IS HALF AS NICE
HEY HEY GIRL

IMMEDIATE

IMMEDIATE

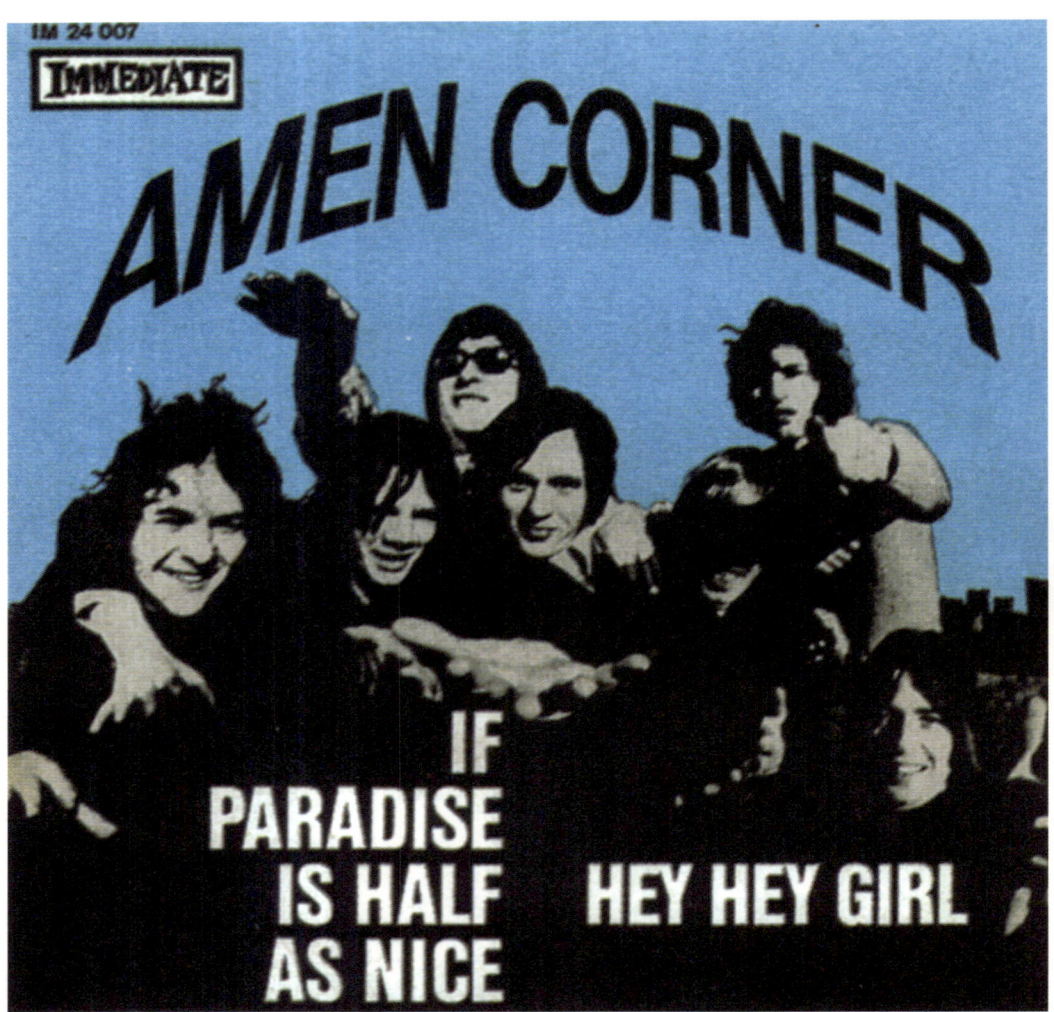

> don't know what Amen Corner are like. But it's no good attempting a tour there without a hit record to back it up. Now The Nice is the type of group that appeals to Americans. Their musicianship is so good. Not that we play rubbish, but we're aiming at the youngsters, and we shall carry on catering for them. But I must admit that The Nice is a too-much group.

Apart from Amen Corner having no joy in the US most of what Fairweather-Low said was untrue. He had started thinking he was Jerry Garcia and decided he was above his audience and was fed up with playing round the ballrooms for £1,500 a night. He wanted to go 'underground'. The group recording a cover of The Beatles' number one "Get Back" for a new single, yet despite another front page *NME* Immediate advert to promote it, the Fairweather-Low produced track was a flop and, frustrated, he left the group. "They have decided to abdicate their role as Britain's number one teenage group. The decision to disband was taken unanimously by the group at a time when they feel they have achieved all that is possible for them within the musically creative limitations of their particular markets", the group's new PR, former *NME* writer Keith Altham, told *Melody Maker*.

Immediate released an album *Farewell To The Real Magnificent Seven*, to 'commemorate' the Amen Corner split, featuring the group's three Immediate singles, with overblown adverts stating: "In 1936 Edward VIII abdicated his crown, his story is in words. In 1969 the Amen Corner abdicated their crown, this is their story in sound." The band recalled how they came away from the Immediate deal with £2,000 split seven ways. Despite Paul Banes' continued efforts to get blood out of a stone, CBS had not been interested in Amen Corner. When "If Paradise Is Half As Nice" was at number one in Europe, Clive Davis had told Allen Klein he did not believe the group were right for the market. Banes did eventually manage to get CBS to press "If Paradise Is Half As Nice" for US release but they gave him no promotional support and it sold just 1,904 copies. Then the company, via their Epic imprint, released their own version of the song with The Dave Clark Five fronting it. An old record industry sage quietly informed Oldham, "You think you're very clever having got a 12 per cent record royalty from CBS but they only have to pay Dave Clark five per cent. So who do you think they're going to work on?"

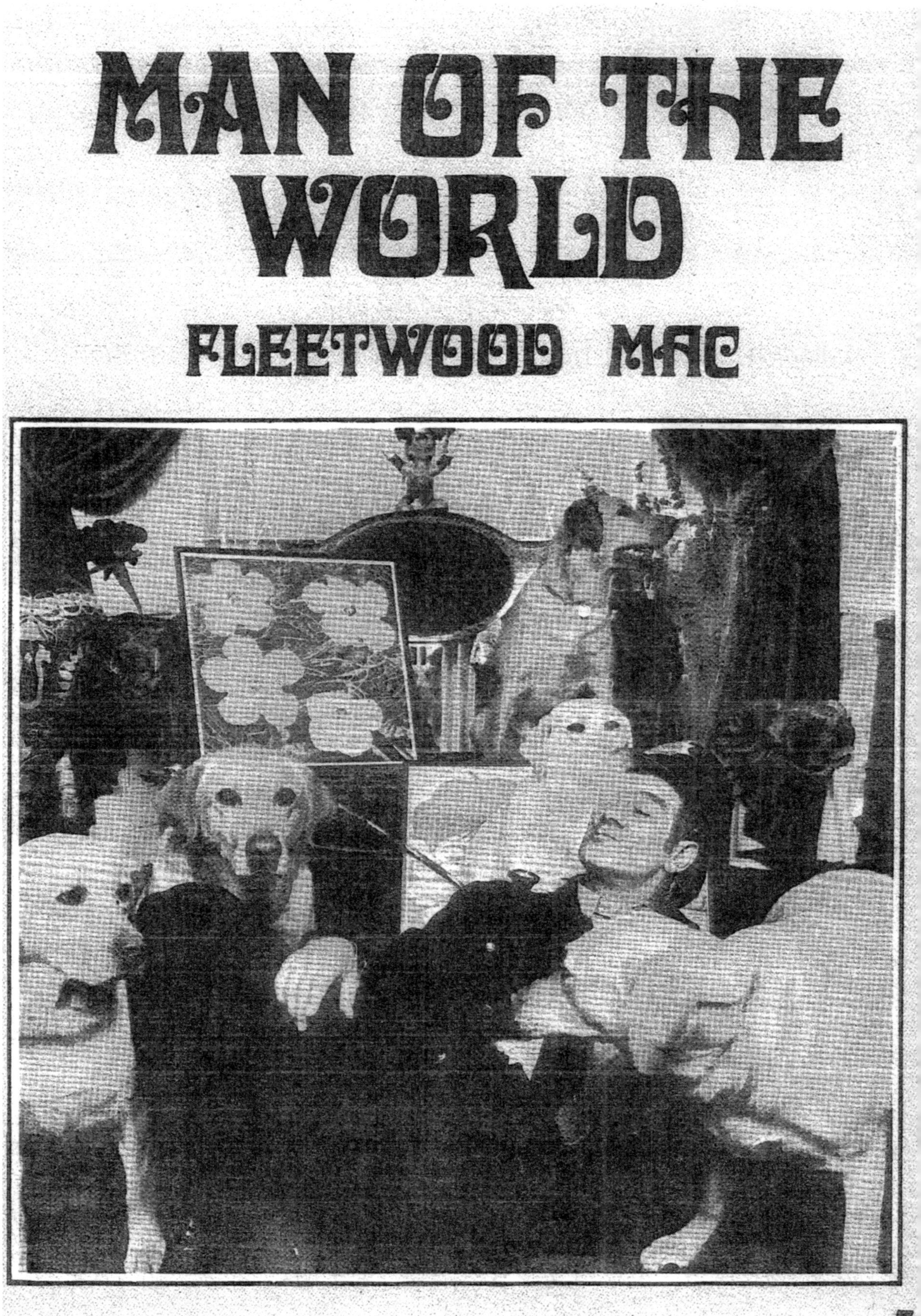
MAN OF THE WORLD
FLEETWOOD MAC
3/

OPPOSITE: ARTWORK FOR AMEN CORNER'S "IF PARADISE IS HALF AS NICE", 1969

FLEETWOOD MAC'S INFAMOUS "MAN OF THE WORLD" SINGLE IMAGE WHICH WAS A FRONT PAGE SPREAD FOR *NME*, APRIL 1969

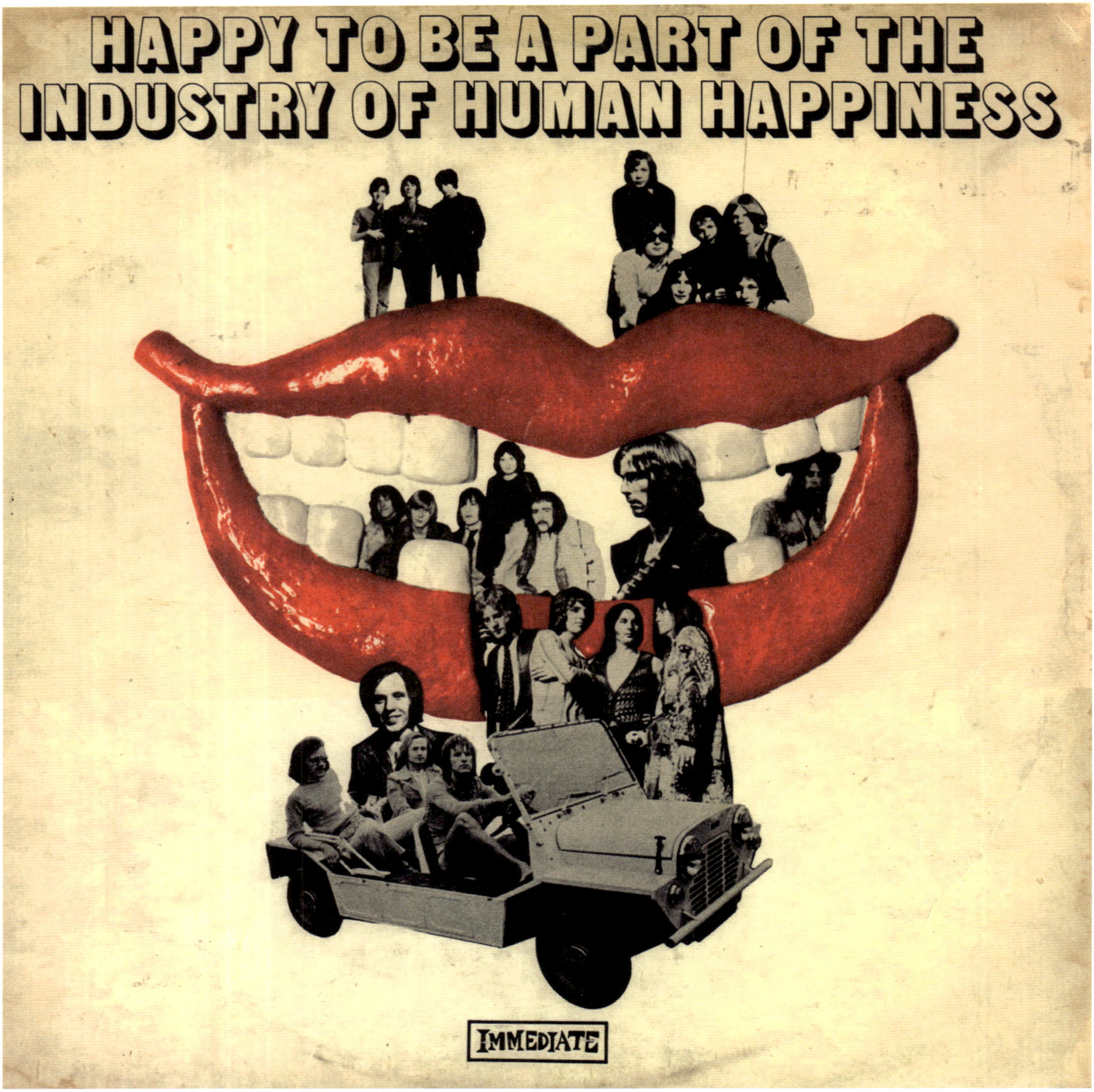
HAPPY TO BE A PART OF THE
INDUSTRY OF HUMAN HAPPINESS
IMMEDIATE

HUMBLE PIE/AMEN CORNER/NICE/FLEETWOOD MAC
JOHN MAYALL'S BLUESBREAKERS/THE SMALL FACES
ERIC CLAPTON/JIMMY PAGE/ALBERT LEE
SIDE ONE
SO FINE/THE AMEN CORNER
MAN OF THE WORLD/FLEETWOOD MAC
WATER ON MY FIRE/ALBERT LEE
TRIBUTE TO ELMORE/ERIC CLAPTON & JIMMY PAGE
ALABAMA '69/HUMBLE PIE
SIDE TWO
COLD LADY/HUMBLE PIE
HANG ON TO A DREAM/NICE
ON TOP OF THE WORLD/JOHN MAYALL'S BLUESBREAKERS & ERIC CLAPTON
RECESS/AMEN CORNER
LAZY SUNDAY/SMALL FACES
A CONMAN SLEEVE PRODUCTION
IMMEDIATE RECORD COMPANY LIMITED 111 GLOUCESTER PLACE LONDON W1

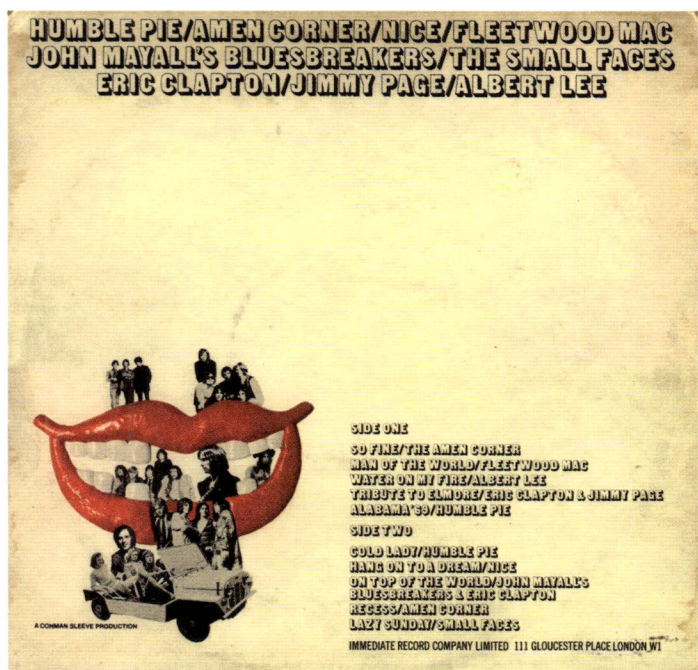

Calder continued his assault on the label's back catalogue. A double a-side single, "Itchycoo Park" and "Lazy Sunday" pressed for the US market, "So Fine" by the Amen Corner surfacing as a possible UK single and he also issued an intriguing "cool low-price package" Immediate compilation album, *Immediate Lets You In*. This was pressed up in vast quantities and featured "So Fine" by Amen Corner, "Man Of The World" by Fleetwood Mac, "Water On My Fire" by Albert Lee, "Tribute To Elmore" by Eric Clapton and Jimmy Page, "Hang On To A Dream" by The Nice, "On Top Of The World" by John Mayall's Bluesbreakers and Eric Clapton, "Recess" by Amen Corner and "Lazy Sunday" by Small Faces. The record sleeve featured snaps of the Immediate 'family' of artists montaged around a huge pair of smiling lips.

Calder looked to the future too, putting a new group, The Hill, in the studio (a single "Sylvie" was given limited release) and working on signing a new major artist for the label, the US singer Scott Walker. Oldham had admired Scott as one half of The Walker Brothers when, during their 1965 heyday, his friend Bob Crewe wrote "The Sun Ain't Gonna Shine Anymore" for them. Having been casually turned on to the music of Jacques Brel by Oldham and Mort Shuman, Scott was now also a solo performer, signed with Piccadilly records boss, Maurice King, for management and recording on the Philips label. In the press, King was blaming Immediate for Walker's failure to honour a fortnight club residency in Manchester and issued a writ against the label. Tony Calder recounts:

> We had Scott Walker. He agreed. He was on board. He was gonna record for Immediate. His manager tried to put injunctions on Oldham and me but in the end he gave up. Scott was ready to record. I negotiated the deal. I mean what a fucking star, but I couldn't deal with him. I was like, "Andrew, you better get your arse over here fast, this guy's not in the real world". Scott was talking about Brel, we were talking about Mort Shuman, he was talking about things I don't know about; he started talking about philosophy. I thought, What's this all about? My idea of philosophy is a number one hit record. I was out of my depth with Scott Walker. I just knew he could have been bigger than Frank Sinatra.

All Calder had to do was persuade Oldham to pay off Maurice King. But King had believed Immediate's publicity and therefore it's wealth and was asking a huge fee to breach the deal with Philips that would then allow Walker free to sign with the label. Oldham refused to pay the price.

OPPOSITE AND TOP:
IMMEDIATE COMPILATION ALBUM:
IMMEDIATE LETS YOU IN, 1969

HUMBLE PIE

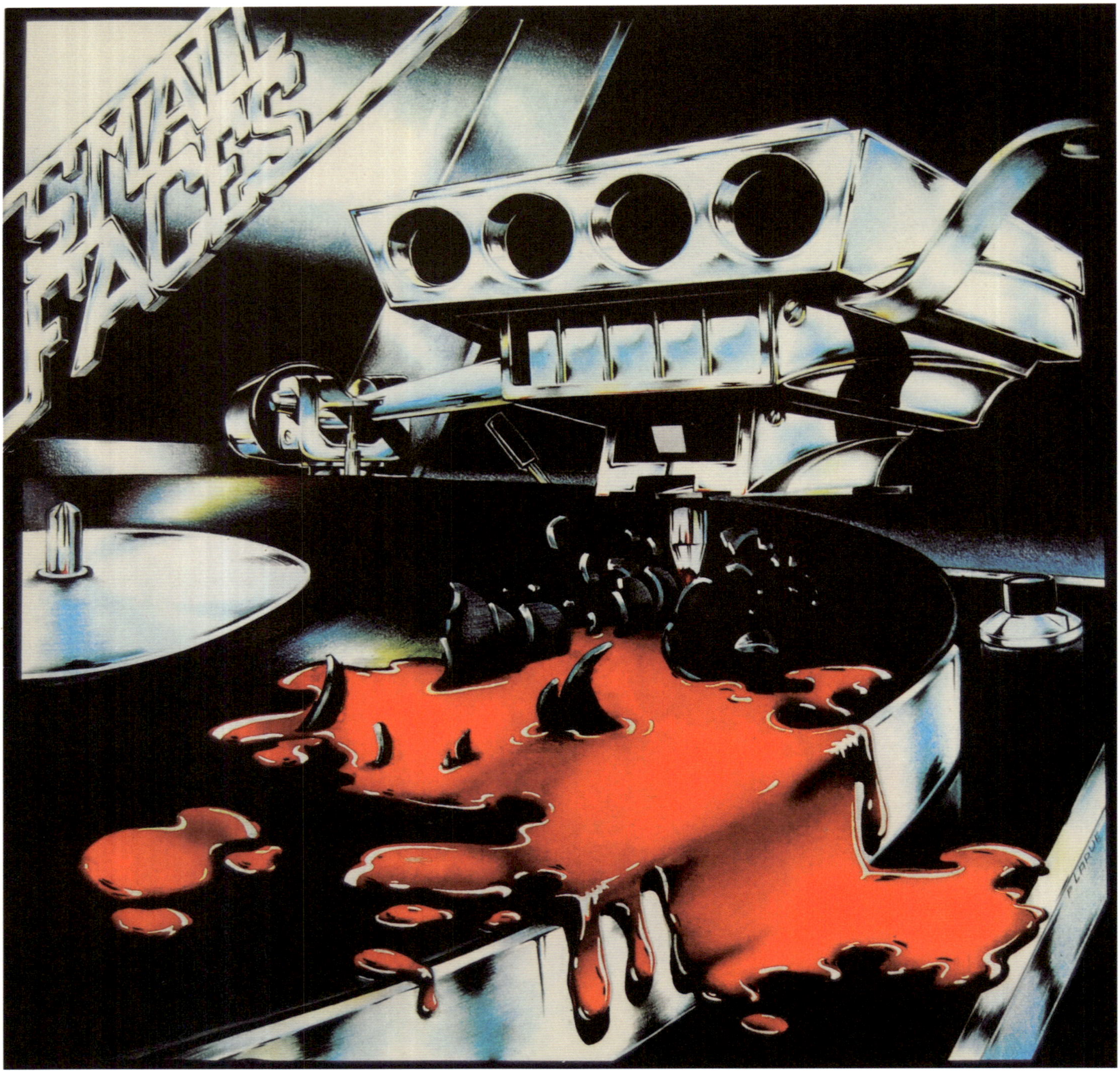
SMALL FACES
P. LARUE

The Scott Walker episode caused a giant rift between Immediate's co-owners. Calder was already resentful over Oldham's questioning of his capability to run the company and now felt humiliated. Calder had shouldered the brunt of the workload as Oldham's attention to, and affection for, Immediate wavered and there was much bad-mouthing in the office. It seemed the only thing they could agree on was Steve Marriott, a shared love that would briefly reignite and unite the two men and Immediate.

bellaphon
CR 3009 STEREO
HERE COME THE NICE · THE AUTUMN STONE · COLLIBOSHER · ALL OR NOTHING · RED BALLOON
LAZY SUNDAY · CALL IT SOMETHING NICE · I CAN'T MAKE IT · AFTERGLOW OF YOUR LOVE
SHA LA LA LA LEE · THE UNIVERSAL · ROLLIN' OVER · IF I WERE A CARPENTER · EVERY LITTLE BIT HURTS
MY MIND'S EYE · TIN SOLDIER · JUST PASSING · ITCHYCOO PARK · HEY GIRL
WIDE EYED GIRL ON THE WALL · WHACHA GONNA DO ABOUT IT · WHAM BAM THANK YOU MAM
IMMEDIATE

IMMEDIATE
RECORD CO. LTD.
45 RPM
IM-8721
A
AFTERGLOW OF YOUR LOVE
SMALL FACES

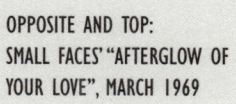

OPPOSITE AND TOP:
SMALL FACES' "AFTERGLOW OF YOUR LOVE", MARCH 1969

The album Small Faces were supposedly recording as the follow-up to the massive *Ogden's Nut Gone Flake* was a record Immediate desperately needed to boost both finances and image. The album had ground to a halt months previously as the group were stumped by how to follow up their "masterpiece". Steve Marriott had caused much unrest in the studio and had more than once walked out on the group, notably after the New Year's Eve gig at Alexandra Palace. The rest of the group had been dismayed to find out he'd got a side project on the go with The Herd's lead singer and "Face of 1968" Peter Frampton, who had played second guitar for Small Faces at a few recent live show. Marriott had produced a Frampton-written Herd single, "Sunshine Cottage" for Deram records and wanted Frampton to become a permanent member of Small Faces. The rest of the group were against the move.

Marriott pressed ahead, rehearsing his side-project with Frampton (having persuaded former Apostolic Intervention teen drummer Jerry Shirley to join up) while playing on intermittently with Small Faces. It had been impossible to keep these developments out of the press and throughout the saga rumours that Small Faces were on the verge of splitting were rife. Immediate took out another front page *NME* advert—infamously titled *The Anthology Of Speculation*—to advertise a new single from the Small Faces, "Afterglow (Of Your Love)". The advert montaged music press news stories speculating on the future of Small Faces, Marriott, Frampton and Immediate itself. Steve Marriott later revealed:

> It was Oldham's put together. By then I had already left Small Faces. The last complete thing we did together was the song "The Autumn Stone", which was going to be the title track of the next Small Faces album, and "Wham Bam Thank You Man". Those two tracks were supposed to be a single but Oldham didn't like "The Autumn Stone" and replaced it with "Afterglow (Of Your Love)". The irony is he wound up using *Autumn Stone* as a title for the album Immediate put out after we split. We had recorded a lot of tracks that we never had a chance to finish. They had titles just to mark the tape boxes, "Colibosher", "Wide Eyed Girl On The Wall", and they were thrown in as instrumentals. The three live tracks on Autumn Stone were from Newcastle City Hall, just after *Ogden's* [*Nut Gone Flake*] came out. We had thought about a live album and wanted to see what

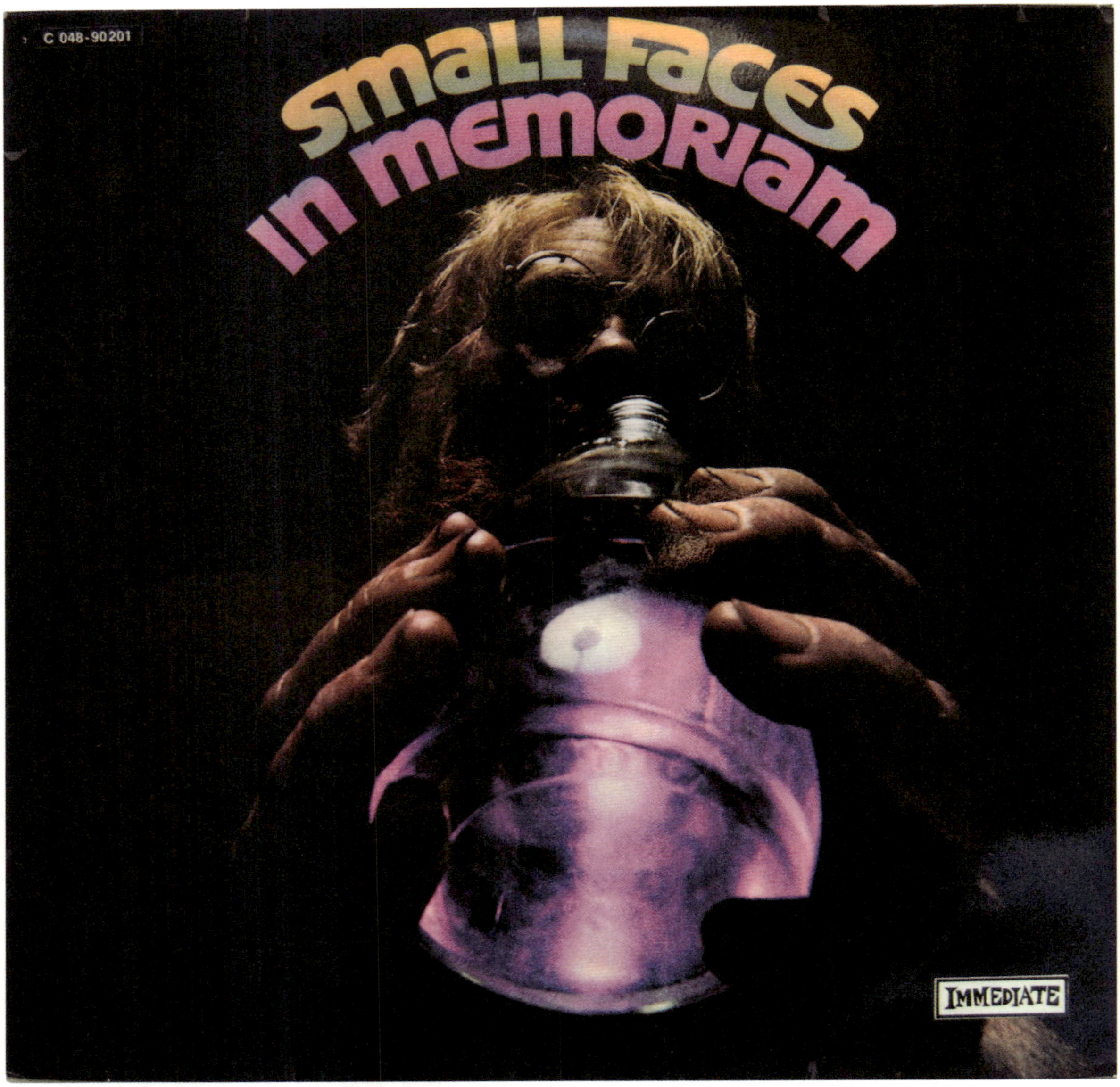
C 048-90201
SMALL FACES
IN MEMORIAM
IMMEDIATE

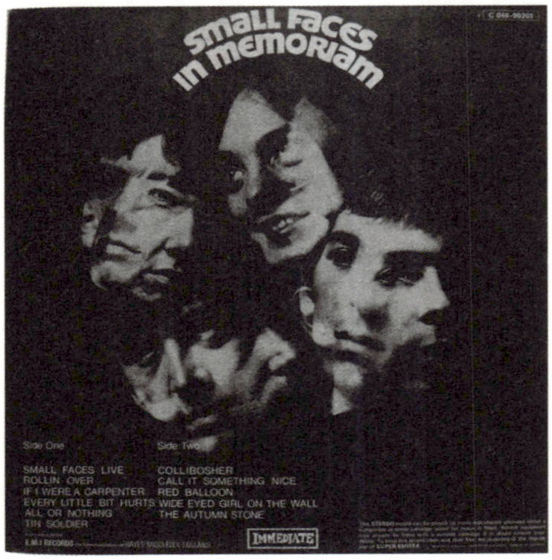
SMALL FACES
IN MEMORIAM
C 048-90201
Side One
SMALL FACES LIVE
ROLLIN OVER
IF I WERE A CARPENTER
EVERY LITTLE BIT HURTS
ALL OR NOTHING
TIN SOLDIER
Side Two
COLLIBOSHER
CALL IT SOMETHING NICE
RED BALLOON
WIDE EYED GIRL ON THE WALL
THE AUTUMN STONE
E.M.I RECORDS
IMMEDIATE

SMALL FACES' REPACKAGED *AUTUMN STONE* NOW NAMED *IN MEMORIAM*, NOVEMBER 1969

OPPOSITE: SMALL FACES ALBUM *THE AUTUMN STONE*, 1969

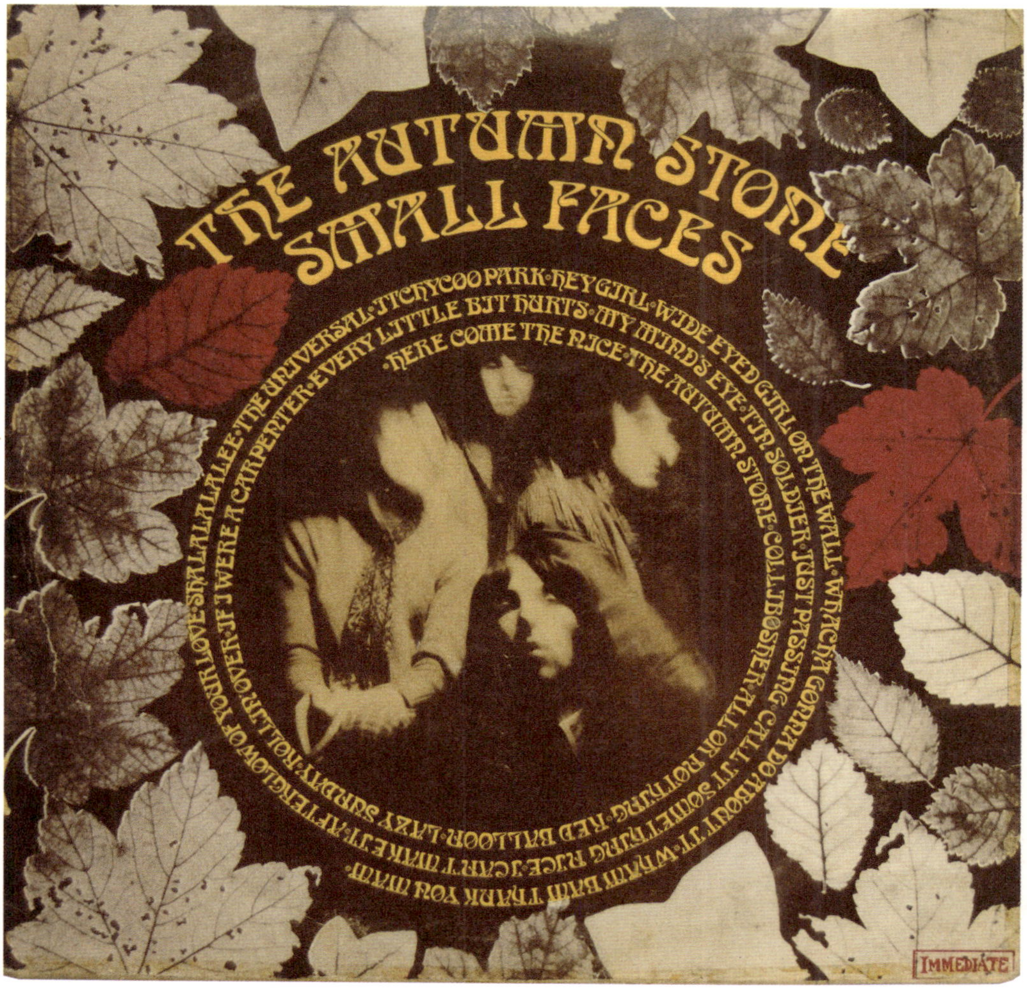
THE AUTUMN STONE
SMALL FACES
IMMEDIATE

it was like. I don't remember too well but I think they recorded a couple of sets—with and without the horn section, at a couple of gigs that were real scream machines. At first Oldham wanted to use the stuff for Small Faces, who were going to continue without me, and Ronnie wanted me to help mix the stuff, so I did. There's probably more of it sitting round somewhere.

With no Small Faces to promote it, the rocking "Afterglow (Of Your Love)" peaked at a disappointing number 36 in the UK with Marriott officially announcing his break from the group soon after, saying: "My quitting is the best thing for them and for me. It will give both of us our freedom." The lavishly packaged Small Faces double album, *Autumn Stone*, which appeared soon after, was a fitting tribute to the group's legacy. Oldham was proud to have been a part of the process, feeling their run on Immediate had been artistically and commercially satisfying for all concerned. The truth was there was little mileage left in the group who had dropped off the pop radar since *Ogden's Nut Gone Flake*, and had never quite made the transition to become the world-beaters they had once promised to be. The lack of success in the US had hurt most, and the in-fighting over the direction the band should take, designed to rectify that, had ripped them apart. A special edition of Small Faces *Autumn Stone* was pressed up for the German market, a double album re-titled *In Memoriam*. Andrew Oldham recalls:

Tony Calder said to me one day: 'Pick a straw.' Then he explained we had a choice. We could either go with three [of the Small] Faces—Kenny, Ronnie and Mac—wherever they were gonna go with their lives or we could follow Stevie. I didn't regard it as a choice. Neither did Tony. Marriott was our man.

Immediate let one-time Cream road manager, Billy Gaff, take over the three remaining Small Faces. Gaff put the Jeff Beck group guitarist Ronnie Wood and singer Rod Stewart in to replace Marriott and Small Faces became The Faces and signed a lucrative deal with Warner Bros Records where they would to go on and enjoy a new lease of life and fame. Marriott christened his new outfit Humble Pie and co-star in the group, 18-year-old Peter Frampton quit The Herd to go at it full-time. Herd manager Ken Howard, recalled:

AFTERGLOW OF YOUR LOVE
WHAM BAM THANK YOU MAN
SMALL FACES

SMALL FACES
IMMEDIATE

Humble Pie Town And Country

Humble Pie As Safe As Yesterday Is
AS SAFE AS YESTERDAY IS
HUMBLE PIE

IMMEDIATE
AFTERGLOW OF YOUR LOVE
WHAM BAM THANK YOU MAM
Small Faces

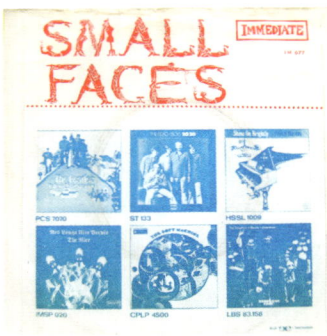

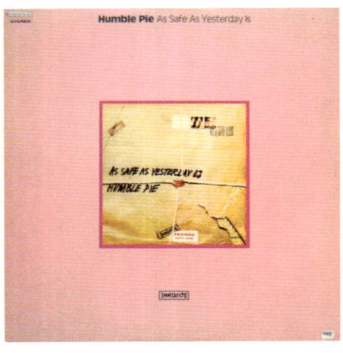

> We suddenly found the van in the street outside the house: its tyres had been let down. They said, 'we're going to Andrew Oldham'. What could one do? One couldn't sue them. It was particularly hurtful because we had a number two record and had notched up three hits with the group. They were poised for very big things. We just thought, Why?

Under Howard and co-manager, Ken Blaikley, Herd were pop fodder featured heavily in magazines aimed at teenage girls and had scored Top 20 hits with "Paradise Lost" and "From The Underworld" in 1967 and had gone Top 5 with "I Don't Want Our Loving To Die" in 1968. But it was The Herd's producer, Steve Rowland, who caused Immediate most problems; he claimed Frampton was under worldwide contract to his Double R Productions until 1971. Rowland fought hard to protect his interest in Frampton and the legal wrangling went on for weeks, with Immediate eventually admitting defeat and paying what was reported to be £24,000 to lift the injunction. Oldham was forced to admit defeat on this one and fronted the money from his own pocket, eager to get Marriott's new group off the ground.

After the expensively delayed start, a front page story in *Melody Maker* welcomed Humble Pie as a "Pop Giant's Supergroup", and told how "two of Britain's biggest pop idols" had been secretly rehearsing for weeks with Jerry Shirley and bassist, Greg Ridley. Immediate took out an advert that spanned the front and back page of *NME*, making an A2-size poster of a David Bailey photograph of the four Humble Pie musicians, to promote the group's debut single, "Natural Born Bugie". The advert was part of a mammoth press promotion, the label's biggest ever, with more full page adverts in *Record Retailer*, *Rolling Stone*, *International Times*, *Oz*, *Black Dwarf* and *Time Out*, as well as special posters and window displays for the 140 shops in the WH Smiths chain. The first 50,000 copies of "Natural Born Bugie", written by Marriott but sung by Frampton, were encased in an expensive colour sleeve featuring a David Bailey photograph of the group. Immediate had already recorded Humble Pie's debut album, *As Safe As Yesterday Is*, and planned, they said, "the most complete packaging concept ever" for its release. The press release read:

> Humble Pie (The Beginning Or The End Of Speculation)
>
> Small Faces, place: anywhere/time: recently. Herd ditto. Steve the Marriott, your very own advert for Unicef (except his tubes sing much better than Danny Kayes ever did) a dozen hits as one of the four Small Faces, waiting for their heads to overcome the name—Sha La La La Lee doesn't make it tonite, or any night. The Herd, Peter Frampton's on the same wave—I can't remember the number but it had to be two-thirds of Frampton wailing around a swiss cottage hook and a walker brothers middle eight for relief. Waltham Cross' own Jerry Shirley came to us through an apostolic intervention with reincarnated hands (they've got to have been around longer than 17 years) VIP's and Spooky Tooth had been the home of bassist, Greg Ridley, until Marriott and Frampton said its been a buzz but there's got to be a change-and we'll call it Humble

EXPRESS
AS SAFE AS YESTERDAY IS
HUMBLE PIE
IMMEDIATE
FRAGILE
WITH CARE

DESPERATION
STICK SHIFT
BUTTER MILK BOY
NATURAL BORN WOMAN
AS SAFE AS YESTERDAY IS
BANG!
ALABAMA '69
I'LL GO ALONE
A NIFTY LITTLE NUMBER LIKE YOU
WHAT YOU WILL
FRAGILE
WITH CARE
ARRANGED: HUMBLE PIE
A JOINT PRODUCTION FOR BEATRICE NOKES
AIR MAIL
PAR AVION
FROM
IMMEDIATE RECORD CO LTD
111 GLOUCESTER PLACE LONDON W.1.

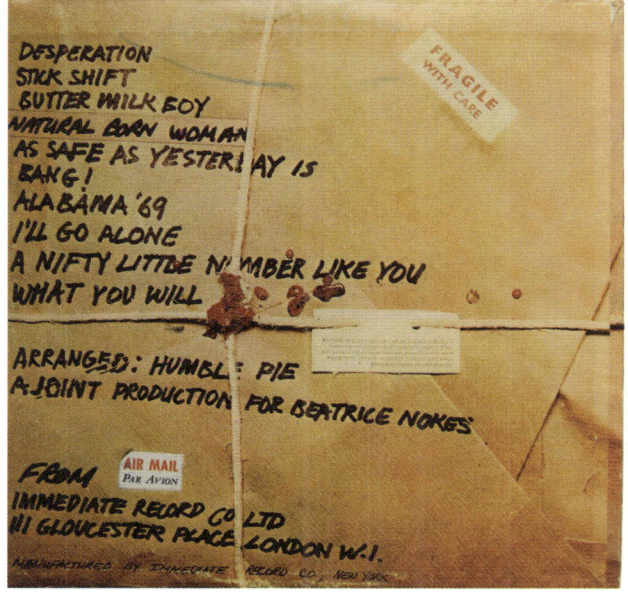

OPPOSITE: TWO INCARNATIONS OF "AFTERGLOW OF YOUR LOVE" BY SMALL FACES AND HUMBLE PIE'S DOUBLE COMPILATION ALBUM, *TOWN AND COUNTRY* AND *AS SAFE AS YESTERDAY*, 1969

AS SAFE AS YESTERDAY
HUMBLE PIE, 1969

HUMBLE PIE
NATURAL BORN BUGIE WRIST JOB
IMMEDIATE
IMO82

IMMEDIATE
RECORDS INC.

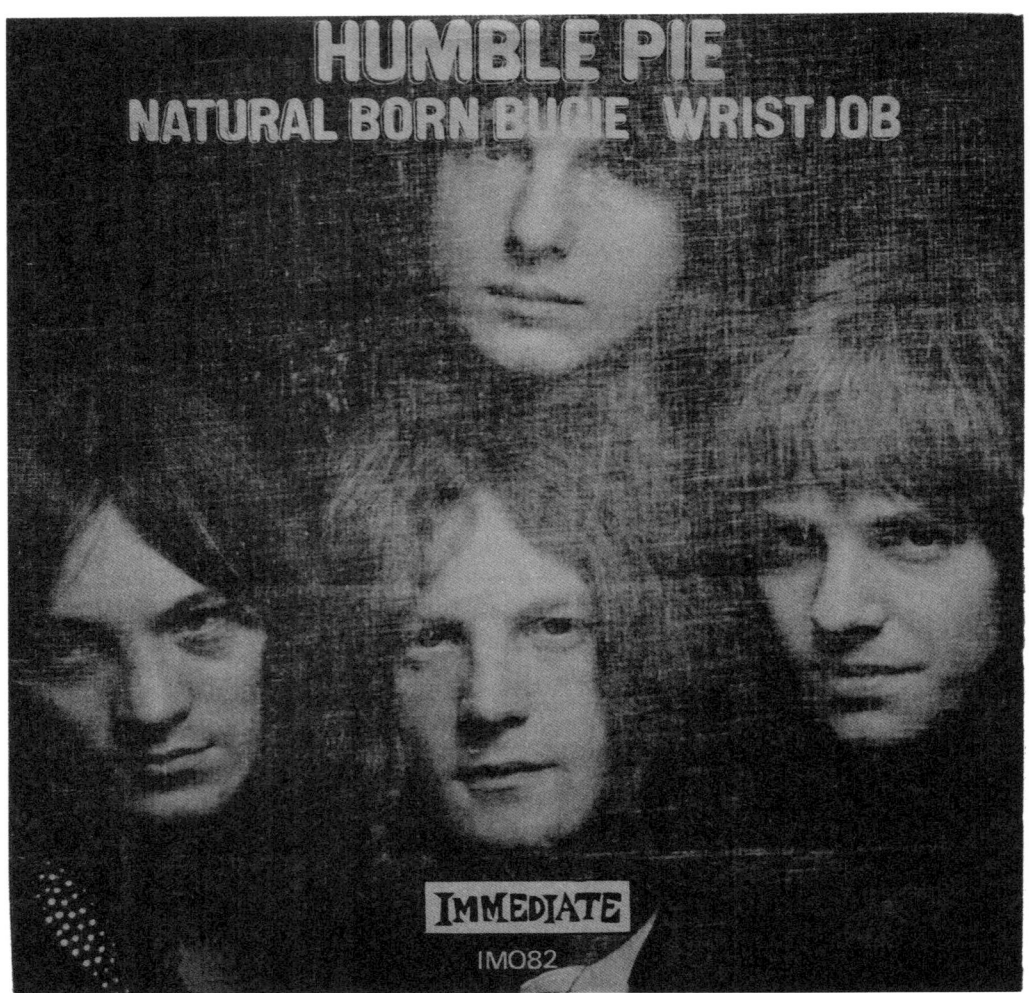

Pie. So, Frampton, Marriott, Ridley and Shirley said let's form a group, not a supergroup, that bag is for ICI and ATV, and to be a good group for us and all we've got a lot of getting together to do. That was six months ago. First of all we would go down to the Magdelan Laver Village Hall as a record company to see how the blowing was going. It was, then we went down as people for a buzz, and more. Humble Pie now have an album As Safe As Yesterday Is and single "Natural Born Bugie" with "Wrist Job". We love it all, we hope you do. And for those of you who said what are Humble Pie up to, just listen. And for those of you who have forgotten "Lazy Sunday"'s and swiss cottage riffs, we don't mind, we've got Humble Pie, so have you, and so have they, and that's what counts."

Humble Pie debuted live at Ronnie Scott's jazz club and in press interviews to promote the new single, Marriott said: "I've never been so excited about anything as I am about the group. We're going to be a heavy music band." Still only 22, Marriott was careering from mod to rocker, hoping, he said, to avoid the "old pop star bit" with his new group. "The single doesn't lay any schmaltz", he told one interviewer and, prompted by accusations that it sounded pretty close to The Beatles track "Get Back", he explained: "It's a bit like "It's Not Easy" [from the Rolling Stones *Aftermath* album], with a sound like the Bill Black Combo."

NME's Nick Logan was sent down by Immediate in a limo to meet Marriott and Jerry Shirley and join the group as they rehearsed for live shows in the village hall near Marriott's home. Marriott expounded on "Natural Born Bugie":

> People have said that they expected something a little more original from us, and there is some justification for that. The next one will be more original. But we never took the song that seriously. It just came to me, as I was sitting on the toilet playing my guitar. I literally wrote the words in ten minutes. They're nothing and the top line is rubbish. But the back track is great and that's more important to me than the vocal track.

When the group performed the single on *Top of the Pops* Frampton said he was just glad he didn't have to spend two hours being made up with obligatory eye-drops dolled on to

IMMEDIATE
HUMBLE PIE
NATURAL BORN BUGIE
WRIST JOB

IM 082 IMMEDIATE
HUMBLE PIE
NATURAL BORN BUGIE (Marriott)
WRIST JOB (Marriott)
AMEN CORNER

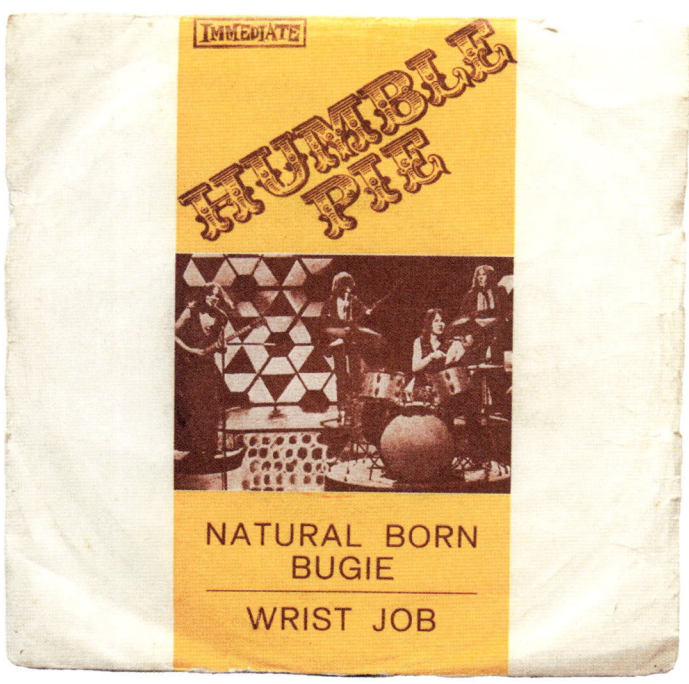

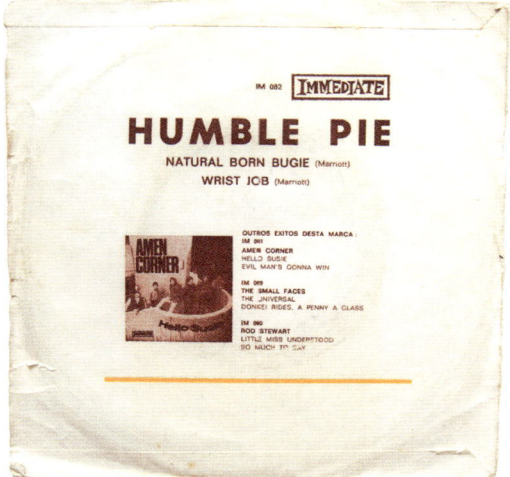

OPPOSITE AND TOP: UK AND US RELEASES OF HUMBLE PIE'S "NATURAL BORN BUGIE" AND "WRIST JOB", AUGUST 1969

make it look as though he was about to cry, the way he had been for previous appearances with The Herd. Jerry Shirley recounted:

> Once Oldham got wind of the fact that we were gonna get Humble Pie together he came up and stood at the plate. There were other managers at the time and other record labels interested, but Oldham just came up and said: 'I'll do this, however you wanna do it, whenever you wanna do it, lets go to bat.' He had this remarkable knack of spotting a hit single. We recorded this little song that was a Chuck Berry rip-off that was called "Natural Born Bugie". The term Bugie back then was considered derogatory because it had the same kinda connotation as the word 'nigger' today; as in the bugie man. We had no idea, we thought it was like boogie-woogie. The song was a throwaway that Steve had come up with a direct rip-off from "Little Queenie". Oldham came into the studio at Morgan and said, 'that's the single'. We said no but within five or six weeks it was number one across Europe. Steve had been very much the front man in Small Faces but when it came to Humble Pie in the early days it was much more Peter Frampton's band. Steve just wanted to relax and groove. It was Peter and I that put the band together. I got in because Peter wanted a drummer that sounded like Kenny Jones. Really Steve just wanted to kick back and play a little guitar and not be the manic front man, that's really where he was at in the beginning. He wanted to see Greg Ridley and Peter shine more than himself, and then it all changed because Steve just had this very powerful presence on stage and after a while as Humble Pie went on he was being encouraged by all those around us, management wise, to take the forefront. Anyway, it was his natural way to do that.

"Natural Born Bugie" reached number four in the UK with ten weeks of strong sales to come and made number one in Holland, Belgium and Germany. The "most complete packaging concept" was used for the group's debut album, *As Safe As Yesterday Is*. The sleeve was made to look as if it were a parcel wrapped in brown packing paper, tied by string, with album information as the address and the photo's of the band by David Bailey tucked away as mock postage stamps.

With Marriott's new denim and hairy rock image and sound, Small Faces fans hoping for more Lazy Sundays in Itchycoo Park were left disappointed by Humble Pie's debut LP (one US rock critic calling it "heavy metal shit-rock"). The album was produced by Andy Johns (the brother of Rolling Stones engineer Glyn Johns) at Olympic studios. This was the other half of Marriott's moon—he shared co-writing credits with Frampton on the album's title track and had written the lion's share of the rest of the album. "Strong-arm music" he called it, with Shirley practically declaring war on his drum kit; searching to find more soul than ever on his vocal intensity and attack. "Buttermilk Boy" caught them at their best, a few organ thrills but basically just a couple of guitars, bass and drums, with some clever vocal switches between Marriott and Frampton.

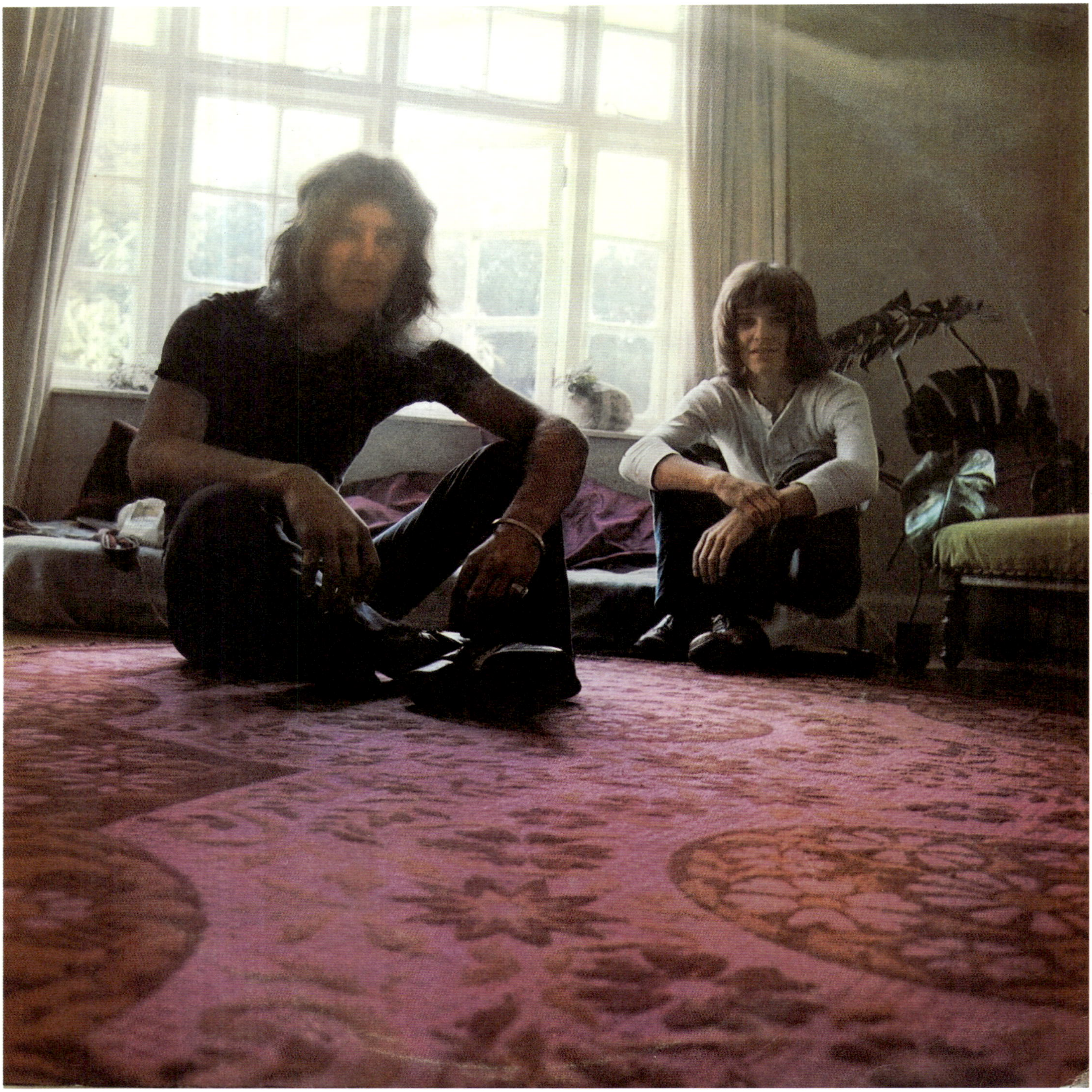

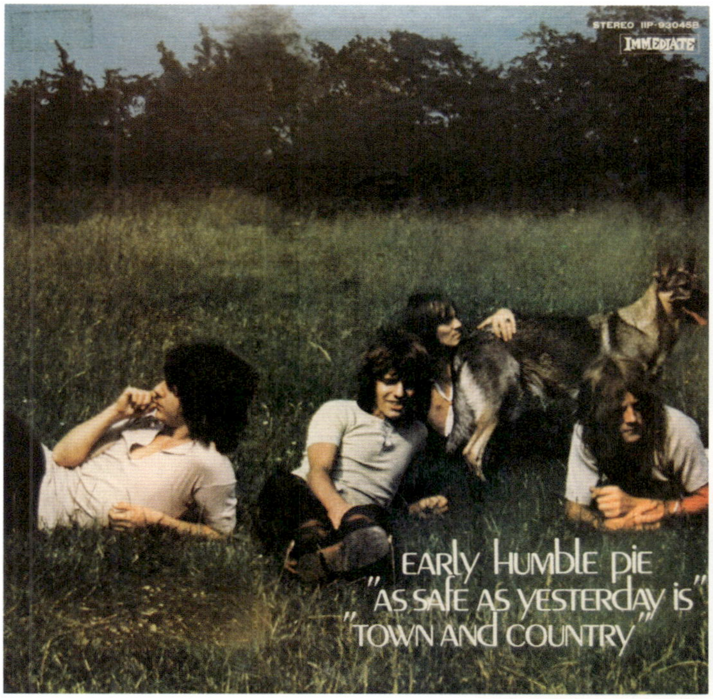
STEREO IIP-93046B
IMMEDIATE
early humble pie
"as safe as yesterday is"
"town and country"

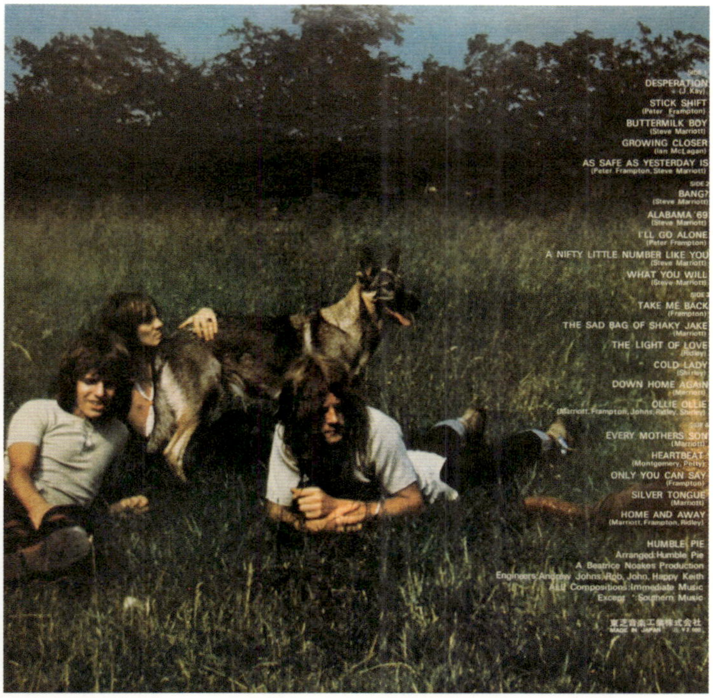
DESPERATION
(J. Kay)
STICK SHIFT
(Peter Frampton)
BUTTERMILK BOY
(Steve Marriott)
GROWING CLOSER
(Ian McLagan)
AS SAFE AS YESTERDAY IS
(Peter Frampton, Steve Marriott)
BANG?
(Steve Marriott)
ALABAMA '69
(Steve Marriott)
I'LL GO ALONE
(Peter Frampton)
A NIFTY LITTLE NUMBER LIKE YOU
(Steve Marriott)
WHAT YOU WILL
(Steve Marriott)
TAKE ME BACK
(Frampton)
THE SAD BAG OF SHAKY JAKE
(Marriott)
THE LIGHT OF LOVE
(Ridley)
COLD LADY
(Shirley)
DOWN HOME AGAIN
(Marriott)
OLLIE OLLIE
(Marriott, Frampton, Johns, Ridley, Shirley)
EVERY MOTHERS SON
(Marriott)
HEARTBEAT
(Montgomery, Petty)
ONLY YOU CAN SAY
(Frampton)
SILVER TONGUE
(Marriott)
HOME AND AWAY
(Marriott, Frampton, Ridley)
HUMBLE PIE
Arranged:Humble Pie
A Beatrice Noakes Production
All Compositions:Immediate Music

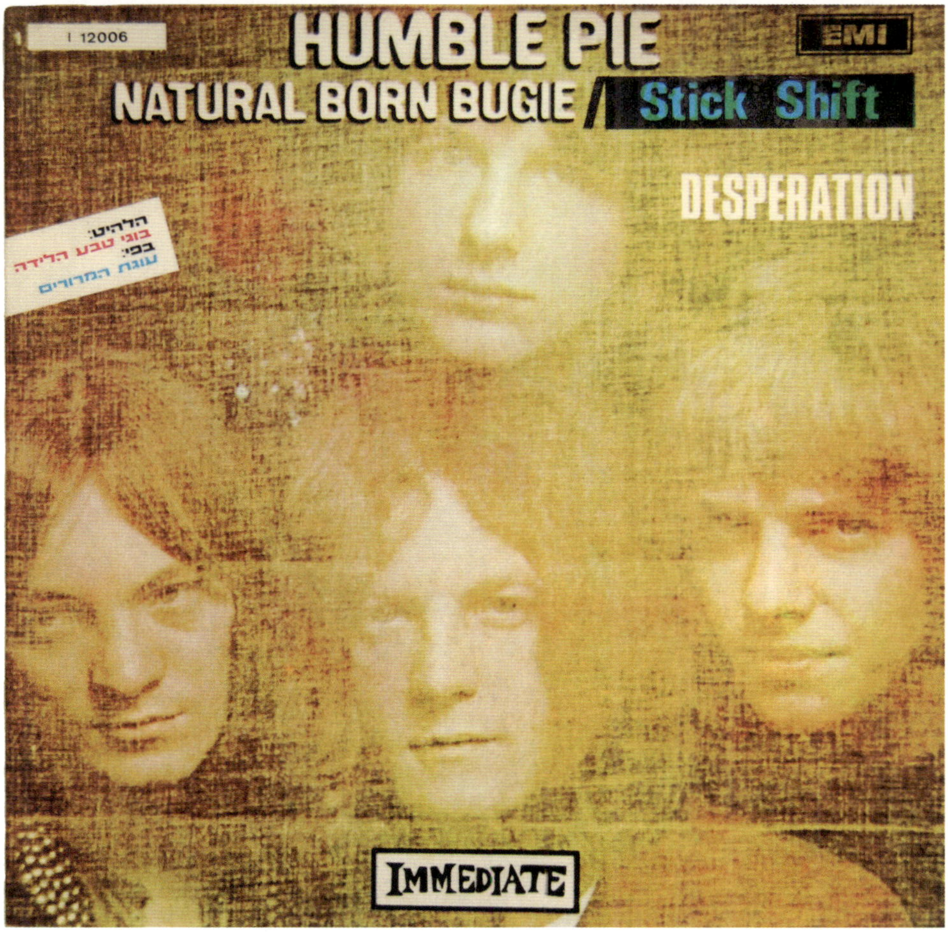
I 12006
HUMBLE PIE
EMI
NATURAL BORN BUGIE / Stick Shift
DESPERATION
הלהיט:
בוגי טבע הלידה
בפי:
עוגת המרורים
IMMEDIATE

OPPOSITE: THE INFAMOUS *TOWN AND COUNTRY*, 1969

HUMBLE PIE'S "NATURAL BORN BUGIE" AND "WRIST JOB", AUGUST 1969

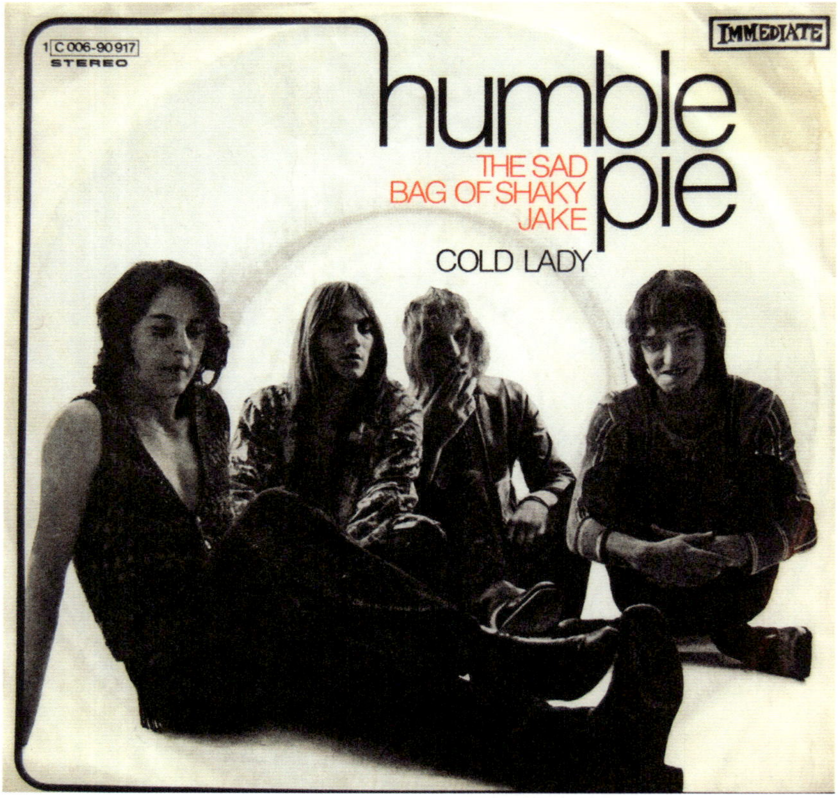
1 C 006-90 917
STEREO
IMMEDIATE
humble pie
THE SAD BAG OF SHAKY JAKE
COLD LADY

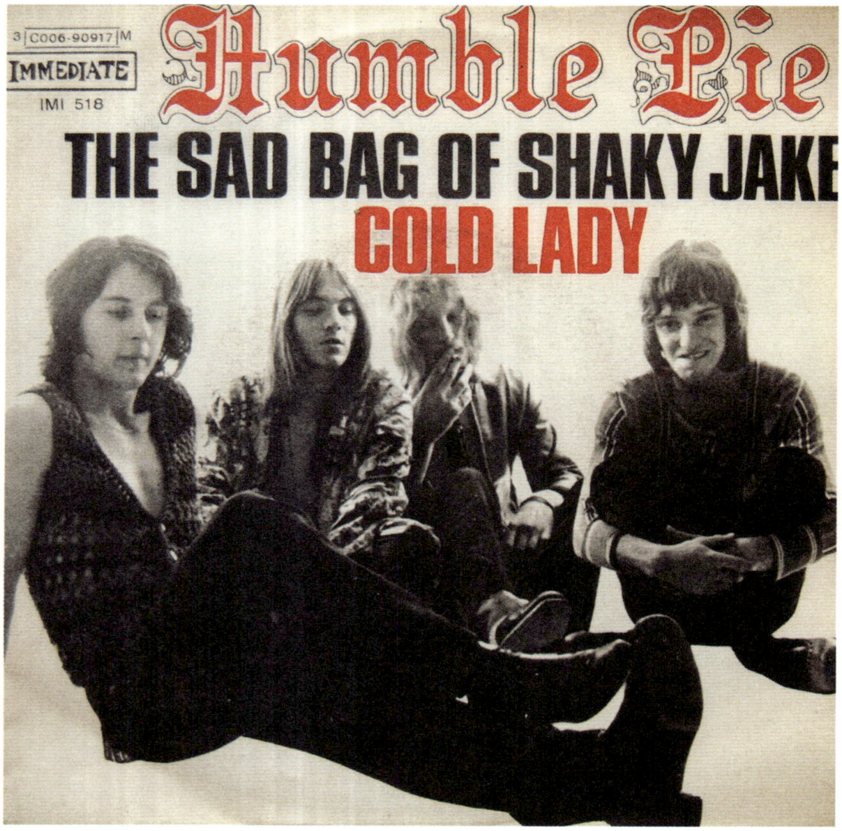
3 C006-90917 M
IMMEDIATE
IMI 518
Humble Pie
THE SAD BAG OF SHAKY JAKE
COLD LADY

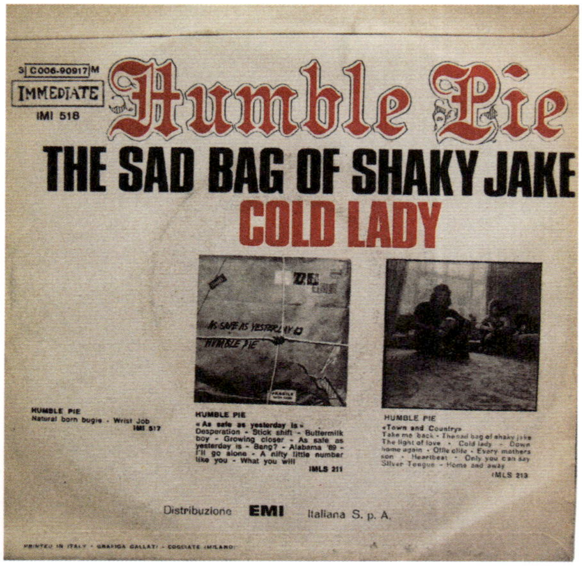
3 C006-90917 M
IMMEDIATE
IMI 518
Humble Pie
THE SAD BAG OF SHAKY JAKE
COLD LADY
HUMBLE PIE
Natural born bugie - Wrist Job
IMI 517
HUMBLE PIE
« As safe as yesterday is »
Desperation - Stick shift - Buttermilk boy - Growing closer - As safe as yesterday is - Bang? - Alabama '69 - I'll go alone - A nifty little number like you - What you will
IMLS 211
HUMBLE PIE
«Town and Country»
Distribuzione EMI Italiana S. p. A.

ABOVE AND OPPOSITE: US AND UK RELEASES FOR HUMBLE PIE'S "THE SAD BAG OF SHAKY JAKE" AND THE B-SIDE "COLD LADY", 1969

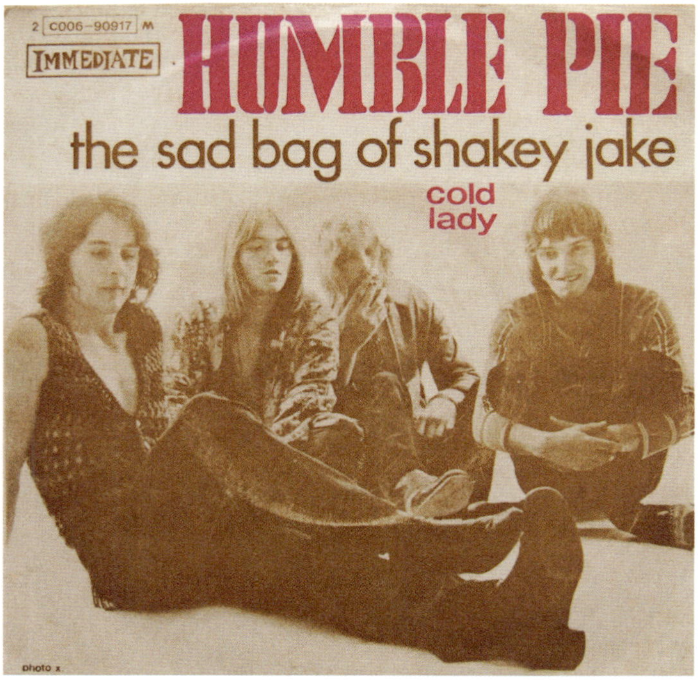
2 C006-90917 M
IMMEDIATE
HUMBLE PIE
the sad bag of shakey jake
cold lady
photo x

At least Marriott was now feeling up to touring and he took Humble Pie on the road in Europe with festival shows in Italy, Switzerland, Belgium, and Germany. Amsterdam's The Paradise Club became the band's main base of operations as they hit the television European promo circuit. The delay in launching the group over Frampton's contract meant the group had already recorded their second album and Immediate rushed to release it. *Town And Country* showed a lighter, more acoustic and country tinged, sound than on their earthy rock debut. "A little more contrived but a lot more relaxed", said Marriott in interviews. He added:

> There's more clarity on it than the first. People criticised us for being muzzy but it was meant to be that way because it was like a live thing. There's more recording technique on the second. The first was not representative of what we are doing now. I am really pleased with the second album much more than the first.

The album, again produced by Andy Johns at Olympic studios, came with another fantastic UK adverting campaign, and there were a couple of obvious singles, Marriott's take on Buddy Holly's "Heartbeat" and his own song "Down Home Again". Promotional copies of a second single, "The Sad Bag Of Shaky Jake", were sent out to record stations as the band embarked on their debut UK tour, a package called *Changes 1969*, which was advertised via a front cover of *NME*. Humble Pie were supported on the tour by former Instant act, Samson and also David Bowie, who was scoring with his first hit, "Space Oddity". The stage show, designed by Sean Kenny, stopped in at such august venues as the Queen Elizabeth Hall. Jerry Shirley remembers:

> Sean Kenny came up with a bizarre set that had this huge white elephant with smoke blowing out of its ass. Oldham was very committed to being on the road with us. The other bands on Immediate he was bored with or weren't pulling his chain. He gave us that great big Rolls Royce to travel England in with Eddie driving. That was our tour vehicle. In the UK on the tour with David Bowie we were still doing a lot of the acoustic stuff as a reaction to all that supergroup publicity. We were trying to say, don't expect too much, give us a chance to grow, we haven't found our niche yet. It was going to America that made us realise we had to get down and do some serious rock and rolling.

Another standout was "Wrist Job", an organic aching soft-rock number—a real Joe Cocker touch—and, in 1969, that was no bad thing. "We've done our second album already and it has got a beautiful sound", Marriott said helpfully while promoting *As Safe As Yesterday Is*. Steve Marriott recalled:

> My missus helped me with the whole changeover scene. You need someone who can give you advice and understands. If Humble Pie hadn't happened, I would have stayed on in the Small Faces, bringing everybody down. I never ever thought I would leave Small Faces. I thought it would just go on forever. But it feels like Humble Pie has been together for years. I just want to be part of the band and do my job. I don't have to freak out anymore. I can relax and play music.

Special displays and posters were distributed to all the record dealers in the UK, but after a good first week, in at number 15 in the Record Retailer charts, sales for *As Safe As Yesterday* dropped off, with many questioning why the hit single was not included on the album—a practice, Oldham wryly reflected, that had once endeared the Rolling Stones to their public.

THE AMERICAN DREAM

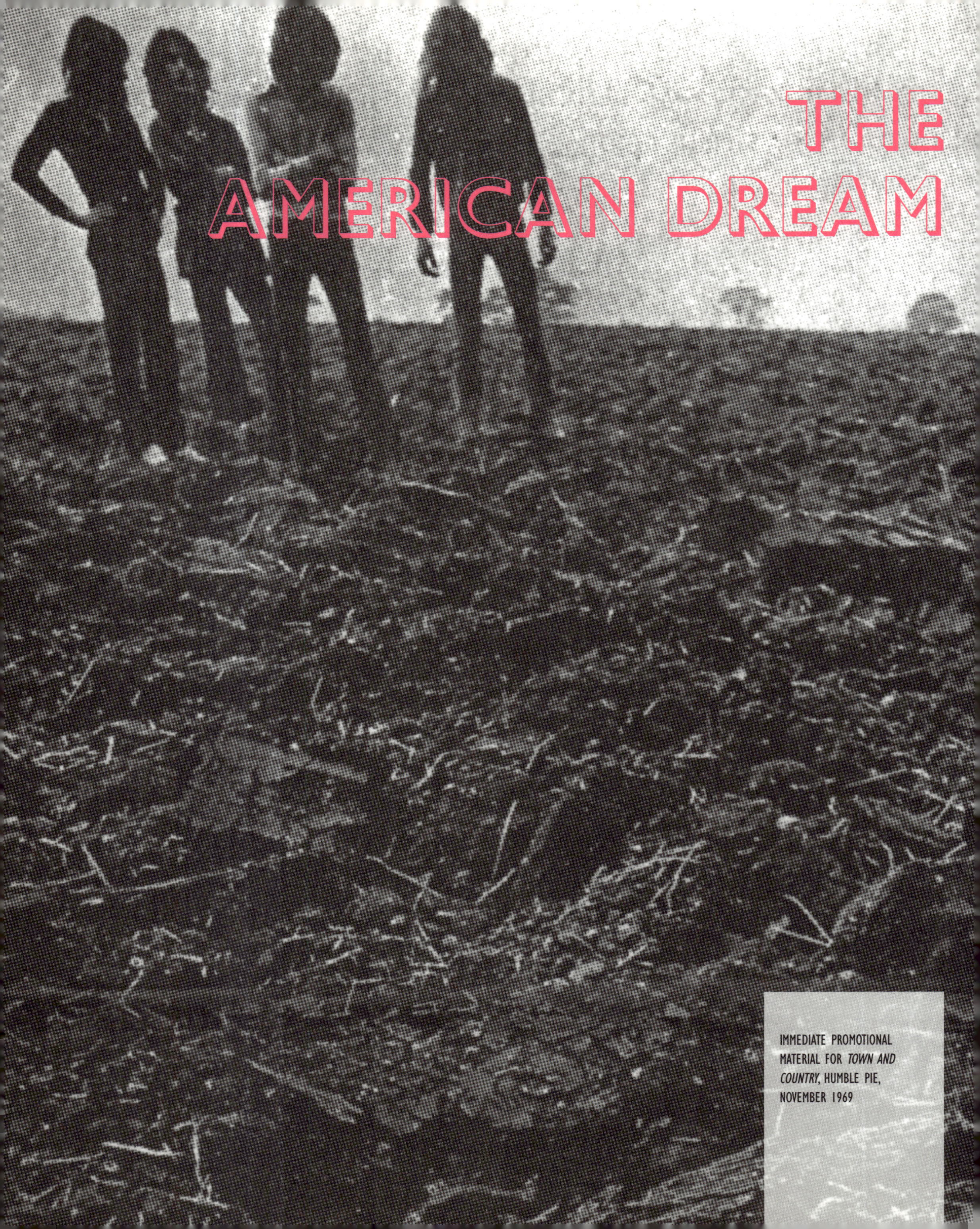

IMMEDIATE PROMOTIONAL MATERIAL FOR *TOWN AND COUNTRY*, HUMBLE PIE, NOVEMBER 1969

umble Pie headed to the US full of great hope. Here, finally, was an Immediate group fit for purpose. Post-Woodstock, hairy, heavy album rock now totally dominated the airwaves and there were many UK acts cashing in big time. Rolling Stones had returned as popular as ever, Led Zeppelin were going down a storm and Blind Faith (another 'supergroup', made up of Cream's Eric Clapton and Ginger Baker with Traffic's vocalist Steve Winwood) had been commanding up to $25,000 per concert.

Humble Pie were confident and ready to get down to what Shirley had called some "serious rock'n'rolling" on a six-week US college tour—the first time the US would get a taste of Marriott's talent in the flesh. Immediate's two-year US distribution deal with CBS had now expired and Oldham and Calder were expecting to attract new US bidders for the group and/or the label, ideally making a play for some of the serious money that was flying about. Oldham was buoyed with thoughts of getting a second clean crack at the US with Humble Pie.

There was, however, a clause in the original Immediate/CBS contract that allowed CBS a third-year option on US rights for Immediate product. As the first two-year period had been so extremely problematic and unsuccessful it was taken as given CBS would not go down that road. So it was a soul destroying moment when CBS President Clive Davis, handed Immediate's US office manager, Paul Banes, a cheque for $50,000 and another $6,000 for royalties owed to Immediate, and informed him CBS were going take up that third-year option.

Oldham claimed that CBS had repeatedly breached it's obligations and that the third-year option was unenforceable. In a court affidavit, Oldham claimed that CBS and the defendant, Davis "willfully and maliciously purported to exercise the option to extend the agreement for another year (to 31 July, 1970), not for the purpose of distributing Immediate records, but to suppress Immediate as a competitor in the US and Canada, and to injure the plaintiffs financially". He went on to claim the CBS relationship with Immediate had been, almost consistently, one of market foreclosure, arbitrary refusal to distribute and "wanton disregard for principles of fair dealing". He repeated Clive Davis' words as told to Klein that "Immediate did not know anything about the US market and that Immediate artists were not the right type to have alongside his new CBS signings as they did not fit into his ideal". Why then sign up the label for a further year?

Oldham compared the way CBS treated Immediate to the way UK record companies between 1955–1964 had treated US labels—paying large advances for the US product, and then burying it while they recorded and promoted their own cover versions for a bigger return. CBS, Oldham insisted, had "destroyed" Immediate as an independent label in the US. Figures were compiled that comparatively showed sales of Immediate records in the US and the UK, from 1 August 1967 (the start date of the CBS agreement), to present. In the US there had been approximately 375,759 singles and 159,990 albums sold, while during the same period, EMI distribution of these records resulted in sales of close to a million singles and 500,000 albums. "This", Oldham pointed out "despite the UK accounting for only six to ten per cent of the world market for records, as compared with the US which accounts for 50 per cent". Andrew Oldham legally stated:

> On or about 11 April, 1969, I engaged the defendant, Clive Davis, in a lengthy telephone conversation regarding Immediate's and my own dissatisfaction with CBS's efforts on our behalf. The gist of my remarks were that Immediate had suffered long enough at CBS' hands and that the agreement had been breached so many times by CBS that it was effectively of no force and that Immediate should be free to secure adequate distribution of its records in the US and Canada from other sources. Davis, after substantial personal abuse of me and other Immediate employees, stated that 'to teach us a lesson' CBS would exercise its option to extend the agreement for an additional year and during that period would do nothing with the records. Davis said, 'we've got you the way we want you and we'll keep you there and we'll tie you up for another year' and he did not wish to speak to me or hear from me or anyone from Immediate.

If Immediate allowed Davis to get away with it, Humble Pie's career would effectively be in paralysis in the US. Steve Marriott who had suffered more than most through CBS' attitude to Immediate product and was keenly aware of the repercussions Davis' decision could have on his new group. Oldham felt he had no choice but to fund the launch of a $7 million lawsuit against Clive Davis and CBS for malpractice, the amount he estimated Immediate had lost in revenue already at the hands of the label. Davis' power, arrogance and ego were threatened and he employed a team of top New York lawyers to pick through Oldham's Affidavit, creating a seemingly never-ending paper trail. Davis was known for rewriting history to his own ends and while I worked on his memoirs I got in touch with Davis who sent a bizarre fax back which said: "Andrew Oldham was always at or near the cutting edge. He was very informed and professional, always receptive and responsive. We enjoyably shared much success."

After dropping the lawsuit on Davis, Immediate issued a statement to the US press to declare they were going independent in the US, disassociating themselves completely from CBS. In the statement they admitting that "innovating a new direct distribution plan in the US" was a major change for the company and "as of the moment, pressing, distributing and promotion policies have not been finalised". The statement concluded:

> This policy has been adopted after careful consideration by Immediate as the only method of servicing, distributing and promoting our product in the US to gain the same efficiency, total responsibility and complete involvement that we feel our

> **TONY STRATTON-SMITH, ALTHOUGH HE MAY BE DEAD, WAS A SHIT-FACED LITTLE GIT WHO STOLE OUR FUCKING TAPES**
> PAUL BANES

> **OLDHAM OVERDOSED AND PASSED OUT... I SPENT THE NEXT TWO HOURS WITH HIM TRAIPSED AROUND MY SHOULDERS WALKING UP SUNSET BOULEVARD. EVERYONE KNEW OLDHAM BY THIS POINT, THEY KNEW WHAT A PROBLEM HE WAS AND HE WAS A BIG PROBLEM**
> DAN CREWE

INSIDE SLEEVE OF *IMMEDIATE LETS YOU IN* ALBUM, 1969

product deserves. The label will continue to be distributed throughout the rest of the world by EMI and independent US release dates are scheduled for Humble Pie and The Nice.

Tony Calder recounts:

We had no alternative but to go independent. We were no longer welcome at CBS and Oldham had made sure that we weren't welcome at any other [US] record companies because by then these executives didn't want to be told they were arseholes. It was a very brave move to make at the time, even today there's no such thing as a successful UK independent set up in the same way in the US.

As Paul Banes remembers:

Overnight, Oldham came in and said, 'we're doing it ourselves, get on the phone'. We got on the phone and called all these independent distributors in [the US]. Oldham took out this amazing, quadruple-page spread for Humble Pie in Billboard, fucking unreal, the label looked great, the whole thing. I went on the road with Humble Pie in [the US], did the whole tour, going back to the office in New York when I could. Six and a half weeks on the road with Humble Pie wasn't the easiest thing in the world as we were working on $8 each per day. I would get a call from Oldham, he was coming in to New York with Steve Inglis and Sean Kenny. I picked them up at the airport. Oldham had this concoction he would drink consommé soup and vodka. He would get out the tin of soup heat it up, fill up the tin with vodka, tip that in and then we would go out.

Setting up as an independent in the US cost Immediate close to $50,000. Over the course of a few weeks Paul Banes arranged for the RCA pressing plant to make Immediate records, pressing up 40,000 copies of Humble Pie's *As Safe As Yesterday* album and 25,000 of the groups (re-named for the US) debut single, "Natural Born Woman". The most lengthy and difficult ordeal for Banes was getting the backing of US independent distributors. Agreements were eventually drawn up with ten of the biggest and most powerful in the US, including Universal Schwartz in Philadelphia, guaranteeing the label coast to coast distribution. Although each of the new US distributors had their own promotion men—in order to guarantee the fullest coverage for Immediate product—five independent promotion men were hired at $2,000 a month. Banes had also collected a complete dossier on US radio stations, DJs, trade publications and underground magazines and he and Oldham spent an afternoon visiting the key radio stations in New York.

There was also a $15,000 budget for advertising Humble Pie in the US with flashy fold-out adverts in *Billboard*, *Cashbox* and *Record World*. Oldham was funding all this from his own wealth, despite having insisted he would no longer prop up Immediate. Befuddled by drugs and drink, he seemed to be acting out of wounded pride more than anything, and amazingly it was working out. He gave several interviews about Immediate's new position in the US trade press under headlines such as "Immediate To Go Direct in US" and "Immediate Goes Indie".

Oldham told *Cashbox*: "All acts on the label are self-contained. They write their own material and produce themselves." Advance copies of "Natural Born Woman" started to receive airplay throughout the US and made on the "up and coming" chart of trade magazine *Record World*. *As Safe As Yesterday* picked up glowing reviews in the US press. Billboard praised "a strong commercial package and underground-orientated numbers". *Record World* called the album: "Head-turning rock and roll, a very powerful smile, moving from heavy rock to country funk to poetic folk-jazz, Humble Pie display considerable talent and energy. Keep tabs on this set, they could be big."

A show at the packed Fillmore East in New York, supporting Butterfield Blues Band and Santana, was "considered one of the happiest pop events of 1969" by *Cashbox*. "Humble Pie are well on their way to innovative rock stardom", reviewed the influential weekly:

The act begins quietly with a solo song by Pete accompanying himself on acoustic guitar. Greg Ridley then sings his solo with Pete going him as second guitarist. The non-electric segment ends with Steve singing lead on a Scottish folk song done in three-part harmony. A quick switch to amplification and the group is off on an extended jam of Dr John material, "Walk On Gilded Splinters" and "Gris Gris Gumbo Ya Ya". Humble Pie's presentation is much like Crosby, Stills, et al's, in that they both feature beautiful and intricate vocals in which different people take over lead. The music moved from Country, to Blues to real jazz and on to straight rock with an enviable fluidity. And Stevie's guitar work was frighteningly good (frightening because very few people in this country have heard of him). Given six months, with a national tour under its belt, Humble Pie will return to the Fillmore topping the bill.

Oldham flew in and out of the Humble Pie tour (it had been his idea to include an acoustic segment in the set) partying hard on drink and cocaine. A live album of the tour would later surface, recorded in LA at Whiskey A-Go-Go, as the band rocked out on covers such as The Yardbirds "For Your Love", Johnnie Kidd and The Pirates' "Shakin' All Over" and Ray Charles/Eddie Cochran's "Hellelujah, I Love Her".

While in the US, the brother of US record producer and songwriter Bob Crewe, Dan, handed Oldham the keys to his weekend home, within easy commuting distance of New York, in the countrified Connecticut, a classic New England five bedroom, swimming pooled mansion, set in eight acres of land. Humble Pie and various UK acts such as Joe Cocker would drop in between gigs for a party. Dan Crewe recounts:

In California, Humble Pie were appearing at Whiskey A-Go-Go and Oldham was recording them for a live album. He was in the control booth and he overdosed and passed out on the control panel. He was literally dead meat, I was scared to death, I thought he was gonna die on me. I spent the next two hours with him traipsed around my shoulders walking up and down Sunset Boulevard, trying to keep him alive. Later that night Whiskey A-Go-Go burnt down. Everyone knew Oldham by this point, they knew what a problem he was and he was a big problem. He was getting antagonistic in social situations, very apt to throwing tantrums and getting into fights. It was not the kind of thing you would eagerly get involved in. There was a lot of talk about CBS having attempted to destroy Immediate, both Oldham and Tony had the feeling that there was a plot to bury the label. By this time Oldham had become pretty damned outrageous and arrogant and would say some terrible things to people, he was no longer being very political. Clive Davis is the kind of person to say, very quietly, 'kill 'em, make the label go away'. Why else would a company that had the rights to somebody who had a track record of making very substantial hits be buried? Either they weren't producing records that were right for the market or CBS was going out of their way to snuff them out.

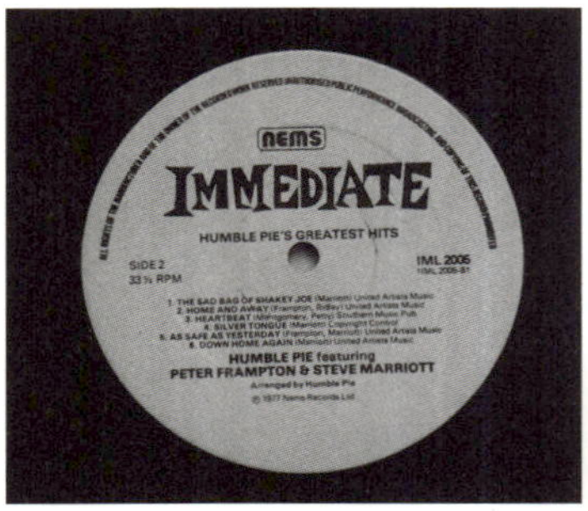
nems
IMMEDIATE
HUMBLE PIE'S GREATEST HITS
SIDE 2
33⅓ RPM
IML 2005
HUMBLE PIE featuring
PETER FRAMPTON & STEVE MARRIOTT

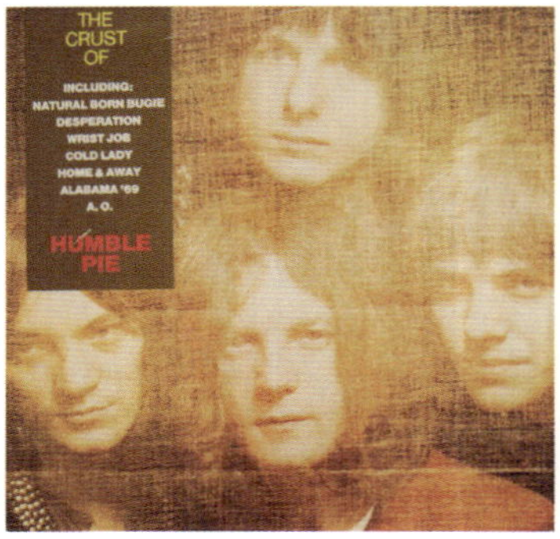
THE
CRUST
OF
INCLUDING:
NATURAL BORN BUGIE
DESPERATION
WRIST JOB
COLD LADY
HOME & AWAY
ALABAMA '69
A. O.
HUMBLE
PIE

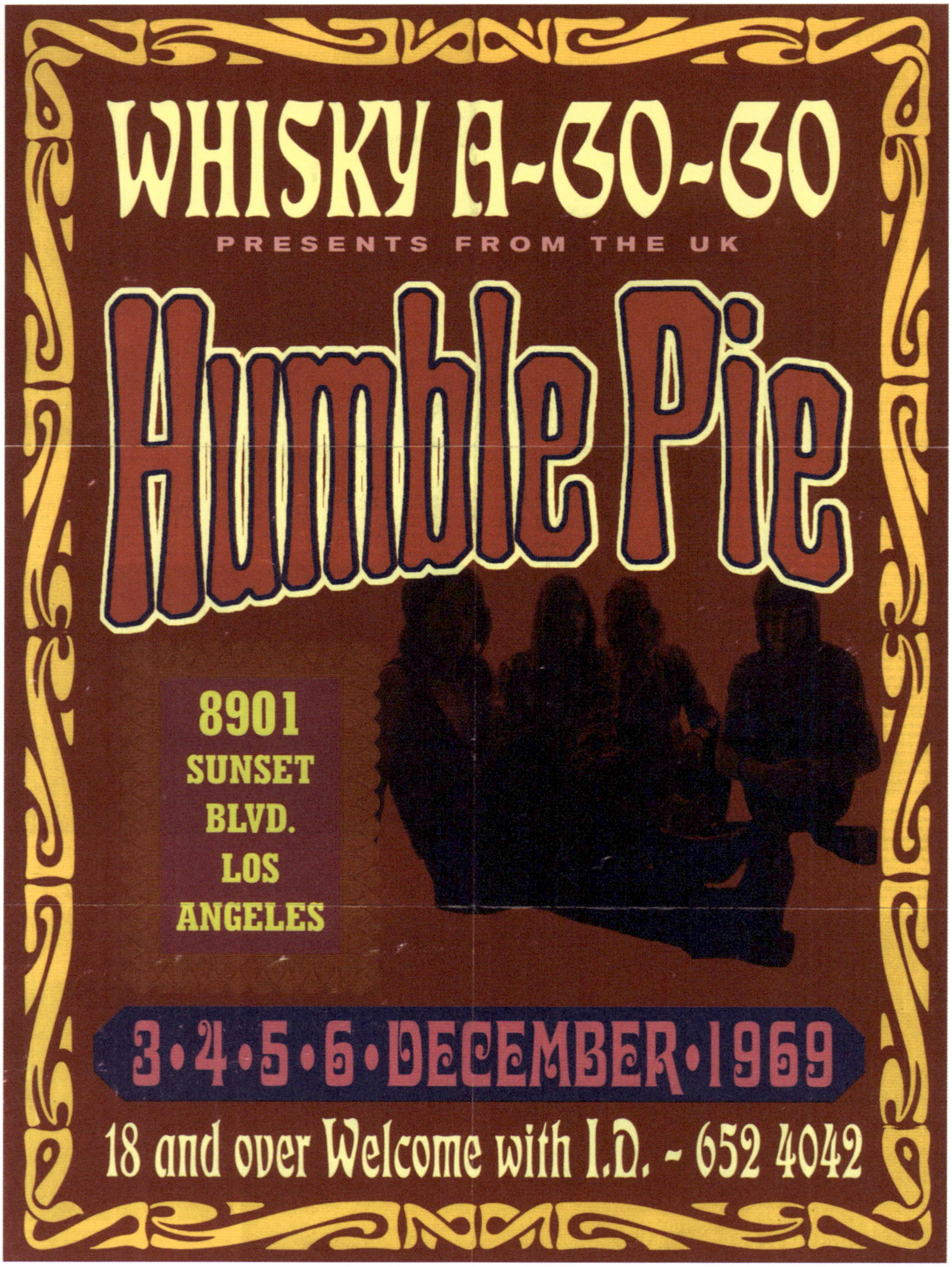
WHISKY A-GO-GO
PRESENTS FROM THE UK
Humble Pie
8901
SUNSET
BLVD.
LOS
ANGELES
3·4·5·6·DECEMBER·1969
18 and over Welcome with I.D. ~ 652 4042

TOP: THE GERMAN RELEASE OF *THE CRUST OF HUMBLE PIE*, THE BAND'S GREATEST HITS COLLECTION, 1983

AN ORIGINAL HUMBLE PIE POSTER FOR THE DECEMBER 1969 WHISKEY A-GO-GO GIGS

The Nice's manager, Tony Stratton-Smith, was confused by Immediate's new independent status in the US. In the UK the group's third Immediate album, Nice, proved what a huge act they were becoming, debuting at number three in the UK charts. It was part live (recorded at New York's Fillmore East, with versions of Bob Dylan's "She Belongs To Me" and their own "Rondo 1969"), and part studio, with more classical posturing on a track based on Lalo's Spanish Symphony.

Immediate coupled a poppy take on the Tim Hardin song "Hang Onto A Dream" with "Diary Of An Empty Dream" for a single and a head-in-the-oven suicide picture was featured on the sleeve. The group were due in the US for their third visit and wanted to hire a 60 piece symphony and philharmonic orchestra for a couple of showcase dates in New York and LA. Immediate sounded out Joseph Eger, conductor of the New York Symphony Orchestra, and discovered his fees would be astronomical.

Meanwhile, The Nice headlined New York's Fillmore East and played with Eric Clapton and his current rave, Delaney and Bonnie, at Philadelphia's Electric Factory. Paul Banes also organised television shows and various radio promo spots for the group in the US. Immediate redesigned and retitled the Nice album for release in the US and independently pressed up 250,000 of the album, Everything As Nice As Everything Mother Makes It, expecting to do some serious progressive rock business. But now came the hammer blow. CBS threatened legal action against Immediate's independent distributors, blocking the release of the album. CBS then pressed up 250,000 copies of the same album at their own plants and charged it to the Immediate account. To add insult to injury CBS didn't promote the album and it was left to gather dust. Stratton-Smith remembers:

> My last meeting with Oldham was at the Speakeasy when we threatened to have a punch up as a result of the way he was failing to give any support, when the Nice badly needed it in [the US]. We were stuck with Oldham at a time when he was distributed by CBS but at Clive Davis' personal instruction he was not allowed to enter the CBS building. So it was very amusing to be with a record company that was itself on an answering machine in a Central Park apartment. Nor could we go to CBS because officially we weren't their artists, we were Andrew Oldham's artists. We couldn't get any action on the records. It was very frustrating.

This was what Stratton-Smith had spent every waking hour of his miserable life waiting for, trying to break The Nice contract so he could jump start his own record label. He used the chaos in the US as excuse and cut all ties with Immediate. The Nice took with them an album in the can that Immediate had paid for and Stratton-Smith set up Charisma Records to release it in the UK. Paul Banes recounts:

> Tony Stratton-Smith, although he may be dead, was a shit-faced little git who stole our fucking tapes. The Nice live tapes we recorded in [the US] for the album after Everything As Nice As Everything Mother Makes It cost us £2,500. Andrew paid for it out of his own pocket. Stratton-Smith went into the studio in London, where the LP was being mixed, paid the bill, walked out with the tapes and set up Charisma records on the back of that LP. That LP did 170,000, it was the biggest album The Nice had, it was what we had been working toward all the time, because the whole thing with The Nice was to see them live. They got an album that cost them fuck all and it cost us heavy grief. CBS were saying Immediate is us. We were saying, 'no it's not because you haven't done anything for our records'. The fact that you haven't put them out is a restrictive trade thing in [the US]. We went to court with the Kennedy's lawyers.

The whole thing was complete mess. The position taken by CBS now made it untenable for Immediate to continue as an independent in the US. Oldham was in a state of alcohol and drug dependent breakdown and couldn't see clearly enough to make any certain decisions on how to move Humble Pie's career forward in the US. The Nice could piss off but the disappointment and confusion on Steve Marriott's face was hard to take. Calder had let the books boil and was refusing to face the reality of the situation, convinced the label could still thrive in Europe, if only Oldham would pour in some more money. It wasn't really Stratton-Smith's fault though. The captain, Oldham, was blown away; "burnt out like a light bulb" Keith Richards would later quip.

> ANDREW OLDHAM WAS ALWAYS AT OR NEAR THE CUTTING EDGE. HE WAS VERY INFORMED AND PROFESSIONAL
>
> CLIVE DAVIS

DRUGS, DRUGS AND MORE DRUGS

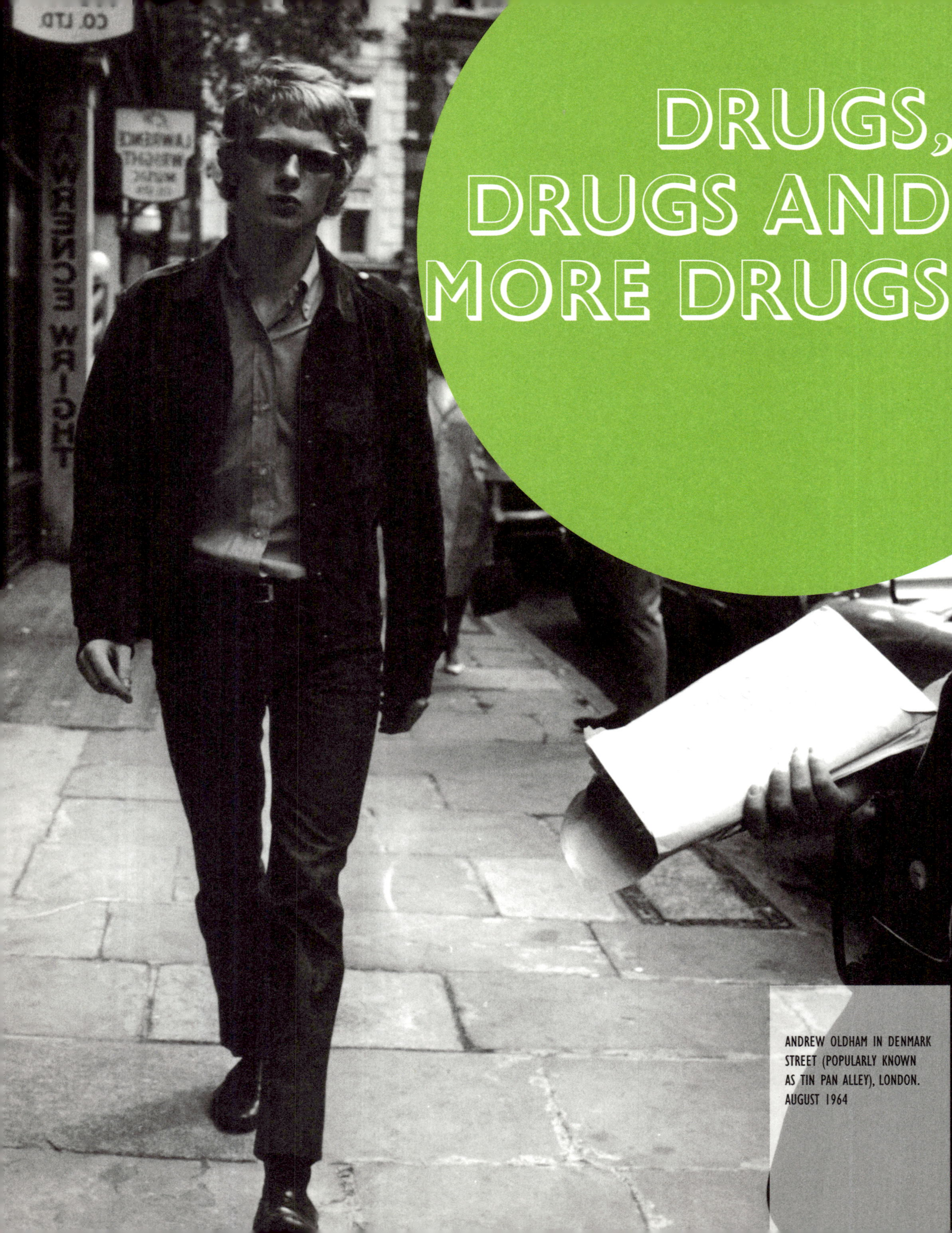

ANDREW OLDHAM IN DENMARK STREET (POPULARLY KNOWN AS TIN PAN ALLEY), LONDON. AUGUST 1964

PHOTOGRAPH BY RICHARD CHOWEN/EVENING STANDARD/GETTY IMAGES

After saving his life in LA and witnessing the disarray Immediate was in New York, Dan Crewe flew back to London with Oldham to try and help the man and the company. After the Rolling Stones, Immediate had been another example of Oldham not having to grow up. Now he would have to. The UK sales of the recent Humble Pie and The Nice albums had barely made a dent in the cash Oldham had splashed out to keep the dream alive in the US. Crewe went through the Immediate books. They were in a mess and one particular entry deeply troubled him.

Immediate had recently paid US major label, United Artists, $50,000 as part of a settlement regarding a 1967 deal which had gone badly wrong. However skillfully you tried to manoeuvre around the fact, this payment put Immediate heavily in debt. Just prior to Oldham making the distribution arrangement with CBS in the US in 1967, Calder had also made a deal for US distribution with United Artists. To allow Immediate to go with CBS, United Artists had demanded $225,000 to terminate and void their contract. The payments had been staggered, so that $25,000 of the debt had been paid back in 1968, the $50,000 was 1969's payment and the final $175,000 was due in 1970. Tony Calder recounts:

> Andrew was at one of the sleep treatment centres in London, the Bethanie Nursing Home. It didn't bother me, you never knew if it was him or the drugs talking. A pal of mine, Martin Davis from United Artists, called and said, 'Do you wanna make a deal for Immediate in America?' The deal was done in three days. They paid the money, $50,000, and they were gonna put the records out. Then Andrew came out of the Bethanie and started screaming, 'fuck United Artists!' and flew off to see Lou Adler in LA for Monterey, bumped into Clive Davis and did the deal for Immediate with CBS without even speaking to me. They were now the ultimate record company in [the US]; Lou was dealing with them, they had Janis Joplin. I was calling him at the Bethanie Nursing Home. I said 'could I speak with Mr Oldham? They said 'he's asleep and he'll be asleep for another week'. How can you do business like that? I went back to United Artists and asked to get out of the deal. Sid Shemmel was their lawyer, the boss of United Artists in the US was this huge overweight guy, Mike Stewart. I heard him say, 'screw the bastards' to Sid Shemmel.

This preposterous piece of company management Oldham accredited to the cumulative effects of the drugs and the heady times. He blames nobody (not even himself) for this bad business: "Our legal counsel was drugs, drugs and more drugs" he said.

Crewe also took a close look at Oldham's own private financial affairs and found overdue demands for a personal UK tax bill of approximately £600,000, pertaining to Oldham's Rolling Stones earnings. It was part of the same Inland Revenue effort that would drive the Rolling Stones to leave England to take up residence in tax havens. Dan Crewe said:

> They had committed to paying a lot of money to United Artists on the debenture and they thought rather blithely that this would be no problem, all they would have to do was have a couple of hit records. Immediate was living way beyond its means, living as if it was always gonna be successful. Neither Andrew Oldham nor Tony Calder thought of the consequences of over-commitment without having the resources. The people who run the company ultimately have to take the responsibility. This is where the drugs start to cloud your thinking. You think that if we do something that's very grand, people will think we are successful and therefore we will be successful. There was more hype than reality.
>
> There was little or no money and there was a lifestyle that nobody wanted to put a stop to. Andrew and Tony got the crest of a wave and rode it. They never realised when the wave was over, and in order to sustain themselves they had to rethink the process, reinvent themselves. They could not sustain themselves in this kind of childish, 'we are indestructible' mentality, 'everybody else are fools, all the record people, they're all fools, all the important people in the industry, they're fools'. The proof of the pudding is no-one is that special unless your really watching what your doing. Oldham was in a state.
>
> I advised him to close Immediate down, it was a farce, and Oldham would be much better off making a deal for the artists directly with a label, letting them take responsibility of the overhead. If there was gonna be any success at all, stick with what you know best, produce and promote. I never had great overwhelming respect for Tony, I don't know what he was doing, he was supposed to be the business head of the company, he was supposed to control it and he wasn't. So in the long run he was never an asset. Oldham had a partner who was not doing what he had to, even if that meant saying, I can't do this, I'm out of here. Instead he was virtually doing the same things as Oldham, it was self-delusional.
>
> Oldham hadn't got the message yet about what he had to do for himself, he didn't realise that his problems lay within himself. He had become a drug addict and an alcoholic. He operated from his waking hour in a constant state of drug addiction, alcohol or both. I spent my time mostly looking at how to salvage Oldham. That was my focus. Oldham had every bank on the phone. I was amazed at the tolerance of the banks and why they hadn't foreclosed on him. I would go in and talk to the banks but it was really like sticking your finger in a dyke. There were leaks everywhere. It was just horrific.
>
> Oldham was out of his mind as far as using, and he had this constant conflict with his then wife. It's hard to lay the blame in any one place in a case like that, there was enough blame for everybody and Oldham did nothing to help the situation. It was awful to come over there and give him nothing but bad news. He owed everybody, he had a high overhead, he had mortgages, he had loans, and he had overdrafts. I never saw so many overdrafts. Banks just allowed him to run up these huge amounts

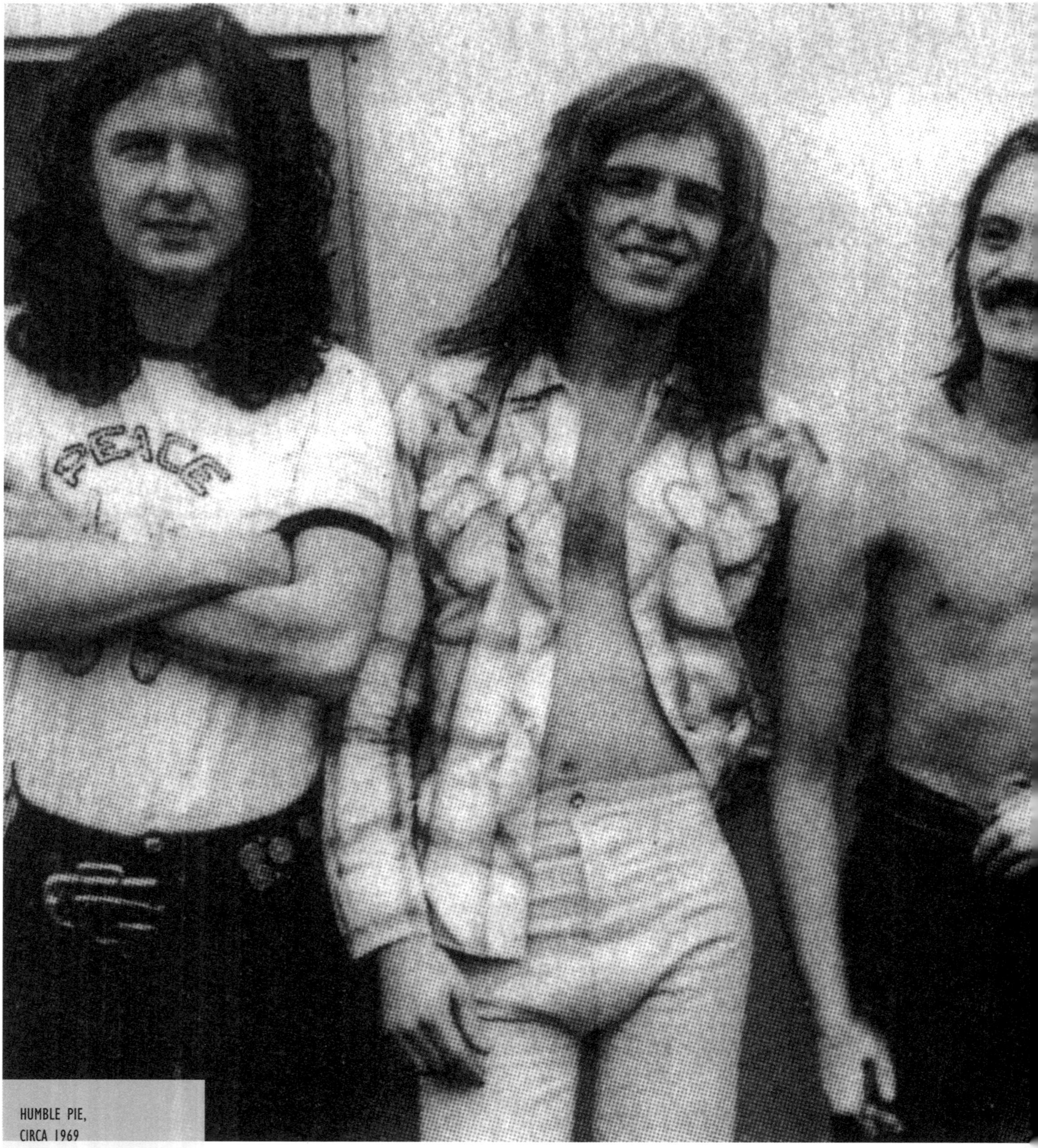
PEACE

HUMBLE PIE,
CIRCA 1969

of overdrafts. Part of that was that the banks had not caught up to the world of the music business, so they looked at a lot of the flash and believed it. Oldham would pull up in his Rolls, take the banker out to lunch and that took care of the problem for a while but that can only last so long. Oh God, what a mess. I advised him to put the label in liquidation mainly to protect Oldham. The truth of the matter is he came out of it by the skin of his teeth. He didn't come out of it clean with everything intact. He came out of it with not having to be a bankrupt—but just barely. He would be on drugs where he couldn't talk, his mouth would just go to mush and he would drink on it.

Ken East, Managing Director for EMI UK recounts:

Andrew came in one day to EMI, he was getting into trouble, and we could see he was. EMI were fairly safe because if we didn't sell the records they were his, we manufactured them at his expense. But it was of no interest to us for him to get into trouble because it's good business being lost. He was very independent, you couldn't tell him anything because he knew it all, likewise Tony Calder.

Oldham was never a dishonest person just nutty that's all. I never worked out the relationship with Tony Calder, whether it was a love-hate relationship or whether Tony tended to push Oldham into areas he couldn't get out of. When you got the two of them together it was like an act, on their own they were different people. You could sit down and talk more sensibly with Tony but things would never really turn out the way they should turn out. With Oldham you couldn't agree on anything because he never had the ability or the mood to talk business in any way. He was just so up in the air about everything. Other people that had to deal with him at EMI and I don't blame them, would say, 'oh Christ is it worth it, the aggro that this fella creates for us'. Most of these people were in sales, and they were the most affected by the things he did. But of course it was worth it because we had got a business going and he was selling a lot of records. Indirectly that reflected on the credibility of EMI. We performed properly for Oldham, which wasn't always the easiest thing to do. There was no way EMI could keep Immediate going, it was beyond repair, they were still running around Europe buying doors for elaborate offices.

Calder describes the state of Immediate at the time:

By the end of the 1960s when we should have had major success in [the US], there were now coming in rules and regulations; there were certain people's arses you had to kiss. Whereas before people were kissing our arse. Oldham didn't want to kiss arse. I wasn't concerned about Oldham's mental state, my main concern was trying to keep the company going. We nearly merged with Chris Blackwell at Island, we sold singles, and he sold albums. We had a meeting, we were gonna put the two companies together and it all fell apart when Oldham came out of the clinic and met with Blackwell, then it was all off. I don't think Blackwell liked the state he was in. Then when I got my stomach ulcer I just snapped. Oldham's efforts were totally destructive to the point where one us had to go.

Freddie Bienstock, Owner of Carlin Music recalls the collapse of the label:

When it looked as if Immediate going to collapse, Tony Calder came to see me and tried to arrange a deal, telling me how well the company was doing. In the afternoon Oldham came over and I said to him, 'listen, Tony Calder was painting a rather optimistic picture about the prospects of the company'. Oldham told me, 'don't believe a word he says, it's all bullshit'. Oldham was living in this big house in Richmond and he hadn't paid his grocers bills for the longest time, he owed over £200. I happened to be visiting when the grocer appeared to collect his money. Oldham let him in and gave him a joint. Two hours later this grocer was bumped out of his head, the happiest grocer you ever saw, he never got a penny but he was in great shape. Oldham told me that should the police come to his house he had a secret passage that went underground that he could get through and out somewhere. Oldham made a lot of money and blew a lot in the craziest way, and Tony Calder was quite some help in that.

Paul Banes describes his encounter with Oldham and Calder in their Immediate offices:

It was five days before Christmas 1970. I got back to the office in New York and Oldham and Tony are in the middle of a discussion. They tell me to go and take a walk. I went out and when I came back, Tony says: 'We've broken up. I'm leaving and going to Antigua.' I was sitting in New York holding the baby and we've got a song called "Going Home" by Ten Years After, a track Immediate Music had an interest, on the Woodstock album, we had 15 minutes, it was worth a £1 million. Anybody with the right attitude would have known what we already knew about the Woodstock album. The only person who didn't was Danny Crewe.

Tony Calder remembers being bought out by Oldham:

I was hemorraging, walking around bleeding. He bought me out neatly within 24 hours, it was 30 December, it was done privately, the money didn't come out of Immediate, it all came out of his Rolling Stones income

Malcolm Forrester, Head of Immediate Music remembers:

Tony had bottled out. He wasn't there. There was a hand written letter from him on aeroplane paper, advising Oldham what to do to save the company. It was almost unintelligible. We were told Calder was getting bruises all over his body, we actually thought he was really ill. When he and Oldham fell out the staff had split into two camps, there was really bad atmosphere. We purchased accountants and lawyers, in London and New York, as if they were going out of fashion. I fell in behind Tony, you never saw Oldham. He was rarely in.

The move from New Oxford Street to Gloucester Place was not a good move. We were always leasing premises when we could have bought them. When Calder went to Antigua I started working more closely with Oldham.

Calder was long gone, bought out for around £26,000, plus a UK house and the house in Antigua, a claimed salary, Mercedes 600 and forgiveness of monies owed. Oldham, still just 26, was living alone in the penthouse above the deserted Immediate Gloucester Place offices, clinging on to the last vestiges of power. Every night Oldham would leave a note out at night for his butler Ted, a retired sailor, telling him what he wanted for breakfast and what record he required to be woken up with. Mario and Franco at the Trattoria Terrazzo restaurant in Soho insisted, after all the good years, Oldham eat for free and there was the new steady supply of the mood elevator Ritalin to stop him wallowing in the badness of his private and professional life. To handle the Immediate liquidation he hired a top London accountancy firm, Stoy Hayward, experts in insolvency work. The creditors meeting was held at the firm's Wigmore Street offices. Oldham remembers:

On the day of the creditors meeting Dr Robertson did his job, I was pretty calm and couldn't be bothered to hit anyone. He even helped me sort out what to wear, a purple velvet jacket and grey flannel trousers, advising against a suit as that spelt money to the vultures.

Martin Spenser, Specialist in Liquidation and Receiverships of Stoy Hayward:

Oldham was the largest creditor, all told he had sunk about a quarter of a million pounds into it. The outside creditors were relatively small. In a normal case if you have a company that is liquidated and there are, say, 100 creditors on the statement of affairs, you can expect that roughly ten per cent of the creditors will turn up. With the Immediate liquidation, the receptionist rang me up about half an hour before the meeting, quite frantic to say that there were over 100 people milling about in the reception. When the meeting started, there was an overflow of another 80 people outside the boardroom and the impression I got was that most of them weren't creditors but people in the industry who had come along to either support him or scorn him or to find out what the score was. Some of them had even brought their own booze.

I'm sitting with Oldham and Malcolm Forrester at this boardroom table and people were cramming up against the table, pushing forward, they were virtually on top of us. It was more like a pop concert. It was unusual and totally different from any liquidation meeting I had been in, more like a social gathering than a formal thing. It was quite daunting and I had never handled anything like this. The creditors normally have a go at the directors for losing money but in his case although there were creditors who had lost money it wasn't substantial. They all knew him.

The only problem I had was trying to get order out of all these people because they were in the music business and to them it was a joke. I had great difficulty in reading out all the information about the company's history and they weren't really interested. They were talking amongst themselves, they were smoking, one or two were swigging from bottles. Normally the director has to answer specific questions raised from the floor, they get put through the mangle because the creditors want blood. The realisations of the company were put into a bank account, and the preferential creditors, the Inland Revenue, the Ratings Authorities—if rates were due, and employees for 16 weeks or more would get the first bite, then the second bite would be the liquidator for his fees and if there was anything left it would be distributed to the unsecured creditors *pro rata*. So if Oldham was owed £250,000 and the other creditors were £50,000, he would get five-sixths of what was left in the pot. But I don't think there was ever a distribution to unsecured creditors, Oldham didn't get anything back.

Steve Marriott, *NME*, talks of Oldham's honesty during the Immediate liquidation:

Oldham was great about it. He just said, 'we're going under, mates'. He warned us all. He said, 'get out now and sort yourselves out, get other labels because I don't want any of you going down with the company'. He was a great bloke, a right old blagger, but underneath all the front he was a very nice man.

Jerry Shirley of Humble Pie remembers Oldham's reaction to the Immediate liquidation:

He did us the biggest favour that any single manager has ever done any band. As soon as he knew Immediate was going down he said, 'call Jerry Moss at A&M'. We said okay. Oldham said: "You're not getting the point here, call Jerry Moss and he will sign you." Oldham would have had the ability to hang us up in all kinds of legalities, which he chose not to do, he chose to give us a career that he felt we deserved. When Oldham said call Jerry Moss he also told us to ask for $400,000. We did and we got it.

Malcolm Forrester recalls the loss of Immediate music:

Dan Crewe was excellent at the creditors meeting. It was a funny meeting. Twinkle standing up while all these people are asking, 'where are my royalties?' and 'why haven't you paid the bills?' and she says 'can I have my tapes back?'. We closed Gloucester Place and I went to work at his house in Richmond. At that moment in time we still had the publishing company, I was putting together this long list of songs Immediate Music owned, it was just incredible, a massive amount of songs we owned the copyright on. But the money wasn't there to pay United Artists. We owed them the remaining $175,000 on the $225,000 debenture deal. There was this clause in the deal, failure to pay meant forfeiting the entire Immediate Music publishing catalogue to United Artists. If the money had have been there it would have been paid. I don't think Andrew had that much money at that moment in time.

This great catalogue of songs. Even then I'm sure I was thinking the amounts involved seemed small. It was incredible. I think United Artists made $175,000 within four months of taking over Immediate Music. EMI own the catalogue now and over the years it's been worth millions and millions of pounds.

"I wasn't interested in Immediate in the last years at all", Oldham would reflect in a 1972 *Melody Maker* interview:

I started losing interest in the whole thing about six months after I parted company with the Rolling Stones. By that time Immediate had proved its point, so it became pretty boring. The last thing I was interested in was Humble Pie. At the business end, the people there started believing the bullshit we were putting out about ourselves. In the last year, there was nobody really sitting there looking after the money. If the business had been run properly there was no reason why the company should have failed. But I don't feel bitter about that. I lost $250,000 personally. I'm the biggest creditor to the company. But it was worth it. Anything you learn out of is worth it. There was £85 left in the Immediate kitty after all the hassles. I really can't complain about it. Nobody really got burned, they can scream and holler all they want but nobody really got burned. That's the way God planned it.

> I WAS HEMORRHAGING, WALKING AROUND BLEEDING. OLDHAM BOUGHT ME OUT NEATLY WITHIN 24 HOURS. IT WAS DONE PRIVATELY, THE MONEY CAME OUT OF HIS ROLLING STONES INCOME
>
> TONY CALDER

JUDGE FOR YOURSELF

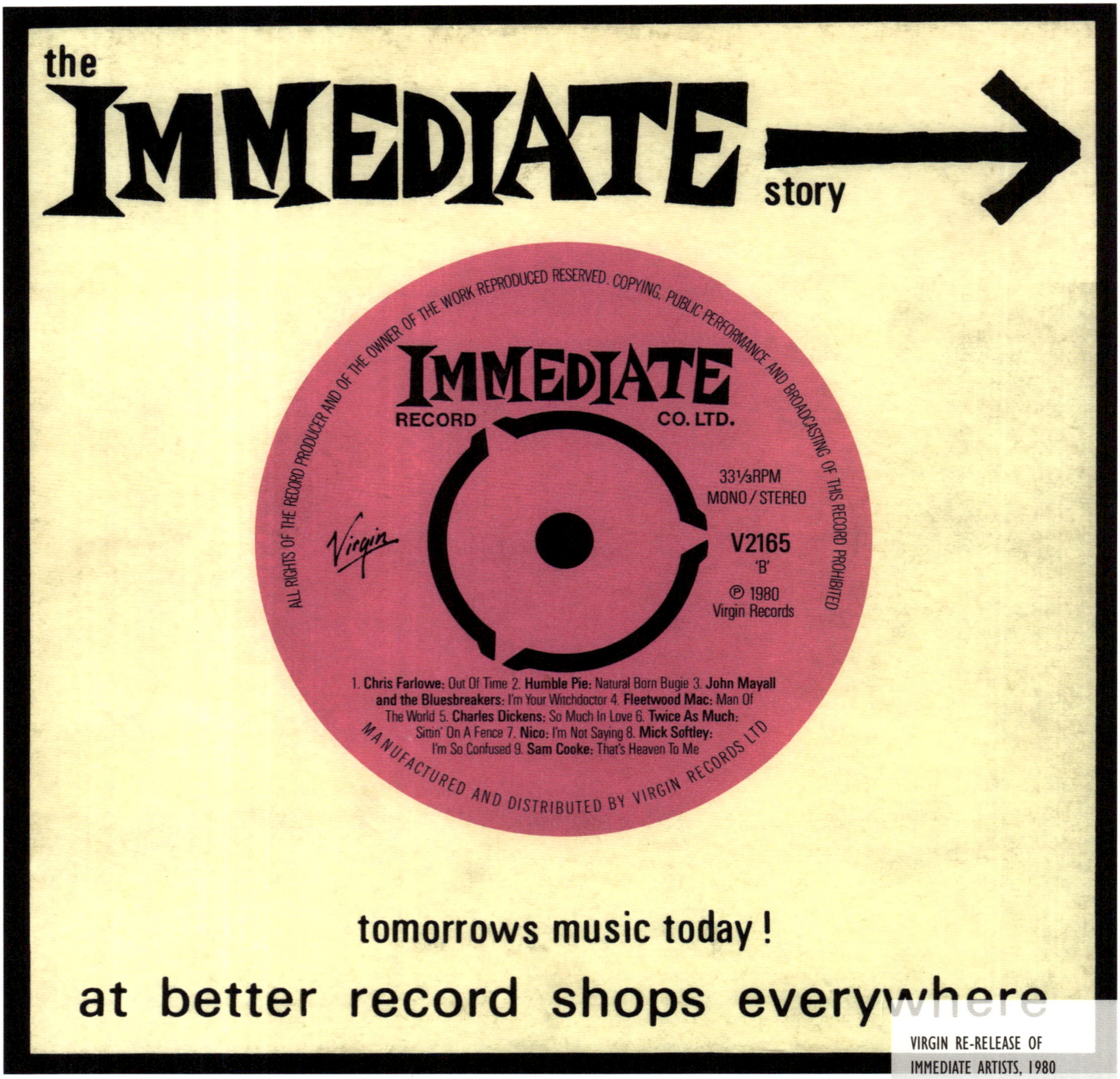
the IMMEDIATE story
ALL RIGHTS OF THE RECORD PRODUCER AND OF THE OWNER OF THE WORK REPRODUCED RESERVED. COPYING, PUBLIC PERFORMANCE AND BROADCASTING OF THIS RECORD PROHIBITED
IMMEDIATE
RECORD CO. LTD.
Virgin
33⅓RPM
MONO / STEREO
V2165
'B'
℗ 1980
Virgin Records
1. Chris Farlowe: Out Of Time 2. Humble Pie: Natural Born Bugie 3. John Mayall and the Bluesbreakers: I'm Your Witchdoctor 4. Fleetwood Mac: Man Of The World 5. Charles Dickens: So Much In Love 6. Twice As Much: Sittin' On A Fence 7. Nico: I'm Not Saying 8. Mick Softley: I'm So Confused 9. Sam Cooke: That's Heaven To Me
MANUFACTURED AND DISTRIBUTED BY VIRGIN RECORDS LTD
tomorrows music today!
at better record shops everywhere

VIRGIN RE-RELEASE OF IMMEDIATE ARTISTS, 1980

What happened in the aftermath of the liquidation? Don Arden was given the gold eagle Lectern he had admired in Gloucester Place but nothing else was salvaged from the building—they couldn't even get the chandeliers down. Together, Oldham and Arden got up to a bit of naughtiness, earning a £10,000 advance from EMI on a single by group that didn't exist. "And whattya call this group", Arden told me the EMI guy had said in the A&R meeting with him and Oldham, after listening to the fruits of a raucous recording session involving Oldham, Ron Wood and Peter Frampton. "Grunt Futtock", Oldham growled. "Amazing", said the guy from EMI (as Don's stifled a laugh) and signed the cheque. Then Oldham quit the UK for good to take up residence in the US, thus avoiding the huge tax bill that was pending. He later told me:

> The Rolling Stones and I were paying a third of everything we earned in [the US] straight as withholding tax, then when we'd bring back the 66 per cent to England, they would want to tax us on the 100 per cent. Well we didn't have it—it was gone. It had taken them three years to arrive at the figures so it had all been spent.

> If we'd had enough to settle the bill both the Rolling Stones and I would have had the option of staying in England, but we didn't. The only way we had of getting out of paying the bill was this flaw in the law—if you left the country and didn't return for three years you were forgiven. That's what we all did; the [Rolling] Stones by mainly going to France and doing their Exile On Main Street, me by going to Connecticut and New York.

Oldham had lost ownership of Immediate Music publishing, the multimillion money-spinner, to United Artists Records. The company was taken over by EMI in the late 1970s and EMI control the Immediate Music publishing to this day. Oldham's contributions to Immediate Music earn him about £26 a year. Paul Banes feels EMI have not honoured the exact and generous terms Immediate Music afforded its songwriters (largely under joint ownership deals, ie. Avakak Music for the Small Faces and James Page Music for Jimmy Page) nor that United Artists should actually have taken control of the catalogue of Immediate Music works in the first place—but that's another story (as is much of this tale).

The liquidation had seen Immediate Records Ltd go under but the rights for the label outside of the UK remained under the control of Immediate Records Inc, the US company Oldham and Calder had set up way back in 1967 on the back of the CBS deal. Oldham solely owned Immediate Inc (having bought out Calder in 1969) and once the deal for US rights wound down with CBS in mid 1970, he was free to assign rights for the back catalogue (outside the UK) to new companies. There had been no satisfactory conclusion to the $7 million court case he brought against CBS. In a deal that ran until 1975 Immediate Inc licensed the rights to Immediate in Europe to EMI (they also had rights to Canada too). The concept of reissuing, particularly before the introduction of CD, was still in a primitive state but select albums from the Immediate catalogue would still sell in reasonable amounts, particularly 'hits' compilations or work by artists who had gone on to bigger things.

In the US, Immediate Inc licensed a smooth repackaging of the two Immediate Humble Pie albums—Marriott's band having by then made huge inroads in the US—to Humble Pie's then current label A&M for a 1972 double-album release and then licensed the back catalogue to Sire. When Oldham struck the deal with Sire (Seymour Stein's new label) in 1975, it was all over the trade press, with Immediate credited as "one of England's first independent companies to succeed in the progressive field, paving the way for today's giant British indies like Island, Chrysalis, B&C, Charisma and Virgin".

"A great part of my life and energies are tied closely to Immediate". Oldham told the press.

> Sire is the probably the one company that I could entrust with the repackaging and marketing of Immediate. They were there on the scene during the Immediate years and have a first-hand knowledge of this all-important period in pop music. With their other repackages, they have proven that they have the necessary historical consciousness to produce a tasteful and authoritative package that will appeal to collectors.

This claim was backed up when Sire released a splendid two record LP, *The Immediate Story*, with Oldham taking a hands-on approach to the packaging.

In this period advances from US deals and royalties from EMI earned Oldham approximately $250,000 and none of the Immediate acts received any royalties, which caused some consternation among certain artists. However, the Ltd/Inc books showed, with rare exceptions that no acts were owed any royalties due to advances and recording bills. To make this clear; when the label had gone under in the UK, there was not one major act on Immediate who was in the black and up until that point there had been, it was widely accepted, a fair accounting. Artists from Small Faces to PP Arnold and Billy Nicholls were all on wages during their Immediate years and, in most cases, had rent paid. £400 sounds like nothing now but it was a lot when you only sold 180,000 singles and no Immediate act sold any considerable amount of albums, bar Small Faces with *Ogden's Nut Gone Flake*. Oldham had poured vast sums of his own money in to Immediate; notably the advances on the Small Faces and Amen Corner, buying out on Frampton's contact to get Humble Pie rolling, the price of going independent in the US, the lawsuit with CBS, plus the constant bailing out and propping up over the years, including costs such as supporting Humble Pie on the road. In short, Oldham was owed some payback—and this he took. And if Oldham had not taken the $250,000, it would have gone to the Liquidator, Patrick Meehan or Tony Calder.

167

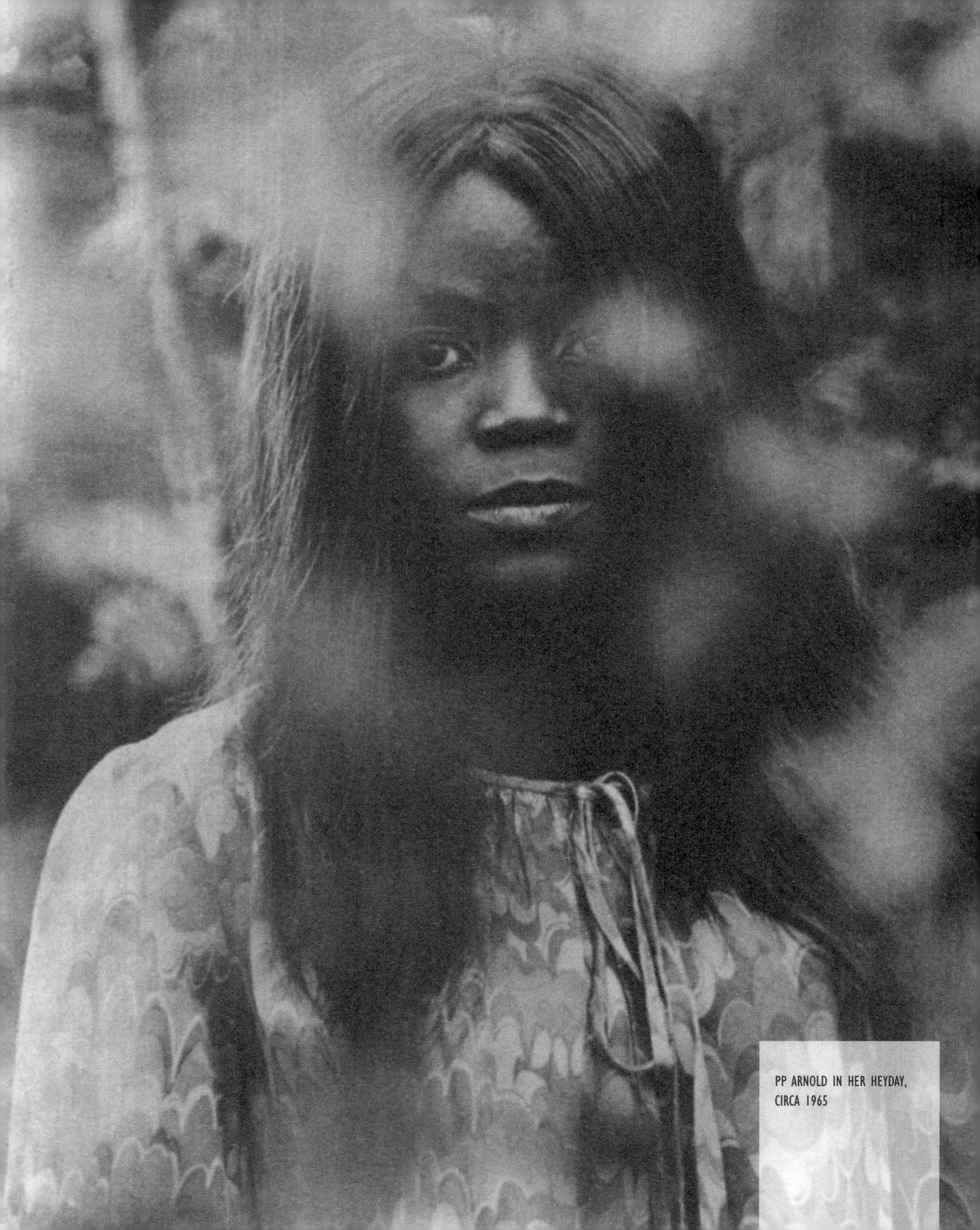

PP ARNOLD IN HER HEYDAY,
CIRCA 1965

Yes, Calder was back on the scene with a new business partner, Patrick Meehan Jnr (who with his dad, Patrick Meehan Snr, had run World Wide Artists records, controlling the early career of Black Sabbath). Calder and Meehan, acting under the company name, Nems (Brian Epstein's old company that Meehan had purchased in late 1969), bought Immediate Records Ltd from the liquidator for around £20,000 in 1976. On closer inspection, it has been claimed, what Nems actually purchased from the liquidator were the Immediate Records Ltd assets and not the contracts or obligations, hence no need to pay royalties—if so it would have been typical of Meehan and Calder's eye for exploiting loopholes in every given situation. Nems now owned the UK rights to the Immediate catalogue, and, Calder and Meehan felt, perhaps even more—discreet inquiries were being made. They had big plans for the back catalogue.

Oldham, meanwhile, had travelled to Paris in 1975 and signed a new deal via his Immediate Inc for licensing on the Immediate back catalogue with Charly Records owned by Jean Luc Young, a maverick entrepreneur rumoured to be financed by the Corsican mafia. Luc Young had just completed the purchase of the back-product from the Sun, Red Bird and Blue Cat record labels and his capture of Immediate made the front cover of UK trade magazine, *Music Week*. Oldham was more than happy to do it. He liked Luc Young. Shortly after they met they had a near death experience when local football hooligans attacked Luc Young's house just outside of Paris and the pair had to defend their families with shotguns and machetes. This is the kind of event that can bind people together. "He was independent, he cared about things, and it was perfect for the kind of figures the Immediate stuff was going to do", Oldham told me later: "It was a respectable home for that time." Paul Mozian, one of Allen Klein's key men was now working for Oldham. He said:

> We called Jean Luc Young 'Kid Cash'. Jean Luc was a young guy, like a scallywag, a street ruffian that had some money, we could never really figure out where his money came from. He wanted to establish a record label, he really had the hots for the Immediate thing. He was so delighted to be able to get the licensing for Europe. We were staying at the Paris Hilton and the management were not overwhelmed with Andrew. He had a tendency of insulting other guests in the coffee shop. He would just say stuff to people, he would tell people to get out of his way, 'you're wearing an offensive pullover', it was outrageous. I would cringe, thinking 'this guy is gonna kill him'. You wonder, what am I supposed to do if this guy tries to kill him, should I help pull this guy away or maybe the guy should just hit him in the mouth once and maybe that will break the problem he had. Maybe it was just a deathwish that he had for a couple of days, he used to live out movie-scenes and do stuff like that, he was being a character in his own play. He wanted to be a tough guy so he would say stuff to people and 99 per cent of the time he would get away with it. This sort of thing escalated at the Paris Hilton, to the point where they wanted us to leave and were threatening to call the police. Of course they wanted him to sign the outstanding bill, which must have been $4,000 at this stage.

> There was much commotion in the lobby upon our departure as Andrew leapt on the front desk, threatening a hotelman that he insisted was a hold over from Nazi occupation. Both our ladies were crying at this point and we made a hasty exit. Kid Cash came up with £10,000 and I was actually able to go to his bank account in Geneva and cash the cheque. Then Kid Cash brought the [Immediate] stuff to the UK and that's when the trouble began, between the Meehans, Charly and Andrew: What did you really license and how can you license something you don't own? We had to go sort it out, I met Don Arden in England who was gonna help Andrew against Patrick and Tony. I guess Andrew figured Don Arden would be a good powerhouse at the time.

Calder had been lured back from Antigua to run OPAL records, the black music subsidiary of Nems, and found himself in the middle of Meehan's plans for the (bought back from the liquidators) Immediate Record Ltd. Nems had already signed Marianne Faithfull and planned to reform the Small Faces, make a video for "Itchycoo Park", re-release it and get a new LP out of the group.

Meehan had not taken kindly to Luc Young's decision to make what Nems claimed was hay and mischief on their turf with the rights he acquired from Immediate Inc. Oldham, who had, since the collapse of Immediate, worked for Motown as a producer and gone on to produce albums by Donovan and Humble Pie, was approached by Calder to join the Nems group as 'director of special projects' or 'executive catalyst'. There was talk of an Immediate II with everyone working together. Oldham agreed to meet up at the Midem Music Festival in Cannes for a discussion to clear the air—prepared to drop the James Caan act and play David Geffen for a year.

Calder had been put in a compromising situation via Meehan (who appeared to want to make cash and screw over the art and artists of Immediate with Nems), one that seemed to betray his original commitment to the Immediate artist driven ethic he'd pioneered with Oldham. After selling his share in the company to Oldham in 1969, for what some claimed was a lager amount than the already stated £26,000, he'd been laying low in Antigua (in the former Immediate Inc owned mansion). The liquidator had chased him all over town for the Mercedes 600 and eventually seized it, selling it on to The Who's Pete Townshend.

To assist Meehan in this new Nems venture, one has to wonder at what Calder's driving forces were. The deal would certainly see not only the artists but also the producers; Mick Jagger and Keith Richards, Steve Marriott and Ronnie Lane, Shel Talmy, Andrew Oldham and more, getting screwed. Probably, Calder, finally enjoyed having one over Oldham and realised this high-profile Immediate relaunch in the UK (and its fallout) would cause his former partner much anguish. It must be stated that however quasi-crooked Calder and Meehan's actions appeared to be with regards the royalties situation, what they were doing was perfectly legal—the English law having allowed them to buy back a package from the liquidators that was all assets and no obligations.

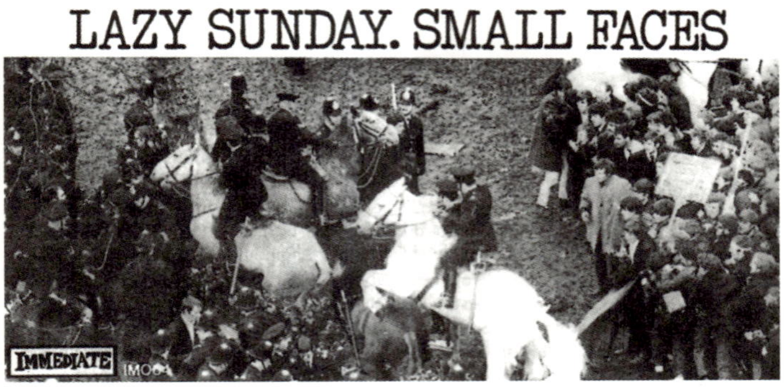
LAZY SUNDAY. SMALL FACES
IMMEDIATE

DON ARDEN CAME ROUND AND PUT A GUN IN MY MOUTH. I WENT TO THE POLICE
TONY CALDER

Oldham appeared in Cannes on a yacht navigated by Don Arden. Arden now managed Black Sabbath and had a huge beef with the Meehans (Patrick Jnr and Patrick Snr) regarding their business dealings with the group. When initially asked about the ensuing events, particularly about the claims of a gun being put in Calder's mouth, Arden joked: "What's the matter? Did someone forget to pull the trigger?" Tony Calder recounts:

> It had nothing to do with Immediate II. It had to do with Patrick Meehan's father trying to make Don Arden bankrupt. Patrick came to stay with me in Antigua and said, 'come back and change World Wide Artists Management into Nems Records for me'. We bought from the receiver what rights the receiver had for Immediate for the UK only. Andrew was busy running Immediate Records Inc, which had the rights for the rest of the world and did a deal with Charly for France and Belgium. But Don Arden came round and put a gun in my mouth. I went to the police.

Oldham exited the Cannes Croissette with the sound of machine gun fire in his ears. Immediate II was definitely off the agenda when Oldham discovered his ex-wife Sheila Klein and Tony Calder were living together. Nems went ahead with their plans for Immediate and in 1976 "Itchycoo Park" made it back in the UK Top 10. Nems paid the group £4,000 to make a *Top Of The Pops* appearance promoting it. Small Faces also played a reunion gig at the Rainbow Theatre in London. *Ogden's Nut Gone Flake*, the single "Lazy Sunday" and more of Small Faces' greatest material was all re-released in the UK. Chris Farlowe's "Out Of Time" was also a chart hit second time round for Nems and was backed by a *Best Of Farlowe* album. Amen Corner, The Nice, Humble Pie and PP Arnold albums were also released—with all artists claiming they received zero royalties.

A sort of uneasy truce existed between 1976 and 1983 about the carving up of territories—with continued allegations neither company pay royalties to artists: Nems by dint of the unique package they'd bought off the liquidators and Charly because Luc Young just kept moving from place to place and was largely untraceable. In the mid 1990s, it was reported that Luc Young was chased to court by MCA in the US over Charly's (it was claimed) fraudulent re-issuing of the Chess catalogue. MCA were granted damages to the tune of $7 million for "flagrant infringement of copyright"—and Luc Young was subsequently believed to be hiding out in tax havens around the world, or even, some said, laying low in Chelsea.

It was understood Oldham had made his Immediate Records Inc deal with Charly in 1975 for five years, and for Europe only, but Luc Young just kept on pressing the records and was controlling the Immediate back catalogue on everything outside the UK. This was not an uncommon state of affairs—Luc Young was really following the lead of the major labels at the time. For instance, it has been suggested that, when EMI's deal with Immediate Inc for Europe and Canada wound down in 1975, EMI kept on pressing up records in India and shipping them in through the back door.

ADVERTISING FOR SMALL FACES SINGLE "LAZY SUNDAY" DEPICTING THE FAMOUS RIOTS IN LEFTBANK, PARIS WHEN 10,000 PEOPLE TOOK TO THE STREETS, APRIL 1968

And we wonder why the records business turned in to Rome and crumbled—they never pay an act today what is owed less than a lawyer would cost because they know the act cannot afford to defend themselves. Old small royalties add up and cover the overhead at the top.

At Nems, Meehan eventually off-loaded Calder and, in 1983, following the advent of CDs (when re-issuing back catalogue was about to go boom), sold Nems to Castle Music for what was described as a "lotta, lotta" money.

Over the next 17 years Castle put out almost everything and anything Immediate had done on CD and reputedly did not pay royalties, instead making pony deals with the acts they needed for PR. They allegedly paid PP Arnold and Chris Farlowe £10,000 each and came to a private deal with The Nice, while all the smaller acts got nothing. Interestingly, a brazen Billy Nicholls kept on releasing his *Would You Believe* LP/CD via his own website. Castle were said to have paid more for the Small Faces to climb aboard, giving Small Faces drummer Kenny Jones the money to start looking for his royalties in earnest (Kenny claims he only started receiving royalties in 1997, when he was handed a reputed £250,000 plus figure). That figure has been called in to question too, as the Small Faces were only on a four per cent royalty at Immediate (that amount being generous for the 1960s when, for instance, The Beatles were on two per cent royalty). So if Small Faces made a generous 32p per album sold, on a 100,000 sales that came to £32,000—minus recording and living costs, that's zilch.

Castle largely restricted their Immediate operations to the UK, while Charly continued to exploit the Immediate back catalogue worldwide—the dispute over who owned what was resolved via a private joint-ownership agreement, which seemed to serve only to legitimise Charly's involvement. How Luc Young had managed to stay in the game up until this point is a mystery—although it has been alleged that Luc Young backdated his original licensing agreement with Immediate Inc sometime in the 1990s to cover up for what he had been doing, perhaps, some said, with Oldham's help. If so, one can only presume a large amount of cash changed hands, and perhaps Oldham still had hopes of rocking Castle's boat.

In 2000 Castle was acquired by Sanctuary Records who spent big on repackaging and issued endless high-end CD box sets and compilation hits packages of Immediate product, as well as straight up album reissues. Royalties, unless you had the sort of backing Kenny Jones persevered to get, were still said to be hard to come by. It is the kind of thing (fancy high-profile repackaging with no recompense) that can drive a penniless act who had one moment of worth with Immediate to drugs, drink, depression or death. It is perhaps surprising that Sanctuary, the largest independent record company in the world, do not question Charly's role in the Immediate back catalogue, with a view to them, Sanctuary, legitimately owning the whole cake. Having largely bowed out of proceedings after the firearms incident in Cannes, a clean and healthy Oldham, following the publication of *Stoned* and *2Stoned*, was finally ready to deal with the maligning and mishandling of his record label—which, particularly the grumbling over lack of royalty payments, had damaged his own reputation. Perhaps he made the mistake of confusing being well with being right.

In 2002 Oldham and Immediate Records Inc were plaintiffs in a High Court case against Sanctuary and Charly. Oldham was after rights and royalties or master recordings he had paid for and leased to Immediate, and/or rights in acts (ie. Small Faces, Amen Corner) that his money, not Immediate's, had paid for.

Oldham ended up representing himself at the Old Bailey. It was rumoured he had run low on funds and did not trust his lawyer, Nick Kannar, having found out Kanaar had been in conversation with his former client Luc Young—something he did not fully inform Oldham of. Perhaps these conversations were about the other dealings Oldham and Luc Young may have had: but whatever they were about, Kannar jumped ship. The judge, Justice Pumfrey, who recently died aged 56 from a stroke, told Oldham he would walk him through the legalities and make sure he understood everything. Alas, the finer points of English law are not something you can pick up overnight. Oldham chose an outfit—striped brown DKNY four button suit—and took off his earrings, before being told by an emissary from Allen Klein that the judge was alleged to "bat for the other side" and butched-up, basing his performance on the Old Bailey appearance by Terence Stamp in the opening minutes of the film "The Hit".

Sanctuary called on Kenny Jones, Blue Weaver (Amen Corner), Mike Hurst and Oldham's old pal Jerry Shirley. Having Humble Pie drummer Shirley pop up against him was a major shock. Oldham had helped out Shirley following the collapse of Humble Pie, offering him work in the late 1970s in Italy, while over there producing major hits with Francesco Di Gregori. Oldham had Banes and former Poet's singer, George Gallagher, in his corner. His star witness, Stan Blackbourne, the old Rolling Stones/Immediate accountant, had died a few months prior (and his testimony was not allowed in court). The timing of the court dates also unfortunately clashed with Oldham's wedding anniversary and went on while his mother was dying in Oxford. He asked for leave to see his mother but was refused.

Even without these things on his mind, Oldham stood no chance and was easily outmanoeuvred by Charly's QC who slipped and slid his way under any claims Oldham made in expert legalise. Then the Judge turned on Oldham because "Mr Oldham did not get a receipt from Don Arden when he gave him £25,000 in cash for the Small Faces". The lawyer from Sanctuary generally acted fairly and just dealt with what they had inherited/bought from Castle. The QC representing Charly, though, would try and get Oldham to pay huge sums into court or be penalised, each time declaring "but m'lud he lives in Bogotá, Colombia!" The subtext being that Oldham was a foreigner and how dare he come back to the UK and try and use the system for his own ends.

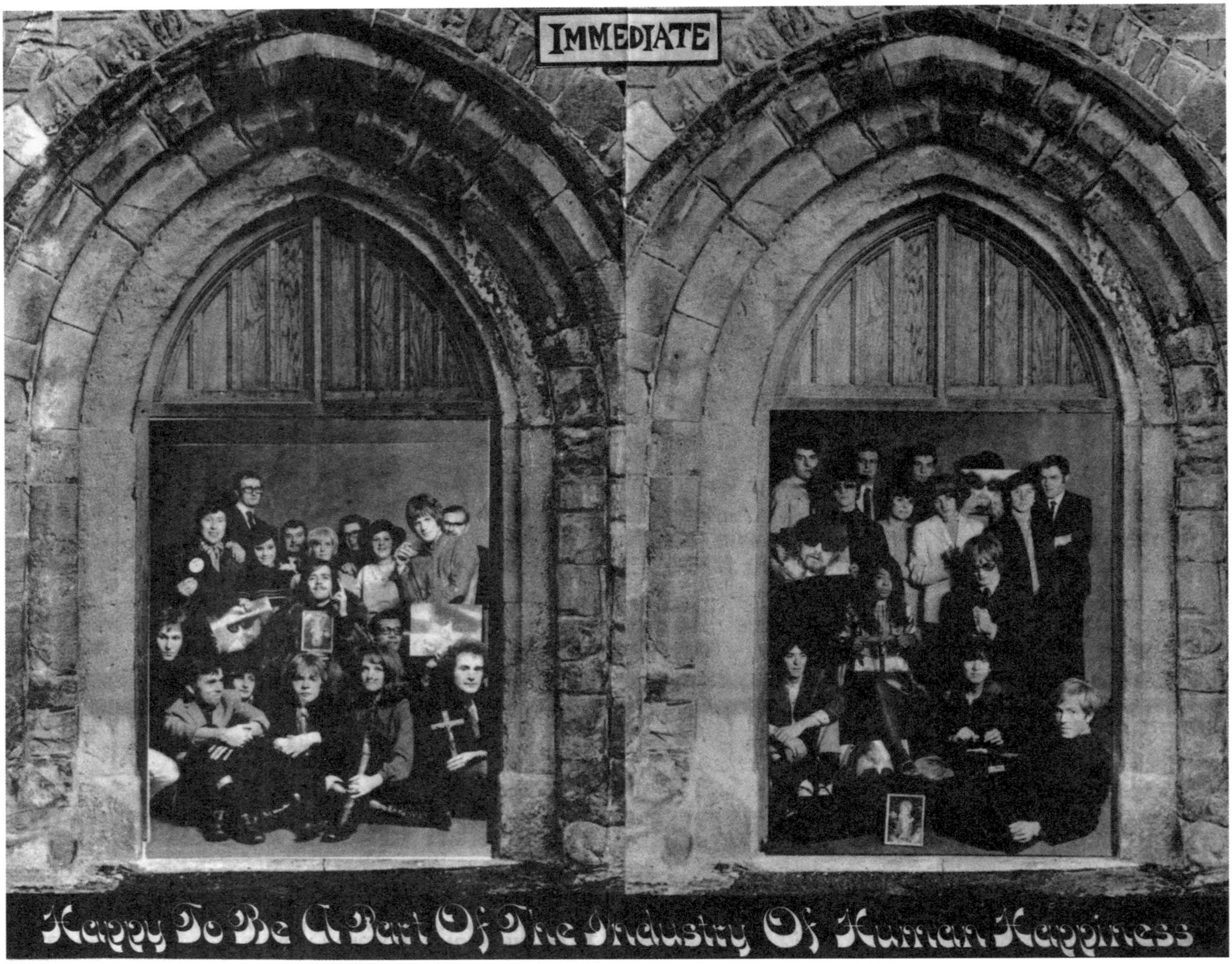
IMMEDIATE
Happy To Be A Part Of The Industry Of Human Happiness

THE ENTIRE IMMEDIATE FAMILY, CIRCA 1967

Paul Banes was amazed by the proceedings. He attempted to explain the Immediate royalty system, which as far as he was concerned, confirmed Oldham's claim of ownership. In black and white, he produced original 1960s label copy that showed Oldham was the owner of many of Immediate's master recordings, ie. they had been privately financed by Oldham and then licensed to Immediate. Banes felt, at worst, this would guarantee payment of the royalties that were allocated in the 1960s to Oldham and all of artists and producers. However, nobody was listening and it seemed to Banes as if the result was a forgone conclusion—the one with the most money wins—but before the verdicts could be announced some fees had to be earned.

Oldham too thought the judge had to allow him royalties on the records ALO Ltd had paid for before and after Immediate Ltd was formed. But no, the judge ruled Oldham had a fiduciary duty to put those ALO Ltd rights into Immediate Records Ltd.

This astonished George Gallagher who had already testified that he had been signed direct to Oldham and his Andes Sound Ltd in 1964 (when Oldham first produced his band, The Poets, and leased the results to Decca Records) and the Glasgow band remained signed to Oldham during the period they had releases on Immediate. "The judge completely ignored my testimony", said Gallagher:

> The opposition's silks were an expensive legal surplus to the event; they surely never have had so little to do. They knew their man; the verdict was a foregone affair. The IRA 'suspects' had more chance of justice in the Diplock courts than did Andrew here: it was a sham. When Andrew went it alone I had already made up my mind on the outcome. I'd seen some of my friends taste good old British justice trying to defend themselves during the miners' strike in 1984. I wish I had had the bottle to just say to the old man Pumfrey, 'you dirty corrupt old bastard it's a waste of time me being here my friend has no chance'.

Even so, Oldham was shaken by Mr Justice Pumfrey's final verdict, that there was an "undisputable" paper trail that led to copyright ownership remaining with Charly and Sanctuary. Having lost the case, Oldham was ordered to pay the £370,000 court costs. Mr Justice Pumfrey ruled that any rights Oldham may have held came to an end with the 1976 Nems agreement. He went on to declare that: "Mr Oldham appears to have been a remarkably effective record producer but it seems his business skills were not of the same order."

It had been a strange experience and, in part, Oldham could even feel some slight relief that he'd lost. Imagine having to account small amounts for artists like Chris Farlowe, PP Arnold and Small Faces who thought they had sold millions. The High Court case was widely reported in the media, much made of 58-year-old Oldham's claim that many of the deals being discussed in court had been made as a result of his dependency on "drugs or drink", having been "out to lunch" for the years between 1967 and 1995.

Prior to the trial, Oldham had alleged that if you buy an Immediate re-release via Charly (most recently releasing stuff via Cherry Red) zero royalties go to any of the artists. Luc Young reputedly once said, in a rare interview, that he was the one who did the work, why should the he pay the artists. With Immediate re-releases by Sanctuary—bar major acts such as Small Faces, Humble Pie, some of Amen Corner, and maybe PP Arnold and Chris Farlowe—Oldham implied the same applies.

At the High Court he had been unable to gain any clarity on the situation. Oldham had tried his best to look out for not just himself, but the lesser known Immediate artists such as Billy Nicholls and David O'List of The Nice and the label's producers such as Shel Talmy, Mick Jagger and Keith Richards—to make sure all involved in the wild adventure finally got their Immediate dues. Having failed, he withdrew himself from the fray, unable to satisfactorily clear his universe. Sanctuary was taken over by Universal in 2007. Luc Young remains at large.

A BIT ABOUT ME

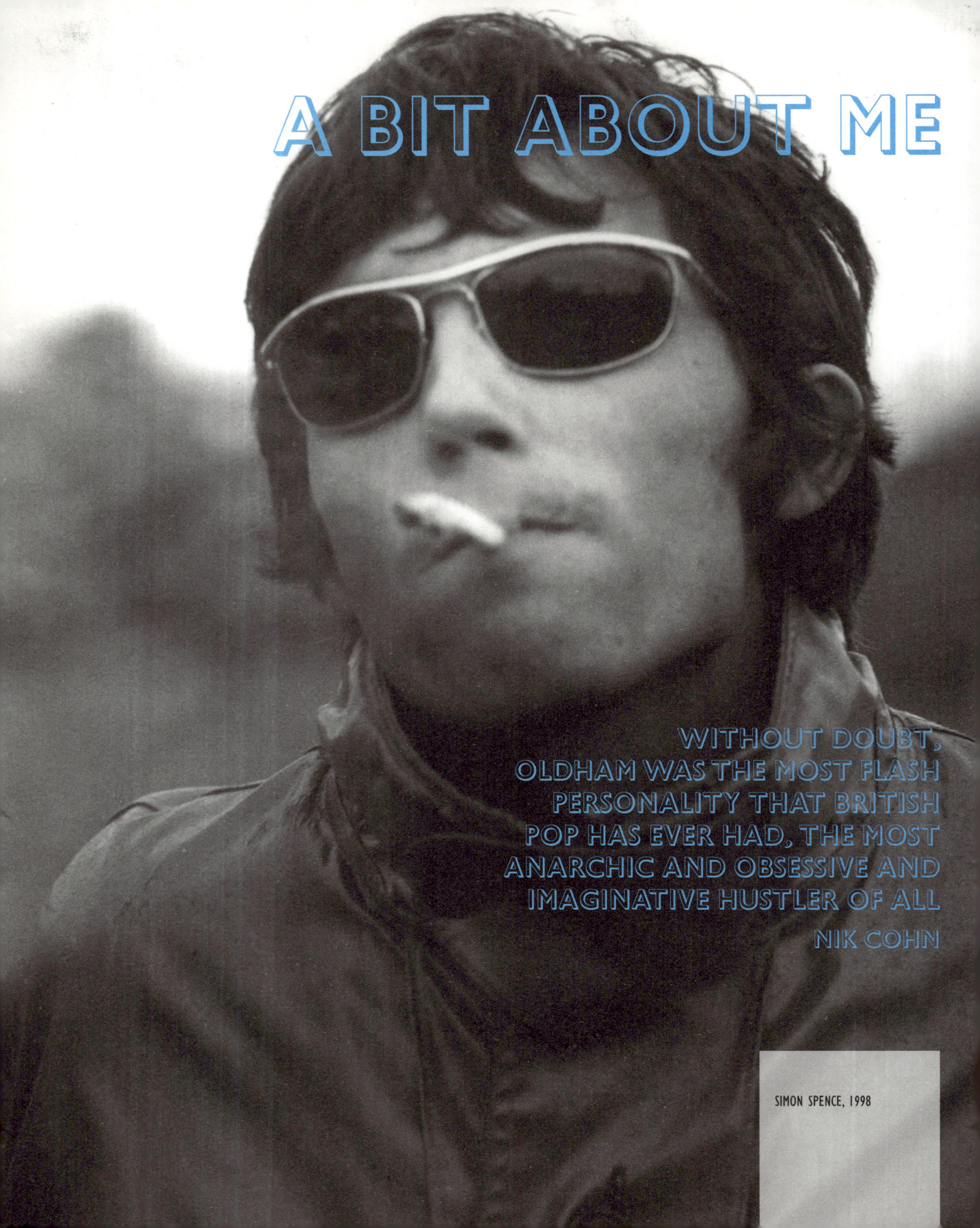

WITHOUT DOUBT,
OLDHAM WAS THE MOST FLASH
PERSONALITY THAT BRITISH
POP HAS EVER HAD, THE MOST
ANARCHIC AND OBSESSIVE AND
IMAGINATIVE HUSTLER OF ALL

NIK COHN

SIMON SPENCE, 1998

In 1990 I read about Andrew Oldham in *Starmakers and Svengalis*, a book given me by *NME* reviews editor, Stuart Bailie. It was a turnaround for Bailie who had previously had to be pulled away from physically attacking me after I had trashed Van Morrison in print.

The chapter in *Starmakers and Svengalis* that focused on Oldham, was addictive stuff. The architect of Rolling Stones' golden 1960s years, their 19-year-old millionaire manager and producer, Oldham—a visionary teenage pop genius in dark glasses, make-up and sharp suits, his story full of drugs, guns, gangsters, cash, chaos and controversy. Then, at the end of the 1960s, when he was just 26, he disappeared in a puff of smoke never to be heard of again. Oldham was mentioned here and there in scores of Rolling Stones books but his huge impact on the group in the 1960s had never been fully explored. Nik Cohn—in his 1969 seminally regarded speed-read breakdown of the era's pop giants, *Awopbopaloobop Alopbamboom*—called Oldham, "without doubt, the most flash personality that British pop has ever had, the most anarchic and obsessive and imaginative hustler of all". George Melly wrote him up "as pretty and cunning as a stoat". Both men also noted Oldham's overt manipulation on the Rolling Stones, particularly Mick Jagger.

I started digging around. Gered Mankowitz—the photographer famed for capturing the Rolling Stones in their mid 1960s prime—assured me Oldham was still alive although, dispiritingly, living far away, in Colombia, South America. He gave me the number of Allen Klein's office in New York, the best way he knew of getting a message to Oldham, then asked that I didn't mention his assistance if I did manage to contact the Loog. The question was why.

There was gossip and hearsay surrounding Oldham. Unhinged after 30 years reclusion, Oldham had said goodbye to the real world and was lost in a drugs and booze hinterland, growing his hair, beard, finger nails, with his mind beset by demons, and his life on a knife edge, reeking of violence. The last thing Mankowitz needed were for the obscene phone calls from Oldham to start again.

Allen Klein had taken over as Rolling Stones' manager after Oldham and he had a reputation as a real mafia heavy. I had the cheek to promise him I was going to ring his office every day until I got a response from Oldham. It worked and after about a week the telephone rang.

It was true. Oldham was nuts. I started sweating and worrying. You couldn't follow much of what he was saying but what he did say, in this low menacing gnash, seemed to have undercurrents of deep portent. I was blown away. Suddenly the phone went dead. Through the crackling, unreliable lines to Colombia—a country which suffered from power surges and blackouts—did I actually hear him say "If you get over here there might be a book in it for you"?

I was a happy 20 when the editor of *The Face*, Sheryl Garrett, gave me the opportunity to find out, paying cash up front for a piece about the trip to Colombia that I was billing as a journey to the heart of darkness to uncover my rock'n'roll Colonel Kurtz. Colombia's infamous drug lord, Pablo Escobar, was full out at war with the authorities and bombs, kidnaps and shootings were commonplace in the capital city, Bogotá, where Oldham lived. As far as I been able to ascertain he had not had visitors from the UK press since he had gone in to meltdown at the end of the 1960s.

Oldham wasn't at the airport to meet me off the plane, grumbling that we had arrived a day early and reassured us that the cabbies were reliable and wouldn't cut our throats. 40 minutes later we were in the lift riding to the top of a classy uptown residential tower, and into Oldham's triplex apartment where he sat in a big room on the second floor, half hidden in shadows, and mumbling.

We stayed seven days. Oldham was on cocaine and drank a tremendous amount of grappa. He was razor thin, wild, wired, almost reptilian in appearance and his eyes bulged as he regurgitated unfathomable tales that went on until daybreak and made my head ache. He didn't seem to need sleep and ate off a tray in front of a giant screen television invariably playing gangster movies featuring Christopher Walken, whose mannerisms and looks he sometimes aped. He rarely ventured out further than the local drug store for more cigarettes. Time for Oldham had no meaning.

He shared some cocaine but mostly slipped off to the bathroom for his own. Between the booze and coke we smoked high-grade marijuana. He didn't smoke many joints normally on account of his hands being too shaky to get it together. The only steady hands belonging to my *NME* photographer friend, Martyn Goodacre, who had tagged along under his own steam.

Oldham showed us his collection of knives, sunglasses and jewellery and spoke about a gun. He changed his outfits quite outrageously throughout the day. He was impossible to fathom. He told me he had struck a book deal in the US sometime in the 1980s for a half a million dollars but had to cancel it when he had caused the writer to have a nervous breakdown. I almost had a breakdown of my own at the airport during a frantic escape full of chaos and confusion. There were elections going on and the streets of Bogotá were full of angry crowds and I vividly remember someone quite deliberately and slowly spitting in my face. There was more terror at the airport and people screaming demands for money. I think they were after the airport tax but Martyn and myself were so high by then our paranoia was reaching dizzy heights (on the plane Martyn thought he saw God and his face froze in terrifying fear for more than ten minutes). Changing at Paris, I fumbled my passport handing it over to be checked and told the guard to, "pick it up yourself". We were detained, stripped, the urine tests showed our cocaine levels to be riding high.

OLDHAM REACTED BY PUNCHING THE MAN'S GROIN AND TELLING THE ASTOUNDED JOURNALIST, 'HE'S LUCKY HE DIDN'T GET KILLED', AS THE MAN WRITHED ON THE FLOOR

SIMON SPENCE

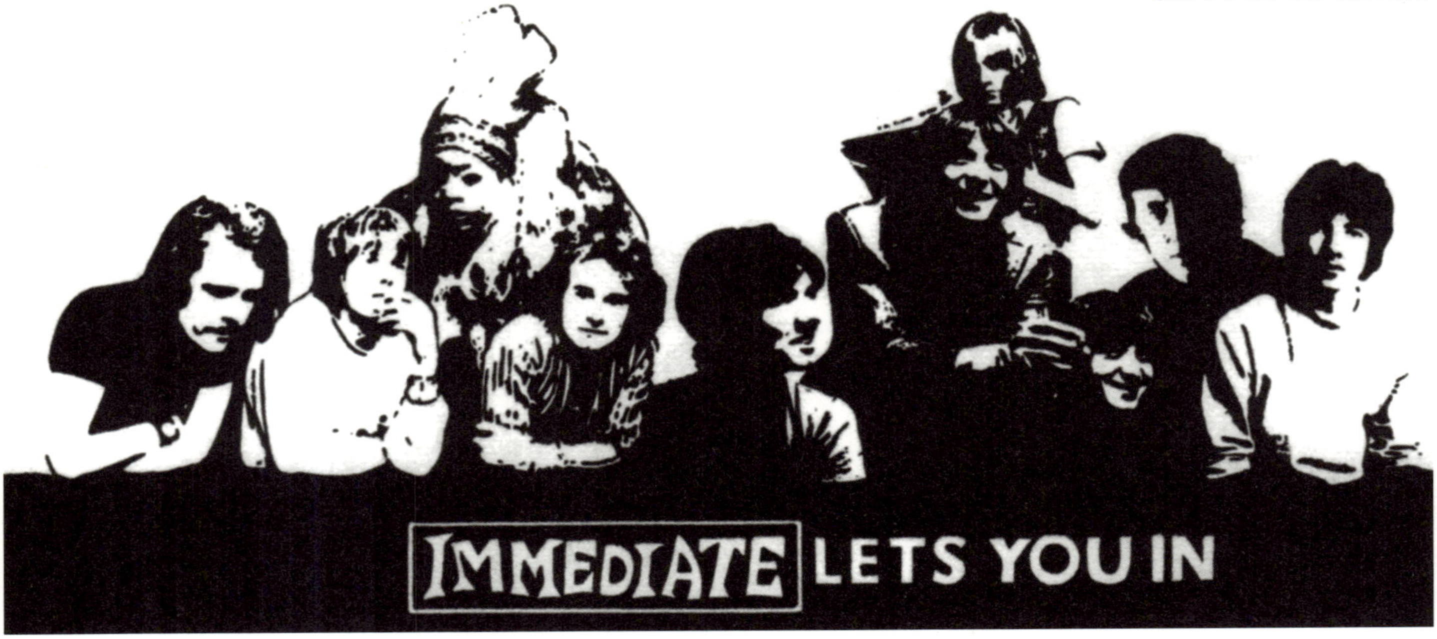
IMMEDIATE LETS YOU IN

I got away from Colombia with a bundle of just decipherable hand-written reminiscences of Oldham's early childhood on fast-fading fax paper and an overwhelming amount of rambling interview tapes to transcribe. When it came to do *The Face* article I couldn't pull one usable short quote from the entire lot.

Six months later Oldham came to London, the possibility of a book seeming more real now, but he stated it would only profile his life up until he was 19—the year he became the manager of Rolling Stones. He holed himself up in an expensive suite in the Royal Lanesborough hotel on Hyde Park Corner for a fortnight where we would start sessions well after midnight and they'd run through the night. Oldham sat in dark glasses, drink in hand, openly snorting coke off the table. A daylight meeting—buying books for research in Soho—was a nervy, sweaty and awkward experience for both of us, but by evening it was forgotten and in the cool of his hotel room the information piled up; an overwhelming jumble of names and events, with the sequences of his formative experiences forever shifting. There would be inexplicable appearances from heavy looking Russians, with heated exchanges, then straight back in to a ridiculous

DETAIL FROM THE *IMMEDIATE LETS YOU IN* ALBUM, 1969

story about a camel hair overcoat he once wore to a French new wave film showing at the Hampstead Everyman—or was it the fake fur zebra-print drape stolen from a strip club in Nice? I was lapping it up. As word got round about the book, he leaked NME a quote about me, "he reminds me of the son I never wanted" and disappeared back to Colombia.

Oldham was born in Paddington, London, January 1944, shortly after his father, Andrew Loog, a US fighter pilot of Dutch heritage had been shot down and killed over Belgium in the Second World War. His mother, Celia Oldham, had emigrated with her mother from Australia to London. She had grown up in the city and in her early 20s dragged up "Andy" between various northwest London rented rooms and apartments. She was a strong single mother. One of Oldham's earliest memories was of finding a flatmate of Celia's dead, with her head in the oven. Before he was in double figures, his mother took a lover, millionaire Jewish businessman, Alec Morris, who was married but whose wife didn't mind. Morris had made his fortune in furniture and the relationship with Oldham's mother lasted throughout Oldham's teens. As a father figure he was totally flash. He drove a Rolls Royce and dressed well and Oldham regularly enjoyed food at the famous Ivy restaurant as a reward for good exam results. Celia, who was half Jewish herself—her father having fled to Australia from Poland—eventually settled in a ground floor apartment in Hampstead and that stylish, artistic suburb of London became Oldham's manor. There were no relations at hand and despite the boyfriend, the family wasn't rich. Oldham's mother worked as a part-time Comptometer (the predecessor of the modern computer) operator, and he learned to be independent. After some experience of plush country boarding schools, Oldham found Marylebone state school grim and in his first year, aged at 11, was expelled for extortion.

When he became famous much was made of the "public-school educated" Oldham. A burst of private tuition helped him though the 11-plus, and Celia hurried him off to board at Wellingborough, which—although a 400-year-old public school near Northampton—was full of local farmer's children. He stuck out, flouncing up from London in tailor-made Teddy Boy drape suits, inventing a long-running dental problem that allowed him to escape back to the city whenever he chose.

Oldham worked hard at being stylish and was full of self assurance, impressing pals by appearing in the audience of the legendary television pop show *Oh Boy*. Precocious, he recalls spending school holidays pounding the streets of London, knocking on the doors of showbusiness impresarios, directors, actors and music companies. At the age of 12 his mother took him to see the West End stage production of *Expresso Bongo*, a black comedy about the music business, featuring manager, Soho Johnny Jackson, and a teen rock'n'roller, Bongo Herbert. It made a lasting impression, as did Elvis, James Dean, Marlon Brando, Jimmy Greaves, Jet Harris and actor, Laurence Harvey. He left the school at 16 with one O-level and no chance of higher education. "Andrew may do well, but not here", said a final school report. Too sharply dressed for Hampstead's burgeoning 1960 to 1961 beatnik, coffee bar scene, Oldham became a sort of proto-mod, perfecting the pose with his first real ally, the infamous Peter Meaden, aka the Face, who later with Phil "The Greek" as bodyguard, orchestrated the early career of The Who. They hung out at trendy clothes shops—John Michael's and Austin's—and hip clubs such as The Scene. They shopped, popped pills, and partied until they dropped. They tried their hand at PR (for John Michael) and gig promotion and started to get a bit of a reputation as a likely pair. Oldham got a write-up and picture of himself in the first ever British men's fashion page, which appeared in the *Evening Standard*, touting grey flannel shirts as the next big thing. His first major piece of luck came at 17, when he landed a job running errands for Mary Quant at her King's Road Bazaar boutique. "The carpets were thick and the teacups thin", he would say, as he watched Quant revolutionise women's fashion. He found himself in the papers again, this time a lead feature in the *Daily Mail*, full of himself for conning Burton's into making him a 50-guinea madras suit on the back of their £2 tailor-made offer.

During the six months he worked for Quant he also picked up night jobs at Ronnie Scott's Jazz Club and at the notorious all-night Soho R&B club, The Flamingo. He quit all three jobs suddenly and tripped off to the South of France, hustling the showbusiness types known to frequent such exclusive enclaves as *Juan Les Pins*. He met theatre and song king, Lionel Bart, for the first time there—hustling him for money—and got work at the open-air Antibes Jazz festival where Ray Charles performed. Oldham kidnapped a London debutante from a well-to-do family and sold the story back to the UK papers for cash and checked out Picasso admiring his own work in an art gallery with a joint.

Back in London for 1962 he charmed himself into a position as music PR, earning a stint with big Top 10 UK solo hunk, Mark Wynter. He also handled visiting hit US acts such as Little Richard, Sam Cooke, Phil Spector and Bob Dylan, and became well-known to London's most-influential music journalists, DJs, managers, agents and record company staff.

A fortuitous meeting with Brian Epstein in the Birmingham television studio at a recording *Thank Your Lucky Stars,* featuring Mark Wynter and The Beatles—making their first television appearance—led to Oldham landing the PR job for the Mop Tops, taking great pride in getting them in *Vogue* in early 1963. He had the ability to make the acts "feel like a million dollars", remembered Kenny Lynch, another of his early UK PR clients at the time, "and he had more front than Selfridges".

Next came Rolling Stones, but Oldham was still holding out on sharing those golden years with me. Nonetheless several publishers showed interest in our material. We kept in contact until Oldham relaunched Immediate Records with his original partner in the label, Tony Calder, in 1993. The band I fronted at the time had just been dropped by Pete Waterman's PWL—the promise of Kylie producing our debut album and our own label, PWL Rock, failing to materialise. We took the opportunity to

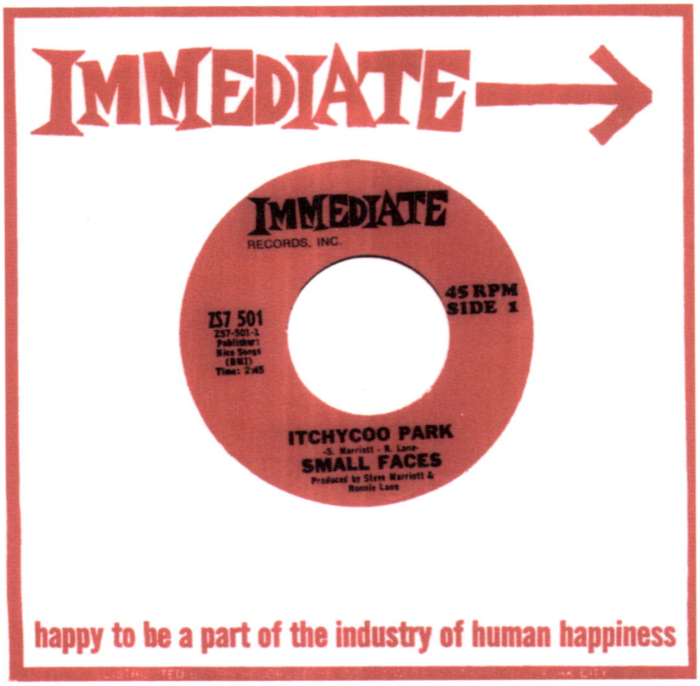
IMMEDIATE
IMMEDIATE
RECORDS, INC.
45 RPM
SIDE 1
ZS7 501
ITCHYCOO PARK
SMALL FACES
happy to be a part of the industry of human happiness

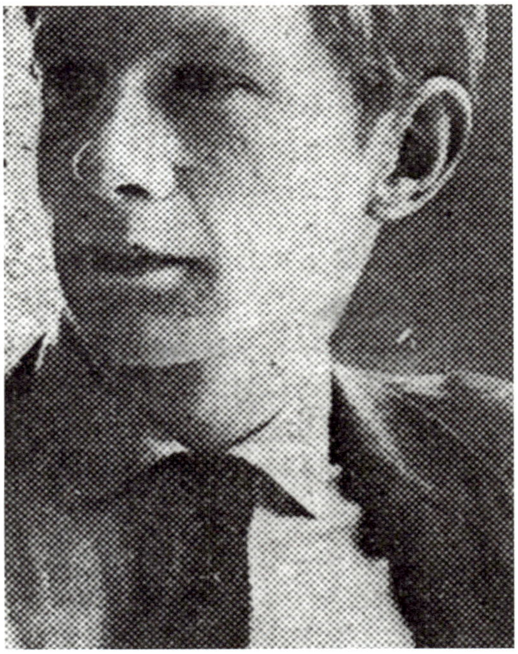

TOP: ITCHYCOO PARK BY SMALL FACES, APRIL 1968

BOTTOM: THE FIRST EVER PRESS APPEARANCE OF ANDREW OLDHAM, *EVENING STANDARD*, CIRCA 1965

jump on board Immediate III, snapping up a few grand advance, delivered in £50 notes in a brown paper envelope.

Oldham returned to London to promote the venture, greeting me with a Nazi salute and immediately snorting half the six grams of coke he asked me to bring him. Journalists queued up to talk to him in his room at the Draycott Hotel in Chelsea, where a large framed still of Al Pacino in *The Godfather 3* had pride of place on the coffee table. Goodacre's Colombia shots of him ended up on the cover of the *Independent Magazine*. He was a great read as a, "legendary... brilliant... eccentric gangster", swigging from his bottle of grappa, veering drunkenly between warm geniality and raging indignation. A songwriter passing through made a comment about the physical attributes of his Colombian actress wife, Esther, to which Oldham reacted by punching the man's groin, telling the astounded journalist, "he's lucky he didn't get killed", as the man writhes on the floor.

Rolling Stones biographer David Dalton—then finishing the Marianne Faithfull biography—was humiliated as the contents of his bag full of Christmas gifts was unceremoniously dumped on the floor in front of an ragbag assortment of Oldham's business associates and hanger-ons. Throughout his stay in London, Oldham was on a short fuse—interpreting a teasing remark as a slur and reacting by hurling a plate of food at the wall and later found by one journalist "rolling around on the carpet, feet swinging in the air, bellowing, 'we all live in a yellow submarine', at the top of his voice".

Another evening, around midnight, I was summonsed to bring what I had of the book so far. The room was crowded with the Primal Scream wrecking crew and the detritus of a wild drugs and booze party. Oldham was drunk and just wanted to tell me I was finished. What he had said during a ten minute dressing down was difficult to follow but seemed to hinge on the mantra "never hustle a hustler". He escorted me out of the room with his arm round my shoulder and in that lonely hotel corridor he half-apologised for his behaviour, with a you-know-me by now shrug.

Immediate III collapsed without a release and two years went by without news on the book. I had expected someone else to jump on Oldham's story after that kind of publicity but nothing seemed to materialise. One night I called him in Colombia and founding him singing from a different Hymn sheet. He said he'd had a radical life-style change and to meet him in Buenos Aires where he would tell me all about it. I hustled *Arena* magazine for the air ticket and he welcomed me to his hotel suite with a non-alcoholic beer. It was early days on his road to recovery from the booze and drugs addiction that had almost killed him. I watched befuddled as he prepared his daily intake of nutritional pills from scores of prescription bottles on his dressing table. The whole affair was something to do with Scientology. In Buenos Aires, he was producing his fifth album with Argentina's biggest rock'n'roll act, The Ratones Paranoicos, for Sony South America. We would meet in the late morning and he would buy me lunch. He would then go to produce the album and retire early for a decent night's rest. I went to the studio with him once or twice; it was out in the country and had an outdoor pool. The band, Argentina's answer to U2, were open, friendly and polite, despite the fact they had won big prizes on prime time television award shows and sold out stadium gigs. When I wasn't with Oldham, I busied myself booking appointments to meet all the major record companies, having a blast downtown hanging out at the infamous TCT magazine shop, or uptown with transvestite club runners and in photocopying shops like department stores, making up tens of one-off t-shirts.

And now, finally, I had what he told me one morning was his "blessing" to do his biography—this time everything, no holds barred. Back home I got an agent, an understudy of the man who would go on to handle the *Harry Potter* franchise. A year of paper research later and I had roughly outlined Oldham's 1960s heyday to add to our exhaustive beginnings.

In late 1996 Oldham was happy to welcome me back to Bogotá for a month to talk though all the research. He would help me put the book together, without credit, and wanted to okay the final manuscript. He was still clean—his home life now a picture of calm. We camped in his teenage son's room to work on the only computer in the house, and then after a smooth couple of weeks he jetted off to the US for the induction of Phil Spector to Rock'n'Roll Hall of Fame. His wife, Esther, arranged a holiday for my girlfriend and me, taking in the country's contrasting *Miami Vice*-esque areas and the beautifully untouched coastlines.

I set about a year of extensive interviews with Oldham's contemporaries back in the UK and US. He had supplied me with some phone numbers and from there the participants in the book grew until the list reached over 300—from childhood friends though to some of the most powerful and influential people the music business has ever had. Over this entire period I would exchange emails daily with Oldham, an exhilarating time as the book grew to epic proportions.

In 1998 I travelled back to Bogotá on my own for what was supposed to be a final two weeks getting our house in order. This stay stretched to over three months, taking in a Christmas and new year. He was rigorous and we worked every day from early in the morning until late afternoon and finally had about 600,000 words down.

We went for Christmas dinner in a remote hotel owned by an English pal of his, driving three hours out of Bogotá into real guerrilla territory where we heard gunshots, screams and rustlings throughout night. Oldham didn't seem worried and enjoyed driving the mountainous curves in his Lexus at dizzying speeds. I was flat broke for most of the stay in Bogotá, but there were kids with carrier bags full of cheap grass on the streets and I found a games arcade full of 1980s retro machines to while away the evenings.
One evening I blacked-out while trying to pay in a cheap chicken joint, and came around on the floor in a puddle of blood, piss and loose change, returning to work the next morning with a black eye and scabby eyebrow. Oldham didn't mind, he was a real laugh, never taking himself seriously, except when it came to business. He joked at the dinner table, after he dropped a scrap of food on the floor—who would be first too it: Ruby, his beloved dog, or me?

The publishers were happy when the first quarter of the book was delivered but after calling it "titanic" Oldham changed his tune, said he wasn't satisfied and I worried at the news he was taking the work to New York, where he would be editing it with a fresh pair of eyes. I saw that edit when he came to London to deliver it to the publisher. Crucially, it was now all in the first person—and that's just the way it was. Oldham had approximately halved the work and the first volume, *Stoned*, followed his life until just after he met the Rolling Stones— keeping his golden era with them for a second book, *2Stoned*. I was working in Hong Kong when *Stoned* eventually came out in 2000. I was off the front cover but on page one, credited with "research and interviews". It got great reviews in the UK, US and Italy, where Oldham had been big in the late 1970s, and sold well, acclaimed as a key rock'n'roll work.

In 2002, *2Stoned* came out and I received the same page one credits. In the acknowledgments he wrote:

> Simon Spence conducted the interviews and gathered the research upon which both *Stoned* and *2Stoned* were founded. Simon made my life and times his agenda whilst I was losing the first and pissing on the second and for that I say thank you.

Oldham's friend, famed photographer Mick Rock, told me I had got lucky when I bemoaned my lot to him over being dumped as writer. He said if I had met Oldham, as he had, in the wiry coke and smack spattered 1970s, I would have got really fucked over. So I count myself lucky and forever blessed.

OLDHAM WAS FOUND ROLLING AROUND ON THE CARPET, FEET SWINGING IN THE AIR, BELLOWING, 'WE ALL LIVE IN A YELLOW SUBMARINE'
SIMON SPENCE

DISCOGRAPHY

1965

The McCoys
"Hang On Sloopy"/"I Can't Believe It"

Fifth Avenue
"Bells Of Rhymney"/"Just Like Anyone Would Do"

Nico
"I'm Not Sayin'"/"The Last Mile"

Gregory Phillips
"Down In The Boondocks"/"That's The One"

The Masterminds
"She Belongs To Me"/"Taken My Love"

The Poets
"Call Again"/"Something I Can't Forget"

The Strangeloves
"Cara-Lin"/"Roll On Mississippi"

Val Lenton
"Gotta Get Away"/"You Don't Care"

The Factotums
"In My Lonely Room"/"Run In The Green And Tangerine Flaked Forest"

Golden Apples Of The Sun
"Monkey Time"/"Chocolate Rolls, Tea And Monopoly"

Barbara Lynn
"You Can't Buy My Love"/"That's What A Friend Would Do"

John Mayall's Bluesbreakers
"I'm Your Witchdoctor"/"Telephone Blues"

Glyn Johns
"Mary Anne"/"Like Grains Of Yellow Sand"

Mick Softley
"I'm So Confused"/"She My Girl"

The Mockingbirds
"You Stole My Love"/"Skit Skat"

Chris Farlowe
"The Fool"/"Treat Her Good"

Joey Levine
"Down and Out"/"The Out Of Towner"

Jimmy Tarbuck
"Someday"/"Wastin' Time"

The McCoys
Hang On Sloopy

Les Fleur De Lys
"Moondreams"/"Wait For Me"

The McCoys
"Fever"/"Sorrow"

Chris Farlowe
In The Midnight Hour

Julien Protest Quintet
"Satisfaction"/"Like A Bob Dylan"

The Variations
"Man With All The Toys"/"She'll Know I'm Sorry"

1966

Chris Farlowe
"Think"/"Don't Just Look At Me"

The Poets
"Baby Don't You Do It"/"I'll Come Home"

Charles Dickens
"So Much In Love Jagger"/"Our Soul Brother"

Sam Cooke
The Wonderful World Of Sam Cooke

The Aranbee Pop Orchestra
(Under The Direction Of Keith Richard)
Today's Pop Symphony

Goldie
"Goin' Back"/"Headlines"

The Factotums
"You're So Good To Me"/"Can't Go Home Anymore"

Tony River and The Castaways
"Girl Don't Tell Me"/"Girl From Salt Lake City"

The McCoys
"Don't Worry Mother (Your Son's Heart Is Pure)"/"Ko-Ko"

The Masterminds
"Barbara Ann"

The McCoys
"And Down"/"If You Tell A Lie"

Sam Cooke
"That's Heaven To Me"

Chris Farlowe
14 Things To Think About

London Waits
"Softly Softly"/"Serenadio"

The Turtles
"You Baby"/"Wanderin' Kind"

Creation
"Creation"/"Making Time"

The Fleur De Lys
"Circles"/"So Come On"

Chris Farlowe
"Out Of Time"/"Baby Make It Soon"

Twice As Much
"Sittin' on a Fence"/"Baby I Want You"

The McCoys
"Runaway"/"Come On Let's Go"

Twice As Much
"Step Out Of Line"/"Simplified"

The McCoys
"(You Make Me Feel) So Good"/"Everyday I Have To Cry"

Chris Farlowe
"Ride On Baby"/"Headlines"

Twice As Much
"True Story"/"You're So Good To Me"

Mark Murphy
Who Can I Turn To

Chris Farlow
The Art Of Chris Farlowe

Twice As Much
Own Up

The McCoys
Hits Vol. 1

The McCoys
Hits Vol. 2

Chris Farlowe
Hits

1967

PP Arnold
"Everything's Gonna Be Alright"/"Life Is But Nothing"

Chris Farlowe
"My Way Of Giving"/"You're So Good To Me"

Nicky Scott
"Backstreet Girl"/"Chain Reaction"

The McCoys
"I Got To Go Back"/"Dynamitey"

Twice As Much
"Crystal Ball"/"Why Can't They All Go And Leave Me Alone"

Apostolic Intervention
"(Tell Me) Have You Ever Seen Me"/"Madame Garcia"

Nicky Scott
"Big City"/"Everything's Gonna Be Alright"

PP Arnold
"First Cut Is The Deepest"/"Speak To Me"

Mort Shuman IV
"Monday Monday"/"Little Children"

Chris Farlowe
"Yesterday's Papers"/"Life Is But Nothing"

Marquis Of Kensington/Marquis Of Kensington's Minstrels
"Changing Of The Guard"/"Reverse Thrust"

Murray Head
"She Was Perfection"/"Secondhand Monday"

Warm Sounds
"Sticks And Stones"/"Angeline"

PP Arnold
"The Time Has Come"/"If You See What I Mean"

Australian Playboys
"Black Sheep RIP"/"Sad Day"

Chris Farlowe
"Moanin'"/"What Have I Been Doing"

Small Faces
"Here Come The Nice"/"Talk To You"

Small Faces
The Small Faces

Small Faces
"Itchycoo Park"/"I'm Only Dreamin'"

Billy Nicholls
"Would You Believe"/"Daytime Girl"

Billy Nicholls
Would You Believe

Del Shannon
"Runaway 1967" (unreleased)

Del Shannon
London Album (unreleased)

Chris Farlowe
"Handbags And Gladrags"/"Everyone Makes A Mistake"

Rod Stewart
"Little Miss Understood"/"So Much To Say (So Little Time)"

The Nice
"Thoughts Of Emerlist Davjack"/"Asrael (Angel Of Death)"

Small Faces
"Tin Soldier"/"I Feel Much Better"

1968

PP Arnold
"If You Think You're Groovy"/"Though It Hurts Me Badly"

Twice As Much
That's All

Chris Farlowe
"The Last Goodbye"/"Paperman Fly In The Sky"

Chris Farlowe
The Best Of Chris Farlowe (Vol. 1)

Small Faces
"Lazy Sunday"/"Rollin' Over"

Various
Blues Anytime Vol. 1

PP Arnold
The First Lady Of Immediate

Small Faces
Ogden's Nut Gone Flake

PP Arnold
"Angel Of The Morning"/"Life Is But Nothing"

Various
Blues Anytime (Vol. 2)

PP Arnold
"First Cut Is The Deepest"/"Speak To Me"

PP Arnold
Kafunta

Various
An Anthology Of British Blues

Chris Farlowe
"Paint It Black"/"What Have I Been Doing"

Chris Farlowe
Paint It Farlowe

Chris Farlowe
"Paint It Black"/"I Just Need Your Lovin'"

Chris Farlowe and The Thunderbirds
"Dawn"/"April Was The Month"

Small Faces
"Mad John"/"The Journey"

Various
An Anthology Of British Blues Vol. 2

John Mayall's Bluesbreakers with Eric Clapton
"I'm You're Witchdoctor"/"Telephone Blues"

The Nice
Thoughts Of Emerlist Davjack

The Nice
"America"/"The Diamond Hard Blue Apples Of The Moon"

The Nice
Ars Longs Veta Brevis

Small Faces
"The Universal"/"Donkey Rides A Penny A Throw"

The Nice
"Brandenburger"/"Happy Freuds"

Duncan Browne
Give Me Take You

Duncan Browne
"On The Bombsite"/"Alfred Bell"

Various
Blues Anytime (Vol. 3)

Small Faces
"Itchycoo Park"/"Lazy Sunday"

Various
European Cup Final 1968 Soundtrack

Various
Tonite Let's All Make Love In London Soundtrack

Various
Gulliver's Travels Soundtrack

Outer Limits
"Great Train Robbery"/"Sweet Freedom"

Excelsior Spring
"Happy Miranda"/"It"

Eddie Thornton Outfit aka Sonny Burke Outfit
"Baby Be My Girl"/"All You"

Michael D'Abo
"See The Little People"/"An Anthology Of Gulliver's Travels"

Copperfield
"Any Old Time (You're Lonely And Sad)"/"I'm No Good For Her"

Twinkle
"Micky"/"Darby And Joan"

Owen Gray and Maximum Breed/Pete Hunt and Maximum Breed
"Sitting In The Park"/"You've Got It Instant"

Jimmy Scott
"Ob-la-di Ob-la-da Story"/"(Part 1: Anullo, Part 2: Dub)"

Samson
Are You Samson

1969

Amen Corner
"(If Paradise Is) Half As Nice"/"Hey Hey Girl"

Fleetwood Mac/Earl Vince and The Valiants
"Man Of the World"/
"Somebody's Gonna Get There Head Kicked In Tonite"

The McCoys
"Hang On Sloopy"/"This Is Where We Came"

Chris Farlowe
"Out Of Time"/"Ride On Baby"

PP Arnold
"First Cut Is The Deepest"/"The Time Has Come"

Chris Farlowe
The Last Goodbye

Small Faces
"Afterglow Of Your Love"/"Wham Bam Thank You Mam"

Small Face
Autumn Stone

Amen Corner
"Hello Susie"/"Evil Man's Gonna Win"

Amen Corner
The National Welsh Coast Live Explosion Company

Humble Pie
"Natural Born Bugie"/"Wrist Job"

Humble Pie
As Safe As Yesterday Is

Various
The Beginning British Blues

Amen Corner
"Get Back"/"Farewell To The Real Magnificent Seven"

Amen Corner
Farewell To The Real Magnificent Seven

Humble Pie
"Natural Born Women"/"I'll Go Alone"

Various
Immediate Let's You In

Amen Corner
"So Fine"/"So Fine"

The Hill
"Sylvie"/"The Fourth Annual Convention Of The Battery Hen Farmers Association (Part 2)"

Various
Blue Leftovers

Small Faces
In Memoriam

Humble Pie
Town And Country

Humble Pie
"The Sad Bag Of Shaky Jake"/"Cold Lady"

The Nice
"Hang On To A Dream"/"Diary Of An Empty Day"

The Nice
Nice

The Nice
Everything As Nice As Mother Makes It

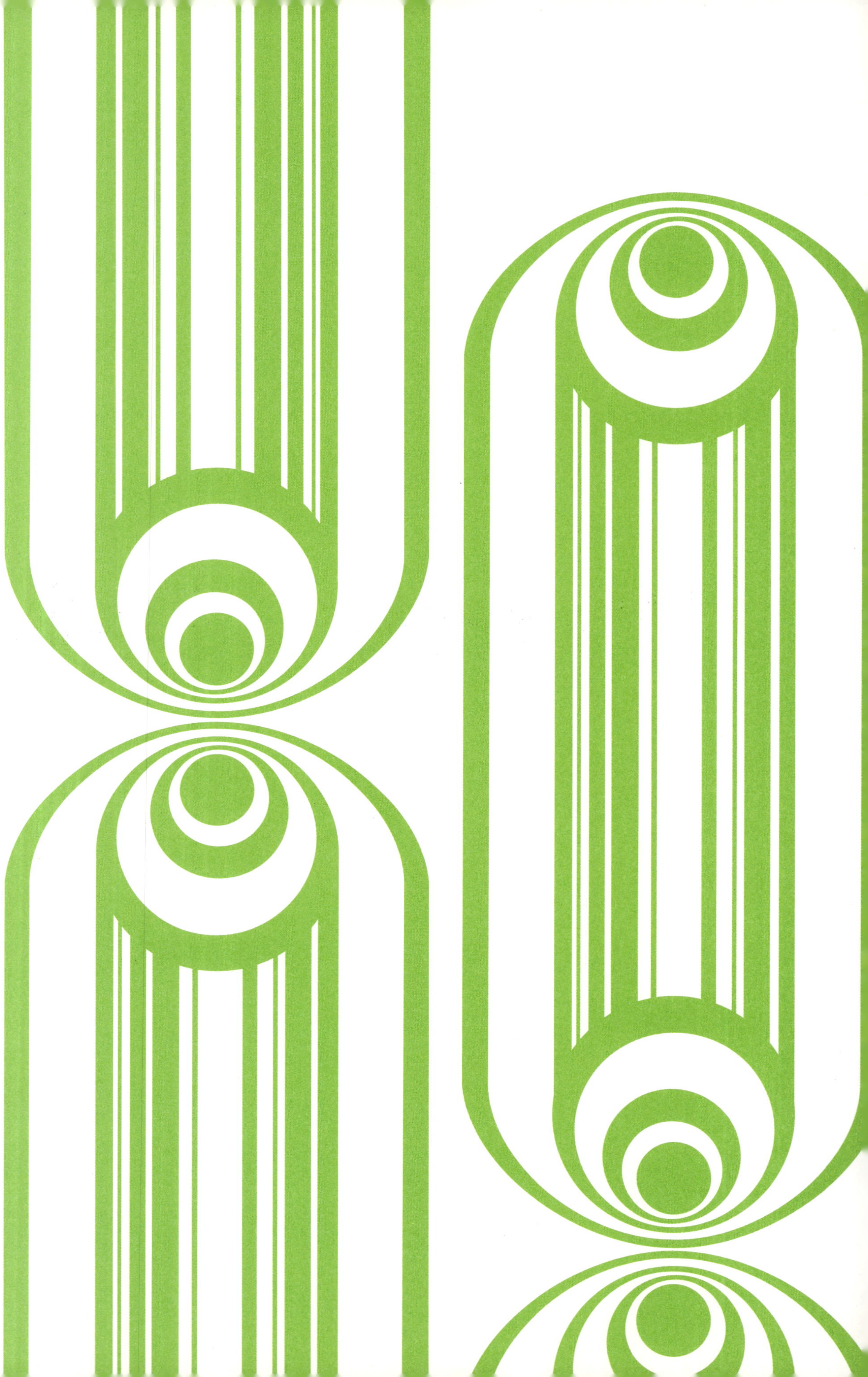

ACKNOWLEDGEMENTS

Shirley Murtas for you know what.

Andrew Loog Oldham for more than you'll ever know.

The Immediate Records alumni for doing it.

Breda and Iggy, Mum and Mick, for being grand parents.

Joan and Walter Carroll for solid gold.

Esther Farfan for the invasions and the Colombia beyond cocaine.

In another life: John Godfrey and Matthew Collin at *i–D*, Sheryl Garratt at *The Face*, Helen Mead and James Brown at *NME*.

For being Fabulous: Ronnie, Russ, Martyn, Hodge and all who sailed with us.

Styling by Barnzley and hair by Dominic Hefti.

Pete Towndrow and Daniel Dwayre for never minding the ups and downs.

Raven Smith at Black Dog for stepping in late and seeing it through.

This book is dedicated to Thalia, Theo and Sylvie.

Simon Spence

COLOPHON

© 2008 Black Dog Publishing Limited, London, UK.
All rights reserved.

Text: Copyright BDP and Simon Spence. Simon Spence has asserted his moral rights as the author of the work.

Edited by Raven Smith at Black Dog Publishing.

Design and illustration by Emily Chicken at Black Dog Publishing.

With thanks to Maria Bertran, Camille Chauchat, Blanche Craig, and Matthew Pull.

Black Dog Publishing Limited, London UK
10A Acton Street
London WC1X 9NG
info@blackdogonline.com

All opinions expressed within this publication are those of the authors and not necessarily of the publisher.

British Library Cataloguing-in-Publication Data.
A CIP record for this book is available from the British Library

ISBN 978 1 906155 31 5

All rights reserved. No part of this publication may be reproduced, stored in a retrieval system, or transmitted, in any form or by any means, electronic, mechanical, photocopying, recording, or otherwise, without prior permission of the publisher.

Every effort has been made to trace the copyright holders, but if any have been inadvertently overlooked, the necessary arrangements will be made at the first opportunity.

Black Dog Publishing is an environmentally responsible company. *Immediate Records* is printed on Antalis Edixion offset, an FSC certified paper.

architecture art design
fashion history photography
theory and things

www.blackdogonline.com   london uk